ROTHWELL

Sam Earner

To Debbie, without whose love and support this would not have happened.

Acknowledgements

My sincerest thanks go to the following for their input to this work, whether reviewing draft manuscripts or providing guidance and support through the process: Liz Bates, Fleur Currie, John Earner, Toby Everitt, Charlotte Fowles, Caroline Gowing, Charlotte Madison, Brian Say, Graham Sim.

Special thanks go to Helen Fazal, copyeditor, for her excellent contributions and suggestions to achieve the finished article.

1

Just ten miles from the Nottinghamshire M1 is a country estate of such drama and historic importance that its anonymity is an enigma. The ancestral home of the Dukes of Rothwell, now under the guardianship of Lady Margaret Cadogan-Brandt, it was singled out by Hermann Göring as his residence of choice when Britain fell in World War II. (Buckingham Palace was for the Führer.) What placed this estate above all others is difficult to say. An imposing refined sandstone house set above a four-mile lake that gently curves between landscaped slopes, it was one of many such stately homes. Perhaps it was the intrigue of its miles of hidden tunnels used in previous centuries to hide, imprison, escape. Maybe it was the prospect of acquiring a vast collection of silver or hosting great gatherings in a subterranean ballroom that boasted the largest free-spanning ceiling in Europe.

In the early nineteen fifties, just weeks after her twenty-first birthday, Lady Margaret had seized the opportunity to perpetuate the estate's cover from sight and challenge. She accepted the Ministry of Defence's proposal for a fifty-year lease to use specified areas and buildings to run a sixth form college for future army officers. On expiry, everything was to return to its prior state, but in the meantime generations of young men would pass through its gates to be educated, exercised and prepared for Sandhurst, university and a career in the regular army. Lady Margaret had found the perfect cloak under which to conceal her legacy and Rothwell College was born.

*   *   *

'Any Rothwellians? Get over here!'

Dressed in pristine khaki uniform – all shining brass buttons, sharp creases, bulled boots, a black beret welded to his head – the granite-faced Scot wielded his pace stick, signalling the new boys to cut a line from train to waiting minibus.

Bruce Noble looked around him. This was it. The exotic notion of a professional military career started here, on Monday 8 September 1986, under the hanging grey skies and drizzle of Naveby station.

He hauled his case towards the misted windows of the bus, his suit dampening from inside and out with the dual onslaught of rain and sweat. A jumble of faces stared back as he and another new college entrant dumped their luggage in any available slot and clambered aboard. The dripping, stubborn face of the sergeant major peered around the door at the driver: 'Okay Brian, looks like that's it for this train. Let's get these back to college.'

The new boys were silent as the minibus passed through the stone gates into open parkland. They peered out, trying to catch a glimpse of Rothwell itself, but only the final few hundred yards yielded any sign that the place even existed. Nearly two miles off the main road, its approach was screened by lines of chestnut and cedar, scattered stone farm buildings passing the window before the main college drew into view.

A cobbled courtyard was the drop-off point, enclosed by buildings familiar from the recruitment brochure – the library, chapel, offices and a dormitory block. It was a bustling place with other boys arriving in shared taxis or saying goodbye to parents who had brought them for the start of the new term. Bruce and his companion climbed out of the minibus and made their way to a pair of older students in college uniform standing at the main entrance.

'Welcome to Rothwell, and right here, Chapel Court. You'll need to remember that. What are your names, guys?' began the first.

'Peter.'

'Surname?'

'Falshaw.'

'And you?'

'Bruce Noble, sir.'

'Don't call me sir, I'm just a student, like you. Richard Drayfuss, or Dick. Nothing to do with the movie actor either. Follow me.'

Dick nodded to the other boy who ticked them off a list. They hurried to keep up as he led the way along corridors and flights of stairs until he stopped on the first floor in the heart of the college.

'Right, spiral staircase. You'll need to ferry your gear the rest of the way from here. Pick up an item and come this way.'

They followed the older boy as he scuttled up the tight iron steps and after two full circles the trio emerged through a narrow door onto another corridor, cross-cut by low roof trusses, which led into the dormitories. Bruce was first into his: Dorm Six, one of many on the attic level of the main building.

'Okay, you're the first here. That bed's for the dorm i/c – it means 'in charge'. You can have any other. Get yourself unpacked then meet back where the minibus dropped you at four and you'll be shown where to go for afternoon tea. Until then make yourself comfortable. Washrooms and toilets are on this level on the other side of the building. Just follow the corridor round. Got it?'

'Yes Dick. Meet for tea, four o'clock.'

'Cool. See you later, Noble. And remember to fetch your other stuff.' He turned to the other boy. 'What did you say your name was?'

'Falshaw.'

'This way, Falshaw.'

The fading voices and footsteps left Bruce in silence but for the distant muffled thumping of car doors and

4

crunching of tyres on gravel. He was here. He was really here! The stately home in the photos – the recruitment brochure, the college magazines. Bruce Noble had made it to Rothwell.

Leaving his case, he sped round to the washrooms to see the views to the back of the house. He headed straight into the first room, passing three baths – all open – there would be no privacy. Odd, but no matter, he thought. As he reached the window, the real-life mesmerising glory of the grounds stretched out below him: manicured lawns, slopes, terraces, ornamental evergreens and rose gardens all plotted and swept their way across to a small lake to the north of a stone bridge and a much larger one to the south – the Winter Lake and the Serpentine Lake Bruce had seen pictured in the prospectus. The beautiful vista unfolded all the way along Serpentine Lake's crafted, winding length, and perfect peace paused as a swan spread its wings skywards from the deep green water beneath. This was everything and more that Bruce had imagined and he understood the tales that memories made here would last a lifetime.

He turned to appraise the figure staring back at him from a long mirror beside the window. His modest height and slim build would put him among the smaller, lighter members of the college. He knew there would be challenges ahead. The loads that he would have to carry would weigh no less than those of his heftier companions. And no doubt the premature greying of hair – the silver lick that streaked back from the scalp above his right eye – and a stern, searching gaze from his young blue eyes would attract fire as they had done in previous schools.

For now, Bruce Noble put all nagging concerns aside. He remembered his father's words: 'When you succeed, notice it. Enjoy the view below before looking to the next peak, or you might never know what it is to arrive.'

*   *   *

After tea, the college gathered in the library, a cavernous space with polished oak floorboards that groaned under the slightest movement. The walls were lined with tall glass-fronted bookcases containing shelves of dull-looking books. Bruce wondered whether any would still be relevant. On the ceiling the heavy decorative mouldings and carvings were intricately painted, but tarnished and flaking. At the far end, partially visible through the half-open door, was the chapel, which appeared to be similar in size to the library.

Standing at the front of the room a tall man in an immaculate uniform surveyed the boys seated before him in rows of wooden chairs. Next to him Bruce recognised the sergeant major who had met them at the station earlier.

'College!' he bellowed. Silence fell.

'Thank you, RSM, and good afternoon, gentlemen. To our new entrants, welcome. I am Colonel Malcolm Hunter, your principal. You will all remember me because I met and selected each of you at the board in Westbury.'

As Bruce glanced around he recognised a few faces from the selection board. It had comprised two days at the Regular Commissions Board in Wiltshire, better known for its main purpose of selecting adult entrants for officer training at Sandhurst. At an average age of 15, Rothwell students underwent a simpler selection process: written tests and interviews, plus being observed to see how they interacted with each other, to decide which of every eighty applicants would be called for selection and win a place at the college.

Colonel Hunter's address was the start of an ongoing cultural immersion, the central feature of which was learning the protocols and rules. Much would be left to the student hierarchy, a well-oiled and disciplined regime from head boy down to the dorm i/cs. Everyone had a position, a function and a responsibility. With his closing words, the colonel did, however, commit what seemed to Bruce like an act of naivety – or was it just his rebellious side emerging? Perhaps the principal was just more used to dealing with adult soldiers, not day one college students.

'The more observant of you may have noticed that we do not occupy every part of every building in the college grounds, and certainly not the estate. Indeed, the main building has at its heart the staterooms, which are strictly out of bounds. And don't worry, you won't stray in there by accident because they are sealed behind locked doors

to be Rothwell's only line of defence from would-be thieves, terrorists, or other unwelcome visitors.

With Tavener on his way home, Lady Margaret stood quietly in her study, pondering the characters she had been sent for the role of security adviser. She walked over to the window and looked out at the garden with its lush lawn bordered by swathes of wild herb bushes. Nestled among the trees beyond the far shore of Serpentine Lake, Rothwell Woodhouse was her usual residence, while the MOD occupied most of the estate and main house. The Woodhouse was sizeable by any standard, very comfortable and adorned with many relocated heirlooms. It was tranquil and secluded among the evergreen woodland of the eastern estate, but lacked the awe-inspiring vistas she had so loved as a child.

Now in her fifties, Lady Margaret had conceded to greying in her long pale blonde hair. Her figure was lithe and athletic, and her sculpted facial structure, generous lips and sapphire blue eyes betrayed perfect lineage. She was as comfortable in overalls or riding gear as she was devastating in Dior couture, standing six feet tall in her heels.

A carriage clock turned quietly on the mantle, the smell of age-old panelled wood and embroidered rugs hanging musty in the air. Among such constants she stood, pensive, thinking of the creeping change that was upon her. In a world that never stands still, technology marched apace, and the impending computer revolution meant that long-hidden secrets could find their way into the open, be traced, fathomed, uncovered. Their protection now required active, not passive, measures.

With few of the Cadogan family remaining, Philip Roberts had become a trusted aide, supporter and confidante. The son of her father's head butler, he was the latest in a line of loyal staff who had served since the fifth Duke of Rothwell. All of Lady Margaret's remaining blood relatives – cousins, nieces and nephews – were living out prosperous lives around the world. But while the contraction of the family and its dwindling lineage had reduced the house's public standing, Lady Margaret remained in the top fifty wealthiest people domiciled in Britain. Placing a reliable figure on her net worth was difficult due to her preferred low public profile, but pundits rumoured estimates between five and nine hundred million pounds. No wonder that the prospect of selecting an unswerving security adviser was troubling to the core. Over three hundred years of heritage would be placed under the charge of a stranger.

Of the three shortlisted candidates sent by her London contact, Tavener was the clear and logical choice. His career achievements, skills and experience all surpassed her requirements. A decorated MI6 operative and respected adviser to a string of British ambassadors and a foreign secretary, Tavener had guarded secrets at the highest level. Moreover, he knew how to find them, too. His values and worldview, his perspective on life, people and events, seemed sufficiently adjusted to the delicate, real reason she needed professional assistance. For Rothwell held knowledge and information that far predated its dukes – back to the time of Christ Himself.

While Tavener accepted the notion of protecting undisclosed assets, Lady Margaret still struggled with the contradiction that such a commitment represented. Could anyone be so blindly accepting, loyal and disciplined? But such concerns were now academic. A series of troubling incursions around the college grounds had started a flurry of security issues for the military staff. They were fixated on the potential for attacks by IRA terrorists. Lady Margaret was alone in her realisation that other reasons could explain such events. She had to act. Reluctant deliberation was now a luxury. She would put any small misgivings about Tavener aside and accept his status as the best candidate. He would be hired.

*   *   *

'Hey geed: pocket flap! Sort it, or it'll be points!'

Bruce halted in the corridor as a senior boy behind him barked the first of what would be a long list of college protocols to be learned. 'Geed', slang for GD or General Duty, referred to members of the junior year.

'You'll get all the rules explained tonight,' the boy continued. 'In case you were wondering, one of them is about looking smart at all times, and you have a jacket pocket flap half tucked in.'

The college was active from seven in the morning until ten at night, and the first full day had felt long to Bruce. After dinner was prep, a two-hour silent period when seniors went to their studies and juniors worked in cubicles stretched along either wall of a long corridor-like room, each containing a desk, chair, shelf and curtained side. Casually termed 'cabins', the boys personalised them with posters, books and ghetto blasters. The last of these led to an explosive cacophony of rock and pop music as earphones were unplugged on the bell that sounded the end of prep.

Bruce recoiled at the deafening noise from stereos in wild competition. He couldn't continue to work under such conditions and headed straight to the library, even though there was little left to do so early in the term. He caught the eye of a friendly boy he recognised from the selection board. Bruce nodded towards the exit and the other followed.

'Dunno how anybody's gonna get themselves four A Levels worthy of Cambridge like that,' the lad started.

'Damn right. Looks like the library's the place when we get into things properly. I'm Bruce Noble, by the way. Weren't we at Tidworth for medicals on the same day?'

'Sure were. I'm Rory McIntyre. Good to see you again.'

'So, what to do, as we don't have any homework tonight?'

'Think you mean prep. We're all public school now, pal.'

'I'm not sure we are. I heard this place is over eighty percent from state schools,' said Bruce.

'Really? So the other twenty per cent are either from shit private schools, or the parents have had enough of paying turd fees, or they're so khaki-brained they couldn't hold on until Sandhurst. Sad twats. Anyway, why don't we go check out that library and make like sad twats ourselves.'

They swept to the end of the corridor, each trying to keep up with the other. By the time they reached the top of the dimly lit library staircase both were running. Rory tripped, careering from top to bottom, a flailing mass of arms and legs, his Doc Marten shoes, their laces untied, and baggy jumper detaching mid-flight. He transitioned into a human toboggan, juddering down the last few polished wooden steps to lie motionless on the flagstones of the entrance hall outside the busy library.

Three senior boys ran over to join Bruce as he bent over his new friend.

'Fuck! You okay, mate?'

'Get a fucking prefect, someone!'

'Whoa, not so fast. Just hold it, you lot. Fella, talk to me, will you?'

Rory slowly started to move.

'Go easy now, fella.'

'His name's Rory,' said Bruce.

'Shut it, geed. If you hadn't been racing him he might not bloody be here.'

'Will you all just shut the fuck up? Can't I even have some peace and quiet when I'm in pain?'

Rory carefully started what resembled a robotic full-motion check. Left arm free. Elevate. Lateral check, forward and back. Roll onto back. Right arm, left leg. Slowly his wiry form, capped with a head of tight dark curls, unfolded into a recognisable human shape. Hmm, thought Bruce. Diligent, peace-loving, clumsy, outspoken, methodical, tough. So this is Rory McIntyre.

'Anything broken? Did you hit your head on the way down?' pressed one of the seniors.

'Nothing broken, no. Didn't hit the swede either – well, don't think so. More skidded down, towards the end anyway,' Rory replied.

'Yes, we noticed. We'll still have to get you checked by Nurse.'

Ten minutes later Rory and Bruce had made their acquaintance with one of the two housemasters. Mr Cowley, the Wessex housemaster, and his wife, drove them the mile to the college hospital. There the eventful evening entered its final act as they were received by a smiling Scottish nurse. Mr and Mrs Cowley departed, leaving Bruce to offer Rory moral support. After hardly five minutes, Nurse Eunice decided that he would stay overnight. In spite of her diminutive stature, Bruce realised she wasn't someone you would dare cross.

would also afford him several yards of vision to help him escape more quickly.

'Stop right there, now!'

The footsteps quickened, thrashing through the foliage. The chasing light grew around the end wall. *Change direction!* Bruce commanded himself, as he broke into a sprint. His mind was in turmoil now: Over the mound? that's what his pursuer would least expect – slower to climb – would put him back near the road – good for navigation, bad for evasion – but was it even climbable? – or sharp left, into the unknown, away from the road?

The light swung onto him as he reached some low-hanging trees which would block his pursuer's view. Bruce struck for the mound.

As the ten-thirty bell rang out, the corridors became termite runs and Bruce hid himself among a column of boys heading upstairs. He knew the mud on his shoes and trousers could mean prying questions. At the top of the spiral staircase, while everyone else headed to their dorms to get changed and collect wash kits, he went straight to the washrooms and began to clean off the worst of the mud in one of the dozens of sinks.

'What the hell are you up to?'

That wasn't long. A house prefect had Bruce in his sights.

'I'm really sorry. I got lost outside and wanted to sort this before I made a mess of the place.'

First card into play.

'You numb twat, not in the bloody sink. I've got to clean my teeth in that. Just get them in a bag or something for now, and use the outside tap and boot brushes behind Kitchen Block tomorrow. Okay?'

'Yes, okay. Sorry, I don't know your name.'

Second card played.

'Don't worry. You'll be introduced to all the prefects tomorrow evening at house prayers.'

And he was gone. A hulk of a guy, yet his bark was worse than his bite. He was firm, but somehow Bruce felt that he was on his side and was probably trying to shape him into something better, smarter, stronger.

The following day there were no lessons until the afternoon. The morning was all about kit issue. It began with general kit for the academic side of college life, and extended to various sports items which would be needed for the gruelling sessions run by the PEO, the physical education officer.

But by far the greatest amount of kit was for the cadet force, among which was the real eye-opener, the personal rifle. For Bruce this would be the standard 7.62mm self-loading rifle or SLR. He learned that this long-barrelled weapon had been designed for Cold War defensive use. It was semi-automatic so you could fire just one round at a time but it reloaded itself instantly. The magazine held twenty heavyweight rounds and some reckoned it could kill a man a mile away if the bullet found the target. A few senior year boys who showed the strength and aptitude got either a GPMG – a general purpose machine gun – or a sniper's rifle. The GPMG was a fully automatic big-brother, belt-fed version of the SLR, but with a rapidly changeable barrel for when it glowed hot during prolonged use. The sniper rifle was also 7.62mm calibre, but bolt action, so the marksman had to reload himself. It carried a 12x magnification sight and a nightscope, and could achieve reliable kills at six to nine hundred metres. The college even had a few 9mm sub-machine guns, but those were viewed as space-saving items for truck drivers and equipment operators, hence not the weapon of choice.

It was a stark contrast to the first day stationery issue at Bruce's previous schools.

As he soon learned, their life would quickly settle into a well-trodden routine: lessons in the morning and the first part of the afternoon, followed by sport. Mondays were the exception with CCF – the Combined Cadet Force or Corps, as it was known – from two until six. Evenings were filled with two hours' prep followed by a combination of more prep, a range of physical activities from boxing to basketball, or perhaps music, drama, or even building things at the technology workshops.

Rory rejoined the throng in the dining room for afternoon tea and 'stickies' – yes, this was a total cultural immersion, they looked like cakes to Bruce. Buoyed by the excitement of the first night's events, he drew his new friend aside.

'How are you, mate? Head got the all-clear then?'

'Well, my partner in crime, it's fine thanks. But best to avoid the hospital if you can. Nurse is sweet but likes to talk. Man, can she talk. Don't think there's anything she doesn't know about me.'

'You won't believe what happened on my way back from the hospital.'

The pair slipped away, unwittingly sinking into the mystery at the heart of Rothwell. By the end of Bruce's account a mission had ignited within them to explore the tunnels. They both felt a compulsion to prove themselves. They knew that the stakes for getting caught were high, but how could such a large area be effectively patrolled round the clock through the entire year?

The whole stranger-in-the-dark thing did create unease, however. Bruce hadn't a clue who had chased him, or whether he had been identified. Could it have been a passing teacher with an overzealous regard for the rules? How naive! What if Bruce had been a serious intruder and had attacked him? Whoever he was, he was a fool – unless he was supremely confident in his abilities, or had a gun.

3

'Good morning, my lady.'

'Mr Tavener. How may I assist you?'

Tavener accepted the gestured invitation to sit and began without any small talk. 'I have conducted an initial security assessment of your asset ownership. Notwithstanding my limits of knowledge, the first consideration is that your concept of using the college as a guise is actually the greatest risk to the asset's discovery.'

About to ask him to drop the jargon, Lady Margaret was stopped in her tracks. She looked him over, as if her appraisal might send his words back whence they came, but the figure of the man and the words he had spoken remained. Tall, thin and straight as a dagger, grey eyes set in a gaunt, sallow face, he held an empty, unyielding gaze.

He sensed her mood, and continued, 'I'm no statistician, although my time around the City has shown me something of the science. Having a hundred and fifty testosterone-fuelled young men, youths whose emerging identities are predicated on boldness and initiative, means they would be most likely to seek out and then ruminate all too publicly on Rothwell's secrets.'

This was a catastrophe unfolding. Time and tide were not merely moving, it felt like they were now engulfing her.

'Go on.'

'It's not an easy position to extricate yourself from, I acknowledge, and—'

'Not easy? I am thirty-four years into a fifty-year commitment with the Ministry, Mr Tavener.'

'I understand, my lady.'

'Do you? Do you really understand, Mr Tavener? I hardly think so.'

Tavener paused. Lady Margaret scanned the floor, exasperated.

'So, how do you explain why the guise has worked for thirty-four years?'

'And it continues to work today, my lady. Yet we live on a cusp between human revolutions. The industrial now gives way to the information revolution. Computers, telecommunications – these are starting an unparalleled change which began with the advent of solid-state electronics.'

'I do not doubt your knowledge or its validity, Mr Tavener, but could we keep the technological discourse light and get to the point?'

'Indeed, my lady. To put it simply, hitherto there have been few external stimuli to get the chaps of Rothwell thinking or prying. But from now on, the cross-pollination of telecommunications, computing and commerce will mean the emergence of more knowledge – faster and more frequent – in open society. It will be new knowledge, or worse, conjecture. And conjecture will be inevitable in the light of the many unanswered questions lingering over Rothwell since time immemorial. Yes, I have been doing my research, ma'am. The turmoil will be compounded by the eventual lapse of restrictive periods for many World War Two secret and top-secret files.'

'What do you mean by "Rothwell's unanswered questions"?'

'There are too many unexplained events and features, my lady. Take the tunnels, for instance.'

'What? Is that the best your research has brought you, Mr Tavener?'

He continued unabashed.

'Tunnels laid with rail tracks that ran in many directions and for miles, yet in reality carried nothing to nowhere: no coal, no produce, there were no destination habitations nor onward transportation hubs, and no underground storehouses or even rooms.'

'And how would you know exactly what lies beneath this great estate, Mr Tavener, if you have not looked within those miles of tunnels?'

In the softest tone, he closed, 'It's what my reading of your own estate journals, maps and other documentation indicates, ma'am.'

She paused to absorb the blow.

'The correct form of address, even after first use, remains "my lady". I am not the head of the royal household.'

The exchange had become a game of chess, with Tavener manoeuvring around Lady Margaret's defences in pursuit of information. She realised that giving more away might be required to enable the asset's protection, but not yet. Her trust in him was still fragile.

She returned to the central point. 'If the students are my greatest weakness, what are we to do?'

*   *   *

The first few days unleashed a torrent of new experiences for Bruce: an A level syllabus to tackle, protocols to learn, tasks to complete and challenges to meet. Besides academic study, students were also to become professional engineers, so one morning a week would be spent at the workshops. Located near the college hospital, these were housed in a barn complex and included facilities for everything from woodwork and metalwork to robotics and vehicle construction. To supplement the major sports of rugby, hockey and cricket, were twice weekly minor sports – taken less seriously and with a choice as wide as imagination would allow or instructors could be found. Karate seemed a natural choice for Bruce, who had attained his brown belt in Shotokan.

Rothwell's long list of time-filling, energy-sapping activities ended with minor studies – anything creative that was not academic or sporting. The choice was limitless, as long as you could justify spending time constructively in your preferred activity. Bruce had yet to decide on that. Art seemed so predictable, chess tedious, brewing was not allowed, and even if he had played an instrument, music was deemed to be an evening pursuit.

As the days passed, the barrage of new experiences began to slow and the new entrants started to get a true sense of one another: physical characteristics, personalities, strengths and weaknesses all made their first appearances. Rory was shaping up as the strong, usually-quiet-but-with-occasional-outbursts type. His physical strength was not obvious, it was more a hidden resilience and mental toughness. This made sense when Bruce learned that his passion was mountaineering – not hill walking – mountaineering, with ropes, ice axes and crampons. Then there was Justin Hepburn, smooth and self-assured, a rare entrant from a private school. His film-star looks were delicate rather than rugged. He was neither an inspiration nor a threat, but usually spoke sense and would be listened to by others. As most did, he got his nickname, but 'Pretty Boy' wasn't considered to be a match winner. Emerging on the extremes were Carl Loevenger, brimming with arrogance, and Shaun Dodd, so naturally retiring that the others wondered how he had been selected. Loevenger had an opinion on just about everything and believed getting ahead in life was about who could shout loudest and dominate most, or as he put it, 'Impose your will upon the enemy'. Shaun was the total opposite, rarely spoke, and in a group would need the path to do so cleared for him. Yet he left listeners awestruck when his few words of wisdom eventually landed. The first history lesson offered a fine example.

'*The battle is won or lost before the first shot is fired –* Sun Tzu. What would you say to that … Dodd?' asked Mr Fisher.

'I suppose you could take the view that if a battle really is to be fought, sir, then all is already lost – to the enemy within each of us, the fear of the other,' came Shaun's reply.

Obnoxious Loevenger, or 'Obbo' as he came to be known, couldn't contain himself.

'Dodd, what the hell are you doing joining the British Army with an attitude like that? If we're going into battle we've all failed? What the hell is that about?'

'It's a long answer, Carl, but to sharpen the contrast for you, would you advocate that those seeking to study and professionally prosecute armed conflict should believe that it reflects the best in mankind? that, given other possibilities, it's preferable to engage in battle to solve our disputes? Surely that attitude would imply a startling misperception of warfare, and military power should not be entrusted to such ignorance.'

'You sound like a CND advocate or a left-wing academic, certainly not a future army officer. Soldiers need strong leadership, not fanciful philosophy, mate!'

Obbo dug further into his position, and nobody was much surprised. What surprised Bruce, though, was the disquiet he felt about which of these two characters he thought should be a general and which would be a general. As he wondered, Bruce feared that perhaps he was a left-winger too.

*   *   *

As autumn turned to winter, the uphill trot to the top rugby pitch became a trial of hardiness. Frozen pitches meant many developed shin splints, a condition where sharp pain was experienced in the front lower leg muscles when running. It was so commonplace that it never crossed the boys' minds to report it to Nurse at the daily sick parade. They just ran with gritted teeth to get warmed up and ease the pain.

It dawned on Bruce that enduring the practice session on the razor-topped icy turf was a form of battle immersion: there was an aim, rules and well-matched opponents, who were simultaneously the source of potential glory but also the obstacle to success, threatening defeat. He was not a natural rugby player. His lean physique lacked the bulk which allowed others a measure of arrogance as they delighted in crushing smaller opponents into the mud. His modest fifth-fifteen team (out of seven) soon grew tight; letting each other down with errors, or worse a failure to commit to a crucial tackle, was unthinkable.

What impressed the new entrants most were the examples and powerful leadership shown by the various rugby coaches, whether one of the teachers or occasionally a gifted student from the first fifteen. A series of missed tackles on one of the quickest guys, Jason Beam, presented the head boy with just such a teaching opportunity. Jason's team started a nice routine of getting the ball to him and he would side step, then outpace all opposition to make tries of fifty yards or more. The head boy, Damon Green, got upset when Bruce's side failed to change the plan and stop the points leak. The next time Jason got the ball and made his first twenty paces, Green dropped his whistle and tore after him. The players stood and gawped as Green reeled Jason in and tackled him so hard that he swept both legs clean off the pitch with a crack of shin bones before landing on top of him, the pair sliding in a cloud of dew, grass and crystallised dirt five yards from the line. That was a clear signal of what was expected, and soon enough Bruce and his friends made sure they closed Jason down, no matter what it took.

Another mandatory pursuit was cross-country, which was a favourite for developing students who were under par. The results of individuals' Personal Physical Assessments sorted them into broadly 'fitter' and 'less fit' categories, and this day the fitter were tasked to take the less fit out for a light five-mile jaunt along a variation of the route all had previously covered. So it was that Bruce was assigned to lead such a run for just one other boy, Simon Webb, one Tuesday morning in October.

A stocky lad from Essex, Simon had an easy-going character and got on well with everyone, but he wasn't made for running, so the PEO believed that more practice was required. The pair wound their way south, past the top of the Mall – the road to the main parade square in front of the college – and round the perimeter road by the cricket pitch. After a couple of miles, with Bruce setting a steady pace, they entered the captivating beauty of the rolling parkland. That was when Bruce needed to break wind, so he promptly let go.

'Bloody hell!' came Simon's astonished reply. 'That was amazing!'

'Er, sorry? Why's that?'

'If I did that I'd shit myself.'

'Do what?'

'Fart on the run, of course. How do you manage it without a problem?' Simon could hardly contain his curiosity.

'Well, what can I say? Just lucky, or naturally gifted, I guess.' The words and logic escaped before Bruce could stop them.

'You silly tosser, Bruce. "Naturally gifted." Wait till I tell the guys.'

He had a point, but he had asked the dumb question.

'Get down!' Simon suddenly hissed.

'What the hell?'

Simon grabbed Bruce by the arm and dragged him down into the cover of some roadside bushes.

'Mate, what are you doing?'

Simon silently pointed down the road. In a lay-by about fifty yards ahead a black Range Rover was parked facing away from them. They could see two people sitting in the front, but their view of the back seat was obscured by a tree trunk.

'How did they get here?' Simon whispered.

'They probably just got on the wrong road. It could be anyone.'

'It can't be just anyone. It's inside the estate.'

Bruce acknowledged that Simon was right. The most likely explanation was that they were friendly forces, folk who were allowed in the estate. Yet, on reflection, they did look out of place to Bruce, wrong somehow.

'Okay, I'm with you, buddy. I get it. What shall we do?' he asked.

'What shall we do? You're the expert running farter. You decide.'

The face said it all. Simon had done his part, now it was Bruce's turn. Bruce thought for a few seconds and then set out his plan. 'First, let's make a mental note of everything we can, then we'll report it to the RSM.'

'Roger. Black Range Rover, two people inside – maybe more but can't be sure – male or female, can't tell, registration plate, can't see,' Simon answered promptly. He looked at Bruce expectantly.

Bruce quickly considered the options before he spoke.

'Okay, okay, I got it. We need to sneak through the woods towards their three-quarters – although pale skin, blue running vest and white shorts aren't the best for that, so better go slow. It has to be covert – no run past for a close-up and even less a chat. We must get away unobserved.'

'Let's do it!'

'Whoa, not so fast, Simon. There's a missing piece.'

'What?'

'Do you think we're both going to creep around? That just doubles the risk of detection for the same information.'

Simon paused. 'Good point, we can cover two tasks here.'

'Exactly. How about I sneak in to get the details as you run past through the woods? But keep a distance and just look straight ahead as if you haven't seen them. They'll fix on you and I can get closer with a lower chance of detection.'

'Hang on, what happened to getting away unobserved? And what if they're hostile? You know about the rumours. What if the IRA have decided we're next?'

'I don't think they'd go to the trouble of attacking just one student. That would be cold-blooded murder – not making a political point, just an execution.'

'Great, but I'm not convinced.'

'Fuck it! You're probably about to run past MI fucking 5, so let's just do this and get back to report and look like turkeys in front of the entire military leadership.' Bruce was consumed by an impulse to act. He felt the window of opportunity closing. Instinct drove him to be harsh and get the task done.

'So it's okay if it's not your neck, eh? You're an idiot, Noble!' Simon retorted. Yet with that he had broken cover and was off. Bruce had to get into position, fast.

The target vehicle was on the side of the road, atop a small rise. Bruce's only sensible option was to head round its right side while Simon jogged past the left. Running at a semi-sprint, he scattered branches and undergrowth in an effort to time his approach with Simon's, but Simon's fury had taken over and caution was abandoned.

As Bruce got closer he realised that he had no real idea about specific aims. What did they say a moment ago? Christ! Gone blank. No, wait . . . vehicle details. He peered over and memorised the number plate: D247 XYA. A brand new plate from August. 24/7 was convenient to retain, as was almost the last three letters of the alphabet. Then the crucial part – descriptions of the occupants. He had to go far enough around to get even an oblique view of their faces, and if they glanced towards him the game would be up. They would easily see him in his Chariots of Fire outfit.

He pushed out wider onto a new course, creating extra space for when he would be at greatest risk of detection.

SAM EARNER

The nearest faces were already showing their first basic clues. Something seemed strange, but what? A few more strides . . . slower now . . . refining the approach . . . getting close. Stop. What could he see? Dark skin, strong jawline, a black woolly hat – how original! maps on the dashboard, binos in hand, what else? what else?

The Range Rover's V8 exploded into life. He could see Simon in the woods opposite, a few yards short of the vehicle. The engine bellowed and the wheels spun, spraying a wall of dirt into the undergrowth as the vehicle's back end slew round and it sped away around a bend out of sight.

Simon halted in his tracks. Bruce stayed down, frozen among the undergrowth.

'What now?' Simon yelled.

Bruce got up from behind a bush and shouted: 'Report!'

And they turned for the college, flooded with energy carrying them home at speed.

*   *   *

'Thank you, gentlemen. That's all for now. You've done your part. Now remember, absolutely no mention of any of it outside of this office. If you tell, be assured it will come back on you.' Mr Willis – chemistry teacher as well as officer commanding the CCF – concluded the incident of the mysterious black Range Rover in the woods with uncharacteristically harsh words. Beside him, adjutant Captain Pearce and RSM Pitcaithly looked on grim-faced.

Simon and Bruce looked at each other, dumbfounded. They left the office Willis shared with the other two men in silence.

'I don't believe it,' Simon started.

'Not here, dummy,' said Bruce.

He steered him to the end of the corridor and out into the courtyard behind Kitchen Block. In a hushed voice Simon resumed, 'That was just so weird. Like, they listened to us alright, but talk about poker faces.'

'Yes, I know. I was taken aback too. I suppose if you don't know what or why, the best policy is to say nothing at all. The thing is, if they say something and it's wrong, that could be a problem. It doesn't matter if it's IRA or MI5, but if it gets around the rest of the guys the speculation will be rife – blabbed in Naveby on a Saturday night before you know it.'

Simon shrugged. 'Okay, that's it then. I remain officially baffled, and definitely unrewarded. But one thing's for sure, I'd have been in the shit if those guys had reacted differently.'

So that was the end of it, for then at least. They split, agreeing that it would never be mentioned. Bruce knew that Willis had got one thing right – if they shared this with anyone it would leak and God only knew where that would lead.

4

'This is the second sighting in a month now, George. There was the incident last week with the three boys from 66 Entry reporting an unknown vehicle inside the estate, and now this. We will have to press our colleagues in the MOD to get whoever is supposed to provide our security to take a proper look, or get Special Branch on the case.'

Gathered in the spartan white-washed CCF office, college adjutant Captain Gavin Pearce was holding a hastily convened meeting. Opposite him a beleaguered George Willis looked on blankly. At his desk in the corner RSM Gordon Pitcaithly drummed his fingers in frustration.

'Agreed. We've done everything the MOD advised,' said Willis, head in hands now. He looked up to address the others. 'We've been patient, taking measures to avoid exposing the boys to being targeted en masse. We have observed and collated and reported, but surely the initiative is now with the IRA?' His eyes widened to invite a solution. 'Gavin, can you get onto your chain in the regular army? Maybe they will at least have some authority to call for assistance in this matter. My TA chain of command would be a waste of time, if not a liability.'

Pearce and Willis turned to Pitcaithly for his reaction.

'Well, of course. Do it! We're sitting bloody ducks, for Chrissakes. And now we have the double peril of hoping a total of five lads will keep their mouths firmly shut.'

'We'll have to be very clear this time,' Willis continued. 'We need to get across how a developing picture has become vivid enough to justify more active measures or some form of proper external support. We know that MI5 have priorities far above this place, and they will not commit any sort of support easily. No doubt Special Branch will be the same.'

'There is another card to keep up your sleeve too, but to use subtly and only if required. If they won't help, we may have to help ourselves,' said Pearce.

'Sir, with all due respect, that's bloody naive,' said Pitcaithly.

'RSM?'

'We have an armoury full of all sorts – more than a weapon per man for a hundred and fifty students, plus ammunition to match. You mention anything risky and the first thing will be your firing pins and ammo getting pulled in by the MOD.'

'I didn't mean that. In fact, it never crossed my mind,' said Pearce. 'I meant stuff like contacting the Nottinghamshire constabulary or private surveillance agencies.'

Pitcaithly glared at Willis.

'Sirs, I think we understand each other. I'll see you at lunch.'

The door slammed, leaving Pearce and Willis standing in silence looking equally lost and foolish.

*   *   *

While evening meals were a relaxed affair where students would just turn up and join the queue, lunchtimes were semi-formal. Various academic and military staff sat on each of the sixteen tables, plus the college principal at the top table. It all ran like clockwork. Usually two courses, and the most junior students would cover all the chores from carrying trays to serving and wiping down tables. Colonel Hunter would invite a different group of boys each day to sit with him and practice polite conversation, while the more polished or crusty of the masters would correct poor etiquette on the lower tables. The part everyone most anticipated with quiet curiosity was the grace, which the students took turns to recite to the assembled throng. Today it was Bill Patel, an Indian guy from 66 Entry.

'Thank you, gentlemen,' boomed Hunter over the growing hubbub.

All went quiet and Bill stepped up. After a theatrical pause he announced: 'Rub-a-dub dub, thank God for the grub,' and he strode off to laughter from across the floor.

'Nice one, Billy!' called John Turner, a senior year student on Bruce's table.

'Alright, Mr Turner, that'll do. I trust you will put in more effort when it's your turn,' said Mr Chittern, head of maths.

'Actually, sir, I think that was pretty well thought through. Certainly had the desired effect,' Turner fired back. Mr Chittern glowered and John gleefully accepted getting his card marked yet again. For him rules were the waves over which he sailed his ship of adventure. He just loved pushing the boundaries and getting a reaction. Yet he was genuine and honest – no hidden agendas or back-stabbing from John Turner.

'So, young Noble, is Rothwell what you expected?'

Mr Chittern's question was obvious and straightforward but it caught Bruce off-guard. In his seat next to the head of table, he was in the prime conversational test position from which reputations were made or lost fast. He had to answer. Cutlery was set upon plates and the table came to rest. The other boys stared at him, as did Mr Chittern. Bruce was caught between two conflicting demands. His fellow students wanted to see if he was going to show himself as being a 'greasy geed' – one whose main aim was to please a member of the hierarchy, to say the right thing. But he also knew this was a perfect opportunity for the establishment to learn who they had really selected.

'It's pretty much what I expected, sir,' he began. 'Fair, busy, demanding, and with a very talented bunch of guys.'

'Oh thanks, Brucie. Pay you later,' came John Turner once more.

'He said talented, not talkative, Mr Turner,' snapped Chittern.

'Go on, Noble. What else?'

Bruce wondered how many more questions he'd have to answer to complete this exercise in small talk.

'Well, the college and grounds are fantastic. I never thought I cared for historical buildings but these are quite something.'

'Christ save me,' exclaimed Turner. 'He's supposed to be a future army officer and what impresses him? The bloody architecture!'

The table erupted in laughter, the other boys enjoying the revelry provided by Turner's mischief. The distraction changed the dynamic, and a frustrated Mr Chittern turned from Bruce to another junior and attempted to continue. Neighbouring tables and their masters glanced towards the din. Now it was Chittern who had to watch his reputation.

On the way back from lunch Bruce saw a head of tight black curls heading down Chapel Hill in front of him.

'Yo, McIntyre, you old dog. What's happening?'

'Just heading back to my basket. Got to drop off some items,' Rory replied, sharp as ever.

'Good call. I need to pick up some sports gear.'

They headed into the basement and followed a narrow corridor with a miniature tramline running through it. Bruce guessed it might have carried laundry trucks or goods trolleys in years past. Along one wall were students' lockers ordered alphabetically and by entry number. Bruce and Rory's were situated just a few yards apart.

'So Rory, how's the climbing going? Top call for a minor sport. But where do you do it around here if we don't have a climbing wall?'

'Cottam Crags. It's only a few minutes away and good enough to challenge my technical and rope skills.'

'What sort of level are you at?'

'Well, I've managed to scrabble a couple of E1 faces, but I lead HVS.'

'Qué?'

'E1 is kinda the bottom end of expert climbing – it goes up to E7, which to an untrained eye would look like a vertical slab of rock. HVS is a grading below the E scale and stands for 'hard very severe'. Then there's 'severe', and so on, down to the starter's level of just plain 'difficult', which is easy.'

'Er, right . . .'

Just as they were losing themselves in Rory's world of outdoor escape a couple of senior year boys stepped between them. They turned to face Bruce.

'You Noble?' started the first. He was the taller of the pair, sporting an extravagant shock of blond hair, gelled in a high wave like a fashion warning beacon.

'Y-yes.'

'Well, you better sort out your priorities, pal, or you can think about getting you and your whimsical bollocks out of this man's army.'

Bruce tensed. Time slowed as his mind started to race, both confused and alert. Behind the would-be assailants he noticed Rory's startled expression.

'What have you got to say for yourself, twat?' the blond tirade continued.

'Sorry, but what in hell are you on about?' Bruce inwardly recoiled at his hastiness. Some instinct had landed him in confrontation mode and this was uncharted territory.

'You and fucking architecture. At lunch. We heard you.'

'Why don't you failed bullies get lost if that's all you have to complain about.' Rory was off, characteristically speaking before thinking.

'I'm sorry, I heard something like an attempt at English but couldn't make it out. What about you, Tom?' continued hardman one.

'Yeah, think I heard some sort of primitive grunting from somewhere, Jez.' Hardman two had found his voice.

A few yards further along the corridor, behind the seniors' backs, another boy from 67 Entry started quietly towards them. Bruce knew his face, but he wasn't in many of Bruce's classes and they hadn't got to know each other.

'Well, Noble? What a twatting name too, Noble.'

'Noble twat! That'll do for a call sign. Should see him through until he decides to do the decent thing and leave military leadership to non-architects.'

The twins burst into laughter.

Rory didn't take well to being ignored. 'Have you had enough now, failed bullies?' he sneered.

Hardman one, Jez, seized him by the throat and slammed him backwards against the lockers.

'I can fuck you up right now, you gobby little shite! Want some?'

'Yes, I want some. Why don't you give some of whatever it is to me?'

Their fellow 67 Entry had arrived.

Jez tightened his grip as Rory squirmed, his face dark red. This was about to explode. Jez turned to look at the new arrival, momentarily silent, instincts alive now, absorbing the potential threat. Arrogance drained from his face. They could all sense the vibes like static in the air. It was clear this stranger had absolute confidence in himself.

'Who the fuck are you, geed? Can't you see I'm busy. Why don't you piss off, if you know what's good for you.'

'No, no, I think I'll stay. *You* can piss off, though. Would you like to walk or fly?'

They locked stares. Animal instincts pulsed within each of them, screaming out who believed in himself and who did not. Any fool could tell he meant business. In the blink of an eye the game was up and new guy had won.

'You fucking freak! I'll have words about you – fucking loser,' was Jez's parting shot, but he had released his grip on Rory, his sidekick was in retreat, and the new ally was melting him with a laser stare – no overt aggression, just absolute certainty, oozing control and self-belief, all effortless.

Jez and buddy skulked away, spitting insults under their breath in a vain attempt to save face. Bruce gave the newcomer a smile of admiration.

'Thanks for stepping in. My God, what the hell was all that? Rory, mate, you okay? Thank you, too, Rory. Man, you don't take any shit either, do you?'

Bruce's appreciation was mixed with unease about how he had reacted. What had the incident meant – about Rothwell, and the army too? Was this bullying part of normal life? Why had he been so slow to react, to recognise an impending threat, and when the aggression came upon Rory why had he been so inert? His head spun.

'To be honest, I was more stupid than cool,' Rory said. 'I had no idea what was going to happen if he started on me – like, really started.'

'You would have hammered him,' came the new friend's reply. 'Sorry, I should introduce myself. Arthur Rose, but it's just Art to my friends.'

'Well, Art, thank you. Thanks for taking the risk and getting involved,' said Bruce.

'You're welcome, both. I couldn't stand back and let that idiot desecrate the values that attracted me to what I had thought was an honourable profession. This man's army doesn't stand for bullying.'

'I don't know how you figure I would have hammered him,' said Rory. 'What would you have done if he turned on you?'

'He'd have hammered him, too.' Bruce's words were out before he could think. Rory grinned in disbelief at the mutual appreciation society that was gaining pace, but Art underlined the grain of truth in all of it.

'No, he's right. I won't go into it now, but I've learned something of how people tend to react in these situations. Rory, you say? Rory, you would have beaten him. The way he behaved shows a real hole in his character. He unknowingly seeks to redress that, but only knows one way – to chase the control that he feels he so lacks. You, on the other hand, you are genuine and have real fire within.'

'Och, I dunno about that.'

Rory's modesty had brought his native Scot's accent strongly through and Art and Bruce couldn't resist a chuckle. Rory looked at them sharply but decided to ignore it.

'How do you know that Art would have beaten him then, Brucie?' he asked.

'The look of the whole thing: posture, body language. Everything shouted a certainty in yourself that was beyond conceit. It was assured, founded on something real.'

'He's right, Rory. In my modest experience, anyone with real abilities tends to believe in themselves. They don't need to throw their weight around to prove it.'

'Real abilities?'

'Is everything alright there, gentlemen?'

Mr Cowley had once more demonstrated his uncanny knack for appearing from thin air right behind an unsuspecting clutch of students. This act of apparition was legendary. Some thought he could pass through walls, ghost-like. The moment something went wrong, or someone was up to mischief, the Wessex housemaster would arrive.

'Well, an answer please. Someone?'

'Um, fine, sir, all fine thank you. Why do you ask, sir?' said Bruce.

'Never ask why, Noble, once you have furnished a reasonable response,' Cowley smiled, and with that he slipped past and away.

Art finally broke the spell. 'Right guys, best we were away to lessons.'

'God, yes, of course. Thanks again,' Bruce replied.

'Welcome.'

And with that Art disappeared towards Class Corridor.

'So what exactly are his abilities?' Rory mused. But the moment had gone and they would have to ask Art another time.

5

'Gentlemen, allow me to introduce Mr Tavener, who has just joined the college as our new lab technician.'

Mr Willis was standing at the front of the class at the beginning of a chemistry double lesson. It was straight after rugby, when it was dark outside and the boys were hollow inside.

'Gentlemen,' nodded Tavener, surveying the expectant faces, his thumbs inserted into the lapels of his white lab coat.

'I should add that you will also see Mr Tavener during CCF. He recently took a TA commission and joins us there as an extra pair of hands for general infantry skills and leadership training,' continued Willis. 'And he has special experience and skill in mountaincraft, so will be assisting Mr Marham with our more prestigious outdoor pursuits expeditions.'

'Right, so a face we won't forget then,' muttered Justin.

'What did you say, Hepburn?' came Willis's inevitable challenge. Tavener stared at Justin.

'Nothing sir, just, um—'

'Don't worry, sir. Hepburn hasn't set his hair quite right after rugger and he's still traumatised.'

Like a flash, Hughes' reply rescued Hepburn. Dominic Hughes was one of a group of razor-sharp, perceptive and genuinely selfless guys. Everyone had heard Hepburn's comment, yet all, Hepburn included, got Hughes' reason for taking the mickey. Hepburn accepted the hit on his image and Willis let it roll, allowing the tactic to register with the class. This seemed to be another example of the purpose of the place: in subtle but powerful ways, the whole college machinery was geared to prepare students in every way possible for training at Sandhurst and a long army career – by getting them to learn about people.

Tavener stood without speaking during this brief exchange. Bruce watched him from his seat at the back of the class. He seemed an odd combination of a man. His TA commission showed he must be competent in the disciplines Willis mentioned, and he certainly must be qualified to assist Marham, who as an experienced alpine guide was no joke in the hills. But for Bruce, something didn't fit, didn't feel right about him. It was almost like having Bruce Lee as your waiter, or Sean Connery handing out the hymn books at church. His demeanour wasn't anywhere near that of a stereotypical TA officer, or a lab technician.

Tavener strode out of the room. An air of intrigue inhabited the brief silence as seventeen pairs of eyes remained fixed on the closing classroom door. Someone had to say what they were all thinking.

'Sir . . . sir . . . may I ask what Mr Tavener did before coming to Rothwell?' asked Mike Heskell, a beaming ginger-haired lad from Cornwall.

'Heskell, I would like to get to the lesson now and you will have ample opportunity to ask Mr Tavener for yourself. But, as you make a point of it, I will briefly sum up what I know – that he has done a similar role as technical support in a university in the south, southwest, I think. Yes, Exeter, I believe,' Willis replied. 'There you go, your neck of the woods. He has considerable experience in outdoor ventures and his willingness to broaden himself professionally through taking a TA commission would have improved his chances of getting a role here greatly.'

'Right, thank you, sir.'

Willis nodded in acknowledgement and eyed the silent class, each trying to make sense of what they had just heard, grappling to match the story with the stranger.

*   *   *

It was Friday in the sixth of a fourteen-week term, or fifteen weeks for anyone lucky enough to get a place on the winter expedition to Snowdonia. The cycle of serious academic pressure – A Levels made O Levels look like kindergarten – daily rugby, gruelling PT sessions and evening activities, set amid the freezing, dark days of deepening winter, were testing and draining. Yet all were getting fitter and stronger.

Everyone ate like horses, it seemed, but in fact it was the new boys who experienced the greatest transformation, and pressure. The more seasoned guys took college life in their stride. Bruce was putting on weight. From a modest schoolboy 59kg on arrival he had developed and grown to 61kg on the gym scales. His PT assessment results were improving too. He could cut fifty press-ups, ninety sit-ups, sixteen dips, twelve chin-ups, and run a mile and a half in eight minutes. Nevertheless, the morning PT session was the nightmare everyone had predicted. Despite all the rumours and advice, some of Bruce's class seemed oblivious to the 'very light breakfast before PT, eat well after PT' messages from the seniors.

The lesson on this day was entitled Ropes – a session designed to educate and exercise on four hemp ropes hanging fifteen feet high from a gymnasium frame. The students learned how to climb, descend, fix with legs and remove hands, move between ropes, hang upside down, do pull-ups, and climb over people who were already on the rope. When the teaching and trying-out part was over, Captain MacWilliam used the last twenty minutes to beast the boys with all the forms of exercise as taught. That was when a percentage of the number started to collapse, faint, throw-up, or if like Bruce they judged the balance of effort and control right, just look sweaty, pale and ill, which told MacWilliam they were trying properly. By normal school standards, this would be off-the-scale carnage. Here it was required for the structured transformation of privileged souls like the Rothwellians.

Once Bruce had recovered, showered and devoured his stashed food store of Monster Munch, flapjack and Marathon bar, the face that stared back in the locker mirror was glowing with health and vitality. His moment of reflection ceased with the slam of Rory's locker door.

'Any idea when they'll announce who's got on the winter exped?' Rory asked. It was clear that he could hardly contain his enthusiasm.

'Probably you, McIntyre, keen geed,' came the reply from one of the house prefects as he swept towards them, PT kit in hand. Rory turned towards the bringer of hope.

'You're just teasing me there now, Greg.'

'Maybe not, actually. You know, it's not for everyone. Many guys, especially new entry, have had enough after fourteen weeks of this term. They miss home and think of family and Christmas. Plus, there's only two places for junior entry – in the past, junior guys have struggled with fitness alongside the others on these expeds – so they may well pick you for your mountaineering experience. You'll probably have the stamina to keep up.'

An optimistic smile radiated across Rory's face.

'Hey, I'm not promising here, but it's a serious possibility. That's between you and me, mind.'

'Yes sir, bring it on!' the McIntyre roared, once again his mouth outrunning his brain.

Bruce allowed Rory his delight, while reflecting on the curious rhythm of the regime, the cycles, the schedules, how long it felt to the end of term, but how the days sped by.

'Man, the weekends come round quickly here, don't you think, Rory?' he said.

'Not as quickly as they go, but I know what you mean, Bruce. It's weird. Part of me wishes they were longer, yet we don't go home, we can't go to the boozer, so it's just as well Saturday is spoken for with morning lessons and afternoon sport.'

'Which then leaves a Saturday night that feels like any other day of the week, Sunday chapel, and more PT to pass the time.' Bruce shrugged.

'Speak for yourself. Any fool who chooses to fill his time with more bloody PT seriously lacks imagination. Find a hobby, man! Join me at the crags. Why not?'

'I'm not sure it's for me somehow. I did some climbing at my last school and quite liked it, but I didn't love it.'

'Why did you put your name down for Snowdonia then?'

'Ah, that's different. That's getting into the hills, and while I'm no semi-pro like you, Snowdonia in winter really appeals.'

'Okay, I believe you, but what about a minor sport?'

'I should look at getting together with any karate guys – I haven't done it since before my last year of O levels, but I did make it to brown belt in Shotokan.'

Their stares locked as they read each other's minds.

'Arthur Rose!' they said in unison.

'That's it, Rory. He must have some combat skills and I bet they're martial arts based.'

'Cool, still a form of PT, but I suppose climbing is too, so I'll let you off. But it won't fill a dull Sunday afternoon, or Saturday afternoon for that matter, when we drongo rugby fifths haven't a game because there are no teams rubbish enough to match us.'

Eyes met and minds were about to meld again. If Rory went where Bruce thought the scheming Scottish explorer's mind would go, the coincidence would be truly unnerving.

'Say it then,' Bruce commanded.

'Okay . . . *tunnels!*'

'Now it's my turn. *Expulsion.* Your go, Rory.'

'Hang on. Have you forgotten? We spoke about this in our first couple of days.'

'Yes, I know, Rory, and I made the decision to forget it.'

'Okay, how about, *future leader*, or *risk-taking*, or *real experience?* Coming back now? And, by the way, we have no rugby match tomorrow afternoon.'

'Hmm . . . *Trumps.*'

Bruce's logic and common sense had run aground on his friend's higher ideals. Rory's motives were intangible, irrational to a point, but also vivid, true, powerful, irrepressible. He was grinning from ear to ear, challenging Bruce not to decline the idea.

'Okay,' he surrendered. 'Shit. *Shit!* I must be mad to even contemplate it.'

'It's what makes the difference, man. There are leaders and Leaders. Which do you want to be? Who do you want to be for your soldiers? This is real, it's challenging, it's scary. There are consequences if we get it wrong. It's what will build judgement and confidence. But hey, I'll let you think about it. Saturday's not until tomorrow, after all, so no rush.'

'Tunnels? Tomorrow?' Bruce baulked.

'Tomorrow, Mr Noble. Tomorrow!'

A restless night's sleep passed slowly, and morning lessons even more so, as Bruce could not escape his growing anxiety over their plan. He was saddened to learn something unattractive about himself – he feared failure. He was deeply uncomfortable with real risk. There seemed to be much to lose and little to gain, yet shying away from the task would be even worse. If he couldn't face this, who might he be in war? While Rory was relishing the prospect, for Bruce the effects of seeking a real-life challenge were becoming apparent in unexpected ways. He started to question Rory's judgement. Was he about to squander his own career prospects in league with a reckless fool?

'You were quiet at lunch.'

Rory had joined Bruce on the way back from the informal Saturday midday meal. The pair had sensed the need for discretion. While they always sat on the same table if space allowed, today they had guarded against too much contact.

'Just trying to avoid the "What are you doing this afternoon?" type of questions, mate,' Bruce levelled, as they got away from the crowd.

'Yeah, that would be awkward: "No, sorry, can't join you for a shopping trip to Naveby – got tunnels to explore." Hmm, tricky.'

They checked about them for potential listeners to their conversation.

'Right. When to meet? Where? And wearing what?' Bruce asked.

Rory's suggestion of cat-burglar outfit with hiking boots was negotiated to rough casuals with said boots, so they could pop up anywhere across the estate and claim to be out for a country stroll.

It was almost two o'clock before they managed to get away and out into the grounds unnoticed. Plan A was to hook up near the entrance that Bruce had discovered on the first fateful night of term. But having arrived there they realised that entering in daylight was impossible. It was way too open, with autumn having claimed all deciduous foliage and the road too close for comfort. Bugger.

'Brucie, this is no good.'

'Just keep going, Rory. Car approaching.' The Volvo estate passed slowly by. Inside they glimpsed a dark-haired man wearing jacket and tie and a woman with longish greying hair under a cloche hat. 'You don't think that was ...'

'Lady M. Yes, very possibly.'

'Not something you see every day,' Bruce acknowledged.

'Bruce, we know there's a tunnel entrance right behind Kitchen Block opposite the squash court.'

'Too risky.'

'Wait, give me a chance, will you? Let's head in that general direction and see if we can find an entrance between here and the college.'

'Good idea, Rory. And if we meet anyone, we're just starting our walk from this area.'

They turned north along the back of the hospital, crossed the main college drive, then turned right, moving parallel to it, with a dry ditch to their right and the lower rugby pitch on their left. After a few yards the boys saw that the ditch, which appeared to lie between the field and drive, was in fact enclosed on the far side by the outer wall of another tunnel. It ran right under the drive.

Bruce nudged Rory repeatedly and nodded towards the ditch.

'Yes, I can see it. I'm not blind,' he hissed.

They pressed on and soon discovered a collapsed section of tunnel wall with crumbling red bricks that exposed a hole two feet square. The dark opening could easily be missed in the undergrowth.

Rory and Bruce stared at each other wide-eyed, but kept moving and stayed silent, scanning for any possible observers. There were none.

'In!' commanded Rory, shoving Bruce down across the ditch and up to the hole. Bruce obeyed the order and as soon as he arrived at the entrance he flung himself headlong inside.

'Fuck! Where's the fucking floor?' He landed with a thump on a bed of compacted earth, similar to what he had spied on day one. The light above him was momentarily blocked out as a madman came hurtling down.

'Oot the fucking way, man!' Rory hit the ground just inches away.

'I'd move if I could see anything,' Bruce said in a strained whisper.

'Let's just get a few paces away and then get the torches on.'

They switched them on after shuffling ten yards or so into the tunnel towards the college. When the beams shone, they found themselves in identical positions: both torch beams were shielded and pointing to the floor; both boys were in half-kneeling posture. They had instinctively knelt, making their profiles smaller to avoid detection. CCF training was starting to rub off. Rory gave a muted laugh. 'That's bloody sad.'

'I know, Pinky and Perky are picking up field skills.'

They looked around them. The walls were of red brick and extended upwards into arches that formed a semicircle about twenty feet in diameter above the dry mud floor.

'I presume we want to keep going towards the college?' said Bruce. 'It should be more interesting – more junctions, maybe doorways, and so on?'

'Agreed. If we head the other way I reckon we'd just hit fields or come up around the workshops. Plus I want to know what happens at Chapel Hill. The tunnel can't continue straight through the college basement level. It has to change direction or depth.'

They pressed on cautiously, quietly, with torch beams low, constantly checking in front and behind. The few yards back to take them underneath the college felt long to Bruce, but his confidence was growing. A sense of control had emerged amid the challenge. Intrigue and excitement took root.

As anticipated, they came to a junction where the tunnel split at a T.

'I guess right leads under the parade square, and left towards the assault course, and then what, out towards the countryside?' said Bruce.

They agreed to turn right and look for anything of interest, such as connecting doors, which would most likely be under the college buildings. After another fifty or sixty yards the tunnel followed a wide curve to the left.

'Hey!' Rory fired up the first real conversation for what must have been ten minutes.

'What's up? Can you see something?'

'Open your eyes, Bruce.'

Five yards away, caught in their torchlight, the rectangular outline of a door contrasted with the long curve of the tunnel. Now they had to be cautious. They sidled up to the cold, dusty metalwork with its rusted handle, killed the lights and watched and listened. There was no sign, no sound. Despite not being surprised – why should a nondescript old iron door, perhaps unopened for decades, suddenly yield either action or secret? – Bruce's pulse was racing and his heart hammering in the silence. This was a first unknown. They had arrived but didn't know where.

The air was cool, damp and tasted dusty. It penetrated lungs and clothes. After a short while they switched their torches on again. A fine powder of earth hung in the torch beams and behind them they could see boot prints in a thick patch of dirt.

'Oops, footprints. Not good,' said Bruce.

'Leaving signs is never good. How could we have been so dumb? That could really complicate things if anyone ever checks down here.' Rory sighed heavily.

They could feel the weight of risk. The pair stood in silence contemplating their predicament. They had got what they asked for and reality was now mocking them. Then a moment of clarity came to Bruce, like a bright light shining in the gloom.

'If our situation hangs on whether this place is checked on a regular basis, surely that would mean other footprints?'

Rory looked at him expectantly: 'Yeah, keep going.'

'So, if we see any, we can assess how fresh they are and maybe how often the place is checked. Also, whether other students might come here too.'

'Brucie! Gonna call you Sherlock bloody Holmes! So we press on then?'

'Yes, but we have just experienced being caught out by the obvious, so let's get thinking about the next black swan.'

'What's the black swan bit about? Pray tell, o wise one.'

'It's an old fable about nobody ever having seen a black swan, leading to the belief they don't exist. I just mean an unexpected event, born of ignorance, belief, expectation, and so on.'

'So, what is it then – the black swan we need to prepare for?' Rory asked.

'If I knew that, it wouldn't be a black swan now, would it?'

It dawned on Bruce that Rory wasn't getting the subtleties on this one.

The way ahead beckoned and the boys pressed on, bolder, quicker now. Rory's compass and meticulous counting of his paces indicated they would soon be clear of the main building and heading for Serpentine Lake. After the iron door, the tunnel soon became dead straight, seeming to disappear into infinity – a challenging enough view in itself. But having pressed on still further, the deep blackness sank gently, eerily, away and down, as the tunnel passed under the lake. Bruce and Rory came to a halt in the face of this next challenge. How far did it go? There were rumours that a tunnel went all the way to the edge of Naveby – that would be six miles. There was no way of knowing what lay ahead, whether they would find anything of interest, and more critically, whether they could extract themselves if lost, injured or pursued. For the first time Rory was at a loss about the decision to proceed. Bruce sensed this and let the pause take full effect. Eventually Rory spoke.

'Okay then, I guess we need a plan on exactly how far we go, and maybe, like in Corps, what we do if things go wrong.'

'Totally agree, Rory. "Actions on", as they call it. So what would be our action on being detected? From in front . . . and behind . . .?'

'Okay. How about: kill the lights and drop to crouching position. If they're far off and we see their light first, then freeze or withdraw slowly, depending on detection risk.'

Rory looked at Bruce, eager for his reaction. They talked it through as they walked, and just as they had on the first night at the top of the library staircase, they were inadvertently moving each other along apace.

After another thirty yards the tunnel began to level out after its descent. They must be under the lake itself.

Another iron door was set back into deep brickwork on the left side, but this one was different. Its bulk and thickness would have suited Fort Knox – great slabs of steel, punctuated by thick domed rivets. Its circular profile matched the opening set into a hulking metal frame in the tunnel cross-section, and while it stood recessed into the side wall, they could see from the light of their torches that it didn't enclose anything behind. A low hum came from some sort of electrical box above it and the shaft of a hefty metal arm appeared to connect a giant hinge to the back of the door.

'What in God's name is this?'

'It's a motorised door, Rory. It must be to seal the tunnel against a flood. If the tunnel collapsed, the lake water would flood the college basement level. This must be a defence against that.'

'I don't like the sound of that.'

Even to an untrained observer, the atmosphere in this section of the tunnel was evidence enough of the risk. The red-brick walls arched above them seemed to be straining to hold back moisture from the lake. The air was rank with the scent of wet clotted earth, filtered through ageing mortar. Here and there dangled tentacles of subterranean roots, presumably belonging to some sort of vegetation on the lake bed. Water trickled down the walls and dripped onto the sodden floor as a slow chorus of splashes echoed from small pools that had formed there. Cracks zigzagged along the mortar between bricks. They wondered how the place was still standing.

Bruce shone his torch into the disappearing space, punctuated by the start of the tunnel's rise, faintly visible in the distance. 'I'm with you on this one, Rory. How about we just get to the top of the next slope? That's got to be the other side of the lake. Then we quit while we're ahead. We'll get a view beyond and we can decide whether to do more another time.'

'Done!' Rory was quick to reply.

The lake would be about fifty yards across at this point so they expected to find the tunnel rising again soon. Moments later another circular structure appeared, this time in the tunnel ceiling. About six feet in diameter, it revealed a heavy-duty metal cover recessed a couple of feet higher within an enclosing cylinder. This really was weird, and neither Bruce nor Rory could guess at its function. They moved past it with less deliberation than before. They were getting used to strange discoveries.

A few yards further brought them to another chunky metal door midway under the lake, this time on the right-hand side. It was more conventional – rectangular not round. To one side was a keypad set in a grimy black casing with three small neon indicators, of which only one glowed with a flickering red light. Bruce cast the torch beam back and forth, but there was nothing to even hint at its purpose. Nothing except a few footprints set in a drier patch of earth nearby. He shone his torch on them.

'What do you make of these, buddy?'

Rory swung his light onto the spot. 'I don't believe it. If I'm not mistaken that print has a rare and distinguished quality. That logo in the sole plate is same as mine – it's from a pair of Scarpa Fitzroys. Someone has good taste.'

'And plenty of dosh.'

'Or they take their hiking boots seriously.'

'So we'd better to keep an eye out for any other guys with same boots as you from now on. We know what they're doing!'

Their journey beyond the mid-point brought a symmetry of man-made features that mirrored previous ones: another roof assembly, another heavy sealing door. The tunnel rose as expected from beneath the lake then levelled out again. They flashed the torchlights ahead where the beams faded into nothingness. It might run all the way to Naveby, after all, Bruce thought.

'We should congratulate ourselves – mission measured and accomplished,' he announced with cautious optimism. 'But you'll say…'

'… mission is accomplished when we get back.'

'Yes, yes okay.'

'But first, tea and medals,' said Rory. 'Actually, tea and photos – for the adventurer's album, of course.'

He took a cheap Kodak instamatic from his backpack and held it at arm's length, straining to capture the best snap of them kneeling amid the colourless void. Next he pulled a flask of tea he had somehow sneaked from lunch and two sticky buns he'd pinched from the tray beside the hatch in the kitchen. They enjoyed the moment, steam rising from their plastic cups. All was quiet, apart from the sounds of munching cake, slurping tea and runny noses sniffing back the dust.

Suddenly Rory froze, his mouth half-open with part-chewed bun visible inside. His eyes were wide, staring past Bruce, fixed towards the direction they had come from.

'What—'

Bruce started to speak but Rory cut him off with a chop of his hand. 'Do you hear that?' he whispered.

The faint thud, thud, thud of boots on damp earth was getting louder, and with it the glow of an approaching light. The footsteps were urgent, directed, purposeful. The difference in the level of the tunnel afforded the boys a few moments' advantage. They tipped their half cups of steaming tea onto the wet floor, crouched down and setting their torch beams low ran onwards, deeper into the tunnel. Adrenalin coursed through their veins. With no idea of where a quick exit might be found, they had until their follower reached the same level before a full-blown pursuit erupted. The boys would be seen easily, they couldn't move without light.

'Nothing ahead, Brucie. What we gonna do, man? Can't run to Naveby,' Rory hissed.

Bruce succumbed to his instinct to look behind him.

'What are you doing? Look ahead, will you?'

But Bruce's rearward glances became more frequent until they were his entire focus. Instinct had taken over. He had no control but to follow what felt natural amid the desperation. He grasped Rory's arm to guide him. The pair were openly sprinting now, Rory scanning ahead while Bruce fixed on what was behind.

'Rory, when I give the word, we kill the lights and hit the floor, flat on our fronts, heads facing back down the tunnel. You take the right side, I'll go left. Then pull your jacket over your head. Got it?'

'Got it, Bruce.'

The faint umber hue from their pursuer's flashlight had now turned to orange against the red brickwork. At any moment the torch beam would pin-prick into view. But that moment would be too late.

'Anything ahead, Rory?'

'Still nothing.'

'Down!'

Cloaked in pitch blackness they shuffled a few frantic adjustments to squeeze into the sides of the tunnel and cover up. The dull boom of boots deepened as the follower reached the top of the rise. Then the sound stopped.

Bruce spied a shaft of light through the thinner parts of fabric in his jacket. It poured past them. They might as well be under a spotlight. Still, Bruce, still. The light flicked away, then back. Bruce figured how far they had run. Their torch beams had been weak but he recalled a view of a totally bare tunnel. The follower's torch might have been much more powerful. If the stranger continued, they would have to make a break for it and try to outrun him or her, if they wanted to escape unidentified. Otherwise they would be caught.

The first couple of steps echoed down the tunnel, then paused.

'Bloody electrics,' a man's voice exclaimed.

More steps now. When to go? When to move?

As Bruce took a deep breath ready to tell Rory to run, the footsteps became quieter, moving away. No light, no sound now. Gone.

6

'Gentlemen, good morning, and thank you for coming. It's been a couple of weeks since we last met on the matter of internal security. I sense that's long enough for questions to be asked and our various MOD departments to respond, if they're ever going to.'

It was the seventh Monday of the autumn term and Colonel Hunter was hosting a gathering of the military staff in his comfortable wood-panelled office. Pitcaithly, Willis and Pearce were seated in a semi-circle around his large oak desk.

'So, having made our representations, what have we to report?' he continued. 'Gavin?'

'Sir, I have contacted both the Royal Military Police at Southwick Park and in parallel I thought I'd try my luck with the Special Investigations Branch at Bulford. Despite trying to tread a firm but balanced line about recent incidents, I spent most of my time either being passed around between departments or explaining that we are the *army* sixth form college. I did finally get to someone who showed some interest and took a few details. The bottom line is that they will – quote – be in touch.'

'Marvellous,' said Hunter sarcastically. 'George, please. Better news perhaps?'

'Colonel. I headed straight to the civil police headquarters in Sheffield – I thought an approach to the local station in Naveby would risk causing a lot of gossip. Sheffield responded well and took extensive details, plus mentioning that this could be a matter for Special Branch.'

'Thank you, George. That is indeed better news.'

'*Christ.*'

Pitcaithly's annoyance was thinly veiled and too audibly shared.

'RSM? Problem?'

'Sir, excuse me for sounding obstructive here, but in our collective efficiency haven't we rather muddied the waters? I can understand that we may be contacting the right sort of agencies and we need to act quickly, but approaching the various groups in parallel surely risks confusion and could leak the reason we're seeking support. If we suspect that the IRA are sniffing around for an easy headline, why didn't we go straight to MI5?'

'Well, RSM, these are all reasonable points, but if you know exactly how anyone contacts MI5 without giving the game away I'd love to hear it,' said Hunter.

'Sorry sir, but sweet mother o—' Pitcaithly stopped to compose himself. 'Of course it's academic now, but although we might not find MI5 in the phone book or want to risk a mail intercept, wouldn't getting on a train and paying a personal visit to Thames House have been an idea?'

Pearce and Willis exchanged sheepish looks under the principal's glare.

'Gentlemen, we are where we are. I suggest we allow the wheels that have been put in motion to turn,' Hunter said at last.

'And?' challenged Pitcaithly. 'Surely that's not enough? What if the wheels stop bloody turning and nobody bothers to tell us?'

'RSM, there's no need for such an attitude, if you please.'

'With respect, sir, there's every bloody need. We must plan for the worst – assume that everyone we have contacted will do nothing more than leak our news and the people that we should be talking to know nothing about it. First, we need to get down to London, and second, we need to put some sort of contingencies in place for ourselves.'

Hunter glowered at him but he could not escape the embarrassment caused by the collective ineptitude of his commissioned subordinates. But whatever the loss of face, he would not risk the boys' lives by failing to do his utmost. 'You're right,' he said through gritted teeth as he stared out of the window. 'We didn't think this through, did we?' He turned to Pitcaithly: 'RSM, would you please take the lead on devising appropriate internal contingencies? Come back to me when you have roughed out a plan and we'll take it from there. Meanwhile, I will go to London.'

*   *   *

That Monday afternoon ushered in the start of a new era for the college. While the platoons were engaged in the next part of a well-established training regime, their student commanders were summoned to Pitcaithly's office. Six in number, they all held the cadet rank of staff sergeant. They were accompanied by the student CCF commander whose rank was cadet company sergeant major.

'Come in, come in. Remove your headdress, guys. Find a chair and relax. We have things to think about,' Pitcaithly opened. 'I want your trust today, gentlemen, and we need your active co-operation in my task.'

Sober expressions set upon the faces of the students, each marked either with anticipation or anxiety, depending upon whether they thought they had anything to hide.

'Starter for ten: what's the current hot gossip among the student body right now? Well? Anyone? Who's in touch with the troops?'

Pitcaithly had intrigued, challenged and confused his audience in equal measure. There was silence as individuals feared volunteering the wrong information.

'I don't want anyone to incriminate themselves. I'm after any news being shared among the boys that could be in the general interest of the college, I am not concerned with any particular individuals,' he continued in an attempt to loosen tongues.

'Has Lady Margaret died, sir?'

'What? No, I said news not speculation. She's only in her fifties anyhow. And where did that come from? Come on, gentlemen.'

'Is it that we hold the largest silver collection in the world, sir?'

'What? Oh for Chrissakes. No! And that news is well known and is also not correct – it's a wild exaggeration, started by egotistical students, no doubt. But no.'

Pitcaithly paused once more, letting the silence pressure his subjects.

'Sir, I really don't think we've got anything for you, or at least not fitting your general interest criteria,' said Tim Hall, the student CSM. Tentative sighs rippled around the group at his words, which Pitcaithly met with a steely glare.

'Gentlemen, this is your last chance, or you will get to find out what I know you know and are not sharing with me in our collective security interests.'

Their eyes widened in consternation at what they might have overlooked and was about to be played back to them, but not a word was uttered.

'Right, okay,' Pitcaithly softened. 'Well,' he laughed to himself, 'I suppose that's something.' He sat back in his chair and surveyed them, his shrewd brown eyes scanning each in turn. He was taken aback that reports of recent incursions into the estate appeared to have remained secret with their individual reporters.

'I need absolute trust and confidentiality here, gentlemen. What I want to do is revise our usual training syllabus and refocus from broad skills development to purely infantry skills – specifically, conventional and non-conventional warfare, both offensive and defensive, especially in the urban environment. Now what will be extremely helpful is if you all can assist me in achieving this revised approach without alerting the student body. None of them have easy access to the syllabus, and thankfully no junior has ever actually asked to see it. The boys are happy to report for Monday afternoon CCF and do what they're told. It suits me that it stays that way – indeed, it must stay that way. Roger so far?'

'Sir,' the student commanders chorused in acknowledgement.

Michael Raines couldn't resist the intrigue, however. He was as distinctive by his reddish-brown quiff as he was for the near permanent tilt of his head, as if intently listening at all times.

'Sir, so will we actually get to learn why we're focusing on infantry skills?'

The other boys exchanged looks, barely managing to suppress their choking disbelief that Raines couldn't instil a modicum of confidence in Pitcaithly by keeping his mouth shut for just a bit longer.

The RSM gave him a long, searching look. 'I sincerely hope that you'll never need to know, Raines. Now, if I may continue, what I want is for us to switch away from all the peripheral skills and tasks such as preparing for parades, leadership and initiative training. The bottom line is that anything that doesn't directly contribute to fighting and surviving an enemy goes.'

The boys were gripped; they hung on his every word. Their thoughts about *why* were fading fast as the anticipation about *what* and *how* grew.

'I'll prepare a proper list so you know exactly what is in and what is out. This is just a heads-up. But expect stuff like weapons-handling skills, marksmanship, section- and platoon-level tactics and manoeuvres. I want us to be able to function and move swiftly and fluently – to be highly mobile, highly flexible. I want to focus on all types of patrols: standing, fighting, clearance, recce; plus quick attacks, snap ambushes, and operations in built-up areas, especially defensive. I want all this backed by solid and practised command and control, exercised through slick and reliable comms.'

He eyed them in turn as the information sank in.

'Questions?'

The first hand went up.

'White.'

'Sir, the need for security around why we're doing this is acknowledged, but may I explicitly confirm that our not knowing the true context will not disadvantage us if we are called upon to actually use said skills.'

'Why should it, White?'

'It's simply about whether we will know enough, sir. Surely knowing the bigger picture means we might be able to respond better if plans don't work out.'

'A fair point, yet sometimes that can be doubled-edged. Judging when, what and how information is used includes protecting it, and therefore withholding it too. So, trust me, as I say. Anyone else?'

There were no more questions, and the student commanders left, struck by the intrigue and the potential gravity of their task, and utterly committed to honouring Pitcaithly's wishes to maintain total secrecy.

'What do you make of that?' Tim Hall asked Marcus White, as the group headed away.

'We have to entertain every possibility, from the IRA to extreme groups associating themselves with the miners' strikes, or just armed robbers wanting some of Lady M's loot. Maybe we're gonna get called up early to serve – everybody knows the MOD is broke these days. They'd struggle if another Falklands blew up.'

'Shit, I hadn't thought quite as widely as that, Mr Strategy,' replied Tim in appreciation of Marcus's military mind. 'It's time to find out who's good at what among the juniors and seniors alike. We might need to consider a re-brigading of the platoons – even a tactical restructuring – to achieve best effect, if that can be done subtly.'

'And well done you, Sergeant Major. It seems you're the CSM for good reason,' White reciprocated.

*   *   *

'Yo Noble, you jammy geed,' cried Peter Falshaw, as he emerged into the dorms from the top of the spiral staircase. 'You've only made the Snowdon trip. Lucky sod. Eight of us went for that. You better bring me back a sheep or something.'

'Man, that's great news. But how do you know?' said Bruce.

'A few of us passed Tavener putting the list up by Willis's office after evening PT – which is where you'll need to be from now on.'

'You're right, it'll be tough – for the two juniors, I mean, next to the fitter seniors. So who got the other spot from 67 Entry?'

'Guess. And he won't be needing extra PT.'

'Well, I'd rather not presume. Go on, who is it?'

'The one and only Mad Man of Hoy, Rory McIntyre of course.'

Bruce felt a surge of excitement. He was off for a winter walking trip with his closest buddy. If the going got tough, you couldn't have anyone better next to you. He sprinted round the square of attic corridors, searching for the other lucky geed. When he reached Dorm Eleven, Rory was already celebrating to an appreciative audience as he demonstrated lifting his whole body horizontally from the floor by holding just the thin edge of an open door.

'Go McIntyre!' applauded Hepburn, standing in mono-grammed pyjamas with matching dressing gown, his hair perfectly groomed.

'Go! Go! Go!' built the chorus from the rapidly filling dorm.

Unfortunately the din drowned the telltale creaks coming from the door, and when Rory achieved full lift the top hinge ruptured and twisted loose. The cries of the pack reached fever pitch as Rory hit the floor and the door detached, crashing down at the feet of the waiting Mr Cowley.

'Ah shite!' cried Rory, face down. 'That's one cheap bloody excuse for a door. God, you can tell the MOD's skint.'

'Look on the bright side, McIntyre, it will probably cost less to repair,' said Mr Cowley.

Rory realised that the silence surrounding his exclamation was not born of his comrades' astonishment, but their dread.

'Gentlemen, I suggest anyone not wishing to join McIntyre or Goldman on points, plus costs for you – or should I say your parents, Rory – may wish to retire to bed now,' Cowley continued.

The thin walls and floorboards of dorm and corridor shook as twenty pairs of feet made their escape, leaving Rory and Tom Goldman, the unfortunate dorm i/c, to pick up the pieces. Bruce had left last, signalling an offer of support to Rory who nodded in acknowledgement but waved him away.

'My study tomorrow after chapel then, gentlemen,' Cowley closed.

By the time Bruce returned to Dorm Six from the washrooms, the riotous mood had evaporated in the wake of Cowley's appearance. The other guys quickly settled and Richie Parks, the dorm i/c, switched out the light as Bruce slipped through the doorway. In the far corner, in the bed next to Bruce's, Shaun Dodd was reading some hefty tome under a shielded reading light.

'Anything good?' Bruce murmured. He figured that Shaun wouldn't be reading material typical of his peer group.

'Keep it down please, Brucie.'

Even low tones were too much for Richie. Shaun turned the cover towards Bruce with the soft light just illuminating the title. For a moment he thought he'd got Dodd all wrong, *Sex, Ecology, Spirituality*, but then the rest of title shattered the illusion: *The Spirit of Evolution*, by Ken Wilber. He risked a whisper. 'What's that about? Like sex is okay and we should all be doing it because it makes you a better person and stuff?'

'Noble! Shut it or you'll be pressing until dawn,' fired Herr Oberst Parks.

Shaun's eyes shot to heaven in disgust at Bruce's trivial hypothesis. He would, no doubt, enjoy intellectually battering Bruce another time.

*   *   *

The next morning brought fresh intrigue among a minority within the student body. Word travelled fast that Arthur Rose had been granted permission to lead a weekly sports class on his specialist subject. But it was not simply karate or jujitsu, as some had expected, but 'eastern fighting arts'. The buzz was that it would include everything that teenage combat brains could conceive. The morning passed through a distraction of lessons as a number of would-be Bruce Lees and David Carradines dreamed of kung fu, samurai swords and ninja tactics. They couldn't wait until the first session that afternoon.

At 3 p.m., eleven tracksuit-clad wannabes arrived in the ballroom, known as the Great Hall, and headed for Art, who was set up at the far end on the judo mats. Dressed in the familiar martial artist's white gi jacket and less familiar wide black hakama trousers, he bid his new students to sit on the low gym benches bordering the matted area.

'Right, let's make a start. Before we launch into anything I just want to get an idea of what you want, or think you want, from our sessions. That way I can consider how I might best cover everybody's preferences – whether we increase to a couple of sessions a week, and so on.'

It soon became clear that they wanted to learn practical skills, rather than getting an overview of many fighting arts but be next to useless at all of them. Quality, not quantity; transformation, not translation, thought Bruce, oddly calling to mind one of Shaun's occasional mantras. The rub came when the group tried to agree exactly what to cover. Three or four were out for both unarmed arts and something using weapons. Others were more pragmatic – wanting just unarmed skills, preferably comprising both striking and grappling techniques, plus 'real-life moves', aka street fighting.

Art approached the mix of incompatible wish lists with eminent composure.

'Guys, given the spread of skills you seek, I can only offer my best blend and if it's not good enough then I apologise, but you don't have to stay.' They leaned in to hear who would get what from the competing preferences. 'To keep the broadest interest, I will include techniques from karate, judo, aikido and kendo. That will be more than enough – sorry, no ninjutsu, Mike.' Heskell beamed back, delighted to have been considered. Art continued, 'We must begin with a number of weeks of very basic but essential stuff, otherwise we will be wasting our time. Let's make a start. We'll get warm, stretch and begin our practice with posture, balance, stance and *ma-ai* – the control of distance. It might sound boring, but consider an opponent who cannot land a blow or grab you because you move so freely.'

They were hooked.

Art's two-hour session shot by. Much like a great game of squash, the physical effort was secondary amid the near total immersion in the activity. It was only during the walk to the Kitchen Block showers that Bruce realised he was soaked through with sweat – just from holding stances, keeping balance, pushing, pulling and darting in every direction.

'Brucie,' called Rory, pounding up the corridor. 'The admin instructions are out for Snowdonia. You need to get your boots into the sports store for a check.'

'Okay, cool. No, wait a moment. Why? Who asked for that?'

'Old Grainger the stores' manager said that Mr Tavener was co-ordinating a kit check. Anything considered unfit for winter walking would be substituted with hiking boots, jackets and so on from the stores.'

Bruce's fixed gaze broke through Rory's buoyant mood.

'Rory, you say Tavener ordered this? Mr Weirdo from the labs, Mr TA Officer Misfit is co-ordinating a kit check, when Marham could just have told Grainger to pull it together?' Bruce was seething. He dragged Rory into the end of the corridor where they wouldn't be noticed.

'Calm down, mate. If you're suggesting that this is all to do with our wee excursion down under, it's a hell of a leap of faith to think Tavener was there, he's picked-out our boot prints and now he's created an excuse to look for a match. That's a long shot, if you ask me. We're only two out of a hundred and fifty, after all – and he's only checking the exped guys. That's only eight of us. Anyway, even if it was true, what business has he down there? He shouldn't be there either. Christ, the guy's hardly more than a lackey round here.'

But Bruce felt a sixth sense at work, drowning such logic.

'Have you handed your boots in yet, Rory?'

'Just done it.'

'Shit, okay. Did you say anything to suggest that I have my own pair?'

'No I didn't, although since nearly everyone's got their own boots here, it wouldn't be saying much if I did.'

'Right, from now on I don't possess my own boots, understand? I could be totally wrong here, but if I'm right, we need to take every opportunity to be a step ahead. I'll request a pair from stores and use those for the trip. If it's all the same to you I don't want to chuck away a career that hasn't even started yet.'

'Crap. Didn't even cross my mind,' sighed Rory.

'What's done is done so just go with me on this. If we're suspected of anything, it's just a bit harder to confirm if the second set of fresh prints can't be identified. And like you say, if that's his or anyone else's aim, then theoretically they really need to check everyone's boots. So fingers crossed.'

7

It was Saturday, 8 November 1986 and Lady Margaret Cadogan-Brandt was taking mid-morning breakfast after her daily ride across the estate on her favourite mare, a grey Irish hunter named Duchess. She was thinking about Tavener's report that two unidentified individuals had entered the tunnels and ventured under Serpentine Lake. Her instinct to withhold information about her legacy from the man had been overtaken by events, and he was now in charge of Rothwell's modest electronic security measures. When the pressure plates in the lower tunnel section were triggered, he had solid evidence that a plan was required.

Sipping a delicately flavoured cup of Chinese white tea, she pondered her isolation as she watched wisps of steam rising above the bone china. Over and over she contemplated the series of complex, unseen global events that had culminated in the need to hire an outsider, a career professional. The urge to survive until she could entrust her secrets to her own kind stirred within her. It made every contact with Tavener a game of wits as she strove to reconcile short-term protection and long-term secrecy. She was learning how to tackle him. Even simple things, such as the decision to sleep on his information rather than immediately endorsing a course of action at his behest, bought her time and advantage. Still, every incident weighed heavily on her. With two students suspected of snooping, her fear was not that they posed any real threat, but that it afforded Tavener another reason to ask questions. He still had not been told what was kept in the area under the lake.

First things first. She would head to the communications room in the private section of the main house and make sure Tavener was not on the estate. Then she would head under Serpentine Lake to the Archive and take stock.

*   *   *

From their vantage point on the steps of the main house's southern wing, Pitcaithly, Mike Raines and Marcus White were looking out over the perfect greenery of the former Nottinghamshire County cricket ground, which this term was given over to the first fifteen's rugby pitch – avoiding the hallowed centre square, of course. The scene was one of incongruent beauty. The day was blustery, but bright. The sun warmed them but was occasionally blocked by clouds which passed over like speeding chariots. A chill wind tore at the remaining deciduous leaves on nearby beech trees. Ornate arrangements of plants that defined the rose garden had been stripped to dull barbs recoiling against the stubborn winter gale.

A platoon, separated into its three sections, swept back and forth over the sports ground. Another, beyond the bridge, was doing the same on the gentle grassy slope of the lakeside. The distant figures were as black specks on a tumultuous sea – gusts whipped long blades to and fro in a kaleidoscope of emeralds and jades. This vista of raw natural perfection was an unlikely backdrop for young men learning the art of war.

Pitcaithly turned to his two young companions.

'How's the new training regime going, lads?'

'Surprisingly well, sir. The guys aren't stupid, they know something's changed, and they know that nobody wants any questions about it,' said Raines.

'Understood. So why do you think they suspect a change, as you put it?'

'We've got lots more range work and live firing, but concentrated on those over or nearing eighteen, and I guess the rest is intuition – we're serious and it must show.'

'They feel the vibes, if you like, sir,' interjected White.

'Indeed.' The RSM nodded, then turned to observe the group on the rugby pitch. 'See Three Section there,' he continued, 'you need to get your section commanders to use a tactic for getting the guys to move quicker when resuming the advance after going to ground. Tell them to brief their sections that when the commander gets up it's the signal for them all to move. And the commander should get up fast and take a couple of quick steps, as if he's about to sprint. The guys will instinctively get up and start

85

moving quicker in an attempt to keep up. It will make the whole unit more agile in its manoeuvre.'

White and Raines exchanged glances, in awe at the RSM's experience.

'Who's having a go at the defence plan?' Pitcaithly asked.

The question reminded his students that all of this activity was because the college was a potential target – not the hunter, but the hunted. Practising offensive moves was good for gelling teams, but was of marginal value against unknown threats.

'Clausewitz White here is taking the lead on defensive strategies, sir,' came Raines' reply, in a reference to the nineteenth-century Prussian mastermind and father of modern military doctrine.

'And when do you think you'll have something to show me, Mr White?'

'I'm about half through what I would like to achieve, sir. I'm researching in parallel too, so it's taking longer than a Piooma estimate. I'm aiming at a week today.'

'Don't bullshit me with jargon. A bloody "pi" what?'

'Er …' Marcus' eyes widened in trepidation at the RSM's reaction. He looked to his fellow platoon commander.

'You said it, Marcus,' muttered Raines.

'Well?'

'It's Piooma, sir: Pulled it out of my arse.'

'I've heard it all now. Well, I'm glad you aren't doing one of those. That said, remember we're in a tactical setting here, so we need a plan and fall-backs for when it goes wrong, as it inevitably will. Strategies are for wars. We're preparing for battle, so make it real.'

'It remains all the more challenging, of course, not having a clue about the threat, sir.'

'A point you made very well in our first orders-group, young White. But I would think more along the lines of what the threat might be. Nobody knows what it is, I'll allow you that much at least.'

Pitcaithly's words were as dark as the thickening cloud.

*   *   *

It was many months since Lady Margaret had had reason to visit the damp, dusty vault. Her heart always raced when the hydraulic door thudded shut behind her, and she prayed that the electrics would hold, both so she would be alerted to anyone approaching but also so she could get out.

The light from a tired yellow bulb was so dim that bending over the volumes of records for any length of time would result in eye strain. Where to begin? The visit to this place, the standing and staring around the walls at the semi-ordered documents, was a compulsion she could neither contain nor rationalise as her sense of isolation grew towards suffocation. Once or twice over the years sons of the organisation had passed through Rothwell's gates. She craved that a miracle would befall her and she could reconnect to her extraordinary kind again through a name on one of the pages. Perhaps she could get a message out or even contemplate entrusting access to her legacy, so all would not be lost if anything happened to her.

She eagerly clutched the college nominal roll, which Roberts had surreptitiously copied and she had already pored over. She scanned the pages once more, hoping that sheer inspiration, something from deep inside her, would reveal a name. Her eyes moved slowly down the first sheet: *Elkins, Falshaw, Foreman, Jukes, Kane, Loevenger, Nairn, Ness, Noble, Raines, Storey, Strickland, Turner* … When she reached the end she felt a single emotion: hope. The list was not fruitless; it yielded the faintest glow of possibility founded on nothing more than gut intuition. Noble. What a fitting name. But now to search for a connection.

The records stretched back generations, variously grouped – by date, or family, or country of origin – and in some places alphabetical sequences emerged. The most recent lineages would be easiest to trace. Only that way could a suspected positive identification be verified. The method of filing was possibly the best clue to a document's age: from parchment scrolls, to hand-bound and decorated volumes, to card folders from the fifties, including some MOD document covers which had found their way out of the OC's or principal's offices. She decided to start by looking at these.

The dozen folders yielded little. Codenames, contact arrangements, organisations, roles, but nothing to suggest a connection to Noble or any other current student names. The randomness of her endeavour began to smack of hopelessness and naivety. She pressed on, thumbing determinedly through the pages. Nothing ... nothing ... then *Noble!* No, *Nobile*; a foreign connection? *Piano Nobile, RV "Fox", Knossos, Crete [Exp. 31 Oct 58]*. Damn. The words continued to flow past. Deane, Diamond, Newman ... Noble-Franks – Noble-Franks?

> *Entry: 1 Nov 75. Noble-Franks, Jennifer (F); Code: Osprey; Orgs: Bank of England (1966-68); Ostermann Partners (68-84); Gray and Hartens LLP (85-): 1-3 Cornhill, London EC3; Contact: Protocol ZULU.*

Lady Margaret steadied herself lest she should fall prey to a flight of fancy. She noted the key details before continuing with renewed vigour. It could just be a coincidence and she needed to consider other possibilities. Then another curious observation: *Doddy* ... Doddy? Her eyes jumped back to the nominal roll: *Dodd, Shaun (67E)*. Another potential connection? She took the details and completed her sift, finding nothing else. Her cryptic notes would go to Roberts, the only person she trusted to trace names and verify connections.

*   *   *

'Got your issued hiking boots then, Brucie? Nice. Very stylish,' mused Rory, having earlier seen the heavy leather clumps lined up outside stores ready for issue. Their design pre-dated his boots by at least ten years. Bruce just grinned back at his jibe, understanding it was more about flirting with their secret in public than any insult over equipment.

'*College!*' came Pitcaithly's familiar roar.

The student body was preparing for the march-past which would follow the Remembrance Sunday service at Wheatley church. The band was from a regular army battalion, the Worcestershire and Sherwood Foresters Regiment, and when the music erupted Bruce felt as if a primal part of his brain was engaged, the hairs standing up on the back of his neck. This was an elixir of fighting spirit, a unified team acting with singular purpose and flowing with pride. It ran through your veins and changed who you were.

The village of Wheatley lay on the estate's southern flank, only a couple of miles from the house. Its residents were used to Rothwell on Remembrance Sunday, and the locals looked on with respect and admiration as the youth of the day passed by. As the column approached the centre of the village, Bruce noticed a man leaning against a phone box. There was something familiar about his face. He sneaked only brief glimpses, lest his prying eyes drew the stranger's attention. The colour of his hair, his strong jawline, Bruce knew he recognised him, but from where? He racked his brains – yes, that was it. Very possibly a face from the black four-by-four incident in the woods.

He tried to attract Rory's attention.

'Hey McIntyre, is that phone box on your list? I know how you like to spot them.'

'Seen. And I don't think that one's in my wee book, no.'

Rory had grasped the obscure hint and coded back his acknowledgement of the sighting.

'Whoever's talking in Three Platoon – shut it!' came the platoon sergeant's hapless attempt at control, his voice drowned out by a crescendo from the band.

Bruce hadn't been able to resist the opportunity to involve Rory in the incident in the woods, in spite of the secrecy to which he and Simon had been sworn. He figured that planting the seed in his friend's mind could be interesting. Now he had to work out what to say when Rory asked him why he had pointed the guy out to him. Had he been a bit too spontaneous?

After a while the band stopped playing and broke off, heading back to their bus in the village car park. The student body continued the march along the southern estate road back to college. Once back in the building Bruce and Rory joined the queue to hand their rifles into the armoury, which is when a familiar voice piped up behind them.

'Sergeant, I think you'll find it was the lovebirds McIntyre and Noble who were talking in the middle of the march-past,' came Jez-the-failed-bully's first attempt at a back stab.

'I'll second that, Sergeant.' Right on cue – Jez's sidekick, Tom-the-sheep.

'Keep out of this, Calico,' the platoon sergeant commanded Tom. 'You were in Five Platoon on the other side of the band, so you couldn't have heard anything, you moron. But, in any case, so what? Somebody jabbered and I shut them up. That's my role. I doubt if the public heard anything over the band anyway, and I'm buggered if I'm pissing around trying to do anyone for it.'

Bruce stayed quiet to avoid any more distraction from the ugly brothers, but Rory couldn't quite hold that off-the-leash tongue of his.

'Two-nil,' he muttered.

That'll be fisticuffs at dawn then, thought Bruce.

But there would be no fisticuffs the following morning. At 06:45 the college was stood to. Everyone was woken and moved to the library for a head count and a briefing from Colonel Hunter. Most were in pyjamas and dressing gowns, a few early birds part-dressed and semi-shaven, and a handful in PT shorts and vests.

The principal stood on a low wooden platform, resting his hands on a simple lectern in front of him. His expression was grave.

'Gentlemen, you have been called here at this early hour firstly to check we are all present and correct, but secondly because we have just discovered an incursion, the areas affected appearing to be the Great Hall and some college offices.'

A murmur swept through the gathering.

'Because we are not sure of the nature of the incursion, we have first to ensure you are not exposed to any physical threat,' he continued.

Great, Bruce thought, gather us in one place with no armed protection – fab plan – smacked of no plan. Bruce glanced over at Pitcaithly who remained impassive, but Bruce guessed he was sharing the same concerns. Yet the announcement, with its clear tactical flaws and suggestion of risk excited Bruce: maybe there really was a potential enemy out there. He felt a rush of adrenalin. The uncertainty and reality were far more scintillating a prospect than sports fixtures and exams.

A small group of seniors returned from checking the inner college buildings and grounds. That felt more like Pitcaithly's influence – a plan enacted. With the all-clear declared, the gathering dispersed, all sworn to secrecy of course, but stopping a hundred and fifty tongues from wagging seemed optimistic. This, plus the shift of focus in CCF training over recent weeks, meant the game was up. A confirmation of the threat was all that was required to put Rothwell on a war footing.

*　　　*　　　*

'I have been able to verify both names, my lady: Noble and Dodd. The name Doddy was changed by deed poll,' explained Roberts. 'Noble's parents are still called Noble-Franks, but Bruce's birth certificate states only Noble.'

'I understand. Sounds about right too. Anything to throw potential adversaries off the trail. Now, to minimise our exposure in this matter I intend only to make contact with one of them. But which? Does your research offer any clues?'

'Both groups of parents are still married. Dodd's father and Noble's mother are members of the organisation, both inactive.'

'When was their last contact with the organisation?'

'Mr Dodd, now in his fifties, nothing since the Vietnam conflict, but plenty during that period. Mrs Noble-Franks assisted through the 1973 oil crisis, and since 1980 her work has allowed her to monitor the rise of exotic financial instruments. It seems she may have current international connections from that activity.'

'Perhaps she is the better option. If I can make contact with her then it might be possible to safely reconnect with the wider organisation. But first things first. I need to meet with Master Noble and determine whether he is a potential help or liability.'

'And to be clear about Mr Tavener's part in this?'

'Absolutely none, not until I say otherwise. I am happy that he is here to deal with day-to-day security, but I need to know someone for longer before I can trust them and we're not there yet. Perhaps yesterday's break-in will give him something to act upon and I can learn more of the man, decide whether to fully trust him. For now, I need to conjure a miracle.'

'My lady?'

'I need to meet Master Noble without anyone knowing. I want to get the measure of the boy, explain the situation as far as I dare, and set at least two protocols: one for how he can know the precise asset type and means of access, if ever required, and another to cover his contacting the organisation through the utmost secret means. If any part of the endeavour fails to meet with total success it could guarantee our undoing and without doubt young Noble's death.'

8

'Well, that's something you don't see every day: the principal of Rothwell College getting all sorts of encounters – or so he thinks. Suspicious vehicles hiding in the grounds, breaks-ins to the college buildings, dark-faced strangers watching their parades. He's jumping at shadows.'

Frank Bennings, principal homeland security officer at MI5, put down the latest incidents report on the desk in front of him. He pushed his thick round glasses on top of his sweaty, pudgy head to rub his tired eyes.

'You can understand his concerns though, Frank,' returned Joe Cotton, his skinnier colleague.

'And you can understand why we would need ten times the resources if we started chasing around after everyone who added two and two and got five. As if we don't have enough real problems to deal with: threats from the IRA, tracking agents from the Middle East – agents from everywhere for that matter. Only amateurs race off when they're under someone's nose, or break in and leave with nothing.'

'Nevertheless, the encounters are, for now at least, linked to a valid soft target and they remain unexplained. Do I put it on the board?'

'Christ! We have to. That's what's frustrating. I bet it's just some youths out of Birmingham or Sheffield who've got word of the college and are out flaunting a hot motor and entertaining themselves with a snoop. Tricks for kicks.'

'Doesn't explain the break-in, though.'

'Look Joe, any tradesman visiting that place to do an odd job will see things that people will talk about – oil paintings in . . . what is it . . . the Grand Hall, or whatever. And either they, or their criminally persuaded pals, will crack Lady M's no doubt antiquated locks and have a go. If they've got brains, they'll only take what they can sell on, so they enter on a hunch but may leave with nothing if it doesn't work out. Get it?'

'Point taken. I'll still put it on the white board.'

*   *   *

Colonel Hunter returned to Rothwell perplexed. While polite and professional, the MI5 team had made it clear that he would not rank highly on their agenda. He had no idea of how else to protect the college without turning it into a police state and strangling normal activities. That could cause real problems if parents started asking questions and getting involved. Pitcaithly's measures would be effective up to a point, but what if they experienced a direct attack? How would they prevent an outright massacre?

As the taxi sped along the familiar trail from Naveby station his mind ran in all directions. Arm the boys? No. Talk to Lady Margaret? No, no. Should he call for favours from the local regular battalion? Or maybe speak to an old acquaintance who had served with the SAS for some tips on how to turn the odds in their favour? His thoughts tumbled one after the other. Perhaps some solace would be found in the detail of Pitcaithly's plans. The RSM's goal would always be to stop any threat to college personnel. Surely then, he would have a trick up his sleeve if the going got rough? But would he admit that? And should he even ask about it?

*   *   *

As the end of the first term drew near, many new experiences presented themselves. The college prepared for the passing-out parade for the senior entry. The parade itself lasted about an hour, when some senior officer or medium-ranking public dignitary – say a second permanent under-secretary of state – would come and review the assembled cadets. Then would be the open day with military, sporting and novel practical displays, like how to prepare a lightweight Land Rover for a parachute drop. A buffet lunch and a tour of the college buildings and facilities would complete the agenda. The dread among the boys was screwing up a drill move, or worse, fainting on parade. The latter was less of a problem in winter, but they were still coached to wiggle toes and discreetly contract and relax muscles to maintain good circulation when standing still for long periods.

For Bruce, the greater spectacle was the President's Dinner. The preserve of the senior entry, this formal dinner was a milestone on the road to preparing for Sandhurst. Students wore the deep blue college blazer, a white shirt and black bow tie. They were matched nearly one-for-one by their guests, all currently serving or ex-military personnel, either in mess dress or black tie. The variety, colour, cut and sheer splendour of the officers' mess uniforms was the essence of cool for aspiring young officers. Most of the material was in midnight blue, which in fact looked nearer to black. Thereupon were subtle or less subtle panels, piping, leg stripes and so on in reds, golds, greys, greens, blues, depending on the wearer's corps or regiment. To top it were brass or wire rank insignia and embroidered regimental badges, such as the Royal Electrical and Mechanical Engineer's prancing stallion and lightning bolt. Finally came the black mirrors of mess Wellington boots – knee-high finest leather, covered to the heel by tight-fitting mess trousers, plus spurs and gold-braided No1 dress hats for majors and above. An outfit would put you back at least a thousand pounds. And all this to start a civilised evening and end up wrecked, after too much beer, wine, port, and to cap it all, mess rugby. But that was the reward for putting up with the speeches.

*   *   *

By Friday 12 December the college was ready for the long-awaited return to homes and families for Christmas. The boys gleefully packed their cases and boarded shuttle buses to Naveby station or climbed into their parents' cars – everyone that is but for those packing another set of gear, bound for the frozen slopes and peaks of Snowdonia.

The winter expedition group would depart the following day after a dreary night in an empty college. With few students in residence everything operated on a temporary, money-saving footing. The limited lighting struggled against great chasms of echoing darkness that haunted untravelled corridors and empty classrooms. Black, lifeless dormitories gaped back eerily as Bruce passed them en route to the bathroom. This end-of-evening depression was the parting shot of a day whose only highlight might have been dinner, but even that possibility was soundly slaughtered by the woeful lacklustre offerings of a skeleton catering service from the grumpy chef, dubbed Kong for his ever bare, huge hairy forearms, plunging jowls and dark, accusing eyes.

The excitement of the next day more than made up for the previous evening. It was mid-afternoon with daylight already being swallowed by the mountains when the minibus reached the head of the Llanberis Pass. The boys craned their necks to gawp at fading views of snow-clad rock reaching out of sight into the low cloud. Quarter of an hour later, the eight boys and two staff were installed in the holiday cottage that would be their home for the next five days.

'Everyone in the living room in ten minutes, guys. Mr Marham wants to brief us!'

Seb Wyatt was excited. These were not normal college conditions. Yes, they had volunteered for some healthy, challenging activity, but most of all for sheer bloody outdoor fun. In no time, all were gathered; the anticipation was palpable. Marham was keen to acknowledge and respect the eagerness on display.

'Okay guys, just want to put a bit of shape on the next few days: outline the routine, look at some of the possible routes – always weather dependent, in winter especially – and confirm arrangements for your onward journeys home after we're done.'

Maps were prepared in waterproof cases, and boxed rations and emergency medical kits were shared around before it was time for Mr Tavener and John Turner's combined attempt at being chef for the night.

The open-plan kitchen and living area meant a hungry audience looked on keenly to see what dinner would bring. However, with no red wine to drown a bit of flavour into the army ration tins of so-called beef bourguignon, Rob

'Rambo' Blanchard-Jones was all too quick to provide his field seasoning of Tabasco sauce. With dad being a former SAS sergeant, Rob took his soldiering very seriously.

Tavener took over and faces cringed as he started measuring out the third teaspoon. They were mighty relieved when Turner stopped him. It tasted surprisingly good, which didn't say much for the original rations. With no TV on offer, or booze for the seniors to enjoy, the cottage soon fell quiet as staff and students hit the bunks for an early night.

Next morning the peace was broken by the return of the minibus crunching up the stony lane, its engine struggling to haul it safely to the cottage. The boys were still upstairs in their sleeping bags, but now awake thanks to the noise. They listened as doors slammed and muffled voices exchanged words briefly below. A few moments later Jamie Philpott, 66 Entry Wessex House, appeared round the bedroom door and started searching in his rucksack.

'What's going on down there?' Rory yawned.

'It looks like Tavener's keen to impress Marham. As if the world's most expensive hiking boots weren't enough, he's just been to the camp at Capel Curig to get a read-out for the day's weather.'

'What's that about his boots?' said Rory, still in semi-stupor.

'Scarpa Fitzroys, like yours, you greasy geed.'

Rory's eyes widened. Slowly he sat up and turned to see whether Bruce had heard. Bruce was looking straight back at him, his hands cupped over his mouth.

The dot-printed computer read-out was the basis of the 08:00 announcement that the weather that day would be iffy – bad for anything risky, but good to get into the hills and experience the new environment. Kit was loaded into the minibus and the group headed for Moel Eilio, which would serve as an ideal space to practise map reading, winter walking, survival and rescue drills. Just three miles north-west of Snowdon and barely ten minutes from the Llanberis cottage, they reached the start point.

'We'll be doing all our walks as a single group,' started Mr Marham to the huddle around him. 'Why would I prefer to do that?'

He paused. A couple of hands went up.

'John?'

'Because we have only one instructor, sir?'

Tavener glared at Turner, his face reddening and cheek muscles pulsating as he ground his teeth in irritation.

'Not really what I was meaning,' Marham replied.

Hands went up again. 'Is it in the event of an injury? If a casualty has to be treated but can't be moved and someone has to navigate off the mountain to get help, you need two adults or qualified people to be capable of achieving both tasks,' said Rory.

'Spot on, Rory. And any other reasons?'

'Morale, sir,' came Blanchard-Jones, always taking the view from the trench. The lack of response prompted him to have another go. 'How about learning quicker? If there are more people, there will be more interactions, discussions, questions and stuff,' he offered.

'Both morale and learning are correct, Jones. Especially the part about "stuff".'

'Thank you, sir.'

'You're welcome. Right, who wants to lead us to the first waypoint?'

They strode off and quickly gained altitude. The pace was getting too much for Bruce when they stopped for Greg Matthews to check his map, with Marham making a few teaching points as everyone huddled round. The difference in strength and fitness between Bruce and the seniors still showed, despite a term of intense physical training. Rory was in his element, however; red-faced, with a constant grin and a permanent icy drip on the end of his nose.

The teasing views of the lakes and old slate spoils of Llanberis were smothered as the expedition entered the cloud base at around a thousand feet. The temperature dropped and a keen wind whipped the dense, moist air over the mountain's sweeping grassy sides, now thick with snow and revealing only traces of the longest marshy blades. Hats were tugged down tight over eyebrows and ears to protect exposed flesh, their orange windproof jackets soon clad in a thickening layer of ice. Thank God he had bought a pair of fibre pile mitts, thought Bruce. His hands were toasty.

'Okay gentlemen, let's stop here and get some hot drinks and snacks on board.'

Marham led them into the lee of the hill. It was still exposed, but nestled in a dip it avoided the harshest wind.

'When we're done with refreshments, Mr Tavener and I will guide you through some rope work so we know how to walk as a group with a safety rope.'

The group spread out into an evenly spaced line and learned how to join the rope, move, signal, and what to do if someone fell. It seemed to Bruce that arresting a fall this way was more a confidence-inspiring measure than a guarantee that the faller would be saved and not take others down the mountain with him.

At the other end of the line from Bruce was Rory, who was talking to Tavener, his voice moving from excitable to argumentative. Bruce could only hear bits of the dialogue, but the tone and gestures were clear enough. Rory appeared to be tying and re-tying the rope and getting irate with Tavener when he seemed to insist on doing it differently. Rory the stubborn mule had made his acquaintance with Tavener the twat, thought Bruce. The others looked on bemused. Finally, Marham intervened, the two separated and the march continued, this time with Jon Archibald taking the map.

Moel Eilio's comparatively gentle features meant that weaker team members could begin to adjust to the cold and the different type of physical exertion of hill walking. The varying depths of snow were the major factor separating this experience from a summer jaunt across open grassland. The effort drained leg muscles, and shin splints from frozen rugby pitches felt like barbed wire in the veins. With the effort came internal heat and sweat, so a longed-for stop to rest and take on fluids meant you could start to freeze in moments. Hypothermia was the silent stalker of which all were warned and constantly vigilant. That was how this environment could seduce you with its beauty then drain you to death in minutes.

*   *   *

'Good morning, my lady. You are awake very early today,' said Roberts tentatively as he entered the sitting room of Rothwell Woodhouse carrying a tray of tea.

'Yes, I awoke around four o'clock and couldn't settle since,' replied Lady Margaret. Roberts' sympathetic expression drew her further. 'I had a terrible dream. At least, I hope it was a dream and not a premonition.'

'You have had much to contend with recently, my lady, and we have a not inconsequential challenge in how to engage young Master Noble next term.'

'That's my fear – that I foresaw something terrible for him.'

Roberts slid into the soft chesterfield sofa opposite Lady Margaret's and listened.

'Are you able to distinguish between a dream and a psychic insight, my lady?'

'From the relatively few visions I have experienced over the years, some of which you will of course recall, and from my wider knowledge of matters of the mind, I can usually tell the difference. That is worth its weight in gold, or perhaps not, on second thoughts. How much would a thought in fact weigh?'

The two laughed. Lady Margaret clasped the tea cup. She needed to laugh, to break the tension and see past her inner torment.

'You see, dreams are born of an ancient mental construct, the so-called magical mind. Magical mind is prevalent in modern humans only in the dreaming state of consciousness, but long ago, ancient man would have perceived of the world this way in his waking state. An example you may have heard of is the caveman who would look up at the moon as he walked, believing it followed him. This is a normal part of ontogenetic development; that is to say that as children we all navigate our ancient roots during our psychological development to adulthood. So children who are young enough would experience the moon in the same way as early mankind.' She took a sip of tea and shook her head in self-mockery. 'Listen to this drivel. Now who's guilty of jargon and inciting boredom?'

'No, please, it's fascinating. Do continue, if you will, my lady.'

'Well, thanks to magical mind, dreams do not follow normal physical rules. Things get mixed up, mutate, and impossible things can happen, or things that are possible in the real world cannot be done. We have archetypes that reflect key metaphorical forms from our phylogenetic, or evolutionary, past. Conversely, my visions have never had those qualities or entities. They obey the rules and forms of remembered real events, or constructed, imagined events, which one might think up while awake. The problem is that my experience last night had some of each. It was experienced in the first person – as if I was looking through my own eyes, rather than observing myself in the scene. It was in colour, with sound – such terrible sounds – and with motion. That's like a vision.'

'And what of the aspects that corresponded with being a dream?'

'The scene was unclear, obscure. It's difficult to properly articulate.'

'And the sounds?'

'It was a sort of wild howling. I know it sounds ridiculous.' She frowned and gazed out of the window momentarily. 'Yes, a sort of ebbing and flowing of booming and howling. Quite bizarre.'

'How did young Noble feature in the experience?'

'I sensed his presence – either in the scene or that this episode somehow related to him. I actually saw nothing of him. It was purely kinaesthetic.'

'Perhaps having dark dreams is inevitable if you're contemplating involving Noble in our situation, our world. One can only hope it's that, and not a re-awakening of your sight.'

*   *   *

Snowdonia was tough but awe inspiring for the young Bruce Noble. The boys were confident in the skills and leadership demonstrated by Terry Marham, whose experience as an alpine guide showed. Nothing fazed the man. He loved this, it was his passion. Away from the college he was quite different – the students could do no wrong and so learned a great deal.

Tavener was still a conundrum, he didn't seem to know how to relax and be himself, whatever that would look like. Although he was efficient and committed, too frequently he appeared to be working at the limit of his knowledge and experience. The second day's excursion to the daunting hulk of Tryfan was a case in point. The mountain rose into a slate grey sky, an intimidating mass of granite with the bladed spine of a colossal stegosaurus. Steep faces swept down from all sides of its frozen form. The group made a rapid ascent over rock that ran wet from the angry sky. Having negotiated the Heather Terrace, they threaded their way directly to the summit via the South Gully.

After a brief stop it was time to try out the famous leap between Adam and Eve. These two protrusions of rock stood above all else, each the size of a large wardrobe. Each student was invited, but not required, to make the five-foot jump from one to the other, which the gentle wind allowed that day. To the north side a cliff fell away for hundreds of feet into the chasm between the central and north buttresses. Beyond this was seemingly infinite space reaching out to the surrounding valleys, which threatened to pluck you from the mountain top and swallow you whole. It was not for the faint-hearted.

'So you understand the aim, and the risks, guys. But that's adventure training – the risks make it real. Who fancies a go? And it's fine if you don't,' said Marham.

The wind whipped lightly around with an eerie anticipation, while above hung the threatening black clouds, like the torn curtains of the gods.

At first nobody responded. Then John Turner stepped forward.

'Okay, let's see if I can make a fool of myself,' he said, attempting to forge his irrepressible nature into steel for the benefit of the rest.

Bruce felt a creeping menace coil in his mind. The others didn't look nervous, but focused. But Bruce detected fear swelling within himself while he watched. Turner began to clamber round to the stones when suddenly Tavener crashed in.

'I think I should go first, Turner. We should never ask those under our command to do anything that we wouldn't do ourselves.'

John stopped and looked to Marham whose deadpan expression signalled that this was a pointless intervention. They made way and hoped for a spectacle.

Tavener hauled himself up onto the first rock. He got to his feet and steadied himself, for a few moments buffeted by the wind. He pushed himself off, leaping for the opposite rock. His launching foot seemed to be too far from the edge of the first rock. Slipping on the wet granite, his trajectory was short of the target.

'Jim!' Marham shouted.

Tavener hit the side of the second rock at chest level, his arms flailing, attempting to hold on to the top edge. It was like a scene from a cartoon. The boys' shock turned to embarrassment as he gave up flapping and slid haplessly down the rock to land in a heap at its base.

'Are you okay?'

Marham strode over to check what was broken, but nothing was broken, except the boys' faith in the man.

With Tavener squatting on a small boulder, suddenly lost for conversation and eye contact, the others started taking turns at the jump. But something was holding Bruce back. He didn't know which confounded him most – the surprise at feeling fearful, or the humiliation of being the only one who would refuse to accept the challenge. Seb Wyatt and Rambo Blanchard-Jones were waiting to go. Bruce would be last of all. He felt trapped. The other successfuls were now looking on, chatting and laughing, relieved that they had done it.

The wind started to gust, a couple of blasts at first, but it quickly became a semi-gale. As soon as Seb cleared the gap, Rambo followed. As the gale took hold Bruce knew it was now or never.

'Hold on, Bruce!' cried Marham, looking all about him and into the skies to assess the changed conditions. 'Were you hoping to do it?'

'I've got to say, not really, to be truthful.'

He was struggling to stand in the turbulence.

'What? Are you kidding, Noble? It's only five fucking feet, you chicken!' fired Jon Archibald. Bruce's heart sank. What a time to find out Jon could be a twat too.

'It's just as well,' Marham shouted against the buffeting of the wind. 'There's no way anyone could attempt it now. Let's head down.'

Even Marham's words were being torn from the mountainside. The elements were battering the group on the outside and Bruce felt truly beaten inside. A failure. A cowardly failure. How the hell could he ever contemplate leading soldiers now?

*   *   *

The trip back to the cottage was horrid. The air in the minibus grew thick with the stench of sweaty bodies and bog mud mixed with melting snow. Condensation so heavy that it ran in beads down to the metal sills covered the windows. Some wiped the moisture away for a view outside in the hope of staying travel sickness as Tavener angrily threw the bus around every bend.

Marham was studying a map which he had opened out on his knee, apparently oblivious to the other man's driving.

'What's that, sir? Are you plotting our next excursion?' asked Michael Raines.

'Why are you asking, Mike? Do you want a good one to go out on before you start Sandhurst next year? And please, let's at least call it a route. Excursion sounds like a Sunday school outing.'

'I just thought it must be engrossing if it allows you to ignore Mr Tavener's rallying demo.'

'Know much about driving, do you, Raines?' Tavener called over his shoulder. 'Why don't you just piss off.'

Marham's mouth fell open. He looked to Tavener. 'Alright Jim, he's just making a point, and I must admit I'm not getting a great look at the horseshoe on the map at this speed.'

'Does that mean we can take in the summit tomorrow, sir?' asked Rory.

'Why don't we take in Crib Goch, if you think you've got the balls, McIntyre,' came Tavener again.

'Anytime you like, you …' Rory started before swallowing his spite.

'It would be pointless anyhow,' said Jon Archibald, taking another easy bite from what was left of Bruce's self-belief. 'If Brucie here didn't fancy Adam and Eve, he'll shit himself on Crib Goch.'

Bruce couldn't even meet his gaze, so low was he feeling about the failed test of mettle.

'Archibald, why don't you shut your mouth if you've nothing constructive to say and no leadership to offer someone who's hit a challenge,' said Michael Raines, only three weeks away from entering the hallowed grounds of the Royal Military Academy. 'Is that how you're going to deal with your soldiers? If they can't do something, you're going to write them off and give them shit? Is that all you are?' He stared his quarry cold and Archibald shrank at the words of his CCF platoon commander. 'Think about it,' Mike concluded.

Bruce saw right then just a little more of what leadership was about. Challenges, successes, failures: their meaning and power were all created within, by what we choose to believe.

The next day would afford the first of two windows of opportunity to attempt a highlight route. The weather would dictate the chance to attempt a defining, challenging and awe-inspiring ascent and traverse. Poor weather would bring another day of safer activity – a more mundane expedition, which could include Snowdon's summit, accessible via a number of routes and with many escape options.

In his bunk the next morning, Bruce was trying to shrug off a heavy night's sleep when he heard Tavener relaying the day's weather report to Marham. Their voices echoed from the sitting room downstairs.

'It's mixed,' said Tavener.

'Is that it?' came Marham's reply.

'Pretty much. It'll be changeable, blustery, with sporadic heavy sleet or snow interspersed with clear spells, if that's more what you were after,' said Tavener.

'It was and it wasn't,' sighed Marham. 'I was considering Crib Goch, but if it's no good we'll simply head up Snowdon.'

'It depends how we play it. I thought an alpine guide would like the challenge of measuring a window for that traverse.'

The two voices faded as the men headed towards the kitchen. Bruce looked around at the faces of Jamie Philpott and Rory staring back from their army sleeping bags. For once the roles were reversed. Philpott was waiting for somebody else's reaction to tell him whether to sing delight or crow frustration. Bruce was uneasy at the way Tavener had thrown the gauntlet down for Marham, but he was unsure how to judge the situation. This was one for Rory.

'Mate?' Bruce whispered, eyebrows raised to invite a verdict.

'Tavener's a cock. Why does he always need to try and impress? And in such a cock way? He's so fucking unsubtle it's not real, trying to suggest taking a risk with a weather window when Marham's already planned for it by allowing two days for the big one.'

'Let's hope Marham sees through it and tells him where to get off,' said Bruce.

9

Word soon got around about Rory's verdict on Tavener's behaviour. As the minibus wound its way up to the car park at the head of the Llanberis Pass all were silent. The team hauled themselves and their kit out and headed for the start of the Miners' Track as the weather opened into the full stride of a north Wales winter's day.

There was a palpable urgency about their pace. Few words were being exchanged among the group, and Marham appeared to be measuring the mood closely: where the maverick Tavener brought concern and doubt, Marham brought reassurance. Bruce was surprised that even the boldest adventure seekers behaved squarely in line with the pack – no thrill-seeking suggestions, just a sense that everyone wanted the weather to stay bad enough to justify heading for Snowdon's summit and not dice with Crib Goch. They knew that many had died there, blown clean from the jagged ridge of rock along which only the boldest climbers dared to pass.

The Miners' Track soon joined the western Pyg Track, the final few yards of which steepened as it drew closer to joining the Snowdon Horseshoe. Then they would have to decide which way to go. As they approached, Bruce's thoughts flirted with the prospect of a cuppa and chocolate bar in the summit cafe. Marham reached the junction of paths and stopped to regroup just as the weather settled – all perfect stillness, the sunshine flooding across the mountainside. Shit.

Bruce watched Tavener and Marham. Tavener couldn't contain the grin that spread across his face. He eyed Marham who met his gaze briefly before breaking to survey the furthest horizons for the next weather front.

'Carpe diem, Terry!' came Tavener's first provocation. 'That cold front has been going through since breakfast so we could have an equally good window of clear weather now. And what a glorious scene for the boys to take in.'

Marham didn't react but continued an extended examination of the skyline in all directions, unrushed by Tavener's comments. He seemed to be deliberately ignoring the man. Bruce's pulse quickened. There would be no opt-out on this one if they decided to go.

'Who's got the ropes?' Marham started. Two hands went up. 'And have you all remembered to pack your harnesses in the top of your rucksacks?'

'No sir, mine is halfway down under my spare warm clothing,' said Jon Archibald.

'Just dig it out,' said Marham. 'Everyone get them on now. Okay, let's do it. If we get on with it we won't need to rope up. Let's go!'

There was a flurry of activity as harnesses were donned and the group got into the order of march rehearsed over previous days. As a junior member of the party and with least experience, Bruce was placed second from the front, behind Seb Wyatt. Behind Bruce was Terry Marham and at the rear was Rory, the most experienced student, followed by Tavener, who had got his way to play hero in the last-man role. Bruce could see Marham's logic in having a solid tail to the party, but mixing oil and water in Tavener and McIntyre was a risk in itself.

Deep sighs and continued silence confirmed that this was more adventure than anybody felt ready for. Rory's words rang in their ears and they prayed that Tavener's optimism about the weather window would be justified.

Marham's deliberations made even more sense when the distance to the start of Crib Goch was considered. It took Bruce a while to realise that the half mile or more via Crib y Ddysgl was merely to get to the start of the arête. Then it began. The mountain fell away precipitously on either side of the knife edge of rock. So sharp and angled was the ridge that in places it was possible to sit astride its crest as if on a steep rooftop. Few sections afforded an opportunity to indulge any instinct for self-preservation by walking alongside rather than on top of the crest, to provide something to hold and avoid the sensation of walking a tightrope. This looked like pure treachery, even under perfect conditions.

The first hundred yards led out onto the knife edge proper. Either side opened into a gaping chasm which many would find hypnotically beautiful. Bruce struggled to appreciate the panorama as he rapidly shrank into a state of semi-terror. His heart raced and his legs lost their strength, his whole body trembling at the sheer danger from which there could be no going back. This was a challenge too far and he sensed he was losing control as his mind burned for it to end, for him to escape – now! He had to control the panic, had to override all instincts and consciously relax. He forced himself to focus on detecting where his muscles were tensing, wasting energy and creating psychological stress. He tried to pick an area, a muscle group, and consciously command his muscles to relax, to disengage, like taking a fist and making it open into an empty hand. Such control was a near-insurmountable challenge. Then the first shaky step brought a slip.

'Shit!'

There was no containing the tension.

Marham cut in. 'Relax, young Noble. Relax and focus on placing your feet. Notice your balance. Listen to my voice. Regulate your breathing, and allow full, flowing, easy breaths all the way in and out.'

His words were an instant lifeline and Bruce's mind seized on them, wrapped into them for refuge, but most importantly, did their bidding. These few words focused panic into purpose. They were a productive distraction, starting a virtuous circle: *focus, notice, reg-ul-ate – flowing breaths – fully in – fully out* … Better!

The red ridge of volcanic rock continued its pattern of spikes and spires, rising and falling, with powdery snow covering its bronze hues. Bruce glimpsed for the first time what appeared to be the end of the ridge. From there the path would veer right and wind down to rejoin the eastern end of the Pyg Track leading back to the car park. A patter of chit-chat had established itself along the line; they were starting to relax and appreciate both the challenge and the magnificence of the scenery.

Bruce glanced down to his left and noticed a swirl of mist hugging the contours of a large depression. It was a trifling thing amid the flood of sunshine which bleached the pristine snow all around. Yet there was a stubbornness about it, the moisture prevailing rather than ebbing away. If anything, it was growing slowly thicker.

'Sir, is there a name for that phenomenon?' he asked, pointing to the coiled tail of mist.

There was no reply. Bruce slowed, planted his feet and cautiously turned to see what was up with Marham and why he hadn't answered. The man had also stopped and was looking at the spectacle with concern. Then he started the same intense scrutiny of the horizon as before. A light breeze had taken hold – light but steady. To the distant northwest the skyline was occluding with white cloud, the top line of which was smudged thin into the blue sky far above. By now the rest of the group had come to a stop behind Marham. The cloud grew and started to take on a strange anvil-like shape.

Marham looked around making eye contact with each of them.

'Everybody okay?'

'Sir,' came the chorus from his obedient troop.

'Last few hundred yards. Stay focused. Let's go!'

And they were off, with a renewed tension coursing through each of them. The signs were clear and the clock was ticking. Paradoxically, the focus of attention on the threatening storm had quashed Bruce's fear. The pace had quickened. They became fleet of foot, shifting to a rhythm that only young men and fell runners could produce. They skipped over the rocks, and whenever a more forgiving footing allowed, their eyes darted to the rising menace of cloud and the gale powering it towards them.

'Eyes on the prize, people!' barked Marham. He needed to keep their attention directed ahead, not distracted behind.

'Sir! Mr Marham, sir!'

The unmistakable Scottish tones from behind announced Rory had a problem. Tavener was down. Rory had stopped without hesitation to maintain the link with the end of the chain. Everyone planted themselves firmly on whichever patch of rock they found themselves. This was an unwelcome delay.

Bruce strained to see what was happening. Like a whippet Marham skipped over the rock back towards Tavener. As he grew closer, Tavener looked up, forced himself upright again and started into a hobble. They appeared to exchange a few words and Marham turned to the front once more, hands thrashing to get everyone moving. The opportunity to rope up had passed.

Within a minute the cloud engulfed them and the first blast of wind erupted, funnelling skywards from the steep rockface below. Bruce scrabbled to grab a handhold as the force took his pack, lifting and spinning him onto the leeward side of the ridge. He redoubled his grip and looked about him. Wyatt, who had been only a few yards ahead, was shrouded in dense, freezing cloud. So too was Marham. Bruce stayed put. The gale pulsed and occasionally this brought a gap of clear air.

'Keep moving ahead whenever you can, but stay low – three points.'

Marham's words, almost washed away in the tumult, reminded them of the rock-climber's rule to maintain three points of contact with the surface at all times.

They were now moving at a snail's pace, clinging to the granite lest the next gust should sweep them away. There could only have been a couple of hundred yards left, but the appalling visibility meant it may as well have been ten miles.

From the rear of the line came more cries. This time it sounded like Tavener. He was yelling against the gale, and when gaps appeared in the mist he could be seen frantically waving his arms above his head to get attention. Bruce saw Marham heading to the back of the line again. A few seconds later there was a prolonged clear spell which revealed the entire team.

Bruce counted along the line, spotting everyone. Except Rory. He could see Tavener and there were no rock features to hide Rory from view. Where the hell was he?

Marham reached Tavener and all eyes fixed on the pair and their intense exchanges and gesticulations. Something was wrong. Marham peered hopelessly over the side. His arms dropped; he looked utterly defeated. Then the horror Bruce wished to ignore took hold. Along the line shocked faces looked to each other. They peered down into the valley far below where Rory's shattered body was partly visible, lying contorted and bloodied against the jagged rock.

Some slumped to sit, crestfallen, weeping, men to boys again. In an instant their friend and Bruce's soulmate was gone. A hot knife tore through Bruce as reality and emotion collided. His sadness and bitter resentment could not undo what had happened nor allow him to escape it. A ghost weaved its way into Bruce's mind that would forever steal any hope of happiness.

Marham tried to compose himself, then turned and led them away, desolate, as the weather front cleared and the sunshine returned to mock them.

10

The college minibus dropped Bruce at Chester station late afternoon the next day, Wednesday, 17 December 1986. The tragedy on the mountain had cut short their trip. He was numb, barely uttering a word to the others as he dragged himself out of the vehicle, across the road and inside to Platform 3.

From Chester, the train ran to Crewe, where Bruce almost forgot to change for the direct service via Birmingham to Bristol Temple Meads. There someone from the family would collect him – he didn't know who, but Mum would have it sorted, just like always. Having survived an invasion of sailors, who for reasons unknown to Bruce decided to change carriages at Crewe then continue celebrating the start of their leave by getting blotto until staggering off at Birmingham, Bruce settled back in a near empty carriage. He watched gold pinpricks of distant street lights pass in the winter darkness. Now he could return to his melancholy without distraction. His eyes stung with tears as he reached for his Walkman, hoping Annie Lennox could soothe his mood, but 'Miracle of Love', while mystifying, simply intensified it. Was his sadness a good thing, he wondered. Deep down Bruce knew he had to acquaint himself with the newfound tormentor, whether he liked it or not.

Eventually, as 10.30 p.m. arrived, the train screeched its way to a halt along the sweeping curve of Platform 8 at Temple Meads station. Bruce alighted to an empty concourse, which meant a brotherly pickup from the car park. Mum would have come to the platform, his brother was less sentimental.

'Wilkommen, mein Bruder!' came Pete's hallmark salutation.

'It's good to see you, brother, very good to see you, in fact . . .' Bruce trailed off, despondently.

'We've heard the news, buddy. Got a call from the college around seven this evening. Get in and I'll tell you more, if you're not too knackered to hear it.'

Pete fired up his pride and joy, a Triumph Dolomite Sprint, and they catapulted through the near empty streets, its sixteen-valve engine howling through Janspeed pipes, showing other drivers what a car should go like.

As they drove, the sensory assault of Pete's rallying took second place when he announced that Bruce would be back on a train in the morning.

'Sorry, buddy,' he said with a sympathetic smile. 'The police need to interview all members of the Snowdonia trip as soon as possible to get statements while memories are fresh.'

Or while we're still in shock, thought Bruce.

Mum was home and eager to greet them at the door as they arrived, her mood uncharacteristically subdued.

'Hello Bruce.' She embraced him in slow solace. 'I'm so sorry, my dear. What a tragedy! I am so so sorry.'

Charles Noble-Franks stood staunchly beside her, upright, his arms by his sides, no expression on his face. The chin-up demonstration.

Bruce didn't care. He choked. Jenny detected his sensitive state and kept things calm and light, and he was soon doing his best to take on a much needed late night dinner for one. Just being back home at Christmas was better comfort than he expected, even though the turmoil would resume tomorrow. As the youngest, Bruce was the last to leave home. His other two brothers and two sisters were older, settled and married.

'Okay Mum, Dad, I'm away.'

Pete was heading out to wake the street en route to rescuing his wife Denise from her company Christmas party.

Bruce, Jenny and Charles chatted until gone 1 a.m. – the late hour was necessary to let their food digest before sleeping, apparently. No harm there. Drained as he was, sleep wouldn't have overcome Bruce's sorrow without some help.

'It was Rory,' Bruce finally got to saying, 'my closest friend at Rothwell. I can't believe it – he was a climber, too. Someone's having me on, aren't they? He was probably the best among us in the mountains.'

His voice cracked and he stopped, not wanting to get even more upset. Jenny and Charles exchanged looks but remained silent, just allowing him to let it out. But it was too late to start recounting the whole story and Bruce had to rest before morning.

There would be no train drudgery the next day. Jenny drove the family Golf and after three and half hours they drew up to a near-deserted Rothwell parade square in front of the main house. Half a dozen cars which must have belonged to families of other boys who had been on the trip, plus two police patrol cars, were already there.

Colonel Hunter greeted them in the entrance hall, his face lined and grey, looking much older than his fifty years. 'Mrs Noble, good afternoon. I'm so very sorry that you have had to visit under these unthinkable circumstances.' He looked at Bruce. 'There are a few officers here, Bruce, and if you're happy to start right away, one can see you now.'

'Of course, sir. That's fine by me.'

Bruce wanted the whole business completed sooner rather than later. Then he could return home and try to forget it all.

He took in the scene of the hall, which had changed since term ended. To the right, outside the secretary's office, stood a magnificent Christmas tree at least eight feet tall. It was adorned with red baubles, each as large as a Christmas pudding, and painted wooden decorations – a stocking filled with presents, a bell and a reindeer. Winding around the tree a few turns from top to bottom was a silky ribbon in emerald green with gold wording: *Peace and Joy*. Bruce hung his head briefly, dejected, as the Colonel and Jenny chatted.

'Do you have any idea how long they might need, Colonel?' Jenny asked, glancing at Bruce with concern.

'I'm told it would be best to allow a couple of hours, maybe longer depending on what comes up. And they will probably need to conduct more interviews in due course.'

'I understand, thank you. It's all quite awful. I can barely imagine what the poor boy's family must be going through, as well as his friends, and you all – the college staff.'

The three said nothing for a moment, hardly daring to look at each other. Colonel Hunter tried to lift the mood.

'Is there anything we can get you while you are waiting for Bruce, Mrs Noble?' he asked.

'Well,' she turned to Bruce, 'darling, if you don't mind, I plan on taking a look at the garden centre we passed at the estate entrance. Is that okay with you?'

'You might as well – and maybe take a look round here too,' Bruce suggested. 'If that's okay, sir?'

'By all means, please do, Mrs Noble.'

Jenny headed off to the garden centre and Bruce went to find an officer to take his statement.

*   *   *

In a corner of the large courtyard of the Cadogan garden centre, Jenny wandered along a collection of open-sided barns and stalls displaying seasonal offerings. She stopped to examine a line of spindly firs that were missing branches and rather out of shape. Another shopper, so well wrapped against the winter air that her face was hardly visible, sidled up and joined in her contemplation of the display.

'I suppose it's inevitable this close to Christmas that the selection of trees is limited,' said Jenny.

'Perhaps not, if you're prepared to pay a little more and know where to look. The Nordic Blue spruces are particularly attractive this year,' came the reply.

'Blue spruces? Whatever will they think of next? White deer?'

'Oh, now those they do have, but not here. Would you like to see?' said the woman. 'Follow me.'

The cold ran through Jenny's very core as a long-past sensation returned. She drew a slow, deep breath and wrestled with her rising alarm to make eye contact. She nodded.

The pair meandered past the other stalls and then headed diagonally across the courtyard. The woman led Jenny into a barn on the opposite side. As they moved in deeper, the darkness cloaked them from view. They reached a small door along the far wall, a quick glance behind confirming that no one had followed them. They ducked through it and into a gloomy passageway lit only by a few arched openings high above, down a flight of dusty stone steps and through an even smaller door to emerge into the damp chill of a tunnel.

The brisk pace and concentration needed to stay with her leader focused Jenny's energy and alleviated her stress. The minute or so between stalls and tunnel was time enough to compose herself.

'One moment while I get this thing to light,' said the woman. She snapped the cheap plastic switch forward and the torch threw out a pitiful yellow glow. 'So, just to be sure then, I challenge: *Amulet.*'

'Um, well … *Osprey.*'

'Accepted. Sorry about all the fuss. How do you do? Lady Margaret Cadogan-Brandt, at your service.'

'Jenny Noble-Franks, and I am very well, now, thank you.'

'It is regrettable that such appalling events should provide a timely opportunity to make contact. I had already intended to do so through your son, both for my own reasons and for the organisation. However, my hand has been forced and now circumstances embroil you both.'

They exchanged information swiftly, intensely. Lady Margaret knew she risked compromising them both, now that incursions into the Rothwell estate were known not to be happenstance and one of the boys suspected of having delved into the tunnels had come to a grievous end. She was isolated. She needed a reliable link to any elements of the organisation that still existed outside. And Jenny had to protect Bruce, who could be the next target for a professional killing – if that was what had happened.

The possibility that Tavener had a hand in eliminating a potential witness to the location of the Archive had changed circumstances completely. Such action could not be justified as an act of absolute protection of assets. Tavener would never admit to foul play – that would confirm something much bigger, that another party or organisation wanted the Archive's existence kept secret at any price. If that came out then the game would be up and Lady Margaret would be in a perilous situation, and so too would Bruce Noble and his family.

Lady Margaret fixed her gaze on Jenny. 'You were never to know the reason for this rendezvous, and so neither would you have known the speed with which events are unfolding and how quickly the net could be closing on us all.' She reached into a tatty hessian holdall and pulled out two metal contraptions. 'I know not for how many years you have enjoyed a peaceful life, and how long it has been since you trained. I don't even know if you have ever used such things as these.'

Jenny's eyes narrowed at the sight of the implements. The first was a slender double-sided blade about six inches long contained within an elaborate and expertly crafted frame and spring mechanism. The assembly had a pair of fine leather straps to secure it inside the forearm under normal clothes. The second device would be similarly attached, but this time to the outside of the opposite arm. It was simpler, a concealable steel shield which covered most of the outer forearm.

'My training involved basic blades and pistols, plus all the usual improvisation techniques. But I think I can guess how this works. It looks like an ancient assassin's tool,' said Jenny.

'Correct. Just make sure you clear your dominant hand fully and quickly away from the body, should you need to deploy it.'

Jenny's eyes widened, trying to take it all in. 'The net must be closing very quickly indeed,' she said.

'I have no means of confirming anything concrete, only intuition about the potential immediacy of any threat. It's just in case. I'm so very sorry, Jenny.'

Jenny shook her head. 'No need for apologies. We actually have far less control over our lives than most of us realise, don't we?'

*   *   *

The pale December sun had set before Bruce and his mother were finally allowed to depart just after four. It would be a long day by the time home drew into sight around 8 p.m.

'So one hour was optimistic then, my darling,' said Jenny as the car crackled its way along the chippings of the main drive and out of the estate.

'Yes, but that wasn't a surprise. One thing always leads to another.'

'What did they ask you, Bruce?'

Bruce stared through the windscreen and let out a deep sigh. 'What's the point when Rory's dead?' Jenny said nothing, letting Bruce vent his feelings. 'Okay, well we went in to all sorts of things, some really tenuous stuff from way before the trip. I'm not used to police investigations and those plainclothes . . . were they CID? . . . those blokes anyway, they know how to be patient and let you talk, then ask another question just when required.'

'None of this will help Rory, but it might lead to a resolution for his family. Did they say that you were to remain silent on the whole matter in respect of any court proceedings?'

'Oh, yes. God yes!' Bruce exclaimed. 'Better remember that. It goes for everyone, so officially I can't even say anything more to you.'

'It doesn't matter, darling. You just do as you have been instructed. It's fine, and I will explain to our beloveds that they are to leave you in peace over the matter.'

As they started south towards Mansfield the lights from another car leaving the Cadogan garden centre sparkled in the side mirror, highlighting the drops of moisture that clung to the chrome frame.

The miles passed. Onto the southbound M1 after Mansfield, heading towards the south of Birmingham and the M42. After nearly an hour Bruce was convinced that the same car which emerged behind them at the garden centre was still following them. Maybe he was wrong, he couldn't be sure that he had never taken his eyes off it. It could be any set of headlights. Any whose nearside light unit was slightly misaligned, throwing an occasional but noticeable dazzle as the road undulated.

On the A42 near Ashby-de-la-Zouch Jenny took the slip road for the Leicester to Burton-upon-Trent trunk road.

'I don't think we need this exit, Mum. We should just head straight for the M42.'

Both were getting tired and a simple navigation error was the last thing they needed.

'Are you sure, Bruce? Check the atlas.'

'Sure I'm sure, just get back on!'

'I'll go round. But quickly check, would you?'

Jenny headed round the large interchange, towards the exit for Burton, then continued back towards the A42.

'Got it – here, I'm a hundred percent on this, Mum. Just follow round and get back on the A42.'

'Calm down, Captain. I trust you. You're really growing up – Mr Future Army Officer.'

Having rejoined the A42, there it was, the car with the dazzling nearside light. Could they have blundered in exactly the same way? Spectacular coincidence if so, thought Bruce. He could tell nothing about the vehicle past the intermittent glare in his tiny side mirror. Yet instinct suggested that this was suspicious and the tension in his stomach would not abate.

About a mile later, Jenny nailed the accelerator and sped past a couple of cars, overtaking them before the end of a section of dual carriageway.

'In a hurry?' asked Bruce.

'They looked slow and I didn't want to keep sir waiting after my earlier navigational error,' Jenny replied.

The suspect vehicle was now a few places back and Bruce hoped they might lose it in the natural flow of traffic. But why would anyone want to tail them? His foreboding was as irrational as it was stubborn.

'Having mentioned regaining time, Bruce, you should prepare your teenage self,' said Jenny. Bruce's tension was back in an instant. 'I'll be stopping shortly. I forgot I needed some groceries – a large brown loaf and two pints of milk. There's a service station along here somewhere, and this stretch of road is a lot quieter than anywhere we will find in Bristol this evening. Let's hope they have what we need.'

'What . . . shopping . . . now?'

'We're low on basics and I'm not venturing into Bristol city traffic if they've got some here. You can go in and get them for me. Oh, and I need tomato purée and a green pepper for a recipe. And check if they sell *Beautiful Homes*. I deserve a treat. Get an alternative if not.' She looked across at him and grinned: 'Please.'

Bruce rolled his eyes: 'Is that it?'

'Take my purse. Should be enough cash in there.'

Minutes later the Shell station appeared. The shop was open, but deserted.

'You jump out here, I'll wait round the back. I don't want to cause an obstruction if I'm not fuelling,' Jenny said.

Bruce headed inside to search for items impossible.

As soon as Bruce had disappeared, Jenny pulled up in the darkness behind the station shop. The car which had been trailing them since Rothwell entered the forecourt and trundled slowly past the petrol pumps and round to the rear of the shop, stopping a few yards behind Jenny's Golf.

The passenger got out, looked around him, then strode up to Jenny's car along the driver's side. His right arm was hanging down, slightly away from his side, to reveal the extended, slender shape of a semi-automatic pistol with silencer. The car engine was running and the lights were on, exhaust fumes swirling in the damp air. He moved to the driver's side blind spot of the Golf, raised the pistol in a close quarter stance and took aim, but the lights from the dashboard cast their glow into an empty seat.

'Looking for me?' whispered Jenny from the dark recess of a doorway at his back.

Her would-be assassin spun round searching for his target but his eyes were not adjusted to the pitch blackness. She reached out to pull him onto the hidden blade and out of view. The dagger entered upwards, deep under his ribs. He fought to resist her grasp as she smashed her shielded left forearm up and into his face, disorientating him and breaking his nose. Next she hammered another blow down onto his gun hand. The life was rapidly draining from him, blood pumping out of the deep wound in his chest. As he started to fall she swung him further into the recess at the shop's back door.

Jenny heard the click of the driver's door opening followed by the sound of hard-soled shoes approaching across the concrete that covered the whole area of the petrol station. A hoarse, accented voice cried out: 'Sergio!'

Silence.

In the darkness, Jenny felt her way to the dying man's right hand to locate his gun. The hand was empty. The second man started to walk towards her. She knew he would stay clear of the unlit area, taking a wide arc to try and locate her from a distance. She had to be quick. She felt for the catch on the mechanism of her hidden dagger, pressing frantically until it retracted the blade into its housing with a snap. Panic rose within her as her efforts to locate the gun became desperate. The second assailant's steps echoed round towards the cover of her car. Alone and a man down, his progress became measured, halting. Jenny sensed the stakes were weighing heavily on him. She afforded herself a moment longer than instinct dictated to systematically sweep the body and floor in search of the weapon.

'Who's there? Sergio? Answer me, or I fire!' trembled the voice.

The pistol had lodged in a fold in the victim's bomber jacket. Shaking, Jenny retrieved it, using both hands to turn it round and take a proper hold. The simplest action seemed to take forever. She could hear the man's feet shuffling into position now, and the faint clang of his body and gun contacting the bodywork of her car. She closed her eyes to imagine his position. She pictured him leaning over the bonnet.

She pinched a finger of her left glove in her teeth to remove it, then staying low pivoted to face the second attacker. Aiming the pistol with her right hand, she slowly started to rise. She extended her left hand out, high and to the side. He caught the vague shape of her pale hand against the darkness.

As Jenny gained height the faint outline of the man came into view, exactly where she thought he would be. She moved her left hand slowly back and forth. Her assailant shifted to fix upon the pale shape and set to shoot.

She fired. Two quick rounds. The first ricocheted off a brick wall far behind, the second found its target and the man slumped from the bonnet, his gun clattering onto the concrete next to his limp body. Blood pulsed from a gaping wound to his throat.

Jenny put her left glove back on and returned the pistol to the hand of the first attacker. She swiftly turned off the engine and lights on their vehicle, then removed her gloves and coat, folded the coat inside out and put both into a plastic bag in her car boot. She jumped into the driver's seat and pulled forward into the light at the edge of the building just as Bruce appeared around the corner at the end of the shop.

'Come on, darling. You took your time. Jump in.'

'Sorry Mum, I spent ages trying to choose you a magazine. They didn't have *Beautiful Homes*. Nor any green peppers. I hope the other items are what you wanted.'

'It doesn't matter. I didn't much like the look of this place after all.'

11

On Monday, 5 January 1987 college returned to a winter wonderland. The imposing sandstone buildings stood bright and tall, under-lit by snow which lay two foot deep across the grounds. All normal sounds were muffled, as if by magic. Breath lingered thick on the air and a cloak of mist hung at roof height, weaving between the branches of cedars laden with white powder.

A flurry of returning students criss-crossed Chapel Court, among them anxious new faces: 68 Entry was joining today.

'Hockey in the Elephant Hut then,' cried Craig Parsons, an ardent hockey addict of 67 Entry.

'Why the Elephant Hut?' Bruce asked, as they shuffled rucksacks and kit bags towards Chapel Hill.

'You said you'd be trying for the firsts – hockey – right? We can't play knee-deep in snow, so practices and selection will be under cover until the ground staff clear the pitches. Rugby players will be pissed off, though. They'll have to do extra gym work to pass their time.'

The next afternoon Bruce made his first visit to the Elephant Hut. After fourteen weeks on site, the estate still had places that could surprise. A purpose-built sports hall in the style of a Nissen hut, it was situated about a mile from the house on one of the many concrete roads that spread like tentacles out to the edges of the estate. It had a pristine floor covered in industrial grey paint superimposed with court lines for tennis, basketball and indoor hockey. Red-brick walls rose to around head height, topped by a roof of corrugated metal which towered overhead in a great semicircle. The highest point must have been fifty feet up. Its shape was just like the tunnels – Bruce grinned at the irony, but the grin soon faded as the events of just a few weeks ago flooded back. No tunnels now. No Rory McIntyre.

In navy tracksuit and fibre pile jacket, Captain MacWilliam scanned the hut, checking that everyone had arrived. Accompanying him as talent spotters were Messrs Willis and Cowley, also wrapped warmly in tracksuits, duvet jackets and bobble hats. Overhead, the electric bar heating apparatus hung above the centre of the playing area, appearing to be more for decoration than output.

'Let's go then, guys. We'll do this in groups of six-a-side to give a bit of space and see who's who. Grab a coloured bib,' commanded Captain MacWilliam.

Play lasted for around ninety minutes, with lots of team changes and substitutions to give everyone a fair chance. Somehow Bruce got selected for the first eleven. He suspected that this was largely thanks to a flash but risky left-handed reverse stick run through the opposition defence, finished with a near miracle pass threaded to Craig, who stuffed home the goal.

As he left Kitchen Block after showering, he spotted a police car and unmarked white van at the end of Chapel Court. Three men, one in uniform, were standing by the vehicles chatting and appearing to refer to notebooks. Bruce assumed that police and other investigators were still around, albeit in the background. Word had soon got round about Rory, and Colonel Hunter had officially confirmed the sad news in chapel that morning.

The next day Bruce and his classmates headed to their morning chemistry lesson with Mr Willis. To get the students into the swing of things after the Christmas break, he announced that he had a simple experiment to try. The odour of sodium hydroxide permeated the lab and measures of hydrochloric acid had been set out on the work benches. Tavener was lurking around in his lab technician role. He was keeping a low profile. That was no surprise, thought Bruce, given the incompetent fool he had made of himself in Wales. He avoided eye contact with Bruce, yet there was no repentance in his face. Twat. The guys hadn't needed to be impressed by him, just protecting Rory would have done. He had achieved neither.

'Hi Bruce. You fancy abandoning chess this term and trying something more interesting for minor studies?' asked Arthur Rose, as they dragged their lab stools out to sit down.

'Name it, Arthur. It can't be more convoluted, antiquated and pompous than chess.'

'Crafting ancient weaponry.'

'I'm not sure about that. What's the attraction?'

'It's got everything. For a start, you learn workshop skills, which is fun and useful in itself, but the best bit is learning how to craft what are actually lethal weapons . . . many of which are either highly concealable or can be disguised,' he tailed off in a whisper.

Bruce glanced around to check that everyone was absorbed in their work and not earwigging the conversation.

'Why do they need to be concealable? And how do you know all this?'

'It's an interest passed on from my father who had a passion for history and archaeology. It's from his years in the Far East, so it's mainly oriental stuff – swords, knives, bows, fighting sticks, throwing stars, that sort of thing. Many items were born of dual usage, such as farm tools modified for fighting; if these weapons could be concealed or disguised, then in days of old attacking peasants could bring a nasty surprise. That was extended into infiltration and siege warfare, where folk would take normal domestic items – baskets, cages and household implements – into fortresses then transform them into weapons once inside.'

Once again the Rose magic had struck. Bruce was captivated.

'That's fascinating. How come your father was in the Far East?'

'Bruce, you ask too many questions sometimes,' replied Art with a smirk and shake of his head. Bruce accepted that as the signal to drop it.

*   *   *

After a weekend confined to college by further snowfall, on Monday afternoon CCF training notched up another gear. While the TA ranges were frozen into inactivity and live firing practice was suspended, the intensive focus on field skills, section and platoon manoeuvre, patrolling and ambushes, would be extended into the night.

'Next weekend we will conduct the first of a series of night exercises to translate daytime tactics into a night-fighting capability,' announced Rohan Millington, the new cadet company sergeant major of the now senior 65 Entry.

'Perhaps we'd better describe that as an operating ability, Mr Millington. After all, we're not off to war,' MacWilliam laughed uneasily, glancing at the gathered student body.

'Yes sir, quite right. So to avoid a bugger's muddle we'll spend a couple of afternoons trying to communicate and manoeuvre blindfolded.'

The boys looked at each other, not knowing whether to laugh or wait to be told it was a joke.

'It's Marcus White's legacy, so laugh if you want and think of him looking equally ridiculous probably doing something similar at Sandhurst right now,' continued Rohan. 'Sounds shit, I know.' At this their chuckles erupted into outright laughter.

'For Chrissakes, Rohan lad,' cried Pitcaithly.

'But we're going to do it, and then we'll see who's laughing,' Rohan continued resolutely.

Grouped into their sections and platoons, the students moved to stand in separate open spaces just as they had done the previous autumn. Each took the issued pieces of cloth and tied them round their heads to cover their eyes.

The effect was bewildering. On the one hand, it was ridiculous. Since there was nothing to focus on, nobody could relate to an instruction to adopt a firing position or move tactically. But Bruce noticed other senses coming to the fore. At first, hearing was everything. Then smells became far more evident. The slope of the ground and feeling of soft, uneven earth or snow-covered grass underfoot was transformed into internal images and perceptions. After a few initial giggles they became quiet, trying to hear commands and judge each other's proximity. A natural competitiveness instilled discipline upon the exercise. Judging distance was a huge challenge and people varied greatly in what they perceived to be five or ten metre tactical bounds between prone firing positions.

Then out of the blue, *crack, crack, crack* . . .

'Take cover!' shouted Bruce's section commander.

Boom! A thunder flash exploded at Bruce's right side. The hiss of another passed overhead. *Boom!* The unmistakable exhalation of a smoke canister popping into life brought choking fumes across the section.

'Gun group to the left flank! Rifle group – three hundred, centre, enemy patrol. *Rapid … fire!*'

He barked fire-control orders and directed them towards an imaginary enemy, crossing the four rugby pitches of the west field until all were soaked with sweat and trembling with exertion. They crawled, shuffled position, fired, darted up, zigzagged ahead to dive down into another fire position, and repeated the pattern between ten and twenty times. When the advance stopped, the boys assumed that the imaginary enemy had been destroyed by their imaginary fire, so they indulged themselves with gasps of smoke-free air.

'What the fuck do you think you're doing, you lazy fuckers!' screamed Seb Wyatt, their new platoon commander from 65 Entry. 'Fucking re-org. Now! The enemy won't wait for you to catch your breath.'

He liberally put his boot into various ammo pouches to get everyone into post-attack defensive positions.

'What's up with you, Webb, you jerk?' he shouted.

Simon was on his back and rolling in agony. Seb's boot had missed his ammo pouch and cracked a rib instead. So hospital for Simon and the OC's office for Wyatt. Bruce surveyed the carnage. Not a normal afternoon playing soldiers, he reflected. This was serious – too serious. And it wasn't that Seb Wyatt had morphed into a psycho. Sure, it was his first day in his new command appointment as a student platoon commander, but the guy was usually reasonable and easy-going. The intensity of the training was going beyond causing a stir among them, it was causing confusion and concern. And Bruce Noble was starting to guess why.

*   *   *

Situated behind Rothwell Woodhouse were its stables – a simpler affair than the grand edifices near the college hospital. Lady Margaret would likely never again ride out from the estate's main stables and take in their thick Steetley limestone walls with corners and detailing in castellated sandstone that reflected the perfection of the house to which they belonged.

Roberts quietly worked to get Duchess saddled, the cold penetrating the quilted under jacket and waxed top coverings of animal and butler-come-stable-hand alike. But he would be warm enough mucking out while Lady Margaret exercised her mare.

'How is she today, Roberts?' Lady Margaret asked as she tramped across the frozen mud and ice of the small courtyard.

'Healthy and headstrong – like you, my lady. And neither of you should be risking a fall, in my humble opinion.'

'You know I wouldn't normally, but we will only be walking – along Obelisk Drive, up to Centurion's Gate and back. It's barely a couple of miles each way.'

Roberts returned her gaze, his brows knitted.

'I'll watch out for you, my lady. If you're not back by lunchtime I will come to check . . . with your permission.'

'What if I meet a handsome gentleman and wish to show him around my estate? I might be later than lunchtime.'

Roberts glanced away, smiling but not capitulating.

'Very well,' Lady Margaret continued, eyeing her old Series 1 Land Rover across the yard. 'Sturdy's in her normal spot. You'll need her for Obelisk Drive in these conditions.'

Duchess and Lady Margaret departed, heading northeast along the straight track which divided Evergreen and North woods. The conifers on her right were thick and tall, having been established centuries earlier. They were a welcome shield against the sharp easterly wind which had now taken hold. A pristine carpet of snow lay ahead, and here and there tracks of deer and fox crossed the path. The only sounds to distract from the biting air were the trickling stream alongside the track and skitters of powdery snow being whipped and scattered from exposed branches onto dried beech leaves.

Half a mile before Centurion's Gate, where the estate track met the Sutton road, stood the Cadogan Obelisk, its simple structure a monument to generations of the family since the first Duke of Rothwell in the seventeenth century.

Set on the rolling crest of the drive, to either side the woods were parted to form a five hundred by fifty yard swathe of perfect open meadow. Lady Margaret paused and looked back to savour the scene, which had been landscaped in such a way that the viewer's eyes were drawn across the heart of the estate to the house and lake.

She turned Duchess left through a narrow gap in the trees opposite the obelisk. The densely planted evergreens muted nearly all sound and quickly stole most of the daylight. Duchess's steps fell on the damp, mulchy forest floor which was untouched by snow. Lady Margaret forced herself to focus on the task of measuring her distance from the entrance. Then, just a few feet ahead, the glow of a pencil torch pierced the shadows. She brought Duchess to a halt. The light moved in a peculiar pattern – a right-angled triangle which was vertically elongated. It moved rhythmically as it traced the sides of the triangle: one, two, three; one, two, three. Five cycles. Then it paused. Then five more.

'A waltz,' spoke Lady Margaret towards the light.

'Bitte?' came the reply.

'Vals!' she exclaimed in German.

'Thank you, my lady. Osterman at your service.'

'And how many?' she retorted.

'Fifty, from the point of departure, my lady. And I mean human paces, not equine. And paces rather than yards, and certainly not metres.'

'A waltz danced upon the head of a pin,' she sighed. 'Anyway, this is nearer to seventy.'

Lady Margaret continued to follow the protocol, more for sport now, although it was true that a number of specific conditions had be met to accept an identity.

'Remember,' Osterman continued, 'firstly, you are on a horse; secondly, a degree of tactical variation is to be permitted for me to find a suitable observation point, and thirdly, here you can turn your animal if you need to flee in the direction from which you came.'

'Accepted, sir. Amulet, at your service. My *animal?* Really? Did you hear that, Duchess?' she smiled, peering into the invisible eyes beneath Osterman's dark hood.

'We should be safe enough for a few minutes at least,' Osterman began. 'I got here before first light thankfully. The snow was falling, which should have covered my tracks. And this little angel was invaluable.' He illuminated a curious electro-optical device, about the size of a slide projector. 'It's a thermal imager. Cutting edge. Much smaller than current military grade equipment which is usually vehicle-mounted. The cooling systems are so cumbersome and energy demanding, you see.'

'Yes, quite. Most impressive. So presumably you weren't followed and we are adequately concealed here. In which case, down to business.'

Osterman swept Lady Margaret for electronic surveillance devices, which would be out of range here but could prove disastrous when in range of their operator.

While Jenny Noble-Franks had done her job by remotely alerting the organisation, Osterman could now delve deeper to record and assess the tide of events of recent weeks.

'We will of course focus the spotlight on Tavener's recent past,' he said. 'His high profile – by way of low profile – Crown service means he should be extensively on record there, if you follow me. Such records will be most secret. My guess is that he is acting independently of any other would-be infiltrators. After all, why have teams sneak around the grounds if you have a man on the inside?'

'And what about the attempt on Osprey?' said Lady Margaret, struggling to take in the fact that there were probably two groups of adversaries to tackle.

'We can't say whether that was an attempted assassination or attempted kidnap. Weapons would be drawn in both instances. But she and her family have been assigned a shadow, so they should be protected, as far as they can be.'

'A tiger, not just an owl, I hope.'

'Yes, for this task the shadow has teeth as well as eyes.'

'If there is more than one group, do you think they each want the same thing?' asked Lady Margaret.

'That is the question. We suspect Tavener is a risk to the Archive. However, it's getting so out-of-date, and times are changing so quickly, that in any case it's fast becoming disinformation. We estimate that three-quarters of living descendants were never told about us; parents and grandparents hoping their families would never be drawn into our world.'

'And the others? The men in the black car? The break-in?'

'That all smacks of amateurism. We consider that they – and *they* could very well be two unrelated groups as you intimated – fancy a silver raid. Be careful with any tradesmen you hire. Get Roberts to check Tavener's homework. A raid would afford Tavener the gift of a distraction and muddy any subsequent investigation.'

The pair swiftly exchanged final pieces of information, including the organisation's consensus on events and possible explanations for them, and how isolated Lady Margaret had become without active external contact – a consequence of the deterioration of the organisation as a whole.

Finally, she needed to confirm her last bastion of hope if it all started to fall apart.

'At least Tavener doesn't know the combination for the door to the Archive,' she declared.

'He doesn't need to know it. He's got you for that.'

12

As February gave way to March, so the winter snow yielded to spring. It was as if a great sigh was breathed across the lake. The first buds stirred on slender branches and the rich green of perfect turf grew like giant ink blots in the meltwater on the hockey pitches. At last the boys could begin the agenda of sporting fixtures, military competitions, and cultural and social excursions.

'Not looking forward to PT today, not one bit,' said Simon Webb.

'You've got nothing to worry about, Webb – you're the best insulated of all of us,' laughed Craig Parsons.

Simon ignored the taunt. He had a quiet robustness about him. His dependability was shown when he had kept his mouth firmly shut after the incident with the Range Rover in the woods. Parsons' joke fell on stony ground.

With snow still hanging around in the shade, a PT session in the outdoor pool was universally dreaded.

'Parsons, seems you've got energy to burn with all that chatter. Go ahead and fetch a log from outside the squash court. Heskell, Dodd, Hepburn – help him. Meet us in the sunken garden,' MacWilliam ordered.

The log was a scaled-down wooden telegraph pole used for field PT – physical training in army boots and full combat clothing. Favourite activities with logs included two rows of about ten students facing each other and each throwing a log to the other row at the same time: one over, the other under – a good test of team co-ordination and mettle. Missed throws soon showed who would try to salvage the error and who would dive out of the way to save himself. But the number one favourite was the log run: so simple, yet so effective. After all the carrying techniques had been decided and handovers between teams practised, MacWilliam enjoyed the real test of grit when sheer distance, time and exhaustion tore every plan apart at the seams. Changeovers got more frequent, more desperate and more ragged as the boys started to crumble. That was the time to find out who you'd want to be alongside in war, the time when the pressure squeezed every drop of determination from the mentally or physically weaker.

Bruce was confused. Swimming and logs. How would that work?

When they arrived at the outdoor pool, MacWilliam got the group warming up – which they all engaged in vigorously to stave off the coming shock. Set at one end of the sunken garden, the pool was a large D-shape, about twenty-five metres along its straight side, a metre and a half deep, and with side walls which stood a metre above ground level.

Parsons and his three companions appeared carrying the log, warming up rapidly under the strain of their load.

'Well done, lads. This way. Yes, keep coming. Over to this side,' MacWilliam called. 'Heskell, Dodd, get ready to swap sides and all of you prepare to take the log into your arms at chest height facing the pool.'

Out of the corner of his eye Bruce saw Peter Falshaw creep towards the pool and peer over the side, his eyes widening in horror.

'Ready? Okay, shuffle closer, and on my command you will throw the log in.'

Peter looked back at the group aghast.

'One, two, three, *throw!*' yelled MacWilliam.

The log hit the frozen pool with a thud. There was a crack as the ice shattered.

'Okay gentlemen. No need for the shocked faces. The good news is we're not doing a full-on swimming session in the conventional way. Half of you would be in hospital by eleven o'clock if we tried that. Today we'll be practising rope rescue for someone who's fallen through ice. The bad news is that the "someone" is all of you.'

So, same shit, different bucket. We're all going to have seizures, thought Bruce.

MacWilliam explained the drill. Each person would rope up, one at a time, in the middle of a rope section as though in an expeditionary line. Fate was ridiculing Bruce yet again. The line, however, would run across the pool. All the boys had to do was drop into the water and try to keep calm as the others pulled them across and out the other side. This would teach many things apparently, not least including the importance of avoiding thin ice.

'Who's first?'

First test. Who would lead the way and set the mood? Bruce had already seen how many of the challenges that had been faced in only six months showed how a first action can set the tone of what was to follow. From the outset, well-applied leadership, imagination and courage immediately set expectations about the outcome. A good start would instil the will to succeed because there would be the belief that success is possible. Somehow Bruce sensed this in a single moment.

'I will, sir!'

The exact same words came from Shaun Dodd and Bruce in the same instant. They stared at each other, each slightly thrown. The opportunity to put aside fears and literally dive straight in was now in turmoil. There was time to think, to assess, to doubt. They eyed each other. Bruce felt as though each were reading the other's emotions, to determine who had the best chance of getting it right for everyone's sake.

There was silence. In the seconds that seemed to Bruce to last minutes, he realised that curious eyes were fixed on Shaun. And Shaun looked totally comfortable.

'If you're up for it, Shaun, you look like you've got this one,' he said quietly, pleased that he had read the situation.

'Doddsie the brave!' cried a voice from behind.

'You sure, Shaun? you dark horse,' said Jim Willmott.

Shaun stepped forward and tied into the rope. MacWilliam called three of the group to the opposite side of the pool to be ready to extract the casualty and get him into dry clothes. Shaun climbed onto the pool wall. MacWilliam supervised his end of the rope with Craig Parsons and Bruce feeding out the other.

'In your own time, young Dodd.'

Shaun nonchalantly extended his right foot out over the water and plopped in. He went straight to the bottom, then gently rebounded to find the surface, like a predatory crocodile, and calmly exhaled. They couldn't believe what was happening. No sign of the guaranteed hyperventilation and near paralysis. Shaun allowed his body to rotate flat and swam in a leisurely breast stroke across the ten metres to the other side, the ropes trailing him redundantly.

The rest fared less well, gasping and shivering as each thrashed towards the far side. The cold quickly took hold and the final metre or so became a pathetic concession to allow the rope to bundle them clear of the water as their muscles failed. As soon as the last man had crossed the pool, MacWilliam sent everyone away for hot showers to avoid getting colds or worse.

Bodies shaking frantically, the group strung out, most in bare feet with training shoes and towels bundled in their arms. It was every man for himself on the dash back to Kitchen Block. Bitten by curiosity, Bruce caught up with

Shaun. 'How the h-heck did you m-manage that?' he stuttered.

'I presume you mean how did I get through the water with such apparent ease? Well, how do I put it simply? Think the right thing and it's amazing what you can achieve.'

'You mean k-kinda m-mind over m-matter?' Bruce continued through chattering teeth.

'Maybe, but that makes it sound like the goal is to force one intention over another and that would only be required if you perceived something as a formidable challenge, which is where the subtleties begin.'

'Is this something to do with your s-sex book?' Bruce blurted out.

'No, not really, although it would sort of relate to it, in a bit of an oblique way. And it's not a sex book. It's about, er, well, sort of modern philosophy, but to be put into practice rather than a load of theories, if you get me.' The pair had reached Kitchen Block and the life-saving shower room. 'I'll tell you more after prep if you want.'

'I w-want!'

Bruce definitely wanted this mystical mind-magic thing. Whatever it was, it could turn a geek into Iceman.

*   *   *

In Thames House, Westminster, the festering issue of Rothwell College and its molehills of mysterious problems remained unaddressed. MI5's focus was anywhere but on unsubstantiated security threats to an educational establishment. It was not a good fit as a terrorist target, where plenty existed across Britain.

Frank Bennings and Joe Cotton were trawling through the latest incident reports from security units at military establishments and high-priority strategic and domestic facilities.

'Anything from the power stations this week, Joe?'

'Nothing. And Hinckley hasn't followed up with the suspect fishing vessel report either.'

'If people want our attention, the least they could do is stay engaged,' sighed Frank.

'It cuts both ways though, Frank. We haven't exactly rushed to Nottinghamshire to take a peek around Rothwell.'

Both stared blankly at the board, eyeing the scribbled bottom line: *Rothwell – aliens?*

'Rothwell? What's Rothwell about then, gentlemen?'

The voice startled the two out of their navel gazing. Roger Gleeson was a tough, incisive-thinking boss. He headed the strategic asset programme, which was focused on far bigger matters than sixth form colleges, military or otherwise. In fact, Rothwell should have handed across to Special Branch or the CID, but Frank hadn't quite got round to that.

'Well? . . . Bennings?'

'Right sir, yes, Rothwell.'

Frank proceeded to stumble into an elaboration of all the things he didn't know but intended to check. 'So you see I couldn't justify the consumption of resources to investigate it above other priorities, sir,' he trailed off.

'Is that right? You do know that the ill-formed, the unexplained – what you might call the intangible – the bit out of place, is what we are all about? You know that, don't you, Frank?'

Joe stared at the floor, embarrassed, but with a little faith restored that he was right to have kept the subject alive. Frank mumbled in acknowledgement.

'What else do you have?'

'Well, apart from the written report left by the headmaster . . .' Frank hesitated.

'The principal is Colonel Malcom Hunter, sir, late the Royal Army Educational Corps, now General Staff List,' said Joe earnestly.

'And who owns the place? The MOD? The army? Or is it leased?' pressed Gleeson.

'That would be Lady Margaret Cadogan-Brandt, sir, the heir to the seventh Duke of Rothwell who died twenty years ago,' announced Joe. He was beaming, Frank was not. 'The college is under a fifty-year lease from her family for the use of specified grounds and buildings. Lady Margaret is one of the wealthiest landowners in Britain with an estimated fortune of over half a billion pounds.'

Gleeson's face was thunder.

'And how does she protect this great wealth and all its associated lands and chattels, Frank?'

'Oh yes, chattels. She is reputed to hold the world's largest collection of silverware.'

'Thank you, Cotton. Now I want to hear from Bennings.'

'I asked Joe to look into that, sir. Joe, what did you come up with?'

Joe was reddening with embarrassment and fury at Frank's gall, but he'd done his homework and answered with relish.

'Her private security adviser is a gentleman by the name of James Tavener.'

Gleeson's dark mood suddenly lifted. It was as if a storm had fallen silent in the beat of a wing.

'And have you visited the college yet?' he asked.

'No, sir,' Frank admitted.

'Good. Don't bother. You were right, Frank. She may be wealthy, but perhaps this is not centre stage for you – for us. I'll allocate this to another team and if they don't find something of consequence quickly then it goes over to the boys in blue.'

He walked out of the room, leaving Frank and Joe staring at each other dumbfounded.

*   *   *

The handbell was ringing to mark the end of prep in the Wessex pits and all around stereos were erupting.

Lib – ra – ry? Bruce mouthed to Shaun.

At that very moment he found himself staring at a poster of Yin and Yang symbols on the wall behind Shaun's head. The memory of his first night and meeting Rory suddenly jolted him. It was as if a mysterious power were revealing itself to him, wanting him to recognise the circle of life, right or wrong, good or bad. The experience was almost too quick to detect, but too striking to dismiss. In a semi-daze, he got to his feet and went after Shaun.

They found a corner in the library so they could talk more easily.

'So Shaun, what the hell is this thing you can do to turn yourself into Superman?' he began.

'I think it's been growing in your mind since this morning and is now thoroughly out of proportion, my friend.'

'Mate, we all screamed and seized up as the cold took us. You didn't.'

'Okay, okay. It's called NLP, which stands for – and this is not a good start, I admit – Neuro-Linguistic Programming.'

Shaun grinned at Bruce's baffled expression. He continued his explanation.

'It's quite new . . . well, about ten to fifteen years old now. Of course, being whacky, it originated in the States, in California. So there, that's all the bad news out of the way. It's a collection of . . . of stuff that people in different areas of human activity do to get results in their respective fields. It's about what they think and do, and how that can be understood, at least in part, by what they disclose in language, thoughts and behaviour – in how they conceive and express their inner worlds, if you like.'

First Art Rose, aka the Ninja, now Shaun Dodd, aka Yuri Geller, but bending himself, not spoons. Bruce couldn't believe his luck. The questions ran in all directions as he strained to piece together his evolving jigsaw puzzle of knowledge about this mysterious art, or science, or whatever it was. But of course it was both. Too young to attend training courses, which anyway were few and expensive, Shaun had learned it from his father.

The clock rushed towards ten-thirty and Bruce just had to have something more – a taste, a sample of some sort – before the night was out. He begged for a demo or something to take away.

'I give in,' said Shaun. 'Christ, we've only ten minutes left, but okay. This isn't the right way to approach it but let's try. The worst that can happen is absolutely nothing. Quickly – just name a situation where you've had some sort of problem, something you have experienced that could happen again, where you want things to be different, but you don't think they can be.'

Bruce pondered. 'Got it. It's one with fuckwit Jez and his lackey – what's his name? 65 Entry.'

'Doesn't matter. I don't need to know the details.'

'So how are you going to do anything?'

'Trust me. Only you need to know the situation.' Shaun looked very sure of himself, which instilled belief in Bruce. 'As you call that situation to mind, tell me how you would rather be – or what you would rather be able to do – as long as it was sensible, legal, and so on.'

'Yeah, right. Shit, I froze. I want to be like Art Rose, but that can't happen because he's got skills which I haven't, so that can't work.' Bruce stared up at Shaun, confused about where this was going.

'You said you froze. What would be the total opposite of froze? And for now you can put aside anything dependent on Art Rose,' Shaun said softly.

Bruce gazed down at the floor, at the head of an old nail bent and buried in the floorboard, his mind searching, emptying.

'Free? Is that it? It's what came to mind when you said whatever you said, but I don't really know what I mean or what that would be like, so …'

'*So* … it doesn't matter. It's all about what's beneath the word and you have found the word so you have what you need.' Shaun's voice took on a hypnotic quality. 'As you drift off to sleep tonight you can relax as you create a large, bright, vivid, living, breathing image of yourself acting free. And make that image swamp the tiny, distant, fuzzy, grey, motionless, silent image of the old situation that has happened and used to happen. And keep seeing that old image disappear beneath the big, bright, new free, as you repeat and repeat . . . and . . . free. And you're ready to sleep now.'

Bruce surrendered to the strange, almost absurd, form of what was being said. He immersed himself in the words and for a few vital seconds was entranced.

'Bed, you lot! It's half past ten,' yelled the prefect.

*　　　*　　　*

'So RSM, how are plans and training for our defence of the college developing?'

'Well sir, the boys are going along with things in a very mature manner,' replied Pitcaithly, choosing his words for the principal with care. 'It's clear they know something abnormal lies behind the radically amended training regime, but they're all – to a man – smart enough not to ask, so we are progressing well. I have acquired a substantially increased stock of ammunition – or training stock as I will call it – thanks to a number of favours called in with local TA units and colleagues in the regular army. Quartermasters make very useful friends, you know.'

Hunter looked on intently but did not interrupt. The two had found a productive formula for each to get what they wanted. Both knew that independence would be essential to protect the college. The greatest risk remained maintaining the students' adherence to the need for discretion.

'Our next key event is a small-scale test of procedures to kit-up, issue weapons and deploy defensively at speed, which we will do at night with a handpicked group of twenty or so,' Pitcaithly continued. 'That will inevitably raise the stakes. The boys will all be wondering what we're really up to. Therefore, I would like to propose we position it as part of a general line of approach, based on poor MOD funding and a requirement for service establishments to be able to stand up a minimum level of defence against a declared terrorist threat.'

'Perfect, RSM. That fits. The college military hierarchy will need to talk this through in more detail so our stories match if we get questions from the men.'

'Men?'

'Men . . . boys . . . students. They're all three to varying degrees, are they not, RSM?'

'They're not adults yet, sir.'

'So when you said, "to a man" a few moments ago, you were just speaking figuratively?'

'I suppose I was, sir.'

A grin cracked across Pitcaithly's face.

A few hours later the CCF student commanders were gathered in the OC's office, with Pitcaithly taking charge and Willis and college adjutant Gavin Pearce listening in. They were confirming the details for standing to, the act of getting people to their posts at full speed when the call came. Sitting in the circle were Rohan Millington, the cadet CSM, and the student staff sergeant platoon commanders: Jasper Perks, Seb Wyatt, Martin Haynes-Dobbs, Steven

Black and Rob 'Rambo' Blanchard-Jones. Also present was Bill Woodsman, the cadet colour sergeant in the appointment of company quartermaster sergeant or CQMS. He was in charge of all stores, which included equipment, clothing, radio kit and the armoury.

'So gentlemen, is everything clear about what's required tonight? A straightforward procedure from the dorms to defensive posts in the right kit. And fear not, nothing will be that simple. The aim is to find all the glitches and iron them out. Happy?' said Pitcaithly, closing his summary of tasks for the night rehearsal.

A hand went up.

'Mr Blanchard-Jones?'

'Sir, I might be off-beam here, but putting aside the tactics and procedures, won't our exercise bring the curiosity of the main student body to fever pitch? The whole place will be awake by the time we've extracted our eighteen from their beds.'

'Maybe so, but we have to get on and I've seen enough maturity and discretion from the boys already to be relatively comfortable. What we must do is ensure they understand this is precautionary, not preparatory, if you get me?'

Nods circled around the group.

The action began at 04:00, the low point in the human circadian cycle. Dormitory doors opened in darkness, beds were located and shoulders silently shaken to start the cascade. Within minutes all eighteen members of the spearhead team were threading their way down the spiral staircase, wrapped in dressing gowns and heading for the lockers where their uniforms were hanging ready inside.

Their faces blackened and their profiles obscured under netted face veils, the detail cycled through the armoury like clockwork. They each received a self-loading rifle and four magazines of twenty 7.62mm full metal jacket rounds. Heading off under the watchful gaze of Pitcaithly and Colonel Hunter were the 'special elements': two snipers and two general purpose machine-gun pairs. All manner of ancillary equipment and dummy pyrotechnics also went out with their designated teams. Schermuly flares, tripwires, nightscopes, ambush lights, personal radios and dummy Claymore mines were included to test the whole process.

After twenty minutes they were set in their start positions. The plan centred on the main cluster of college buildings, its aim to achieve an all-round defence, which gave optimum observation, making use of urban cover to hide them from view and protect them from enemy fire. Pitcaithly and Hunter made their way around the entire formation, trailed by Captain Pearce and Rohan Millington.

At each manned location Pitcaithly strode around, back and forth over some distance to get a sense of the position's effectiveness. Tucked in bushes beside the Chapel Court crossroads was Sniper Team Alpha. He signalled up the perimeter road and two boys from senior entry came running towards him.

'How did it look from out there?' he asked them.

'All pretty good, sir,' replied Pete Cooper. 'But through my image intensifier I caught glimpses of light under these conifers. Maybe Jon was taking his eye back from his I-I sight and the light from the viewfinder was illuminating his face.'

'Possibly. Good spot, young Cooper.' Pitcaithly turned to the sniper. 'Were you?'

'Sir,' came Jon Watson's grudging confirmation of error, as he dragged more cam netting over his head and rifle.

Pitcaithly, Hunter, Pearce and Millington headed back to the OC's office in Kitchen Block with mixed emotions.

'Are we doing the right thing, RSM? This takes on a whole new complexion when you see our young men in what would be the firing line, if God forbid, anything should materialise.' Hunter spoke with a heavy air.

'I understand your sentiment, Colonel. It would be near impossible to explain if any of our boys were injured or killed, yet I also believe that any reasonably coordinated armed response to a violent incursion would have the enemy going straight to plan B and getting out. They would expect easy pickings – killing us in our beds or a bombing.'

Pitcaithly eyed the principal. Captain Pearce had stayed close by, listening to the exchange between them with increasing concern.

'If I may, sir?' he started. 'I think we can all see the dilemma and accept the risks and anticipated gains of a proactive stance on all this. But eighteen is too few on such a perimeter, even this close in, and we took twenty minutes to stand-to. An attack would be over before we had even got dressed.'

13

The Easter break was fast approaching and with it came an end to the trickle of police visitors in the wake of Rory's death. Life should have returned to normal but the unspoken menace of a potential terrorist attack hung over everyone. A standing patrol now watched over the college each night, from lights-out to the morning bell. Tired faces started to show among senior year students, who had exams ahead that would not be helped by regular stints on guard duty.

The pattern that had developed was both practical and bold. The college hierarchy had placed exceptional faith in the student body to keep absolute secrecy about the defensive regime. A small number of boys acted as lookouts from concealed rooftop positions with nightscopes and binoculars. The assault group – ten boys who had been selected on the basis of age and expertise – would sleep in combat gear with weapons loaded and stowed under their beds, ready for action at a moment's notice.

Meanwhile, Arthur Rose's gruelling but addictive martial arts training continued, with only a small core of die-hards remaining. His teaching now took on a coldly practical style. Bruce sensed that Art too was focusing on the looming threat. There was as much emphasis on evading projectiles by motion and concealment as on direct physical combat. He taught how to use ancient projectiles offensively too – darts and throwing stars, as well as minor incendiaries that could flash, bang and produce smoke when exploding. The final line of defence was the use of concealed small weapons, such as short-bladed knives, and vital armour, such as steel skeleton bars, which protected the forearms or open palms when blocking.

Yet amid all the fuss and alarm, nothing could distract Bruce from the absence of Rory McIntyre. The numbness that had descended after Rory's death lingered as a dull, heavy ache. He found himself as a constant observer of life, drifting through it detached, like a third person. Everyone around him was striving to do well, to realise the opportunity for a great career in the army, but the untimely demise of his close friend had prematurely completed a circle of life and death for Bruce. It now stalked him, always whispering 'So what?' in the face of every undertaking and notion held as valuable or important by others. Whatever happened or was going to happen, all plans, hopes and dreams were constantly challenged by the haunting assertion that all comes to dust in the end. Under this dark shadow Bruce now walked his life's path.

*   *   *

'What are you doing for your major summer sport then, Bruce?' asked Shaun as they descended the steps from Chapel Court into the Great Hall corridor.

Shaun had become more than an occasional friend now, and in some ways had taken the place of Rory, as far as Bruce's needs went within college life. While he had neither Rory's fire or tendency for misadventure, Shaun was a rock of dependability. He never had an agenda, no ego. He was widely read and his capacity for seeing things in different ways afforded him an even temperament and wisdom far beyond his years. Nobody bothered him, not even Jez Picher and his sidekick Tom Calico. He was unassuming and passed almost unnoticed, yet would shine just when required, so he was always credible as a future army officer.

'Bruce?' he repeated. It broke the daydream.

'Sport . . . summer . . . Yeah, well, although I would probably do better at athletics, I think we sweat quite enough in this place, so some long afternoons of English cricket will do nicely,' he grinned. 'What about you, Shaun?'

'Sailing. Thought I'd take the opportunity, and I guess a bit like you I can't really see the point of more PT. I'm also terribly uncoordinated and wouldn't trust myself with hard objects being thrown at me.'

'Like hand grenades?' Bruce teased, poking fun at the future officer-diplomat, but Shaun just smiled back ignoring the attempt to rile him.

Shaun had imparted more of his NLP knowledge, which was simply fascinating to Bruce, and truly useful. It enabled increasing awareness of his feelings, thoughts and problems, and it provided ways to change things, either in himself or the surrounding situation. Based on the self as the creator and controller of the individual's destiny, there was a powerful simplicity about it.

'Shaun, that technique you showed me, about imagining myself as a tree . . .'

Bruce started to shake, as hilarity welled up inside them both.

'What's that, Bruce? You want to dress up as a tree? I think some professional help is required. No . . . sorry . . . that's what we all want to do for a profession, nearly forgot,' Shaun exclaimed, eyes filling with tears of laughter.

'Mocking your profession again, Trotsky?'

Picher and Calico, Tweedledum and Tweedledee, had made yet another untimely appearance. Bruce sensed deliberate intent and malice in the coincidence: the scene was so much like before, when Picher grabbed Rory by the throat. He felt a rush of anger and neither fear nor any shred of concern over expulsion was going to stop him from reacting this time.

'Do you have a problem, Herr Picher?' shot Shaun.

Standing in a quiet corridor just off the Great Hall, their encounter had no onlookers. Jez strode up to Shaun and faced him down, toe to toe, leaning over him to make full use of his half-foot height advantage.

'I've got a problem with Trotskies who should have been weeded out by now, yeah,' he sneered.

But Shaun just held his gaze, not flinching from eye contact for a moment. A broad smile started to spread across his face and Bruce could feel the moment coming. He glanced over at buddy Calico who looked sheepish and passive as ever. Bruce now flowed with rage. He tried to take it all in, to calculate the moves so they had advantage in whatever surprise was possible. Time slowed, as once it had when Bruce stalked the Range Rover in the woods. And like then, the haze of uncertainty would be resolved only by instinct, by intuition, by action. The trigger was coming and it would be Shaun's response to Jez's next move.

Bruce moved freely past Calico and circled to Jez's right side. Jez's arms rose, ready to shove Shaun backwards, but Shaun had turned to concrete and was going nowhere. Jez pushed, but recoiled and had to regain his balance amid his surprise. Confusion broke in his face.

'Fucking arsehole, Dodd!' he yelled. 'Who the fuck do you think you are?'

Up came Jez's fist and in went Bruce's.

The crack of Jez's jaw echoed within the corridor's close walls and blood sprayed from his mouth – a flicking of crimson onto the whitewash, as if from a painter's brush.

Bruce reset his stance instantly and flashed a reverse punch across the turning side of his opponent's face.

'Bruce . . . can *stop* now … listening and focusing only on me!' cried Shaun, as Picher completed his fall into wall then floor. Shaun moved between them and broke the spell. Bruce's eyes were ablaze. He was making Jez pay his dues for Rory and he was relishing it.

'Oh dear, dear, dear. What's this? The conduct of gentlemen, Mr Noble?' roared Mr Kelly, the Lancaster housemaster. 'If you wish to leave the college, Mr Noble, you don't need to decorate the walls with blood to do so.'

The suspension which followed was inevitable – a political move. Bruce would have to be banished for a month or so to placate the family of the injured party. Picher's underlying character was known well enough by the more astute masters and staff at the college, but they lacked firm evidence to shortcut the wasteful process which would first educate and train him before Sandhurst or his future soldiers would expose his true nature, either by testing him beyond his limits or withholding critical support when he needed it.

Shaun respected Bruce for stepping in and he attempted a small measure of reciprocation by offering some NLP homework to keep him occupied during the suspension period. This would complement the physics coursework hurriedly drawn up by Mr Campbell and maths from Mr

Chittern. But Shaun's offering was by far the most intriguing.

'A Testament to the Senses', he called it. The theory, so it went, was that human senses are much more powerful than most people realise. Moreover, one sense is usually more highly developed than the others. The key to unlocking both of these ideas was not solely the biology of the sense receptors – like good hearing – but the quality of neurological connections to and within the brain – good processing. The experiment was twofold: learn and practise enhancing all the senses, and then find the queen, the sense that outperforms all the others. The key would be to detect and recognise micro-signals, the almost imperceptible information that we receive constantly but never notice.

Coursework, fitness, jobs around the house, Art Rose's martial arts routines and Shaun's masterclass would occupy Bruce obsessively for the next four weeks, until Easter passed and the summer arrived.

14

'What do you think you're doing? Get out of my car.'

'Drive!'

'You? What are you doing here?'

With the disturbing discovery by Cotton and Bennings fresh in his mind, Roger Gleeson sat in silence while the principal's secretary regained her composure. The car slipped into Naveby's Saturday afternoon traffic and she tried to think where best to stop for a conversation.

'Next left,' Gleeson ordered.

'But I had the old cricket ground car park in mind—'

'I prefer the industrial estate, so that's where we will head. Never mind any outdated assessments or contingencies you might have cooked up, they're irrelevant now.'

The car drew up in the lee of derelict steelworks overlooking the Witham canal. Huge wall panels ran with rust, groaning under the pressure of air from the freshening breeze. Weeds stood tall and stubborn along disused rail tracks; great piles of industrial chains lay solid, welded whole and stained ochre by the elements.

'Update me on significant developments since your last report,' Gleeson began.

'That was only a month ago. I don't know what could have happened since then that would be classed as significant.'

'James Tavener. What about James Tavener?'

'What about him? He joined last year, in September, the new college year. And he was on the fateful winter expedition. But that has all been reported.'

'Who else does he have contact with?'

'No one, as far as I know. He doesn't seem to have a wife or girlfriend.'

'Where does he live?'

Lorna was puzzled. Where had this sudden meeting come from and where was the interrogation going?

'He lives on the estate, in a subsidised flat near the college hospital.'

'What is his role at the college?'

'He's the lab technician for the science block, and a staff member of the CCF. He has a TA commission. He also helps with adventurous training – or not, as the case may be.'

'Or not? Meaning what exactly?' Gleeson snapped.

'Meaning he didn't save the McIntyre boy. I heard that he was closest to him on that ridge they were crossing.'

'Anything else to tell me – about him or any other events or people?'

'It's all been reported. That's what I don't understand.'

Gleeson pondered, staring out through the misting windscreen as a rain shower swept through.

'Take me to the station.'

*　　　*　　　*

The return from the Easter break brought few discernible changes in college life. There had been no new security incidents. Indeed, the whole subject seemed to be wearing thin among staff and students alike. After a few wild rumours that some seniors were allowing juniors to take their places on armed standby – for all manner of rewards from music albums to food to high-tech outdoor clothing – the hierarchy was considering stepping down the alert state as exams approached for the outgoing 65 Entry.

Amid Britain's predictably unreliable weather the early summer sports programme picked its way through a minefield of cancelled athletics meetings and rained-off cricket matches. Another President's Dinner came and went, and the after dinner nostalgic wanderings of inebriated guests visiting where they once slept finally put an end to the practice of students sleeping with loaded rifles under their beds.

The college dance was another notable event. Girls from whichever private school had adequately forgotten previous encounters were invited to a social evening involving a buffet supper and disco with the senior entry. All other students were kept well away and rumours abounded that by nine o'clock there was more movement in the undergrowth than on the empty dance floor.

Now back from his month's suspension, Bruce Noble was maintaining a heightened awareness of when his newly declared enemies were in the vicinity. He knew that whatever the logic or risk to his progression to Sandhurst, Picher would itch for retribution, and it was guaranteed to be on an unsporting basis. Bruce figured that Jez would wait until his exams were in the bag, yet he could equally see that such a distraction hanging over him could prompt a much earlier strike. Sun Tzu's sentiment struck a chord with him – he would only win if he out-thought his enemy before any attack. He would sleep nervously until he worked out how to prepare for such retaliation.

'Bruce, Art Rose said to say that your supplies have arrived at the workshops,' said Mike Heskell. The words brought him back into the present and the taste of his now cold treacle sponge and custard.

'That's great news, Mike. Many thanks indeed for passing on the message,' replied Bruce, feigning enthusiasm.

'You heard it first on Kernow Today,' Mike exclaimed with characteristic exuberance. Heskell was anchorman for a mythical Cornish news show, at least in his own mind.

But his message was what mattered and the timing was perfect. It was Tuesday lunch, and next that day was minor studies, which Art had finally wangled so that Ancient Fighting Systems was an acceptable topic. Bruce grabbed an abandoned bike previously owned by a 64 Entry student – now long gone – and pedalled the half-flat tyres for all they were worth along the gravel road to the workshops. He arrived to find Art Rose already there with the special delivery.

'What have we got then, Art?'

Arthur Rose was standing in the entrance to the metalwork shop with a small cardboard box open on the bench in front of him, a frown on his face.

'They couldn't supply the shafts. We have flights and I have steel tips and frangible graphite tips. No bloody use without shafts in the middle though.'

Art had mailed a friend's father who ran a small precision-engineering firm that usually made parts for industrial electrical units. The note in the package stated that the hollow graphite shafts were non-standard and therefore prohibitively expensive.

'To be a little fair, Art, I don't think the ancient Japanese warrior would have had graphite-shafted arrows anyway. Not really authentic, is it?'

'Bruce, the word "ancient" is simply to justify the opportunity. I'll have some bamboo shit to one side in case we ever get asked. This is much more fun, wouldn't you agree?'

Art was referring to his two designs for rather more contemporary arrows. The first used sharp steel tips on heavyweight shafts for momentum and penetrative power. The second used hollow shafts that could be filled with petrol, or a similarly volatile accelerant, ignited by incendiary tips that shattered on impact. At last Bruce understood the reason behind the hastily crafted willow longbow that had stood in the locker untouched since Art had started the project last term – it was a pure ruse. The bow that he'd been developing all the time, the device to propel these objects, was also rather unconventional – a 20/100 lb progressive-draw compound bow, in black, naturally.

Art tutted and sucked his teeth in frustration. 'So what about the frangible shafts? No graphite, no incendiary rounds.'

Bruce had an idea.

'Mate, I did a summer job as a junior projectionist at a flea-pit cinema in Bristol last year,' he began. Art looked bemused. 'It's maybe a bit of a long shot – no pun intended – but the illumination source for the projectors was a brilliant light focused through a concave mirror into the main lens and out to the screen. The light came from high-voltage electricity running through a pair of carbon rods cased in copper. Their opposed tips burned a brilliant white as the current flowed between them.'

'Sorry Bruce, but how does that get me a result here?'

'The rods are weighty and about fifty centimetres long and six or seven millimetres in diameter. If you can drill out an inner core through the carbon then you might have a rigid but breakable shaft to hold the fuel. It would have to sit ahead of an alloy section to be long enough overall, of course.'

'Go on.' Art looked on intently.

'I have friends who still work at the cinema. The rods come by the box load. They would never miss a couple of dozen if you thought it would work. What do you think?'

'I would need a mighty specific drill bit to do the job. But I might be able to get one, thanks to the wonders of medical science and another contact. Do it, Bruce!'

*   *   *

The first few evenings after Bruce's return allowed details to be filled in and colour to emerge among an otherwise bland picture of no change and no real news in college life. A bored Craig Parsons, now with time to spare after the end of the hockey season, was only too happy to spend time after prep one evening conveying all the latest information. Comfortably installed in a pair of old Burlington leather armchairs in a corner of the library, Craig delivered the headlines to Bruce.

First off, while Tavener was still allowed to support adventurous training and continued in the CCF, he was conducting himself much more modestly. Gone was the readiness to volunteer to lead tasks, his eagerness to assert his opinions when planning events. Cold comfort for Bruce. Next was the news that the rumours that the overnight guard regime was being stepped down appeared to have foundation. Nobody slept in combats with rifles at hand any more. Only passive measures were in place – rooftop observation posts were all that remained.

But that whole subject, the most serious potential threat to them all, had become even murkier. Word had finally filtered out about suspect incursions and unidentified persons and vehicles in the estate. Craig cited some claimed examples, none relating to the black four-by-four incident Simon and Bruce had witnessed in the woods. It seemed there had been numerous other events, none of which had been reported. There was talk, folk started to speculate, and the whole thing gained a momentum of its own, whether fact or fallacy. The most troubling part were the rumours that a core of students, identities unknown, were conceiving their own contingencies for armed response.

Bruce thanked Craig for his diligent account and they departed for the dormitories. He was confused, troubled, and disturbingly somewhat excited too. The notion of an inner circle planning a high-risk and irregular scheme came as a natural and unavoidable target of interest. He would seek counsel in his two closest and wisest advisers, then proceed to infiltrate this covert core, if indeed it even existed.

Next day, in the spare minutes between lunch and Wednesday afternoon sports, Bruce caught up with Shaun to continue their review of the homework set for Bruce's brief sabbatical. He needed to understand and recognise afresh what the lessons meant and how to transfer the skills into real life, so they chatted about it at any opportunity.

Shaun had set a range of tasks, as well as prescribing papers and sections of books to browse. The primary practical task of enhancing the senses was most fun and after perseverance it opened what Bruce thought of as a subtle new world. The word 'subtle' was an instinctive and coincidental choice of word to describe his sensory revelations; subtle was also the term used for a level of transpersonal consciousness in a philosophical model developed by a thinker called Ken Wilber, the author of the voluminous sex book that had little to do with sex. This book had been among the more challenging reading Shaun had given him.

Bruce could now invoke heightened states of sensory awareness. By closing his eyes to accentuate sound and smell, he could create sketchy mental pictures of his surroundings. In trying to find two identically coloured blades of grass, he discovered a rainbow within a rainbow. Allowing aromas from food, and more noticeably alcoholic drinks, to drift delicately into the upper nose, rather than snorting in great lungfuls of air, brought forth all manner of olfactory distinctions. Samples of real ale were no longer akin to cold, bitter tea; the most complex brews were a heady concoction of caramel, malt, biscuit, orange, grasses and dark fruits. His kinaesthetic senses – what we feel within our body from our emotions, such as fear or excitement – and proprioception – balance and body position, all became so alive Bruce felt he had lived anaesthetised before this. He was now mindful enough to direct his internal as well as his external awareness. Detecting unconscious processes, such as becoming aware of the sensation of his foot within his shoe, brought a plethora of hitherto undetected emotions, sensations and internal dynamics into his conscious control.

One unusually warm afternoon during Bruce's suspension period had seen him crushed in a crowded city bus from the centre of Bristol. The tiny top windows did nothing to abate the rising temperature and he started to perspire in the sweltering air. That was the first time he tried a technique to use the neurology of imagination to control his emotional response to the growing temperature. He noticed where he felt heat and stress within, and invited his mind's eye to picture the colours, weights, movement and textures that were associated with the worst affected areas. He allowed curiosity to alter colours – reds became cool, dark blues. Heavy acidic skin was conceived as light, creamy, floating in a breeze. He imagined sitting in a large ice chamber, the image of his breath condensing on the freezing air, and the cold clinging to his skin. Absorbed in this mental construct, time passed swiftly. He had loosened his clothing and was sweating, but he remained calm; he could think clearly and felt he could have outlasted the test however long it took.

These insights afforded more rapid growth in martial arts skills too. Movement became elegant, efficient, balanced and crisp. Bruce's modest physique was starting to conjure the first signs of disproportionate power. He was reminded of Bruce Lee. While Lee was a master of his art, he was also no hulk or power machine. He was lightning quick and his speed put great energy into his strikes. Bruce could learn to do the same.

What Bruce struggled with, however, was relating to all the theoretical stuff. Shaun loved philosophy and psychology. He had a natural and deep curiosity which had at its heart the need to explain the *why* of things, and always with people at the centre of enquiry. He applied this so eloquently that the populist military views so often adopted by his peers looked idiotic after Shaun dropped a new context around the debate. But Bruce was lost when it came to recognising real-world scenarios where he could marry theory with practice. How to deploy this stuff so that it led to a valuable insight, a wise decision, a clear result?

'Craig mentioned reports about some group of guys making plans after the armed contingency regime was shelved. Have you heard about that, Shaun?' Bruce said in a low voice as they walked down Chapel Hill on the way to their lockers.

'What's it to you, Bruce?' Shaun replied, checking around them.

'You mean you're in on it?'

'You read the part about pluralism, didn't you?'

'What? Yes, yes. A pluralistic view – that there can be many views – infinite views, possibly, as I recall, I think. So?'

'So, when I say what's it to you, it doesn't automatically mean I'm in the gang or even that there is a gang. It could mean, don't talk about it here, don't reveal your sources, or even don't speak with anybody at all if you intend to do anything about it. Do you get me?'

As usual, Bruce strained to keep up with Shaun's intellect. They had now reached the entrance to the basement. The area was filling up with other students as folk cut back and forth going about their preparations. Shaun shot Bruce a long stare. They understood each other. Security is key and you can ultimately trust but one soul in this world. Yourself.

Over the next few days Bruce reflected more deeply on what he had read and why, out of all possible material, Shaun might have put together those particular books and papers to study. One of the subtler maxims came to mind: that if a seemingly complex problem presents itself but resists being solved by the conscious mind, simply let it rest on the back burner, day in, day out, and sooner or later it will yield. It will yield because while the unconscious mind is instinctive and undirected, it is also the daddy – the source of cognitive power – and is always the deep decision-maker.

That was what happened when it dawned on Bruce that the rumours of an inner circle were probably true. How far advanced any schemes might be, or how successful they might become, was a different matter. But for a rumour, first you need a thought. And whether the original thinker is the first to speak of the thought doesn't matter. And whether the first speaker is likely to be the first to act on the thought doesn't matter either. Intuitively, the rumour proves the thought and among this community it would be both possible and probable that someone would attempt some form of corresponding action. So, when the college hierarchy changed their behaviour in standing down the armed protection force, some among the student body may have interpreted that as a change of rules. And that was perhaps how once untold accounts of incursions had now emerged, and with them the notion that control over security had been conceded.

15

Rather than a May ball, Lady Margaret preferred a more restrained formal dinner to maintain relations and promote the house's interests among the great and good in the City of London and Westminster. Her greatest trial, however, was to maintain a patrician public profile while choking in her private, secretive world.

She would often host a two-day gathering around the late May holiday when guests would tour the estate, ride, shoot game, go boating on Serpentine Lake, and savour the final and main event, the white tie banquet. The guest list comprised a judicious selection of the influential, informative and prospective. The trick was always to satisfy previous benefactors and facilitators, who expected to be invited, while making room for necessary newcomers.

This year Roberts was collating the last replies from a select group of thirty invited guests that included a permanent under-secretary of state, two earls (contemporaries of Lady Margaret's father, the seventh Duke of Rothwell), a governor of a British overseas protectorate, a foreign ambassador, a chairman of a FTSE 100 company, the director of the London Arts Council, the senior partner of an international property lawyers' syndicate and the UK head of a US private equity firm. And spouses.

The management of the event would be different this year. Everything was under Tavener's watchful eye. The extraordinary tragedy of Snowdonia had somehow shifted Roberts and Lady Margaret's reservations about him as a man undisclosed, which is what he had been to them. There now lingered the air of a fool about him. The still-waters-running-deep and hidden agendas had become an image that now seemed less plausible. The tension of recent months had abated, and Lady Margaret found solace in having extra eyes and ears to control this occasion. She had an extra mind too, one whose expertise was to sniff out the unwelcome guest or any ill intent. The cold reality was that, whatever the occasion, nobody in these circles bothered to travel or dress for anything which would not be of potential benefit to them. And there were no rules governing what interests could be pursued or how that might be done. For Lady Margaret, keeping such company usually meant swimming with sharks.

With two weeks until the May banquet, Tavener had joined Roberts in the drawing room of Rothwell Woodhouse. The unlikely duo were hunched over an oak table amid scattered paperwork after repeated examination, discussion and note-taking. Responses to the invitations followed a familiar pattern: twenty-six acceptances, two without partners, and a further two who were substitutes – suitably senior representatives sent to show their superiors cared. What they cared about, of course, was to see who showed and what was said.

'All in order, that's your view then, Philip? This is a pretty usual set of returns?'

'Yes, I suppose. We often get stand-ins. Just never had one for an ambassador before, nor a governor of a UK overseas territory,' replied Roberts. Tavener studied the other man's expression. The eye contact started to become a stare. Roberts continued, 'We've usually had a substitute or two, but it's mainly from the corporates. Lady M can open doors for them, as you can imagine. The public sector tend to just politely decline – prior commitments, and so on. The fact that these cases are both based abroad and they're both sending people is, well, perhaps beyond the call of duty.'

Tavener nodded solemnly and paused to reflect. 'They might be new – new in their appointments, new to the game? Has either attended before? Do they know Lady Margaret?' he asked.

'Neither Sir Donald Trimm nor General Martin Hempstead are names familiar to me, so they could easily be new in post. We held no event last year. General Hempstead wears two hats: he's both the commander of British forces and governor of the Sovereign Base Areas in Cyprus. His posting there is only for two years, as I recall. Maybe you're right and they feel obliged to have somebody represent them.'

'And their representatives are a Dr Matthew Greech, senior crown servant and head of staff for the British ambassador in Czechoslovakia, and Mr Roland Parcelle, senior civil servant and the governor's head of public relations,' Tavener mused, scanning the table in front of him.

'Are they senior enough to justify their attendance?' asked Roberts.

'I guess so. Who else could they send? I mean, would you want some ponce of an RAF fast-jet jockey getting on everyone's nerves? or an ex-Special Forces boss deciding to get pissed to relieve the boredom and give the other half a lecture on life in the real world? It would be a bloody disaster.'

'Agreed.' Roberts nodded.

'So who's new among the other guests?'

They continued through the afternoon, working out who was who, what activities would be required, how to plan the seating for the banquet, considering special needs and preferences, and contracting for the management of catering, accommodation, transport, entertainment and logistics. Security would be Tavener's preserve and he would keep Lady Margaret and Roberts briefed only as much as was necessary with his usual 'need to know is the cornerstone of effective security' mantra.

But as things stood, it was Tavener who needed to know more. His focus was split among competing risks. While nobody seriously expected any stupidly criminal acts –

theft of high-value items, for instance – there existed a triad of most likely vulnerabilities. He considered the top three targets to be firstly the undisclosed asset or assets, then documentation and information, and finally prized items, whether paintings, silver or jewellery. Each in turn had its significance. The undisclosed asset or assets were still a mystery, and a potentially attractive acquisition for whoever might have knowledge of them. The risk to documentation centred on financial and corporate papers and records, which could hold key information on anything from the condition of the estate and its investments to details of owned and beneficiary organisations, including listed companies. Such critical inside information could invite hostile takeovers of weak firms or poison the assets of potential acquisition targets. Finally, considering the prized, and sometimes priceless, items, it was probable that nothing would be taken at the time, just identified and located for a later raid.

These concrete threats were in reality remote; the more obvious one was conversation. The entourage that would accompany the guests – drivers and even house staff – combined with the geographical and temporal spread of activities, meant there would be many opportunities for infiltration. Tavener felt he lacked the cards he needed to win the game. He would be discharging his task with one arm tied behind his back.

The next morning he was granted his request to join Lady Margaret for breakfast to discuss security preparations. The guest list was reviewed and anomalies debated. Once again he set out his case for being allowed at least some further knowledge of the vital but nameless asset or assets which he was hired to protect. He presented the three risk priorities and argued that, with no information whatsoever on the vital asset, he was under-resourced to cover all three threats. The game of cat and mouse resumed.

'I fail to see how one is split three ways, Mr Tavener. Documents and valuables get locked away and that's that,' snapped Lady Margaret.

'If that's true, it would presumably leave me only one location to protect, a location that I do not know. However, the security infrastructure of this estate is Victorian in its sophistication and condition, and with respect, my lady, any modern professional could walk wherever he pleased. I cannot be everywhere at once.' He paused for effect, allowing her to realise she had few places to go. Just as she was about to reply, he continued, 'Could we at least rule out what is probably the largest area which has been off limits for discussion during my tenure – the tunnels.' Lady Margaret shot him a hawkish stare but said nothing. 'I understand that there are miles of empty tunnels, apart from some unexplained ... how can I describe them? ... *constructs* beneath Serpentine Lake. Doors of various sorts, I suppose.'

Lady Margaret reddened, her rage building that he had taken liberties contrary to his brief and was now appearing to delight in trading them like poker chips.

'So, can I rule this area, and indeed all the tunnels, out of my calculations?' he repeated.

'Yes, you can, Mr Tavener.'

'So that is not the location of your vital asset or assets?'

'Correct. It is not. That much I will allow you, I suppose.' She sat back in her chair, experiencing a momentary relief that the discussion had come to an end.

'Then you will not mind if I take a closer look?'

Lady Margaret took her time to finish breakfast. She sat in silence, composing herself in the wake of Tavener's blindside request. He rose from the table and waited, leaving half-eaten food strewn around his plate while he nosed around the dining room of the Woodhouse, a smirk set upon his face.

Half an hour later, the two of them had made their way to the private back kitchen on the ground floor of the main house. In a corner was a white glossed door with an air vent near the top. It looked like a pantry, but behind it was a spiral staircase descending to the tunnel beneath. Tavener followed her down the stairs and into the tunnel where the pair matched each other's steps as they strode through the tunnel towards the entrance to the vault, Lady Margaret bristling with indignation at having been outwitted by a high-handed newcomer.

'If you wouldn't mind, Mr Tavener?'

He turned his back while she punched the six digit code into the keypad. A faltering bleep and green neon light signalled that the electromagnetic locks had released.

'Allow me,' said Tavener, moving forward to haul the heavy door open.

'Wait!'

The motor began to slowly open the door. Lady Margaret reached around the inside wall and twisted the Bakelite toggle of the main light switch. The yellow glow revealed the bare space inside.

'After you.'

Tavener stepped into the dusty space and looked around him, absorbing the few clues the room yielded. Lady Margaret stood inside the door, allowing him to make his examination. His gaze lingered on some faint lines in the dusty tiled floor.

'What was this room used for, if I may ask?'

'This was a bolthole, Mr Tavener. Some years ago the silver room – the strongroom, if you will – was suffering from damp and decay. The surfaces of the walls were crumbling and we needed to have work done but dared not risk even showing what the room contained, never mind the danger that items would go missing. So we thought that this somewhat remote old storeroom could be reinforced and offer a suitable temporary location.'

'But this is less than half the size of the silver room.'

'Yes, it is. That was why it held only the most valuable items. Others were simply locked away in empty rooms on the upper floors.'

Tavener conducted a slow round of the space. He missed nothing but equally found nothing to feed his curiosity. The lines in the dust could have marked where some form of shelving once stood. He tapped the walls here and there and studied the joins between walls, ceiling and floor.

'Are you thinking of moving in?' Lady Margaret said wryly.

Tavener spied a wisp of dust rolling across the worn stonework.

'Hmm? Oh yes . . . I mean, no, of course. Apologies. My thoughts were running elsewhere for a moment. Thank you . . . thank you so much for your candour. I'm sorry that I felt compelled to press the matter.'

'Apology accepted. So where were your thoughts then, if I may ask?'

'With you, actually. They were with you and the fact that I need to share more with you. Also, about all of this – how it all fits together. You see, I need to level with you, my lady.'

They stepped back out into the tunnel and the door eased shut sending a soft boom reverberating along the brick walls.

As they wandered back towards the house Tavener set out his case for greater information sharing. He covered all manner of possibilities for how and why Lady Margaret might be more vulnerable than in previous decades. While the concepts were much as he had described months before, the delivery was different – more tangible were his examples, more imploring was his tone, more sincere his sentiment. The range of potential eventualities apparently ran along two theoretical and perpendicular axes: from the mundane to the exotic and from the likely to the improbable.

'I completely understand how you would never expect such distinguished guests, some of whom you know well, to represent any sort of threat. Let me frame the situation this way: consider them as potential media for more removed and passive threats,' he continued.

'I am trying to stay with the argument and the unfamiliar terminology, but please carry on.'

'The statistical view is to be taken around combinations of factors and variables. Bear with the terminology at little longer, if you can, my lady,' he smiled. 'What are their motivations – what do you have or represent that they might wish for?'

'Go on.'

'What of the second-order effects? Who else would they speak to about you – those with whom they might share their exclusive knowledge? If one day a select piece of silverware or art disappears, it is unlikely to appear on the open market. It is more likely to hang on the wall of a private collector for their personal gratification, never to be seen again.'

Lady Margaret nodded in acknowledgement and continued to listen.

'Now we get back to the central issue. If your vital asset or assets are of an obscure or exotic nature you might attract state intelligence services to come snooping, and not just the British. Much worse would be if such services perceived a threat and therefore felt a need to exercise control over you. That is why I'm having trouble with the fact that two of your overseas public servants are sending substitutes when it would be more normal to give their apologies.'

They had reached the kitchen again. The final few yards had passed in silence. He wanted to give her space to absorb his words, hoping she would now be prepared to open up to him. She was lost in thought, contemplating the best way forward.

Pensively she looked around the kitchen, then wandered over to a stack of clean folded tablecloths. She rested her hands upon them as if to start packing them into a cupboard. Tavener's eyes widened in anger and disbelief. Surely she was going to say something after all that? Finally, staring out over the rose garden and the lake beyond, she spoke softly and slowly, as if in a trance.

'Thank you, Mr Tavener, for your sincerity and thoughtfulness. However, I must tell you it is my firm belief that I would harm your situation if I revealed more than I should, which would still amount to remarkably little. I understand how frustrating for you this must be.

The irony is that my stance is in alignment with your cherished principle of need to know. You see, as you have just demonstrated, you are doing what I had hoped for – providing your expertise on security matters, and from the best possible place: one of calculated ignorance.'

Tavener stormed out, slamming the kitchen door with such brutality that its aged, delicately polished brass handle separated and clattered to earth, ringing as it struck the flagstones. The brass ball circled briefly before rolling to rest at her feet, leaving Lady Margaret to meditate upon the exaggerated stretch of her reflection in its gleaming surface.

*   *   *

College life was temporarily disrupted to give space to the banquet. The Mall was always out of bounds except for official activities such as parades, but the exclusion area was now extended so VIPs could arrive away from prying eyes, whether by car or helicopter.

Guests arrived from early afternoon on Sunday, 24 May 1987. The entertainment and minor social gatherings that preceded the bank holiday banquet swung into life, the choice of activities making for a chaotic scene to the uninitiated onlooker. Students trod a minefield of strict protocols regarding where they could go and when. A routine Sunday afternoon stroll around Serpentine Lake, for example, was disrupted in the final return mile when on rounding the last promontory the boys were confronted with shrieks of Pimms-fuelled melodrama as female guests misjudged where the small jetty ended and the sailing boat began. When the unfortunate students sheepishly tried to circumnavigate the whole embarrassment, canes were thrust in accusation and protest: 'Get out of here, you boys! Don't you know who lets you imbeciles dare to reside here?' It was a regrettable clash of cultures.

The workshops suffered similar disruption. Art Rose was heading over to continue working on his ancient weaponry project only to turn the corner to find the courtyard had been taken over by cars, mainly ones with black privacy glass. Under the warm sun the drivers had found shade in doorways or had opened their car windows to let in a cooling breeze. Everywhere were the clichéd accessories of the watchers for the rich: the inevitable Ray Bans and the occasional Rolex, with dark suits harbouring holstered Berettas as their shady owners scanned broadsheets from around the world. Men strolled about, a couple down to waistcoats showing pristine white shirt sleeves as they worked soft cloths to remove any dust or flies from freshly valeted Bentleys. Here too, cultures crossed. The more humble staff – drivers for public servants, or anyone not in the top ranks of a blue-chip company or enjoying great private wealth – loitered awkwardly. Vauxhall Cavaliers and M&S suits made for little conversation.

Art stopped in his tracks. The nearest chauffeur looked him up and down as a first challenge to entry. He took in the scene. Beyond the gathering he noticed the buildings were totally locked down – not a single door or window suggested anyone at home today. In spite of the general instructions, he had hoped to find this area unaffected by the festivities. Lowering his gaze to disengage his observer, he sloped away, retracing his steps until he was out of sight before pausing to consider his options. On the far side of the courtyard was the lathes room, the dilapidated wooden windows of which had catches that could easily be shaken free. Art planned to enter the woodwork shop and quietly go about his business.

As he threaded round behind the barn complex and turned along the back wall, he heard voices approaching. He darted to the previous corner but no door offered access or escape. In desperation he leaped behind the broad girth of a nearby horse chestnut tree and crouched down. Pressed against its tough bark, he froze, his ear cocked towards the passers-by.

'We'll let things settle, let everyone get comfortable and immersed in the fun,' directed the first man. 'All the while we need to be making ground. The best opportunity will be tomorrow evening, of course, with everybody in one place and no calls until after midnight. You're clear on the areas you're working?'

'Yes, understood,' replied the second man. 'Gaining entry around here should be a cinch, but doing so without leaving a trace is actually less simple. Old locks and bolts, rather than modern Yales, for example. Skeleton keys don't litter the place with cropped ironwork, do they?'

'Just do your best, map what you can, photograph what you can, and be smart.'

Twigs snapped underfoot as the pair strolled past and away.

As afternoon drifted towards evening, word was circulated that any interested guests were invited to join her ladyship in the east stateroom of the Oxford wing at six o'clock. This would be an opportunity to view some cherished heirlooms which were in routine use – not hidden within the darkness of a vault. When Tavener learned the news it did little to alleviate his ongoing fury at what he saw as being deliberately played by Lady Margaret and her amateur pseudo-security strategy. He felt both trust and control slipping away, since the proceedings were only loosely following the agenda. But this was Lady Margaret's home; she would clearly do as she pleased. Tavener therefore left Roberts to supervise the unplanned tour.

The visitors duly arrived and were welcomed into a spacious yet homely scene on the first floor. Tall sash windows with inset shutters allowed the light to flood into the room, despite its eastern aspect. In contrast to the wood panelling which was favoured in the lower and public rooms, the stateroom had period plastered walls in coordinated pastel greens, highlighted with white border detail within individual wall sections. The original broad oak floorboards were covered by three antique Persian rugs; brilliant yellow cadmiums, crimsons threaded with old golds, ochres and indigos spread across the expanse in intricate geometrical design.

They might have expected to find the gilt-edged mirrors set over marble fireplaces, oil paintings of Lady Margaret's ancestors, often seated on their prized steed, and a commanding ceiling centreline of cut crystal chandeliers, but even the untrained eye could not miss the most novel and significant attractions. To one side and away from direct sunlight in an open bookcase, were the four foolscap volumes of *Birds of Africa,* with its exquisite hand-painted illustrations of exotic birds on the left-hand pages, and descriptive calligraphy on the right. Each was hand-bound in elaborately decorated and jewelled fine leather. At the centre of the room opposite the main fireplace stood a solid silver Queen Anne coffee table. On a side table in the far corner was a Chinese vase. Modest in appearance, it was around eighteen inches tall and decorated in light blue and yellow adorned with carp and flowing, vibrant decorations. This piece had once resided in the royal palaces of the eighteenth century Qianlong dynasty.

Around a dozen guests were present, wandering between exhibits once the brief formalities and guided highlights were complete. A low hubbub developed as appreciative eyes took in the marvels at hand. Roberts glanced around and saw that Messrs Greech and Parcelle had stepped out into the corridor. Quietly, he followed.

The pair were strolling towards the far end of the corridor. They exchanged words in hushed tones and seemed to admire the few smaller paintings hanging under ornate brass picture lights.

Roberts held back in the doorway, observing them, watching to see what they would do next. When they reached the end wall they stood still and stopped talking. Roberts quickly pulled back as Parcelle glanced around to the stateroom doorway. Then they returned to their point of interest: the wall.

The corresponding end wall of the stateroom suggested a line for the south-facing outer wall of the Oxford wing. While the corridor turned at right angles where they stood, it ended there too, at a doorway. Could this lead into a bedroom suite? Such a suite would be a very odd shape to have included any space behind what must have been an internal wall, closer as it was than that of the stateroom next door. The two men stood and stared and puzzled. Its dimensions and geometry were an enigma to the observant eye and enquiring mind. Greech raised his hand to tap the wall.

'May I help you, gentlemen?'

Roberts was suddenly at their heels. Greech's hand fell lamely to his side, a guilty schoolboy caught.

'So this is wallpapered . . . the corridor . . . not painted like the stateroom . . .' he mused.

'That is correct. Daylight wouldn't fade the wallpaper here, you see.'

'Ah, of course. Shall we join the others? Probably ought to be thinking about changing for dinner I suppose, eh Roland?'

16

The dinner at the end of the first day was informal and relaxed, the guests mingling over a splendid buffet. The banqueting hall was a venue that impressed upon visitors the longevity and importance of the Rothwell name; from floor to high ceiling it was clothed in tradition and spectacle. Heavy oak panelling clad the lower walls, limestone fireplaces stood at either end and gold-framed canvases of ancestors loomed in between. Deep claret-red walls rose above the picture line to a soaring Gothic alabaster ceiling from which a dozen huge ribbed plasterwork pendants hung down like the tapered hind quarters of cattle carcasses.

Lady Margaret circulated, dividing her time evenly among the gathering, not sitting to dine lest she should spend too long with one group and give the impression of favouritism. Her approach was always to nurture relationships with the human touch, so that acquaintances would become allies, to bridge the gap between mere connections and confidants. That way, long after tonight's merriment, she might receive a call or letter – a courtesy afforded to a respected friend – to tell her of developing economic turmoil in South America, or a disease getting out of control in the Congo. Even hearsay so often has substance. Maybe an invitation to a gala for a foreign dignitary could open doors and assist the organisation's endeavours abroad. Her very best efforts were needed now.

The hours passed by until a jaded Lady Margaret allowed herself a final sip of sauvignon after the few die-hards retired, having indulged the waited drinks service until midnight. At last the house fell silent.

The next day was bank holiday Monday, another Sunday for the boys of Rothwell College. A few had decided to spend a long weekend at home, while most spread their wings locally, taking time away from the college but reappearing for meals and a place to sleep. Caution still prevailed, and observation posts on roof tops accessed via the dorm windows remained in place. The occasional bodyguard would emerge from a car on the Mall to catch sight of a figure holding binos crouching behind a textile cover in the corner of the green coppered roof of the main house. Their quizzical, disapproving looks were soon quelled as word was put round that the military were entitled to their protective measures too. But watchers do not like to be watched.

Through the day a steady trickle of delivery vans, temporary house staff, tradesmen, couriers and drivers came and went as preparations for the banquet moved into the final phase. By eight o'clock everything was in place and the string quartet began to play on the elevated lawn of the rose garden overlooking the cricket pitch and Serpentine Lake. The evening breathed its final warmth, the sunshine holding on just long enough for canapés and aperitifs to be served before guests were invited inside to dine.

Behind the scenes, the activity was gathering pace, pressure building for the chefs and waiting staff. Roberts was used to the fact that planning was entirely necessary yet often useless in the face of reality and put himself to work wherever the moment needed him most. Just as he was supervising the rapid uncorking of more champagne, requested by the already well-oiled wife of a hedge-fund investor and her following of first-timers, Tavener appeared beside him.

'Philip, may I ask, with the greatest respect, why you are opening champagne when your attention would be much appreciated elsewhere?' he asked through half-gritted teeth.

'Such as, Jim?'

'Such as out here, as another pair of eyes for me to—' Tavener checked himself as one of the hired staff struggled through with the first of the starter course. She was followed by a steady, well-orchestrated stream of waiters and waitresses. 'We need to be watching all the guests all of the time,' he hissed.

'I could ignore the request for more champagne, but it would only get worse,' Roberts grinned. 'You need to have a little faith sometimes, Jim. Let things take their course, if that's even comprehensible to you.'

Tavener turned on his heels and walked away. As he rounded the swing door to the kitchen he nearly flattened Lorna Hamble, Colonel Hunter's secretary. Laden with two jugs of water in each hand which she just managed to control, she was caught flat-footed, both in step and thought. Her eyes widened in surprise, and she froze, scrabbling to know how she should respond and what she was meant to know and not know about him.

Tavener smelled fear and instantly detected an out-of-place reaction. He rose to his full six foot two inches and closed upon her, cornering her between door and wall.

'Miss Hamble! I am correct, am I not? Our esteemed principal's . . .?' Still dumbstruck she made to answer, but he continued, 'secretary, that's it. And we have never been introduced. I am James Tavener. You might know of me, assisting in the science department, CCF, that sort of thing. All quite modest stuff, but I appreciate such opportunities, nonetheless.'

'Of course, Mr Tavener, yes. It's a pleasure to . . . well, bump into you, I suppose.' She laughed nervously.

'Yet tonight it seems we are both temporary workers, exchanging an all-too-quiet evening in for a few pennies and a chance to marvel at how the other half lives?'

'Quite so, sir. How ably summarised.'

'Please, it's James to my friends and close colleagues.'

'James it is then. You must forgive me though.' She gave him half a smile and vanished in another flurry of waiters heading to the dining room.

Beneath the sparkling light of the three grand chandeliers, the sumptuous five-course dinner had begun. The quartet set the mood, maintaining a soothing rhythm, the saviour to any awkward gaps in conversation. Folk could engage politely with each other or relax and nod approvingly at the music while savouring the finest estate venison accompanied by a glass of mellow, rich Château Lafite.

Tavener patrolled inside and out, checking secured doors to private rooms, surveying gardens and outer entrances. Every half hour his route took him to the communications room where he would scan the antiquated lighting board for any intrusions or trouble in the main estate buildings or tunnels. This round – nothing. Just a house full of happy guests, waiters in attendance and sweaty chefs taking moments to breathe whenever they could.

It was just after ten o'clock and the evening had progressed without a hitch. Tavener was standing in the shadows at the edge of the dining room when Lorna suddenly appeared next to him.

'So, James, while trying to balance jugs of water I've also been trying to fathom your role here tonight. Something behind the scenes is it?'

'You could put it that way, Lorna, but I regret to say without the intrigue or glamour that perhaps you were hoping to discover.'

She immediately sensed that trusting her instincts to engage him and mix things up a little might have been rash, but the die had been cast. 'Go on. You're just adding to the intrigue now. So what *is* your role? And don't worry, no role is too modest in my eyes.'

'You could say that I'm here to make sure everybody arrives, goes home and doesn't get lost in between. As simple as that. So I spend my time watching and checking that if some merry soul disappears to the loo they actually reappear. That's more complicated if they go as a couple, especially when they didn't arrive as one, if you understand me,' he smirked.

She stood speechless, her mouth hanging open.

'Now, you must forgive me,' he said, pleased with himself as he set off on mission fictitious.

The most important part of the evening soon arrived. The transition from main course, through dessert, then cheeses served with a Dow's '63 vintage port had to be skilfully managed as the diners knew they would have to suffer the speeches before retiring for further refreshments. As silence fell and Roberts, the master of ceremonies, invited Lady Margaret to address her guests, the distant drone of an alarm rose from the communications room. Lady Margaret sensed the impossibility of coincidence and shared an intense glance with Roberts who immediately took his leave as she began her speech.

Tavener was already there when Roberts arrived.

'The Woodhouse, Philip.'

'But that's a fire signal,' replied Roberts aghast, pointing at the upper flashing red unit and then the unlit lamp beneath it which was linked to intruder detection pads around the Woodhouse's doorways.

'Wait!' Tavener scrabbled in a nearby cupboard. Tossing aside a torch, plastic bags and empty jars he fished out a pair of binoculars. He darted back across the room and leaped onto a bench to get a view east towards the Woodhouse. 'I can see a faint glow. Something's alight!'

'We should call the fire brigade. Now!'

'No, I'll head there right away and check it out. Stay here by the phone. It's too suspicious. Tonight? Right now? I suspect a deception is being played.'

'You'd better be sure, Jim. It'll be gone in minutes if we're wrong.'

Less than three minutes later Tavener skidded his Rover to a halt in the driveway of Rothwell Woodhouse to find the end stable alight. In a separate stable of her own, Duchess was crying out and kicking at her door, but neither she nor the Woodhouse were at risk. The three empty stalls would burn out without the flames reaching further; intermittent downpours that had overtaken the early evening sunshine were already dampening the flames.

Tavener stood still, taking in the scene. Violent gusts of wind drove sheets of rain across the yard and under his torchlight the mud glistened a deep treacle black. Duchess started to calm. He looked around for tyre tracks and footprints, lights, motion, sound. Nothing. He checked through the window to the drawing room. All was well. He rushed round to the front door, let himself into the dark hallway and made for the phone.

'Philip? It's just a diversion. The disused stable block has been set alight. Get about the house there. Check the guests. Who's out of their seats?'

'On my way!'

Lady Margaret had intended to keep her speech light-hearted and brief. But while instinct told her to do exactly that and then to attend to whatever crisis loomed beyond, rationality called her to extend it. It would mean that she could contain the situation in one room, where all the guests should be. Her mind switched to another gear, and she sensed the rare but not totally unfamiliar onset of an out-of-body experience. It was as if her mind had divided in any number of ways allowing her to engage with all the demands put upon her.

Firstly, how would she expand her speech and buy time? She would need to slow the process with detail. The welcome extended to overseas guests would now include a potted summary of their businesses, their association with her household, their performance on the lake after a few glasses of Pimm's, and on it would go. Secondly, she would conduct a visual appraisal of the dining room. Which guests were absent? There should be none. Who was in attendance among her staff and aides? Six or seven stood ready around the edges of the room and at the doors, but Roberts and Tavener remained absent. Finally, what were her priorities? If somebody was trying something, a diversion, an attack, a robbery, or even just prying photographers after an exclusive, what did she care about most? Who or what should be protected first?

As she ran through these parallel cognitions, Roberts slipped back into the room and stood near the door. Lady Margaret stumbled slightly in her speech as she caught his eye. He was cueing her towards an empty seat: Roland Parcelle. She instantly concluded this must be a snooping or infiltration incident, not an attack. She nodded almost imperceptibly and Roberts set off again, knowing what he had to do, leaving Lady Margaret in turmoil behind her mask of graciousness.

Moments later the fire alarms rang out throughout the house and the proceedings abruptly halted. Lady Margaret, assisted by the head waiter and sommelier, called for the guests to leave via the main entrance to the house onto the Mall. Tavener returned straight into a tide of confused and noisy guests and was thrust into taking control of events. He was retrieving the guest list from his suit pocket to attempt a roll call when he saw Lady Margaret walking towards him.

'If you are agreed, I suggest we tick people off the list and get them away, back to their accommodation. Those staying here may return inside when I give the all-clear. Now I must move through the crowd and make my

218

apologies,' she said. Tavener returned a firm nod and began his task, pen and paper clutched in hand.

A few minutes later Lady Margaret turned to see Roberts waiting for her by the steps to the main entrance, his expression set with concern. They exchanged a few quiet words before he headed back inside and she over to Tavener.

'Mr Tavener, when you are done here, would you be so kind as to check the strongroom and the tunnel for any lost revellers, staff, or anyone of whom we may not know?'

'Of course, my lady. Where will I find you to report?'

'Roberts and I will check the staterooms. Let's all meet back in the dining room at, say, eleven? That should allow time to complete our checks.'

'Very well.'

Lady Margaret watched Tavener's retreating back heading towards the kitchen en route to the tunnels before making her way up to the first floor and the east stateroom. As she ascended the final few stairs to the corridor, the scene that she feared most awaited her. Initially obscured by Roberts standing before her, motionless and sombre, every next step brought further into view the gaping darkness of the open trapdoor in the corridor floor. Silently she joined him and together they stared down in horror.

At their feet lay the entrance to a lower level far below. Wooden steps descended into an engulfing blackness, where barely visible in the distance was a pair of heavy wooden doors. One of those doors had been opened. More significantly, it had not been closed.

'My God,' she uttered. 'The Dark Hall.'

'We have a big problem. If it's our friend Parcelle, then goodness knows what games are afoot.'

'We cannot have police crawling around this place, Philip.'

'Somehow I suspect that won't happen. There is foul play here and someone's head will roll for their plan going awry, whatever the plan might have been. Whoever is behind this will want it kept under wraps as much as we do.'

Lady Margaret struggled to reconcile the possibilities.

'But who . . . and how do we . . . or how would they—'

'What? Make contact? Ask for him back?' said Roberts. She looked at him aghast as he continued, 'They won't know what's happened to their man and we would do well to capitalise on that while we hold at least some of the cards.'

'What do you suggest?'

'James Tavener. He must have contacts. Networks. Including dirty ones. Maybe he can assist this situation – *facilitate*. Isn't that the jargon?'

She drew a sharp breath. 'But he cannot know about this place. Ever.'

'Agreed, my lady. Nevertheless, perhaps he can make some calls to assist with the slim possibility of locating Parcelle if he surfaces elsewhere?'

'Or recovering a body,' she exclaimed, her hand covering her mouth in shock. 'Do we even have a choice? We must let Tavener try. But great care is required with how we involve him or it will backfire.'

'Indeed,' said Roberts, closing the trapdoor and securing the catch. 'Let's hope this holds long enough for the dust to settle without more surprises.'

17

'Delta-2-1, send sitrep. Over.'

The radio crackled deafeningly in Bruce's ear. He eased back the volume control.

'Delta-2-1. Fire alarms sounding in the main house, which no doubt you can hear. Yes, guests emerging onto Mall. Looks like show's over. Cars arriving to collect. Over.'

'Roger that, Delta-2-1. And please cut the speculation and commentary. Yes, we can hear the alarms. Out.'

'Zero, should I remain in position or evacuate? Over.'

'Stay in position. No alarms sounding in college areas. We are checking now. Could be diversion or deception. Keep eyes on, Delta-2-1. Remember your evac routes. Out.'

Cold comfort. Bruce scanned the two routes along the parapets in either direction to external fire-escape ladders. Both were clear. He watched as below him the Mall continued to fill with aristocracy in dinner gowns and white tie, limousines sweeping in from the estate beyond. Setting his gaze back through the nightscope he peered into the bushes in the near distance, the last bastion of cover for any would-be attackers.

The brief rain shower that had started only a few minutes before had stopped. Suddenly he became aware of heat rising beneath him. He flinched, confused. On the verge of panic, he knew he needed to stay calm. Below, the first chauffeurs arrived. One scanned the scene, looked up and spotted Bruce, now half-standing. Bruce stared down at him. The man did not react. No arm waving or shouting. If there were flames below surely the man would call out?

Bruce steeled himself. *Time, Bruce. Time. Work it out.*

It slowly dawned on him that he was sensing the warmth absorbed by the west-facing copper roof tiles at his back, now radiating the last of their heat to the cool night sky. He reached out and touched a wet tile. The faintest trace of heat met his hand – to Bruce's skin it was as if it had been glowing red.

'Delta-2-1, precautionary. You are to stand down. RTB via dorms. RV in five; my location. Over.'

'Delta-2-1. Roger. Out.'

Bruce switched the scope off to save precious battery power and started inching along the walkway inside the parapet, crouching past dorm windows, aiming to re-enter the building through the nominated opening. As he passed an outlying senior dorm he heard voices, not the usual chatter, but intense, stifled emotion.

'This is such shit, man.'

'Keep your fucking voice down, Rambo.'

'This is *shit,* guys. The place is erupting. I just came past the com cell. There's a fire at the Woodhouse, but it's not a fire apparently. Like a hoax or some shit. Now her ladyship's party is out on the street for another non-fire. Alarms but nothing there. Anybody who wants to make a headline just needs to bung a Molotov through a window and let his buddies take us all in the killing zone with their gats. Then it's into your wagons and high-tail it all the way to the M1. It's that easy.'

Bruce paused, hoping to get more information in the few moments he would dare to delay. The voices continued, eager but cautious. He heard steps as one of the seniors arrived at the window, opening it wider to let in more fresh air. He threw himself flat on the walkway under the lip of the window sill and froze. Face down, he had no idea what was happening above him. For an instant that seemed to last a lifetime he imagined he was under the gaze of the senior student who would now be furious at what he had found. He waited for the impact of a fist or angry shouting but nothing happened.

The hubbub continued in the dorm. Bruce remembered that his radio could crackle to life at any second and give him away. As was becoming uncomfortably familiar, he knew he had to accept the risk while attempting to reduce it. Slowly, painstakingly, he reached to locate the switch and killed the radio. He would be off comms but could plead ignorance if he was called. Why should he need to keep it on for the few minutes journey back to Kitchen Block? It would be best to save that battery too, surely? He slipped away, his mind turning over the voices and identities of those who had spoken.

The next morning at breakfast Bruce found Shaun Dodd sitting at one end of an emptying table. He looked up expectantly.

'You look excited – and tired.'

'I was manning the O.P. last night, so yes, a bit knackered. After all the fuss died down they sent us out again to see our stag through to 2 a.m. But that's incidental. I overheard some loose talk.'

'Like you're about to do, Bruce?' Shaun challenged, raising an eyebrow.

'Shaun, I know what you said about only ever being able to trust myself with secrets, but I am going to indulge in some gossip with you on this one. If I can't trust you, then what is this world about?'

'I'm touched, Bruce, but I think you missed my subtlety. You're right – I meant what I said: you can only ever truly trust yourself. When you accept that then you can decide whether to play by it. If you choose to trust someone, just remember that's the moment in the plan you forego your option for perfect security. It's something you can't reverse. That's all.'

They paused, each eyeing the other before turning to their plates of sausages, bacon, beans, eggs, buttered toast, and mugs of strong hot tea.

'I think you haven't considered the whole argument, Shaun. If I don't share my thoughts, concerns – maybe plans – with you, then it's one mind trying to do it all alone rather than two. Yes, it's a greater security risk with two, but a greater cognitive risk with one. Would you agree?'

Bruce experienced a moment of glee that for once he had matched Shaun's intellect. Shaun reflected before responding, 'Go on then. What's the news?'

Bruce started to relay the story of the seniors' conversation in the dorm. After a minute he stopped. A knowing smile was lighting Shaun's face. A tilt of the head and theatrical attention to Bruce's words told Bruce that he was behind the curve. His news, it seemed, was not news at all.

'What?'

'Bruce, I'm so sorry. I'm trying not to laugh. You see, I have . . . what would you call it? . . . an uncanny knack of being in the right place at the right time. It's partly luck, but there is also a bit of history in that regard for me – so I guess it's also a bit of a sixth sense. I happened to be looking out through the doorway and towards the window of Dorm Four as you headed past in your sniper-man gear. A few of us had not long arrived upstairs to turn in. I left my dorm and walked along the corridor, seeing you passing the windows as I peeked through open doors and empty rooms. But you didn't appear at Dorm Eight, and Dorm Seven's door was shut. I rather absentmindedly dropped my towel outside it to see what I could hear. So you're going to tell me about Blanchard-Jones and his merry crew of frustrated Sandhurst platoon commanders to be? How am I doing?'

'You bastard, Shaun!' laughed Bruce. 'Just when I thought I was keeping up with your planetary brain. What a moron.'

'On the contrary, you should be pleased that you discovered not just the seniors' secret, but also your own,' said Shaun more seriously. Bruce frowned and looked at him questioningly. 'The heat from the roof. I first spotted you from my dorm when fetching my wash kit and I watched as it all unfolded. But do you understand it yet?'

Bruce looked at him, his mouth open.

'Your supersensitivity to radiated heat.'

'Do you mean when I felt the roof tiles? I thought we were on fire.'

'It was the alarms that got you thinking that way. So why did you reach to touch the tiles?'

'I thought they were hot.'

'They're copper, a superb conductor of heat. They would have cooled quickly after the sun went down, then we had some rain, yet you detected the faintest trace of heat, like a fingerprint.'

'Shaun, I'm confused. What are you getting at?'

'The other day you warned Dominic Hughes that the transformer for his guitar amp was running hot, but you announced this from across the room without having touched it or even been near it. Or another time you turned to look at the door in the chemistry lab before Tavener walked in. He was wearing those awful Hush Puppies, so you couldn't have heard his footsteps – but you reacted like it was obvious, like you could see straight through the door. I followed your gaze, wondering what on earth led you to stare across the room all of a sudden. All the untrained eyes around the room didn't even notice or think to question, of course. People too easily assume some other explanation.'

'But what does this mean? And how do you know what to look for, and then to spot it so keenly?'

'That's my boy. Like I said, it's slippery this disclosure stuff, isn't it?' said Shaun, with a widening grin.

*   *   *

The note slid under the door – the faintest whisper of paper against flagstone breaking the perfect silence. Tavener placed his shoe and cloth onto the table and turned to inspect it. Inside a cheap white envelope was a typed note inviting Mr James Brandreth Tavener to a welcome evening of the Cottam Hunt on Thursday, 28 May at the Cottam Arms public house. No name, no signature. The approach struck him as quaint, but also reassuringly antiquated. Very good, he sighed. The meeting was requested for the next day, but by whom? The possibilities were disturbing.

The curious incident of the missing Roland Parcelle had brought Tavener brief amusement. His theory that one of his former brethren might have sent a snooper who had drunk himself into such embarrassment that he had to retire from the dinner too ashamed to reappear was crumbling. His cynicism and patronising high handedness in telling Lady Margaret that the salient thing to do was to wait for Parcelle to resurface in Cyprus had been broadsided by the invitation. He was seething. Once again she had sought his expertise to clear up a mess about which she had withheld the truth. It now seemed that Parcelle should be considered an intelligence asset who had not returned to wherever he should report.

He arrived ten minutes later than the appointed time and sat for a further five in his car. Through the drizzle he scanned across the Cottam village green for any amateur who by now would be ripe to panic and come outside to look for him. But nobody appeared.

Sporting a slightly dishevelled country look of corduroys and leather-elbowed cardigan under a Barbour bodywarmer, complete with fraying flat cap, he strode into the main bar and stopped to inspect the chalkboard before ordering a mug of Marston's Pedigree. He looked around him and spotted his summoner, the man's face partly obscured as he sat motionless in the shadows nursing a half-empty sleever. They made eye contact, but Tavener's gesture offering a refill was waved politely away. Tavener paced directly to the table, frothy-headed pint in hand.

'They must be keeping you busy if you haven't had time to change out of your suit, Inspector,' he announced.

At the bar, ears pricked up. The man met Tavener's opening shot with a cold stare.

'You're in unjustifiably good spirits for a man in your situation, Jim,' said Roger Gleeson.

Behind them, folks returned to their own drinks, deciding to let the strangers sort their business in private. Tavener sat. As the two men leaned in, each taking a long swig from their glass, the hubbub started to return. They took a moment more to size each other up.

'So how is retirement treating you? Got your bus pass yet?' Gleeson laughed aloud.

'Life is very satisfying, thank you, Roger. Especially since I had the good judgement to move on before I lost my sense of humour. I lead a simple life now, in a very beautiful place, as I'm sure you already know. But what about you? Has progress slowed a little – if you are having to come see me, for instance?'

Gleeson gave a rueful smile. He expected nothing less from the man who was a minor legend in his sister service. 'You of all people will know that the visitor can be anyone, and is usually proportionate to the scale of the matter at hand, shall we say?'

'Fire away, but I must say, regrettable a tragedy as it was, I thought the boys in blue did a pretty thorough job after the lad McIntyre's fall. I am intrigued as to why it's come your way.'

'Very good, Jim. But we both know this is not about the boy, don't we?' Gleeson paused, attempting to unsettle his mark. Tavener merely shook his head and smiled in bemusement. 'Parcelle, Jim. Roland Parcelle. Where is he?'

Tavener looked Gleeson in the eye.

'You're kidding me, right? Seriously Roger, you've fucking had the gall and stupidity to waste public time and money coming here – all this classic bullshit, believing that I know the whereabouts of what I now presume is a lost sheep of yours.'

'Let's cut the crap, Jim. You retired from the service, but a man like you never really retires. You might be trying to kid yourself that you're leading a normal life, helping in the science department, teaching outdoor stuff, but you were there that night. You don't miss things when people disappear.' A pleading edge had crept into Gleeson's words.

'I can't be responsible for all her ladyship's great and good at all times. If somebody chooses to leave a social function and not tell anyone, there's not a lot I can do.'

Gleeson grimaced. 'Social function. I like that. Parcelle's a US asset. The Americans are missing a man. Do I have to spell it out, Jim?'

Tavener looked into the distance as he absorbed Gleeson's words. His focus returned.

'Roger, if he were the Pope I still wouldn't be able to help. And what the hell was he doing there anyway?'

'If you're holding back, I strongly advise against it. The Yanks will quickly run out of patience and they have a habit of doing whatever they want in the end. Their way. Which is never a good way for us. So unless her ladyship wants an open police investigation for a missing person, soon to be presumed dead – and that's the least painful option – I suggest you help me keep this under control. British control.'

Tavener stared into his drink, perplexed. 'That's something I'll have to live with, my friend, because I'm all out of answers on this one.'

'Have it your way. But in case you should happen to remember anything, or decide you have something you want to share with me . . .' Gleeson slid his business card across the table, keeping it pinned under his fingertip. 'And if you get into deep water, I might even consider helping you.'

18

Once again Bruce found himself compelled to follow the danger, despite Shaun's insistence that to protect his military career he should abandon plans to infiltrate any secret plot for college self-defence. He couldn't explain it. He couldn't stop himself sniffing around, wanting to sense the risk, to feel alive, even when the trail from the previous thrill-seeking mission in the tunnels stopped cold at Rory's grave.

So how could he approach it? Perhaps he could 'accidentally' overhear some of the suspected players talking and allow himself to become sworn to secrecy around their cause, thereby becoming part of it. Alternatively, he could express his concerns and himself be overheard by one of their group. Or, he could simply reach out to one of them in confidence and see what developed. These seemed the most logical possibilities for the budding spy.

Each option had potential strengths, risks and challenges to its effective execution. Bruce felt that his ability to hold more than one option in mind, only deciding through instinct in the heat of the moment, would surface when needed. It was both thrilling and terrifying. It could invite intuitive brilliance or court unmitigated disaster, as happened in the first hostilities with Jez and co.

And so it ran for a few days as Bruce began to gravitate around the various seniors of Dorm Seven, at breakfast, in the gym, at cricket practice, around the library. A convenient trestle table outside the clothing store next to the seniors' bar presented an opportunity for Saturday night boot-cleaning where tipsy men might pass and he could engage them in conversation.

After a number of false starts and dead ends, nothing satisfactory had transpired and Bruce sought counsel again. To avoid looking totally useless in Shaun's eyes, a non-specific discussion with the resident mystery man Art Rose was the clear alternative.

When the weather allowed, summer sun and long days afforded opportunities for outdoor martial arts training. Wearing old clothes to save grass stains on their precious aikido suits, the outdoors afforded the boys different kinds of space and surfaces on which to train. From their deserted area at the far side of the cricket field, the surrounding landscape in all its resplendent glory was the perfect backdrop. It added a new psychological dimension of peace and reflection. Bruce intuited the melding of mind and body, as the martial art practice itself became a focus to experience afresh what it was to be present and awake in each moment.

But above all, the location afforded privacy. Their numbers had dwindled due to the rigour of the programme and the attraction of less punishing summer pursuits, and Art and Bruce were frequently the only ones training, as it was this evening.

Art was guiding how advanced martial artists read an opponent very early, from the faintest telltale signals which precede a move. Some could even sense whether the upcoming move would be to evade, to dummy or to attempt a winning strike. Art provided Bruce with myriad initial moves, letting him react to defend before pausing to discuss what he noticed, how he reacted and his thought processes. After an hour, they towelled sweat away and downed water as the sun lowered in the sky above the Oxford wing.

'So, Art, this thing with observing the opponent – does that apply just to combat?'

'Meaning what, Bruce? I'm not quite following you.'

'I'm really intrigued by what you said about your father – all that stuff about the Middle East. So, do you read people in general? Are you into that sort of thing?'

'It was the Far East, and no, I don't think I do read people. But tell me what you mean exactly. "Read" . . . how?'

Bruce continued the conversation for a while longer but it was clear that without specifics it was going nowhere. He was glad he had held back from saying anything in pursuit of his true desired outcome: to be spoon-fed precisely how to infiltrate a group. Again, his intuition had told him to wait.

Another week passed before Bruce's patience was rewarded by a mundane coincidence. After a cricket practice match, Bruce and Bill Woodsman of 65 Entry were tasked to fetch the boundary flags. It had been a hot afternoon and lively batting meant that fielders had worked hard, so rather than jog round in opposite directions they ambled round together letting their soaked whites dry in the sun.

Bruce glanced over to catch Bill scanning the lake across to the woods and hills on the horizon. He was lost in thought. Bruce guessed that the scene playing out in his head had no satisfactory conclusion for his companion. Instinct took over.

'It's a lot to defend, isn't it, Bill?'

'Damn right.'

'An open door. It's crazy when you stop to think about it. Unless it's just me.'

'What are you referring to, Bruce? Bit deep, I mean.'

'The issue that's always there, just beneath the surface. The rumours, the unexplained events – like the time the principal had us all mustered in the library after the break-in. It feels like we could be at risk, but nobody seems bothered. It's as if the hierarchy are doing nothing now.'

'What can anyone do? I mean really do, beyond the fairly passive stuff that has had guys up all night for months but achieved nothing?'

'Maybe their achievement was the knowledge that there was no attack planned. But if we were going be hit, there's not much solace in seeing it coming if we can't fire back, is there?'

They headed towards the final couple of boundary flags. Bill stopped and looked ahead, checking they couldn't be heard from the pavilion.

'What are you saying, Bruce?'

'I'm saying we should maybe consider doing something for ourselves, if the hierarchy are so tied by rules.'

'Go on.'

'Basically, Bill, it's simple. If there's a plan for that, I want in.'

Bill squinted into the fading sun. He checked again towards the pavilion, then turned back to Bruce.

'That's quite something to say, Bruce. I'll give you that. But here's the deal: you ever spout shit like that again and risk getting overheard, risk one of the staff thinking we would consider unilateral, unauthorised use of live munitions against unidentified targets ... You're getting the picture, are you, Bruce? And the staff would conclude that only the senior entry could enact such a plan, because only folk like me, the fucking cadet quartermaster, or my armoury sergeant have the keys to the guns and the kit. So that's our careers buggered then, isn't it. So do us all a favour and get back in your box before someone puts you in it, you moron.'

*   *   *

'We have a problem, my lady. I had a visit from, well, not so much an old colleague as a new shadow, let's say.'

'Your language is cryptic – and ominous, Mr Tavener. I'm not sure I'm going to like this.'

'Not one bit, my lady. Our missing person – one Roland Parcelle, or so we were led to believe – would appear to be a CIA operative. He hasn't reported in, and my British contact is concerned that the Americans will take matters into their own hands.'

Lady Margaret turned pale and slid into her study chair as the strength seemed to leave her. 'And what does that mean exactly? Tear this place apart looking for him? He took his own leave of absence, as I understand it.'

'He is missing and they will want answers. All we can do is be vigilant and ready to provide plausible information to any stranger who may appear, or detect any who may seek to conduct their own searches, if you get me.'

'I get you very well, Mr Tavener, and difficult as this may be for you to accept, I very much respect and appreciate your efforts thus far.'

'I have done very little, my lady. The information found me, which is not how I like to do business, I can assure you. But for now, thinking caps on.'

Lady Margaret sat in the stillness of the sitting room at the Woodhouse, enveloped by a sense of déjà vu. The carriage clock turned quietly on the mantle, its rhythm hypnotic, while she looked through the window and into the dark depths of the coniferous woodland beyond the garden.

Roberts entered with a silver tray bearing fine bone china teacups, a steaming pot of Darjeeling and rounds of shortbread.

'You're lost in thought, my lady. Is it to do with Tavener's troubling news?'

Lady Margaret's attention returned to the room.

'Philip, I need you to do something, something for the Archive, something difficult and painstaking and slow. And …'

'No one else can ever know?'

'Quite.'

*   *   *

'So how are your enquiries going, Bruce?'

'Ah, yes. Well, Shaun, my belief that I could be patient when the situation required seemed to reward me with an opportunity, but then it blew up in my face.'

Bruce outlined the encounter with Bill Woodsman. The two boys were chatting in the shade of a cedar tree set comfortably back from the exposed slope down to Winter Lake opposite the college. The weather had been fair of late and the meadow around them had returned to the depths of lush grass which had hosted section fire-and-manoeuvre drills the previous autumn. Shaun took a swig from a can of Coke and passed it to Bruce.

'If it's any consolation, old boy, among all the tedious shit I find myself enjoying, I read somewhere that anyone who is expert in their field has paid their dues. Do you know what that means?'

'Invested their time to become that expert, presumably?'

'Correct, but most importantly they become expert by knowing all the ways things don't work as well as the specific combinations where they do.'

'In other words, I learn more from failure?'

'Much more. Failure carries an emotional charge: it affects you and you remember it. The trick is to learn from it. That way failure makes you wiser, stronger. You just have to see it right. So, what did you learn from your encounter with Bill Woodsman?'

Bruce paused, at a loss to respond to what Shaun had conceived perfect and whole in a single thought. 'I'm not sure. Maybe, and I don't know how, I could have progressed more steadily when things were looking interesting. I just dived in. It was instinct. I wanted to get to a conclusion, to close the deal.'

Shaun held the space, saying nothing, letting Bruce develop his self-analysis.

Bruce shook his head. 'What do you want me to say? I'm lost.'

'Okay, why do you think he exploded, as you described?'

'Because the implications of me screwing up were massive – for him, and others too.'

'Had you considered his position? Did you imagine yourself in his shoes hearing your words?' Bruce fixed on Shaun, wanting to hear more. 'Reacting in the moment is risky. If you had a strategy of infiltration, or even just investigation, you should have thought through things like that.'

'Jesus,' murmured Bruce. 'The only scrap of information which started me thinking such plans even existed was what I overheard on the bank holiday – the seniors in Dorm Seven.'

'And?'

'They expressed concerns and objections, but nobody referred to any actual plans. There was talk but nothing concrete. I heard what I wanted to hear, not what was spoken.'

'What was it that led you to jump to conclusions, Bruce? There must have been something.'

'The emotions involved – the conversation was heated. And the insistence that Blanchard-Jones keep his voice down.'

'But that could have been for the same reasons that Bill chewed you out, don't you think?'

'It seems so now, but ...' Bruce looked ahead determinedly. 'It was like a sixth sense for me. Something connected inside and I was so sure, so sure it was true. Even now I find it hard to accept there is nothing behind it all.'

'Well, Brucie, time will tell. And you need to monitor the outcome. Keep your ear to the ground in case there actually is some secret pact; then you will know if you have a sixth sense – or a blind spot.'

*   *   *

As May gave way to June the end of exams moved closer and with it a sense of anticipation for Bruce. He noticed the absence of uncomfortable encounters with Jez, who seemed contained, focused, but his air of self-discipline – his ability to wait – was unsettling. It smacked of what could be Jez's hidden talent, the ability to cause menace, then to strike from nowhere at a time of his choosing. But Bruce was consoled and pleased to notice his presence of mind in bringing a lesson of Shaun's to bear: pluralism – in Shaun's usage meaning the ability to view a situation from many angles.

Perhaps Jez was not a calculating assassin after all but a coward as well as a bully. 'All mouth, no trousers', as Bruce's mother would say. And if he was waiting patiently, he would have a finite window of opportunity to attack. After the last exams the seniors were not left to hang around the college soaking up public funds. They would be away to undertake visits and attachments to units of the corps and regiments that might recruit them. Then Bruce would need to focus, to expect Jez to find an opportunity to attack him. Of course, Jez would run the risk that the beating could backfire on him if Bruce won the fight for a second time, or if Jez was caught assaulting another student.

The din of the morning washroom returned Bruce to his senses. He looked up to see Art Rose staring at him across the basins and boys heading past having washed and shaved.

'Earth to Noble. Come in, Noble.'

Bruce's mouth opened, but no words came out. Art grinned at him. Finally, Bruce engaged his brain.

'How's the project going, Art?'

'Can I show you this afternoon?'

'Of course.'

Art scanned around the now empty washroom. 'And I have some news to share, just with you,' he muttered.

They met by the Elephant Hut at four.

'Not much need for this place when the weather's fine,' said Art, as he strode to the side door, keys in hand.

'No, I guess you're right. Hockey practice, basketball, cricket nets – is that all it's used for?'

'And what do cricket nets look like when you replace the stumps with a boss?'

'Indoor archery range. Very good, Art, I like it. Hence the . . . er, what's that? A violin case?'

'Okay, it's a bit of a cliché, but sometimes the old ways carry a touch of class.'

'I bet it makes quite an entrance.'

'Let's see, shall we?'

They peered into the darkness which surrounded the shaft of light stretching in through the doorway. Art swept the wall, found a switch and brought the cavernous Nissen hut to life. Massive strip lights buzzed and pulsed into action; fans turned to move air through the windowless space. The nets were in place, ready to receive cricketers on a wet afternoon, but today the boys were alone. They headed inside and Bruce pulled the door closed behind them.

'Help me with this, would you?'

Art rolled a full size archery boss out from behind some side netting. They heaved it onto its stand, then went back to the case, which Art unclipped and opened. Bruce was entranced. Before him lay the first working prototype of Art's highly illegal compound bow and lethal arrows.

'I've got a mix of stuff to fire. To start, I just want to know that I can hit something at twenty-five yards with this thing, and that I haven't cocked up the build so I have to aim at the bloody wall to get it to go straight. Then I can try a few heavy heads in here before we have to rummage around for a secluded spot in the woods to test the incendiaries.'

'Heavy heads? As in armour piercing?'

'Yes, but how thick the armour is another matter.'

Art nocked a plain alloy practice arrow. With his sight set three-quarters low he lined up on the pinhole – the target dead centre – and released. The arrow softly hissed its brief flight before slamming into the top of the boss.

'Whoa! That's nearly dead flat, Art. A shit-powerful bow!'

Art nodded in satisfaction, adjusted his sight and loaded a second. The hall echoed as the arrow thudded to within five inches of centre, still high, but on the centre line.

'That's a nine,' he said. 'One more adjust.'

The third clipped the tiny cross inked at target dead centre.

'Three shots for that. And it was easy. The compound mechanism works a dream. I could hold the aim for as long as I wanted. Here Bruce, you try.'

They stayed for a few more minutes, with Bruce hitting regular tens, if not pinholes. The weapon was expertly constructed, beautifully balanced and easy to master, as well as being collapsible for covert transportation. Bruce studied the design, trying to take in how he might reproduce it. But the craftsmanship was beyond his skills with machines and materials.

'Enough?' asked Art.

'Yeah, cool. Outside now?'

'In just a moment, if that's okay. Shaun tells me – and nobody else, I should reassure you – that you have a bit of an unusual gift, a super sense for radiated heat.'

Bruce tried to hide his surprise that Shaun had spoken of it.

'Yes, well . . . that is . . . it seems like a possibility, at least. Not really been proven, though.'

'I'm intrigued. I know you relish your martial arts practice and this could give you a real niche power – fighting in the dark.'

Bruce struggled to balance his excitement at the prospect and his caution about revealing more. Before he had worked out what to say, Art's enthusiasm had galloped ahead.

'I've been thinking. How about we see where you're at with it? I'll kill the lights. You grab a tennis ball from that bucket, then when I give the word, you try and hit me. Sound like a plan?'

'Er, why not?'

But Bruce's gut tightened as his secret was put under the spotlight. A crazy thought flashed across his mind: *You want to kill the lights, Art, so you'll know how to kill me.* He forced himself to get moving, jogging over to collect a couple of tennis balls from a bucket near the doorway and then returned to stand in the centre of the hall.

'Ready, I guess,' he said.

The lights and fans shut down, their switch contacts sending an eerie snap echoing around the room. Pitch blackness and silence engulfed them.

'Give me a mo, Bruce – forgot to remove my shoes. Okay, you count to ten out loud and I'll move to a different part of the hall. Then go for it – see if you can detect me.'

Bruce did as asked, counting to ten then pausing to scan about him. He reflected that if he wanted a way out of revealing any special talent, the obvious thing to do would be to miss every time. Yet he was also seduced by the challenge. He wanted to find out for himself.

At first he sensed nothing. Art remained motionless and silent. Bruce relaxed, took a long slow breath and scanned around again. Slowly, in his mind's eye, as if floating above where his physical eye was looking, he detected an image. It was a mental picture of Art's body heat. Bruce closed his eyes to remove the confusion between his eyes and his skin, which was actually the sensor. He raised his arm and threw the ball. Clang!

'Not bad, but that's the door to the fuse box, I think, Bruce,' said Art from directly behind him. 'Try again.'

Bruce relaxed and closed his eyes for another count to ten. Now a number of shapes started to emerge: the electrical unit by the wall, ceiling lights, and the entrance door which had been warmed by sunlight. He continued turning. Right there, what seemed like only a few feet away, was the distinct glow of Art's outline.

'I don't want to hurt you, old boy,' he said.

Art remained silent, so Bruce threw the ball.

'That's my head!'

'I tried to warn you.'

'Very impressive, Mr Noble, but we are obliged – by mathematics itself no less – to check that this isn't a fluke. We must test the null set.'

'Do you mean that you want to have a go, to check it wasn't a fluke?'

'Yes, if you want to put it plainly.'

Art grabbed a couple of tennis balls and they took their places in the dark, Bruce finding a suitably random position where he stood still and silent. He was ready. The first minute slipped by. Was Art trying too hard? Perhaps he was a poor sport. Then he spoke.

'I meant to tell you about some news, didn't I, Bruce?'

Bruce stayed put, mouth shut.

'Last night I needed a piss. Right in the dead of night. For some reason I decided to peek outside on my way back to the dorm. I don't know what possessed me to do it, but I took a look all the same. From the window by Dorm Four I spotted lights moving around inside the Oxford wing. I guessed they were night-vision goggles being adjusted or taken on and off, possibly glimpsed some red laser dots too. It looked like a number of guys were searching for something in there. You wouldn't know anything about that, would you?'

'So we're on pause now or finished with the test?' Bruce said. 'Art, I haven't a clue about why that should be. In fact, I'm surprised you should ask me if I knew. How would I?'

'It doesn't matter. You know about the rumours – I just thought I'd check out yet another random Rothwell twilight zone unexplained event with someone I can trust to keep schtum about it. I can trust you, can't I, Bruce?'

'Of course.'

'That's my man! Now, let's head outside and try the warheads.'

'So no test then?'

'No need. You did well and I was just indulging my vanity, which is always best stomped on whenever it rears its ugly little head.'

After careful searching for a secluded spot, Art set about firing both the armour piercing and pyrotechnic arrows while Bruce acted as lookout from the crest above the hollow in which Art had created his mini-range. Thanks to the availability of surrounding trees, an abandoned wooden pallet and the rusting hulk of an old cattle trough, it became clear that the armour piercing arrows were good for about three millimetres thickness of galvanised metal. Anything thicker, such as the frame on which the trough stood, would simply repel them. Similarly modest results beset the fire rounds. Wooden or slightly soft objects, even some tree trunks, would not ignite the pyrotechnic arrows. Striking a hard surface – metal or stone – did the trick consistently, however. It was something to behold, the sound of the bow buzzing when the flights passed the arrow rest, the arrow's hum and whoosh as it flashed through the air, then a sharp crack on impact and soft explosion as the fuel sprayed and ignited.

Bruce rejoined Art as he began packing the bow into the music case. Then the sound of slow hand-clapping broke out behind them. The pair spun round to look straight into Pitcaithly's eyes. Stunned that the RSM had got so close without detection and likely observed the whole thing, they looked sheepishly at each other.

'Very impressive, young Rose. Don't look so worried, lad! Your secret's safe with me. We might need all the help we can get, worse case. And I've never minded distance weapons, especially silent ones.'

'Sir.'

'And make sure you lock the Elephant Hut before you go, won't you?'

'Sir.'

'And return the tennis balls back to where they belong.'

19

Within the US embassy in London there operated the intelligence machinery of a state making its home in a foreign country under the special conditions afforded by ambassadorial diplomatic cover. The Grosvenor Square establishment housed a CIA station, complete with cypher room, quartermaster's department, armoury, debriefing and holding facilities, and state-of-the-art operations rooms. Today, Wednesday, 3 June 1987, the ops unit – codename Piecemeal – was reviewing the Rothwell reconnaissance task.

Buried at basement level in the centre of the embassy were four windowless, hardened and electronically secure conference suites. At 8 a.m. the CIA station ops team and their task leader, David Hurst, were in Alpha suite, huddled around whiteboards in front of eight computer screens and a spacious table covered with large-scale maps and partial building plans of Rothwell College. Sat behind were the recon squad commander, his deputy and the squad's secure communications operator. On the line, by telephone conference facility, was Zack McKinley, CIA head of UK operations, four thousand miles and five hours away in Langley, Virginia. But the time difference didn't matter

251

today; even though it was still the middle of the night in Langley, McKinley had been up for several hours, awakened by news that the team sent to find Roland Parcelle had itself lost a man. The team had been forced to withdraw without extricating their dead comrade – and without finding Parcelle.

'You had two objectives: to locate and recover Hatman, dead or alive, and to gather any potentially valuable information to assist an evaluation of Birdcage,' began the dry, emphatic voice from the conference phone. 'You tell me that you have discovered a potential secret meeting site of a suspected organisation with possible global interests, the motives and specifics of which are uncertain. But that's based on very circumstantial evidence. And you lost another of our assets – terminated – in a firefight from which you had to withdraw without him. Confirm.'

All eyes ran to David Hurst.

'Nearly all correct, sir.'

'Nearly all? I've been up half the night after what should have been a covert infiltration and extraction procedure in a British boys' school. What part did I miss?'

'It wasn't a firefight, strictly speaking, sir.' Several of the recon men looked down at the floor, while others winced at the volunteered information. 'The assailant the team encountered didn't fire back.' There was silence from the teleconference phone. 'He ... he used a knife, we think.'

'You're fucking shitting me now, right? If that's true you can leave with your pension,' the words spat from the speaker. 'You had night-vision goggles and silenced assault rifles. How did one guy force you out like freaking coyotes and kill one of ours? Explain that to me, will you?'

'The NVGs, as you know sir, work on residual light. There was no residual light in the mine. We were blind. Only at the entrance did they have any effect. Further inside we were sitting ducks.'

'Whoa, hang on a minute. Back it up. Nobody said shit to me about any mine on the Zero Three contact brief.'

'One moment, sir,' said Hurst.

Furious sign language was exchanged over the building plans as they resolved the initial miscommunication.

'Sir, the team located the entry point – Hatman paged it as soon as he found it. They went down the steps to the underground hall. There they conducted brief intel collection before continuing the search via an entrance at the back of the hall which led to a tunnel complex set in what might be part of a former coal mine, or possibly an underground coal transportation network. That's where the contact happened, sir.'

From the conference phone, a heavy sigh. 'Is the duty room there?'

'Sir. Here, sir.'

'Has post-op surveillance found anything to suggest that we were detected?'

'Nothing sir. Nothing so far. The place looks normal. No drills, no roll calls in the college, and her ladyship is enjoying a leisurely breakfast, we're told. Oh, and nothing from the Thames House side either.'

'Let's hope it stays that way. David ...'

'Sir.'

'We've got to tie this off for now. One KIA and one MIA presumed dead. So nothing more at Birdcage until I authorise it. Give post-op another twelve hours then get them out. Now I've got to explain this shit to the deputy director.'

The call was terminated.

*   *   *

Very good, thought Tavener, as he inspected the fresh footprints beside the vault. The infiltrators had detected and avoided the pressure plates hidden beneath the mud of the tunnel floor. The prints took him back to his time in Iran. US navy seals prized their kit and he remembered the quality of American military boots that British soldiers could only dream of. There, captured neatly before him in the drying casts of silt and clay, was the self-same four-point star in the tread pattern. He shone his torch on the vault entrance. Neither the soft red neon from the keypad, nor the door and its frame, gave any indication of interference. It occurred to him that if there were no other security measures there was probably no worthy prize inside – or the dated lock system and door could withstand a substantial assault. He set off for the Woodhouse.

Lady Margaret was preparing to receive relatives on a fleeting visit to Britain en route to Austria from Brazil. When Tavener arrived with a rare smile in his eyes she knew he had news, and mercifully not bad news. It appeared that the CIA had probably already come and gone, he explained. They would have been obliged to conduct a physical check for one of their own. It would have been a judgement call – a balance of risk to satisfy as many of the operational response actions as would have been safe to attempt. The logic would run as follows: if Parcelle was missing or captured, he should be located, then extracted, the identity of his abductors established, and lastly his medical condition should be confirmed to enable decisions for any further action. An assessment of compromise risk would be made, and perhaps a reason given to next of kin for their loss. And failing all that, faced with the worst outcome of having no answers for any of it, they would abandon the search, instigate a cover story and manage the consequences.

Lady Margaret absorbed Tavener's sober and lucid explanation. The usual lever would need to be applied: she had to be on her guard to counter his need to know more. But such an enquiry was not forthcoming. He was consumed with the constraints of time, the expanses of real estate to search, and the likelihood that if Parcelle had been abducted it would be for a reason. If that was going to be the play, he would have been swiftly moved off site and contact made with the CIA. Tavener was satisfied that the search team wouldn't return, not for him anyway.

He left her to greet her nephew and his wife. She let an hour pass to be sure that he was back in the science block, before directing Roberts to secure the entrance to the Dark Hall. She figured that enough time had passed since the banquet-night episode to be safe to visit and make sure it was fully locked down again.

Tavener's news had given her mixed comfort. Perhaps the spectre of a CIA visit was out of the way for now. Perhaps they would be back.

*   *   *

Roberts made his way to the main house and headed to the Oxford wing. At the top of the stairs leading to the east stateroom he halted, apprehensive about what he would find, but everything was in its rightful place. The rug covering the trapdoor entrance to the Dark Hall was exactly where it should be. Nothing was disturbed or damaged. As he moved forward, a floorboard creaked. He froze, listening for any sound below. All was quiet. He pulled back the rug, slipped the hidden catch and lifted the trapdoor to reveal the steps beneath.

His torch illuminated the interior of the stairway. The doors leading into the hall from the last step had been firmly shut. Now he had to re-bolt them from the outside.

He looked down at his trainers, reassuring himself that they were the best choice both to be quiet and to run. Unclipping his Browning 9mm pistol from the holster under his left arm, he brought it up and into the aim. Next he placed his right foot on the first step, eased his weight onto it and breathed. As he continued in this pattern he entered a cocoon of attention. All he saw was the doors, all he heard was his heart thumping and blood hissing in his ears.

He made it to the doors. The pounding in his head was deafening now. His lips stuck together as he sought a final breath through his parched mouth. He kept the gun pointing ahead. Trembling, he hovered his left hand over the first bolt. He thrust it home. Then down to the next, then the third and final bolt.

He stepped back and held the gun in both hands, eyes darting over the doors for signs of movement. There was none. He turned and sprinted up the steps two at a time, then slammed the trapdoor closed and rolled to the floor flat on his back, gulping in air as the tension began to leave him.

As his retraced his steps past the stateroom he scrutinised its door. The room was alarmed, with access contacts on the doors and windows and electric eye trips set to catch anyone who broke the beam. While the CIA would easily find a way around such measures, he still checked his own anti-surveillance trick – a tiny splinter of wood hardly the length of a pin wedged between door and frame an inch above the floor. It was in place.

At the Woodhouse the family had quickly moved through the pleasantries of filling in the gaps since their last meeting over three years earlier. Brazil still held all the attractions for escapism to be enjoyed by her ladyship's nephew. Giles Courtenay had never known a day's work since he dropped out of his economics and politics degree course at Warwick, when chasing girls and drinking the cocktails no other students could afford had finally undone him.

Lady Margaret remonstrated with him as Henrietta his wife looked on.

'My dearest Giles, do you ever envisage playing a part in our legacy? When, one day, I am gone there are so few others I could call family, not since your uncle passed.'

'You know my problem, Aunt Margaret. Were I to inherit your wealth I would fret over its management and preservation. Vast sums can only be invested and a market crash means it could be gone overnight. Then where would this place be? I'd be seeking to scratch out an income to pay for a crumbling edifice through the garden centre and turning the house into a museum. I'd end up living in a National Trust site sixty miles from the world's least inviting sea.'

Henrietta broke the ensuing silence.

'Giles, we should take a walk and leave Aunt Margaret to her duties. We don't want to be a burden, do we? Thank you for a sumptuous breakfast, Aunt Margaret. No doubt jet lag will soon catch up so you will excuse me if I take a nap later.'

The pair left, crossing with Roberts on the doorstep. The heavy oak door banged shut, its brass letterbox and knocker tinkling mutedly, and peace returned to Lady Margaret's world. Roberts looked at her face, all too aware of the family issues.

'Philip, it's good to see you.'

'It's only been thirty minutes, my lady, but I understand. Family …'

She gave him a brief smile of recognition, then got on to business.

'Doors secure? Everything in order?'

'Yes, everything,' he said, exhaling deeply.

'Not a pleasant job, I know. And I am most grateful.' Roberts raiscd a hand in acknowledgement. 'Have you managed to make a start with the Archive?' she continued.

'A start, yes. But, as you said yourself, it's painstaking. Even confirming and updating the simplest facts is terribly slow and fraught with complications.' Lady Margaret nodded. 'And then, if the strategy is not triggered in reasonable time, the information could date so easily.'

'Yes, yes I know. But remember the tactics that underpin it. The information needs to be suitably open yet abstract, hinting at a direction rather than declaring a destination. We need to set the conditions for fearful men to react hastily and in confusion, a chain of events whose complexity covers its own tracks.'

'That I understand and it's precisely how I conceived the plan. Getting the right information is challenging though.'

'One day, Philip, some clever person will magically bring it all to our computer screens, I am sure. The world at our fingertips.'

'Which, ironically, is what Tavener sees as impending doom for us.'

'Tavener . . . Yes, I sense that he will have a part to play in this, too.'

*   *   *

Sunday, 7 June 1987 brought a tedious combination of bad weather and a frustrated student community. As rain fell in sheets across the Mall, a clutch of first year students hung around the few armchairs at the end of the Wessex House pits. They were only days away from departing for the summer Outward Bound training or the CCF camp. The seniors were awaiting their summer attachments or visits to regular army units. Holding the whole thing up were the remaining A level exams. These were the side subjects, as far as most were concerned, and included English, French, German and history. The last exam would be on Thursday morning.

Bruce had engaged in all manner of time-killing activities, to the limits a maturing teenager could bear: a leisurely lunch, a fight over the Sunday papers, a walk and further philosophical education from Shaun, and a session on aikido grips and throws with Art. The dreary evening meal was supplanted by a Sunday night Chinese takeaway for at least fifty, which made for a comical order list, organisation of payments and distribution of fare.

A couple of hours after the takeaway feast, Bruce headed to the squash court, looking forward to starting the last week before the break. A note pinned to the corkboard in his cabin had made him smile:

> *Simon Webb is playing Captain MacWilliam in a private squash challenge tonight. Come to enjoy the spectacle but be silent. No lights. All will be revealed. Starts 21:30. S.*

It must have been arranged late in the day, for Shaun hadn't mentioned it during their walk. Bruce decided to slip through the changing rooms and approach unseen, rather than follow the cobbles from the courtyard round and down the slope behind Kitchen Block.

Housed in its own separate building, the squash court was in darkness with no sign of life, but CCF night exercises had shown Bruce how people could easily be hidden under cover of darkness if they remained quiet and still. He tried to honour the trust put in him by creeping in carefully and waiting for someone to emerge and tell him the plan.

It occurred to him that he could sneak up for a peek at the entertainment unhindered if the players were making plenty of noise during the warm-up. He'd lost track of time.

Starts 21:30, he recalled. Instinctively he pulled back his sleeve to check the time, but his watch had no luminous dial and was lost in the pitch blackness.

Then a footstep and whisper interrupted his confusion. *'This way. Absolute silence.'* Bruce closed his eyes to try and pick out the voice. It wasn't Shaun, but it was familiar. They entered the building and ascended the stairs to the viewing gallery, Bruce following the other's cautious footsteps, then feeling his way to avoid hitting his head on the low beams above the wooden staircase. The guys must be staying out of sight, huddling behind the wall overlooking the court, perhaps planning to spring a surprise on poor Simon Webb when his annihilation was complete.

Bruce edged forwards a few feet towards the viewing gallery wall, afraid he was going to tread on someone and blow the whole thing. Then it occurred to him: *Use your talent.* He paused to allow the thermal picture develop in his mind's eye, but he detected little. Then he noticed a faint shape move to his left.

'Having fun?' came the voice.

Bruce shuddered. Had he screwed this up already? What had he done wrong? To stem further embarrassment he stayed silent, awaiting the incoming insult and further instructions.

Out of the void came the first punch, straight into his mouth. Bruce reeled. Then a second cracked his nose. He fell to the floor, a wet warmth of blood starting down his face. His mind froze.

'I'm having fun,' came the same voice, coldly familiar now.

Bruce fought to collect himself. *Move! Make yourself a hard target!* he shouted inside.

'Oh, now that's not fair. Where have you gone?'

Bruce took fleeting solace in wresting even a moment's initiative. He prepared to move again, while through the stream of blood and watering eyes he attempted to detect his attacker's position from his body heat.

An arm wrapped around him from behind and flung him over a waiting leg, tripping him into the wall. His hand scraped the flaking paintwork sending shards underneath a fingernail. The agony bit, let in by too slow an adrenal response, as Bruce's utter confusion held him in a stupor.

'Payback time, eh Noble? An eye for an eye?'

The voice was confirmed. It was Jez. But how was he so effective in the dark? Then Bruce saw a second person lifting something away from his face, seeming to adjust it. Tom Calico, wearing night-vision goggles.

Footsteps on the thin carpet reverberated around the court, warning of the next incoming blow. Bruce's eyes were filling with fluid, and swelling had already started to block his nose. But he had to try something. He got his feet under him, dummied a move to the left, then shifted right. He planted his feet and thrust a punch around mid-body. Fresh air. A hand gripped his ankle and pulled his foot from beneath him. He reached out, seeking to grab something for balance and to stop him being dragged away.

Thrashing desperately, he made contact with a neck, then hair. He felt a splatter of warm liquid on his face. Spit! Another hand took hold behind him, finding his belt. Bruce's mind flashed with thoughts of the aikido moves he had been shown only hours earlier, but nothing was working.

Jez found his grip and launched Bruce over the gallery wall and into the court below.

20

Pain seared through Bruce's battered body. His head was pounding and his lips crusted, set with the metallic taste of drying blood. He lay still, disoriented and confused, trying to find a start point from which to escape his anguish. As he made to raise himself, his outstretched arm slid from under him in a pool of thick red liquid, sending him flat on the floor for a second time. Approaching voices and footsteps deflected the agony and creeping self-pity.

'Quickly now, Philip. I sensed nothing to stop us getting in.'

'And that seems to be true – no lock. But we will have a task to explain our presence if we are caught empty-handed, as it were.'

Torchlight pierced the squash court door as it swept back to reveal Lady Margaret followed by Roberts. But the blurred images meant nothing to Bruce. She knelt beside him to assess his injuries. One pass of the beam proved that he was conscious – just – but badly hurt.

'We must get him in the car and to the college hospital.'

After a day in Sheffield General and an emergency visit from his mum and dad, Bruce was returned to the Rothwell College hospital to recover. Propped up in bed with his left arm in a sling and the wounds on his face starting to heal, he chewed on another grape while looking out of the window into the dense branches of the nearby horse chestnut tree. Had this been rugby season, he would have had company, but today he lay alone in the hospital, staffed only by Nurse Eunice, in a ward with eleven empty beds alongside.

He looked at the white plastic wall clock: 9.25. Although term was winding down – only a passing-out parade remained in the diary – he guessed his friends were either still engaged in routine lessons of some variety or they had been instructed not to visit yet. In fact, this was the first time he had stopped to think why nobody had visited. Then his mind became caught up in thoughts of how he hadn't stopped to think before being duped into going to the squash court.

Next door the rumble and hiss of a boiling kettle, clattering crockery and the slamming of a cupboard door heralded further morning refreshment from Bruce's tornado of a carer.

'Master Bruce, tea?' said Nurse Eunice.

Two plain white cups, saucers and a steaming pot were set down next to his bed, plus brown biscuits that seemed identical to those in army ration packs. By Nurse's standards this was special treatment, which begged a question. It wasn't her style to take tea with the students, so why enough for two?

'You have a visitor. She will be with you shortly – I'm to leave you in peace.'

Bruce watched as she sped around the door. Could it be the police? No! He was in turmoil. They would be investigating the assault, but he wasn't ready. A part of him felt he should simply report Jez, but he knew it would be the end of the other boy's career, even if he did deserve it.

The visitor appeared. A vaguely familiar trench coat – Burberry, thought Bruce, which his mother had often admired – and the same click of court-shoe heels against the floor confirmed that this was his rescuer.

'Good morning, Bruce. Are you up to receiving a visitor? I hope you don't mind,' said Lady Margaret. 'Do you remember me? I found you on Sunday night. How are your injuries?'

'Er, yes . . . no . . . I mean, yes, I'm fine with meeting you. And thank you for saving me. Are you Lady Cadogan-Brandt?'

'At your service.'

Bruce's mouth hung open and he winced as his bruised jaw went too far. She smiled and melted him a little more.

'How's your shoulder? Nurse says you broke your collar bone. And the cut around your eye might take some healing.'

Bruce stared into the sheet and sighed.

'What's the matter, Bruce?'

'We've only just met. I haven't spoken to anyone about what happened yet – I haven't been asked, but the post-concussion recovery period will soon end and then what? ... questions from the principal ... the police ... I feel trapped, but have no real reason to say why.'

She let him speak, her extended pause leaving him little choice but to continue to offload.

'I sense that I must trust you – it's as if I have no choice. I feel utterly trapped and I can't understand why. Oh God, I'm wittering now.'

Lady Margaret softened her gaze and looked on with compassion. Bruce opened his heart to her.

'I was thrown over the balcony. I was lured there, attacked by another student who had help from a friend – useless though he was – then I was thrown from the balcony into the court.' Bruce drew in a sharp breath as he relived the emotion. She said nothing and allowed him to compose himself. 'The student responsible has a reputation as a troublemaker, but has never been caught for anything worthy of real discipline or expulsion. I was suspended after punching him a few months ago when he tried his bullying tactics on a close friend.'

'You're sure it was another student – a particular student, you say. Nobody else.'

'Quite sure. Yes.'

Lady Margaret sighed with relief more openly than she intended.

'May I ask why you are taking such an interest in what happened . . . er, I'm sorry, how should I address you?'

'My lady is conventional – we should try to keep things normal. And I am taking an interest because I found you and I want to know how you are recovering. I am afforded certain . . . let's call them discretions, on the rare occasions when my life intersects with that of the college.'

Bruce was puzzled. Was this just genuine kindness or the beginnings of an enquiry?

'If I may ask, my lady, how come you were there? since, as I understand it, you never come into the college.'

'I suppose it was a rare coincidence, Bruce, although you might say I have a strange talent for such things.'

Bruce's mind went into overdrive. He'd heard it put like that before – Shaun Dodd watching him pass the dorm windows on the night of the fire, a talent for being in the right place.

He looked up, re-engaging with her. Lady Margaret met his stare, deliberately letting the mystery take hold. She wanted him to notice. She wanted him to remember.

'Tell me more about your conundrum, Bruce. You believe that everything points to telling Colonel Hunter the truth so that the student in question can be brought to book, but your instincts say otherwise. Is that correct?'

'Precisely. What grates is that the other boys will think I am shying away from a difficult but justified decision to report him. They'll think I don't want to be seen as a grass or I'm afraid of the consequences. The previous fight and other incidents mean we have history, you see.'

'So, what is the real reason stopping you from reporting him?'

Bruce shook his head. His mind was a tangle.

'I can't say – I really don't know, but I can give you the reason why I *should* dob him in – all the soldiers who will suffer at his hands, from his bullying incompetence. Maybe Sandhurst will weed him out, but somehow I doubt it.'

'Go on. What else? What is your instinct trying to tell you?'

A gust of wind blew outside and thousands of leaves from the birch trees rose in a rustling euphony. Their flickering of alternate green and silver shades held Bruce in a trance, in a moment that felt like it could have lasted forever. Eventually, he turned his eyes back to Lady Margaret.

'This will sound ridiculous. There is a purpose for him. He has a role to play, somewhere, someday. It's like there is a path that he must take and I should not interfere with it.'

Bruce turned back to her for a reaction.

Lady Margaret's breath released and her chest relaxed. Her eyes narrowed and a smile cracked across her face. He had it. He was beginning to understand.

'Then stay true to your instincts. Be ready to explain why you thought you could see in the dark and proved yourself wrong. Speak not a word to your friends of the real events.'

'Which still means I will have to ward off questions when rumours fly after Jez starts bragging.'

'That, Bruce, is the price we pay.'

'We?'

She smiled warmly and departed without another word.

It was barely afternoon when Colonel Hunter and Captain Pearce arrived to make their first enquiries. Bruce had just finished his mushroom soup followed by pasty, mash, greens and gravy. Nurse Eunice was very protective of her patients, so the pair trod carefully as she loitered, attending to sets of already well-folded blankets.

Bruce had only Lady Margaret's prompt about not seeing in the dark as inspiration to guide his impending web of lies. His heart raced, as instinct, strong as ever, met the sheer terror of undoing himself with a single mistake in consistency or detail. The conversation began and with it Bruce felt himself tip into a new abyss. The first few exchanges came and went and he hardly took in their questions or remembered his responses. Concerned looks and a slow pace had Bruce thinking that the still recovering card was working well, even if he hadn't intended to play it.

'So, may I ask what led you to be at the court if you had no intention of playing squash, Noble?' Hunter asked gently.

'I said you might find this hard to accept, sir, and as embarrassing as it is, here goes. I had long wondered whether the stuff we were taught on night exercises – primarily navigating in the dark – could be improved.' The two men's expressions hardened, curiosity tinged with scepticism. 'Well, the first and critical element, it seems to me, is actually seeing in the dark.'

Bruce wove his web and Hunter and Pearce stayed their urge to bring him to the point. Nurse was watching, so Hunter merely eased the conversation along.

'You see, Noble, what concerns me greatly is that you should have brought yourself to such harm. How did the experiment go wrong, if that's what we have here?'

'I understand, sir, and I deeply regret that my exuberance might lead to unwanted questions if word got out about facilities being accessible twenty-four hours a day – without supervision and so forth – I really do. But . . . what did you say, sir? Oh, how did it go wrong? Yes. Well. I was trying out … echolocation.'

The adjutant sighed in frustration. 'Echo what?'

'Like bats use, Gavin. Didn't they teach you anything at staff college?' said Hunter. 'Go on, Bruce.'

'Hence the logic of the squash court, sir. No light pollution from the outside – fine for the visual experiment, but also pure flat walls and no objects. Great for echolocation.'

'Yes, and …?'

'And I . . . well, I fucked up.'

'Pardon?'

'I said I fucked up. Did you hear that, sir?' said Bruce, playing slightly delirious.

'It doesn't matter. Keep going, please,' smiled the Colonel after a glance over his shoulder.

Bruce reached his crescendo. 'I thought I had paced the distance to the front wall of the court and to the viewing gallery wall reasonably well. Then, when I ran the experiment – remember I was in the dark – I forgot I was upstairs. I strode to the front wall and went straight over the top and into the court below. I said it was embarrassing.'

Colonel Hunter sat back and nodded slowly in acknowledgement of Bruce's open and honest account, which was indeed rather embarrassing for a potential army officer. He looked at Pearce, but the adjutant was unmoved. He returned his gaze to Bruce.

'Very well, I see. I will leave aside for a moment the question of why you needed to be upstairs rather than in the main court area. That is because I should perhaps advance the conversation by asking you to explain why, at a quarter to ten on Sunday night, I got a call from the Lancaster housemaster telling me that Mr Picher had reported being in a fight with you which got out of hand?' Bruce froze inside. Hunter was reddening. 'And by the time Picher got hold of Mr Kelly – out of hours, of course – and folk rushed back to find you . . . well, you were already in Lady Margaret's car and away, by all accounts,' he thundered.

'By my account you mean, Headmaster,' interrupted Nurse Eunice. 'And I think you now understand why we medical professionals don't usually allow people with recent concussion to be interrogated. You may leave now, gentlemen!'

The creak as the hospital front door closed behind the officers and the crunch of their shoes on the gravel brought fleeting relief for Bruce. He sat in bed with his eyes closed, slowly shaking his head at the mess he had landed himself in. Again.

Nurse Eunice reappeared and set a consoling cup of tea beside him. She gave him a knowing yet compassionate look.

'I will leave you to your thoughts, Master Bruce.'

Realising the window of opportunity was closing, Bruce wondered if he should enrol Shaun to help resolve the dilemma. Friends would soon be allowed to visit and after that he would be fit enough for more formal questioning. He knew a lot was at stake for the principal and the record of the college. Luckily his parents were being most accepting of circumstances and patient about explanations. What irked was his seemingly endless torture of having to wriggle out of trouble with his superiors and wrestle with his conscience about how to do it. Lady Margaret had struck at a deep, even primeval, level. *'Speak not a word to your friends of the real events.'* Her words resonated within him.

What should he do? If he stuck with his story he would be calling Jez a liar, and one with no sensible motive to lie – he would only be implicating himself. He must have panicked and tried to come clean, believing he might have killed Bruce. But if Bruce changed his story he would look ridiculous. The excuse that he was recovering from concussion couldn't explain away the lucidity and logic of his argument for choosing the squash court to conduct experiments in night vision and echolocation. He clearly wasn't of unsound mind when he gave that account of events. And changing the story could mean Jez's expulsion too. Any possibility that a fight had occurred which had put Bruce in hospital would probably lead to an investigation by local police. Bruce knew they would get to the truth and Jez would be gone, while he would look like a poor loser who had stabbed his adversary in the back when things got complicated. It would also leave him labelled as a bizarre liar. The stain on his character might even be fatal to his career: poor judgement, dubious integrity – not the qualities sought in army officers.

Bruce felt certain that Shaun was the only person who could be trusted to see a way out of the puzzle.

*   *   *

It was Thursday, and unfit for military duties, Bruce was assisting with final uniform preparations among the assembled college parade. This was the main dress rehearsal before the big event the next day. The weather was fine and he made his way along the ranks in their starting positions outside the science block, ready to march towards the Mall.

'Hey Noble, lend a hand would you?'

Sniggering erupted among the seniors at the head of the column. Bruce still had one arm in a sling so a hand was literally all he could lend.

'What is it?' he asked, ready with clothes brush and Sellotape to remove any remaining fluff from otherwise immaculate No.2 dress uniforms.

'Piss off, I'm just kidding. Don't need you touching my rig, thanks,' said Steven Black, one of the cadet platoon commanders.

'So you'll take care of the penis drawn on the back of your headdress then?' Bruce snapped back.

'Hey!'

Bruce strode away as Black fumbled his cap off to check whether he had reason to panic. He did not, but Bruce was out of sight.

'*Parade!*' blasted Pitcaithly. '*Pa-rade … shun!*'

A hundred and forty pairs of boots thundered to attention, the massed crunch of heavy leather on flint chipping reverberating around the surrounding woodland.

'*Shoulder … arms!*'

Rifles were swung across the body, ready to march.

'*By the centre … quick march!*'

The band struck up, the bass drum gluing every pair of feet to the pace. Arms moving in perfect synchronisation, the college marched away. Bruce watched them, alone and dejected. A few of the kitchen staff had gathered by the dining hall door, humble local folk, men and women of all ages. Bruce looked over and Mary, well into her seventies and the oldest of them all, gave him a supportive smile. Bruce was struck by the irony of their contrasting situations. He had all the prospects: expectations of power and respect, travel, camaraderie, challenges, achievements and a fine pension. But she had about her a meekness and a wisdom born of life experience which had tempered possibilities with realities. So there he stood, humiliated, and she with dignity and compassion.

Two hours later the basement corridors ran with students glad it was all over. Caps were off and sweat streamed from sopping hair. Shirt collars darkened with perspiration were loosened and ties ripped away to bring relief from standing like statues under the June sun.

Bruce caught up with Shaun, who he persuaded to walk with him before it was time for a relaxed lunch – no staff to entertain today.

'If this stroll is related to your recent . . . incident, let's call it, perhaps I should go first,' began Shaun. 'Word has it that our friend Jez is on a proper sticky wicket this time. But he is keeping Tom Calico out of it, by all accounts. The prevailing rumour – no doubt coming from Jez – goes like this: you and Jez agreed to a gentlemanly duel. It needed to be challenging but "responsible" was the word bandied around. So you agreed on wrestling—'

'What?'

'Yes, wrestling indeed. In the squash court, because it's secluded and there are no objects in the way.'

'You're kidding me.'

'I know, kindergarten logic here we come, but what can you do? So Jez – and the same sophistication of logic continues, you see – Jez has it that the sparring session took place in the viewing gallery because no outdoor shoes are allowed on the court.'

'Could have brought trainers.'

'No black soles either, but bear with me, Bruce. So you were having your little tussle to decide who's the daddy when lo and behold the court sensor times out the lights.'

'What?'

'Yes, it's good, I'll give him that. There is a sensor overlooking the court. No movement for a certain time and the lights go off.'

Bruce was not enjoying the plausibility of the story. It made his echolocation experiment sound absurd.

'And wouldn't you believe it – the lights go off at just the wrong moment, and whoops, over you go.'

'Arsehole, if that's what he'll be telling Colonel Hunter.'

'No, that's what he has told him, Bruce. They didn't delay interviewing Jez. He wasn't in hospital.'

'Christ. That's not good.'

Shaun and Bruce rejoined the road for the last few yards to the dining hall. A voice came from behind them. It was Bill Patel.

'Yo, Noble. You are to report to the principal's office at fourteen hundred today. Strict instructions. Okay?'

'Got it, Bill. Thanks mate.'

Shaun looked at Bruce. 'You should tell the truth and do the right thing to get this guy expelled. You have nothing to worry about. Everyone knows he had it coming and now you can nail him – for all of our sakes, not to mention his future troops. Whatever he says, it's easy to tell the truth from a lie – stands out a mile, unless you're a super spy, or psychotic.'

21

Shaun had the good sense to leave Bruce to his thoughts over lunch. He could read his friend's inner turmoil but said nothing and looked on as Bruce sweated about what to do, hoping that the instinct to let Jez off the hook would pass. But it was an instinct that remained strong in Bruce, like a compulsion to obey the will of some higher, unimagined power.

He knew he had precious little time to prepare for the inquisition and satisfy the mystery that confounded him. He tried to go back to the basics that Shaun and his directed reading of NLP had taught. Aside from foundational concepts, such as adopting an open and healthy philosophy of life, the first thing to address was management of his own emotional state. He needed to stay calm, and clear thinking should follow. Panic, and it might be the beginning of the end. So Bruce sat in silence at the end of the table, staring into a steaming plate of Lancashire hotpot, letting his mind slow down.

The next NLP recollection presented itself: all behaviour is positive. Every human action has an intent; we do nothing without reason, even if the reason is an unconscious one. Bruce pictured a possible scenario: the principal in his office behind his desk, plus the adjutant, but also Jez Picher. Would they be questioned together? Why might that happen? And what if they were questioned separately? College was one day from the end of term. Picher was one day from qualifying for entry to Sandhurst, beginning in September. Bruce considered that the principal may well seek the truth, but equally that he might not want to find it. Difficult questions bringing inconclusive answers could waste the college's – and even police – time, and it could mess up the army's schedule, where Jez presumably already had a place allocated at Sandhurst.

During the lunchtime hour's grace Bruce let his thoughts run through various scenarios and sequences of how, when and about what they might be questioned. He tried to fathom the logic and permutations of events and outcomes. He explored a few potential avenues of inquiry and consequently felt more composed, although the dual spectres of failing to speak against Jez and being caught out as a liar still loomed large. Stronger than both of those catastrophes, though, was that he could not tell the truth. Jez was on a path towards some future event and Bruce was not to interfere with it. In fact, the mystery felt so profound that if it all went wrong, he should even take the fall and leave Jez to his planned future.

At five minutes to two, Bruce Noble slipped down the stairs from the juniors' cabins and into the hall outside the principal's office. Standing in line were Jez, Captain Pearce and Mr Pitcaithly. Bruce's insides churned at the sight of the RSM. He was a man who would have done his homework and he would be keener than any to root out a bad apple before that individual got anywhere near to being a serving soldier. A shaft of light pierced the gloomy hall as Colonel Hunter flung open his door.

'Come in, everyone. Let's make a start.'

Everyone? They would be conducting this together? Bruce grappled to follow his mental preparations. This was the first junction in the decision tree – being questioned as a group. The approach would remove risks of secondary reporting since whoever followed the first account of events could choose to agree with it or deny it. That would be infinitely easier than being interviewed alone, with no idea of what others had said. Being questioned collectively also heralded the prospect of argument, conflict and even a breakdown of process. Any opportunity to derail the expected outcome could give Bruce a way out.

All lined up in front of the principal's desk. Only Colonel Hunter and his secretary, Lorna Hamble, sat. Clearly this was not intended to be a convivial affair.

'Now, I have heard separately from Mr Picher and Mr Noble their accounts of how Noble came to be injured. And they do not agree.'

Bugger. Bruce knew he would get no confirmation of Jez's story from his own mouth. He had only heard third-hand accounts about the friendly-duel-that-went-wrong scenario.

'And when someone requires hospitalisation for concussion and a broken collar bone,' Hunter continued, 'then we are one step away from involving the police, with the potential for charges relating to bodily harm. However, it is for me to instigate such proceedings if nobody chooses to report it. Which brings us to now.'

A knock came at the door and Miss Hamble got up to usher in Lady Margaret. Hunter rose to his feet.

'Welcome, Lady Cadogan-Brandt, and may I thank you sincerely for availing us of your time this afternoon.'

Miss Hamble poured her a cup of tea. The rest were not offered tea.

'You are most welcome, and please accept my apologies for the slight delay.'

'Then I will continue, if I may? I have heard two separate accounts of a serious occurrence, two accounts which do not agree. Indeed, they are starkly different, and if I am to come to the point, I can relate only to one. The other I find frankly bizarre, if not impossible.'

No prizes for guessing which was which, thought Bruce, who had reached another decision junction. Should he rescind his account and claim it was offered to cover for an innocent event which went wrong, thus admitting that he had lied, even if his lie had been well intentioned?

'But then the plot thickens, does it not, RSM?' Colonel Hunter nodded to Pitcaithly.

'Indeed it does, sir.'

Bruce glanced across to survey the body language among the group. Picher's colour was changing, a tide of scarlet rising in his face as he stared at the floor with widening eyes. *NVGs!* Somehow Jez had screwed up. Pitcaithly must know that the night-vision goggles had been out of the stores over the weekend. The only way Jez could have got hold of them was with Bill Woodsman's permission as key-holder, or by stealing them, thinking nobody would discover they were missing. Bruce's mind froze. How had he failed to factor this into his planning? And if Jez had asked permission, would Bill have allowed it? Would he have checked with Pitcaithly? NVGs cost thousands, so using them outside CCF time would be hard to justify.

'Mr Picher, is there anything you want to add or correct in the account you gave on Monday?' Hunter enquired with an unwavering stare.

Jez hesitated and Bruce found himself in the paradoxical position of being on his side, glad that he was being careful.

'I don't believe so, sir.'

'*I don't believe so.* You must be reading my thoughts, Mr Picher, because I am close to saying those very words about this whole affair. Mr Noble, is there anything you wish to add or correct in your account?'

Bruce's mind was a blur. Jez must have thought it through – or did he fuck up?

'Mr Noble!' boomed Colonel Hunter, shaking Bruce back to reality. 'An answer please!'

When logic fails, let intuition through.

'Yes, sir.'

'Pardon?'

'Yes sir, I do wish to correct my account of events.'

The room stirred with dark anticipation. Pitcaithly turned to look at Bruce, and Hunter sat back in his chair, pen wrested away from notebook to welcome the impending blunder. In the corner of Bruce's vision Lady Margaret shifted in her chair, as if she was reminding him of her presence.

'Well sir, after you left me on Monday—'

'Tuesday, Noble, we saw you on Tuesday.'

'Was it Tuesday, sir? *We?* May I ask who else was with you? I remember only you, sir.'

'I was accompanied by Captain Pearce, Bruce.'

'Ah, right you are, sir. Well, the next day I think it was I thought that my exuberant account of events may have gone too far. You see, I was trying to avoid the potentially serious consequences of what had actually happened.'

'So you are saying you fabricated an account out of a wider pragmatism?'

'That's one way of putting it, I suppose.'

'Lying is another.'

'I admit, sir, that the effects of concussion, which evidently were still present when you interviewed me – until Nurse Eunice stopped you, I believe – may well have undermined my better judgement. So yes, I lied, and we both ended up with a somewhat unreliable outcome.'

The principal's thinly disguised fury was building.

'So what do you wish to say now?'

'Short version, sir? Jez Picher and I met for a duel. As you know from my previous suspension, Picher and I sometimes like to act first and talk later to settle our differences. And from that previous encounter, Jez invited me to settle our score in a rather old-fashioned and gentlemanly way, that nonetheless would still represent a challenge of strength and skill.'

'Oh, sweet jeez,' Pitcaithly exclaimed under his breath.

'So we agreed to a wrestling match.'

'Colonel!' Pitcaithly boiled over in frustration. 'Do we have to listen to this?'

'RSM, please. It aligns with Picher's story. Continue Bruce.'

'We chose the squash court because it was out of the way and it was a clear space. Calico was the referee.'

'Picher, you mentioned nothing of Calico,' challenged Hunter.

'I didn't want to drag Tom into it, sir. He had no part in this of any consequence.'

The principal briefly bared his teeth in frustration. 'Apart from being a key witness. Continue Noble.'

'We pulled ourselves around a bit, getting tired and sweaty – it was almost a joke in the end. But we must have got a bit close to the side and all I remember then was waking up to find her ladyship standing over me.'

'So why were you upstairs?'

'In the viewing gallery? Oh, no outdoor shoes allowed on court, sir. Simple.'

Pitcaithly could suffer no more.

'Why don't we start talking straight for a change? Colonel, may I present my information now?' Hunter nodded. 'Mr Picher, would you explain to me why you requested from the CQMS not one, but two pairs of night-vision goggles from the stores on Saturday?'

'Of course, sir. Tom and I thought that since it was nearing the end of term we had time to do something different. Bill told me a while back that the college had these items on loan so we wanted to give them a try overnight and at least have seen a pair before we went to Sandhurst.'

So far so good, Jez.

'You won't be using those at Sandhurst, I can assure you,' said Pitcaithly. 'Maybe rifle- and vehicle-mounted image intensifiers, but that's by the by. What matters now is my strong suspicion that you got them to give Noble here the surprise of his life and a good beating to go with it.'

'But that's ridiculous, sir . . . if you'll allow me. How would I have got Noble to come to the squash court to surprise him, as you put it. It's impossible.'

'It's not at all impossible, Mr Picher. You just had to send him a note to draw him there under false pretences.'

With that Pitcaithly produced the scrap of paper which had been pinned to Bruce's wall and long since forgotten.

'RSM, let me see that.'

Hunter studied the note and looked daggers at Bruce and Jez. The game was up. Jez flushed and stared with horrified eyes back down at the floor, into the abyss that his actions had opened. Bruce felt panic take hold as he attempted to stay calm and keep alive the possibility of being saved by doubt over the circumstantial evidence.

'Oh, I say!' Lady Margaret remarked with an uncharacteristic shriek. She appeared to be studying something in the corner of the room, behind her armchair.

'Is there a problem, my lady?' asked Pitcaithly.

'No, I think it's alright, thank you . . . as long as your electrics are sound here. She's a very old lady – the building, I mean, not me,' she said with a chuckle.

Colonel Hunter attempted to return from the distraction.

'I have seen and heard quite enough. If a remotely plausible explanation had been presented by you both we could have drawn a line under this episode right here. But all I have heard is lies. You give me no choice. Picher, you are suspended and shall not proceed to Sandhurst, pending a police enquiry. Noble, this will be your second suspension, pending the outcome of the same enquiry. On grounds of integrity alone, I doubt that either of you will ever go to Sandhurst.'

As Jez broke down and Pitcaithly turned to support him, Bruce noticed Lady Margaret stand and slip behind the assembled group. While the scandal registered and chatter broke out between the principal and his secretary, and Captain Pearce, Jez and Pitcaithly, she reached into her bag. Bruce was speaking to nobody, just watching Lady Margaret, dumbstruck.

Suddenly two loud cracks resonated at either end of the office and great plumes of smoke appeared. Bruce instinctively held his breath as thick white gas billowed into the room, quickly overwhelming its occupants. Colonel Hunter slumped forward onto his desk. Pitcaithly and Picher grasped each other then crashed to the floor with Pearce alongside.

Bruce made eye contact with Lady Margaret who was holding a silk scarf over her face. This was her backup plan and he had to try and follow it. Miss Hamble made a lunge for the door, coughing and spluttering as she swayed towards Bruce. Without thinking, at first he let her pass, head down as she bent over to avoid the fumes, but then as she went by he struck a side-palm blow to the back of her head and she fell to the floor, out cold.

'Take this!' Lady Margaret thrust a handkerchief into Bruce's hand. He mimicked her, placing the cloth over his mouth and nose before taking his first tentative breath. The material was moist and infused with chemicals. 'Door!' came her muffled order.

He rushed over and turned the key. Lady Margaret stopped for a moment to survey the scene. All was still. Nothing of concern could be seen from the outside. And in any case, nobody would have reason to venture past the windows, which looked across open ground to Winter Lake. Outside the door faint murmurings and distant footsteps echoed as folk went about their business, ignorant of the drama within the principal's office.

Lady Margaret briefly checked that the others were fully unconscious. She grabbed Jez's note, which lay beside Pitcaithly, then darted behind Hunter's desk and extricated the notebook from under his right arm. Having tied her scarf behind her head so she could use both hands, she started writing in the book. Moments later she replaced it under his arm on the desk and looked to Bruce.

'Get the windows open.'

Bruce leaped over Miss Hamble to get the heavy sash frames as high as they would go. Air started to circulate in the room and eventually the last wisps of smoke dissipated. Lady Margaret tugged her scarf down and sniffed the air gently. She waved a cautionary hand in front of her face then ripped the cloth away and stuffed it into her bag.

'We're clear. Give me that please.'

Bruce threw her the handkerchief.

She watched intently for the first signs of her victims stirring.

'My lady . . . door?' Bruce whispered.

'Gosh, yes. Well done.'

He carefully unlocked the door while watching for anyone who might be regaining consciousness.

Pitcaithly was the first to come to, followed by Hunter and Pearce. Jez and Miss Hamble were last to wake up. Miss Hamble groaned, rubbing the back of her head as Bruce helped her into the nearest chair.

'You hit your head on the arm of that chair,' he said. Another groan.

'Colonel, are you alright?' said Lady Margaret. 'I think we were all nearly suffocated by the electrics.'

'What the …?'

Pitcaithly got onto his feet and shuffled to the corner to inspect the socket into which a standard lamp was plugged.

'Crikey – black as coal!'

For a moment Bruce was dumbfounded. How had she made that happen? He hadn't seen her do anything to set fire to the electrics. Did it have something to do with the half-empty tea cup which now sat on a nearby side table? And what was in that smoke?

'Colonel, are you starting to feel more normal now?' Lady Margaret continued.

'I think so, but what on earth happened?'

'Your electrics shorted. The standard lamp. Overheating electrics and Bakelite plugs make for some very nasty toxins, or so I have been told. Nearly had us all.'

'Indeed.'

'However, the good news is that we reached an amicable conclusion to the saga concerning Picher and Noble.'

The principal's face was vacant, his eyes squinting and rolling like a cartoon character. Around the room others were starting to tune in.

'Your notes. You made notes,' Lady Margaret continued. 'You decided to accept the consistent accounts about the boys' gentlemanly duel. No further action required. To be put down to experience. And the NVGs were a red herring. Thankfully they were not lost but were signed out properly from the CQMS.'

'Well, that's something sensible at least,' said Pitcaithly, as he continued to shake his head, trying to focus.

Bruce couldn't believe what he was hearing. It was as if their memories had been wiped and were now being rewritten.

'I regret, however, that I must leave now. I have another engagement. If you would excuse me, Colonel?'

'Of course, my lady. And thank you again, most sincerely, for coming along. Good day to you.'

'Are we free to go now, sir?' Bruce asked boldly. 'We need to get to the armoury to prep the rifles for tomorrow's parade.'

'Very well, Noble, yes, you may all leave. I have my record and I will notify you if any further consultation is necessary.'

He peered quizzically at his notebook as they filed out.

'Bloody good call, Colonel,' said Pitcaithly. 'We all need some fresh air, I can tell you.'

After the drama of the previous day, 65 Entry's passing-out parade seemed almost an anti-climax. The collective fear of actually passing out on parade guaranteed at least modest interest though. The English June day was warm, a balmy twenty-four degrees under the sun. In khaki wool uniform and deep blue dress hats, standing still for over an hour with a rifle weighing nine pounds meant streams of sweat and an ever vigilant RSM and PEO wandering the ranks in the background, watching for the ones turning pale. If they had to succumb, some wore it as a badge of honour to hit the deck in a perfectly erect posture, although the watching parents didn't relish seeing their darling sons smash their faces into the grit. Bruce sat the parade out, or rather stood to one side, ready to assist nurse by passing cups of water to anybody judiciously taken off the square before they fell.

After the final march-past they changed out of their uniforms to prepare for the afternoon's entertainment. All manner of things were on show, from a section attack to a karate demonstration or land-sailing duel along the lakeside. By five o'clock the parents were saying their farewells and heading home with cameras full of memories and bellies full of tea.

Bruce's plan to join a group heading for the army Outward Bound course based in Tywyn on the Welsh coast had been scuppered by his broken collar bone and instead he had been allocated a place on the college's CCF summer camp, a much more downbeat affair. With only one arm functioning he could wash dishes but not climb mountains, apparently.

When the college had emptied of visitors and uniforms were stowed in lockers, a lull fell upon the place that brought with it a sense of menace. Bruce found himself a few yards up Chapel Hill, standing on the cobbles, not knowing quite where to go or what to do. The lowering sun cast sharp shadows down the slope and a cooling wind whipped traces of dust around the polished stones. Behind and in front, footsteps and chatter echoed and waned, leaving him in perfect indecision.

His brief confusion over what had caused him to stop like this was soon resolved when his attention settled on the Swiss army knife in his back pocket. He headed off up the hill and steered a sharp right around the end wall that enclosed the cobbled driveway. He paced out towards the bridge across the lake, seeing and hearing nobody on his way. The breeze held steady at his back and caressed long waves of meadow grass above the lake shore.

Once across the bridge Bruce checked for onlookers, near and far. There were none, so he navigated the rocky bank down and under the blind side of the bridge, located the paracord and fished out a bottle of Strongbow cider from nature's ice bucket of deep green water. Moments later, hidden from view under the low boughs of a cedar, he prised the crown cap free, wiped the bottle top, lay back and took the first delicious swig, as the warmth of the day rose from the brush beneath him and birdsong enchanted the early evening air.

22

An undemanding CCF camp and a sunny summer holiday at home afterwards afforded Bruce the respite needed for bones to heal and memories to settle. He was indifferent to having missed out on all the derring-do exploits enjoyed by his fellows on the Outward Bound training. Multiple ascents of Cader Idris, early morning dunks in the Irish Sea, endurance challenges, log races, sea kayaking and twenty-four-hour marathons far outshone the potato peeling and leadership tasks of the CCF event, but Bruce was surprised to find himself unmoved.

It was soon September and the start of the new term. Sitting in the taxi taking him down the long drive into college, he took the few final moments of solitude to think through what was important and what was not. As he dragged his case through Chapel Court the stream of new faces scurrying to follow their mentors to the dorms brought a realisation that this year would pass quickly; it was already passing quickly. He sensed a looming destiny that in time would reveal itself to him.

The incident with Lady Margaret in Colonel Hunter's study would stay with him forever. While he said nothing to his parents directly, like an amateur spy he had tried to dangle information or refer to her in passing to test for a response from them. There was no logical connection between Lady Margaret and his parents, as far as he knew, but his gut was in charge and flights of fancy ran in his mind. His father responded, or rather failed to respond, to any allusions with such lack of interest that he was clearly unaware and unconnected to any of it. But his mother, while muted in her reactions, paid attention, and that intrigued Bruce. It led him to consider why – after the trip home at Christmas with its navigational blunders and sudden insistence on sundries shopping at a petrol station – she had suddenly conceived of the need for a new car. And a new coat, for that matter. How had she appeared so composed when they visited him in hospital? He was lucky to be alive, but she couldn't have known anything beyond the pitiful reassurance that would have been attempted in a telephone call. And how did any of this relate to Lady Margaret and her exploits?

*   *   *

'It's not my place to say it, but you look rather down today, my lady.'

'I have received unwelcome if not unsurprising news, Philip. I suppose it was a miracle to have had it at all.'

Lady Margaret was sitting at the Woodhouse kitchen table, eggs Benedict half-eaten, coffee going cold.

Eventually she took pity on Roberts who was hiding his bemusement behind a mask of politeness.

'I'm sorry. What I am trying to tell you is that the overwatch on Osprey is to be withdrawn.'

'Ah.'

'Precisely. We're so fragmented that there is simply no depth to us anymore. Whoever was appointed, or more likely who decided out of some act of charity to provide the requisite service, has done so for nine months now. Apparently they want their life back – or their sanity.'

She shook her head in despair.

'Or they need to earn some money,' said Roberts.

'No doubt it's all three. I suspect we can't even pay them through a secure route any more, but I am concerned.'

'Excuse my naivety, but isn't nine months sufficient time to assume the coast is clear?'

'That depends on the assailants and who or what is behind them. If they're on to us then all they need do is put their overwatch in place and wait.'

'To do what?'

'I don't know . . . to get whatever they didn't manage to get previously, perhaps.'

Roberts gestured to her plate and cup. She waved them away and he began clearing the breakfast table. Outside, the early morning showers had ceded to sunshine which brightened the shady yard beyond the window.

'How are you getting along with our plans for the Archive?' she asked.

'Very well, I am pleased to report. There's quite an art to it in many respects. I like that. Combining art and science. Things have to be right in so many ways. I'm probably halfway there now.'

'That's good news. Very good, indeed.'

'I would be quicker but I have to take such care around Tavener.'

'And I thank you for your patience with that. Any sane person would have been rid of him long ago, but …'

'He has a part to play?'

'He has a part to play. And we will learn it soon enough, I believe.'

*   *   *

The shift to their final year and the return-to-college blues ushered in a boldness among certain members of 67 Entry. A gang of its older students had teamed up with the less academically inclined among the now senior 66 Entry for a Saturday night on the beer in Naveby. The final push towards December exams for some soon-to-be-departing seniors had not dampened their thirst for an outing to dispel the gloomy mood and they led the way to watering holes which had served generations of coal miners and factory workers.

The scene in chapel on Sunday morning was a sight to behold. Bruce looked on, thankful that his newfound antipathy for things adventurous, or any form of limelight which lacked a clear and beneficial gain, appeared to have substance behind it. The entire third row was filled with the walking wounded from a beating in town. The locals didn't care much for college boys, especially loud ones who couldn't hold their ale, and even more especially loud ones who couldn't hold their ale from the shandy-drinking south. The biggest lad, Jamie Philpott, stood six feet five and a full-shouldered eighteen stone. Bruce grinned as he imagined him weighing in to overshadow a lairy, tattooed labourer only to receive a haymaker and wake up with the police standing over him on the pavement. He looked quite the part with a white bandage circling his head from chin to crown.

His thoughts ran to what might have been, had Arthur Rose been on hand. But the only image that came back was Art raising a tactful hand in refusal of any invitation to join them. He would have seen the whole thing as a doomed escapade by the uninitiated, preferring a night in perfecting his craft.

While some things repeated the previous year's pattern, others did not. Only one term now stood between 67 Entry and their CCF command appointments. Word had it that Willis invited information from the presiding senior entry on any special interests or talents shown by their potential successors when he considered who would get what. A hand well-played this term could mean that a budding platoon commander might get one of the six college platoons to lead and train, or a skilled marksman and fieldcraft exponent could head the sniper team. If your bent was radios and communications, there was the post of signals sergeant, in charge of all radio equipment and training.

As the days and weeks gathered momentum, Bruce's pattern for engaging only in what he deemed to be truly important was viewed by some as leaning towards the ascetic, and worse than that was being seen as antisocial – not a team player. That was how, when the hierarchy took the unusual step of holding a dinner dance with St Imelda's girls' boarding school – open to the entire second year and not just the senior entry – folk were not surprised that Bruce volunteered for security duties. 'His loss' was the popular view.

By the time the eagerly awaited Saturday night arrived, autumn had properly taken hold. The passive, observation-based security measures of the summer term had continued, but special occasions when events brought significant numbers together, or might have attracted outside attention through gossip, warranted increased precautions. So it was that as the gleaming white fifty-four seater with smoked windows crunched its way to the end of the chipping-strewn drive, Bruce made the final adjustments to his sniper suit, fitted his magazine to the weapon, checked his radio and slipped quietly away into the woods that surrounded the dining hall.

By half past nine the chill night air was taking hold and a fog had descended, while inside the dinner had finished and disco lights and music burst into life. Bruce zipped his jacket liner up as far as it would go, tucked the cam net into it and hunkered down on his insulating ground mat under cover of some thick bushes. He rolled his head and neck to stay relaxed and keep alert, and peered into the image intensifier sight at his allotted arcs of observation and fire. He soon developed a rhythm, breaking his duty into chunks of time that followed the tracks being played at the disco. The music was loud enough for that to work, but not so loud that he couldn't detect nearby movement by sound as well as sight. That was how he heard undergrowth being disturbed and the distant soft tread of footsteps upon the compacted earth.

The steps were halting, as if someone was trying to negotiate a specific route. A route to avoid detection? Bruce closed his eyes to sense the direction of his target – it was at his back. Nightmare! It would be impossible to turn around without giving his position away. He steadied his momentary panic, realising that some fool from the dance had probably come out for a piss or a cigarette – but not a screw. He could detect only a single pair of feet plodding around, and no tipsy whispering. Tension turned to intrigue. Bruce was probably invisible and somebody was labouring around trying to find a spot, but for what? Then the steps ceased, just a few feet to his right. A different rustling started now, not undergrowth but clothing – a dress perhaps? The subject's breathing became audible, and frustrated.

'Sodding things,' came a voice bridling with irritation. Then a brief silence before the patter of fluid onto earth. The drifting smell confirmed that one of the girls had tired of waiting in the queue for the loo. Bruce shook his head and struggled to contain his laughter.

'What the fuck! Who's there?'

'Calm down. I'm keeping guard – and I can't see you.'

'You pervert! What the hell do you think you're doing creeping around watching girls having a pee?'

'I think you'll find that I was here first, and now you've compromised my position so I'll have to move.'

'So you should.'

Bruce pondered and grinned again, his mission now on hold. 'You don't seem very happy for a girl on a night out.'

More rustling ensued and footsteps finally arrived beside him as she pulled her clothes into place. She peered in to see his face, which was dimly lit by the return of light from the image intensifier's eyepiece.

'Is that a gun?'

'No.'

'No? Bloody looks like one to me.'

'It's a rifle, a 7.62 millimetre British army sniper rifle, so you've nothing to worry about. It's accurate to well over six hundred metres. I just hope you can work out how to use it after I've been shot, now that you're here.'

'Right, well, there's not much to say to that, is there? I mean, what should I expect at a place like this?'

Bruce strained to look up and see his visitor. She crouched to make it easier for him.

'I'm Bruce. How do you do?'

'Bruce . . .?'

'Ah, Noble. Bruce Noble.'

'Camelia Gordon. Very well, thank you.'

'It's a pleasure to make your acquaintance, Camelia. I take it there was quite a wait for the, er, powder room?'

'More than was ideal. I'm glad to be away from the whole sordid thing for a while, if I'm honest.' Bruce nodded in acknowledgement. 'It seems that, unlike you, we are expected to attend such events – part of our social development.'

'Losing your virginity under a tree at Rothwell? That sort of development.'

'Precisely, although we have the autumn chill to thank for sparing us any widespread shagging tonight.'

Bruce raised his eyebrows, as much in admiration as surprise at Camelia's straight talking. 'I should apologise. You must be getting cold. May I offer you my jacket?'

'No Bruce, you may not offer her your bloody jacket, or any more of your easily misdirected attention.'

From nowhere another non-team playing volunteer and self-confessed exam swot in the form of Jonathan Watson of the ruling 66 Entry had appeared. As head of the sniper team, he had spotted Bruce's mini party and now it was time for a bollocking.

'You shouldn't be here, young lady. You have compromised this O.P. Please go back inside.'

Bruce let the new cloud that now loomed over him proceed unhindered, darkening and rolling briefly through his life, as was its destiny to do. He looked down and said nothing, but rued the abrupt end to an intriguing encounter.

'So you're in charge here, I guess?' said Camelia.

'Correct. Head of the sniper team.'

'Impressive. I bet those rifles are accurate for quite a distance.'

Bruce smiled to himself as he detected Jon falling under her spell.

'Over six hundred metres,' he replied promptly.

'Hmm, so why have you put your man where he has a clear view out to what . . . thirty metres? Maybe forcing his relocation wasn't such a bad outcome.'

Jon stiffened in surprise and frustration.

'No need to answer. I probably don't know what I'm talking about. After all, I'm just a girl. Good evening, gentlemen.'

And with that Camelia was away, back through the undergrowth before Jon could recover his pride or Bruce bid her farewell.

*   *   *

As the days marched towards winter and the clocks changed to standard time, bringing in black nights like the covering cloaks of watching wraiths, Bruce was preparing for what had laid at the back of his mind since the last days of summer. And sure enough the moment came.

'You're a man of few words today, Art,' he said one Thursday afternoon as they set up for archery at the Elephant Hut. But Art just focused on setting up the equipment and made no eye contact. 'Art?'

Art stopped, kneeling with one hand on the lid of his bow case, the other hand cupping his chin, pondering. He stared into the case. 'I had a short letter from John Turner at Sandhurst. He was offering an update to a few of us back here who had got to know him and some of his buddies from 65 Entry. You were with him in Snowdonia, of course. He said that they were busy – understatement – but everybody was coping. Everybody including Jez Picher.' Art stood and glared at Bruce.

'Okay, and your point is what?'

'That many of 65 Entry were slightly surprised to see Picher . . . well . . . pitch up at Sandhurst. After what he did to you.'

'So . . .?'

'So how come he got away with it?'

'Art, what are you saying? I don't get to decide what happens to him. Take it up with the principal if you have an issue. And it doesn't affect you anyway.'

'No, no, no. It's not that simple. Hunter would, I strongly believe, do whatever was within his power to prevent somebody who had proven themselves to be unfit to lead soldiers – unfit to be trusted at all – from proceeding to Sandhurst. Conversely, to go there, he would have to recommend him.' Art's expression intensified. 'So how the fuck could that have happened?'

'Art, firstly I don't have to explain or defend myself to you or anybody else who has – wrongly – filled in the gaps for themselves, as seems to be the case. Secondly, once I'd given my account of events, Colonel Hunter made the decision, not me. If that goes against your ideals then you'd better ask him.'

'That's a pity. I was hoping for more from you on this one. You know what I think, Bruce? I think you passed up a crucial opportunity to stop a fool and a bully from going any further because you couldn't shoulder the responsibility of telling a truth that would – justifiably – stop his career before it started. He's going to get command of soldiers. Then he's either going to abuse his powers or make their lives a misery through ignorance and negligence. And that's before anybody gets near a battlefield. You should have shown the moral courage to prevent it.'

Art's face had reddened, his breathing was fast and full as bitterness swelled within him. Having initially chest-poked Bruce he now had him by the collar.

'Art! Take it easy, will you? Look what you're doing!'

Art's fists were turning white with tension. He rolled his grip tighter, twisting his knuckles into Bruce's neck and chest.

'Art!' yelled Bruce.

As if woken from a trance Art released his grip. Bruce sank to his knees in agony, clutching his injured collar bone.

'I made it clear enough what the guy was about and you failed me, Bruce. Don't know what you were playing at, but you failed me. Failed us all.'

23

The bitter November morning brought a thick carpet of dew, soaking the trunks of the chestnut trees across the open parkland of Bristol's Durdham Down. The sun seemed loath to rise into the clear sky above the mist, but that wouldn't stop the dog walkers and die-hard joggers.

'Come on, Poppy! Ready?'

Jenny Noble-Franks hurled the chewed rubber ball as far as she could towards the centre of the park. Her springer spaniel Poppy sprinted eagerly ahead, leaving Jenny to take in the view, wellingtons squelching in the damp earth. She pulled back her sleeve and through a cloud of breath stared at her watch: seven o'clock. Poppy returned within seconds and the game began again a few yards further on.

Fewer folk were about than normal for a Friday morning. A runner puffed by, more dog walkers strolled in the distance. Keen students headed towards the city along the pavement on the far side. Poppy collected her ball again but ran off into one of the copses of silver birch trees which broke up the wide centre space. Jenny walked over see what had attracted her attention.

'What are you up to, you mischievous young lady?'

Poppy wagged her tail wildly and looked up behind the branches.

'Making friends perhaps,' came a voice from behind the nearest tree.

Jenny halted.

'Please relax and continue, Osprey. I am a friend,' said the stranger.

She walked a few more yards, focusing her effort to turn hesitant steps back into normal walking. Waiting under cover of the trees, his hands thrust into coat pockets, was a middle-aged man dressed for a morning stroll: stout boots, jeans, Barbour, tweed flat cap, and cut blackthorn stick in hand. 'I am your owl, and your tiger, if that serves as a suitable introduction?'

'It does, very much. Thank you.' She let out a breath.

He was tall and lean, with angular features set in a pale complexion. Blue eyes shone beneath the few errant strands of grey protruding from under the peak of his cap.

'I have been dutifully keeping watch since last December,' he began, 'but circumstances have forced me to leave. It's been almost a year and I have seen nothing to suggest that you are under observation. Have you?'

Jenny's shoulders dropped as she sighed, deflated. She had grown so used to the unseen protection as to have forgotten about it, but now it was to end she was in turmoil. She scanned the park to check they were far from unwanted eyes and ears.

'I've seen nothing unusual. Nothing.'

'You will have to be vigilant – doubtless you always are – but if we have been compromised then things will happen soon. Watch for any changes as you go about your life and your usual routines.'

'How soon? . . . Oh, what I am saying? How could you know?'

'Days or weeks. A few months, even. If you find yourself celebrating the new year, celebrate being alive too.'

'I'll be sure to remember that,' she replied, shaking her head in disappointment.

The man ignored her mood. 'Good. Let that keep you sharp. Talking of which, I understand you have some rudimentary kit with which to defend yourself. Perhaps you should try my offering too. It's in your shed, under the Flymo.'

'Oh, that thing doesn't even work. Hasn't cut a blade of grass in years.'

'I know. I was counting on it. But make sure you get to it soon.'

The stranger looked over Jenny's shoulder. She started to turn her head to follow his eyeline but caught herself in time before making things too obvious. She shifted her position and surreptitiously looked in the same direction. There was nothing out of place.

'What am I missing?' she whispered.

But when she turned back, only Poppy's soft panting and keen brown eyes awaited her. He was gone.

Jenny struck for home. With Poppy's paws cleaned and her head buried in the food bowl, she slipped out of the house and into the shed. Behind the Flymo was a bundle of hessian sacking the size of large bag of rice, bound with electrical tape. She held it to her body to check she could adequately conceal the contents under her cardigan for the dash back to the house.

She sliced the tape and unravelled the sacking. Inside was an army issue Browning 9mm semi-automatic pistol. How original, she thought, Bruce could have got me one of these. With it were two small boxes, each with twenty rounds of ammunition and a basic cleaning kit. She grinned. As if she would clean the pistol after an encounter that required her to fire it – more likely it would be wiped clean of fingerprints and discarded. Jenny considered where it could best be hidden but remain accessible within the house, before heading back inside.

*   *   *

As November gave way to December, Roberts had finally completed his special task for Lady Margaret. Having waited patiently for the appropriate time, he observed Tavener driving off on his regular Saturday shopping and lunch trip. Whether to Nottingham or Sheffield or even nearby Naveby, he would be away long enough for Roberts to make his move.

He hurried back to the Woodhouse, loaded nine large boxes into the Volvo and then headed to the main house. The college was quiet. Students were in Saturday morning lessons, the cleaning staff had finished for the day, and the coast was clear for him to shift the boxes into the building unnoticed.

Once safely in the back kitchen, Roberts began ferrying them down to the vault. He punched the code into the keypad and as soon as the gap allowed, walked past the creaking iron door. With the shelving already back in place he hurriedly arranged the files, folders and papers in their prescribed order. After the final box had been unpacked, the shelving was full. He steadied himself and deliberated before setting the last and most critical piece of the jigsaw.

An hour after entering the vault he punched the numbers again and stood back as the door shut. From inside his waxed cotton jacket he retrieved a dustpan brush, then retraced his steps to the kitchen, sweeping the tunnel floor behind him to remove most, but not all, of his footprints.

When he returned to the Woodhouse, Lady Margaret was in the drawing room. Given over to more physically active pursuits than conversation, however, the space was more like a yoga or ballet studio than a family room in a manor house. Dressed in full fencing attire, complete with mask and white lamé covering her torso to detect successful hits, she was keeping her opponent at bay. The parrying and lunging was intense, even aggressive. A buzzer sounded as one of them landed a scoring attack.

'Not again! Break, please,' Lady Margaret exclaimed as she withdrew.

The pair downed weapons and removed their masks, letting air circulate around their sweating faces.

'A sabre, my lady? Somewhat heavy for fencing,' said Roberts.

'Still light, but it allows for the use of the weapon's edge,' replied the stranger. 'Her ladyship is a fine sabreuse.'

'Roberts, I should introduce you to Lucien Martell.' The men stepped towards each other and shook hands. 'Lucien, Philip Roberts, my personal aide.'

'How do you do, sir?'

'It's an honour to meet you, Philip. Lady Margaret holds you in the highest regard.'

'Lucien is a longstanding friend of my late husband. As you know, Edward enjoyed many pursuits and introduced me to fencing. Lucien was once a coach to the French Olympic team.'

'The honour is mine, monsieur,' replied Roberts.

He made his excuses and left them to finish their practice. An hour later Lady Margaret joined him in the sitting room where he was studying his notebook.

'You look pensive, Philip, but that's probably as it should be. Did everything go to plan?'

'Apparently – as far as I could tell. I just felt . . . exposed. I could have done with a second pair of eyes.'

'And hands too. I understand. But the pair of us lugging stuff around becomes much more conspicuous. It's an excuse I use to avoid real work, I know,' she laughed.

Roberts looked to the door then back to her. 'May I enquire?'

'Ah Lucien. He is a reliable friend – one of us. He is staying for a few days and I am briefing him in the hope that he can secure some resources to balance things in our favour if further external contacts can be rekindled. I'm taking every safe opportunity I find.'

'We are as a flickering flame in a breeze. We could grow or perish at every turn,' said Roberts thoughtfully.

She eyed him but allowed the comment to stand without challenge, before continuing, 'So you are confident that everything is in place?'

Robert nodded. 'The scene is set. It can either wait that way indefinitely or be found by a passing foe.

'Good. At least we have some sort of insurance policy if we are compromised.'

Roberts grinned, enjoying a brief moment of hope.

'There's something else too,' Lady Margaret continued. 'I intend to send Tavener to Bristol.' Roberts' eyes widened in surprise. 'I want him to provide cover, for a limited time, in place of the withdrawn asset who was protecting Osprey. It's been a few days, so if she is under observation then they should be getting twitchy, ready to act now.'

'But under what pretence? Surely you don't mean to expose the organisation?'

'Heavens no, Philip! I shall explain that Jenny's role at Gray and Hartens includes acting as a fund manager for the Rothwell estate. She suspects that she is being stalked – worst case, to be abducted – so that funds can be stolen, since she has access and authority to trade on my behalf. This emerged in conversation during our periodic telephone call about fund performance, etcetera. Osprey will be working to this brief too, so a similar outcome but via different means, as far as she is concerned.'

'Sounds plausible, but that would be sailing very close to the wind with Tavener. He will assume it to be untrue and his curiosity will be piqued.'

'Quite. So let's see if he puts his hand into the cookie jar.' Lady Margaret paused, watching Roberts contemplating her plan.

'And Jim has obligations in the college,' he said, looking back at her. 'CCF, his lab-technician duties, extra-curricular activities. He will need a reason to be absent. Let me guess . . . his poorly mother needs her son?'

'Precisely, and there's nobody better than Tavener to conjure a story. It would only need to be for long enough to know whether any adversaries intend to move – indeed, whether there *are* any adversaries out there. But also long enough for . . . how shall I put it? . . . .. *natural complexity* to unfold and invite Tavener to show at least a little of any hand he might be playing. That way he either exposes intent in his dealings with Osprey, perhaps by trying to elicit information from her, or he makes a wrong move while under our observation. For example, he might stay clear to allow others to carry out their plans.'

'What, you mean risk Osprey with Tavener? What's the upside to all this, my lady? I can only see the downsides. If he acts in the way you mention, then either he gets information from her about us, or she gets captured and possibly killed by a third party. If nothing happens, then we won't have learned anything new about him, unless you would take that as evidence that he has no suspicious agenda and can be fully trusted.'

'It is a calculated risk. If he is loyal to us he will wish to succeed for reasons of personal and professional pride – the success of his mission. Of course, he may solely wish to succeed to preserve any cover under which he might be working, as you imply.'

'Things could get very messy if he thwarts an attempt on Osprey and later is discovered to be the source of infiltration of the Archive.'

'Exactly. Oh what stakes and confusion! And your words assume that it is the same enemy, but there may be more than one group. Even if there is only one enemy, how would they react if they ever found out they had received information purloined by a self-serving snake? He would have blocked their attempt to get information so he could sell it to them himself. What complexity is borne of so few permutations . . .'

Roberts frowned. 'It's a lot to take in and a lot could go wrong. But one small point of detail, if I may. You mentioned there could be value to us if Tavener discloses intent in his dealings with Osprey or makes a wrong move while under our observation. Who would be observing him on our side? Surely you don't mean Osprey herself?'

'No, Philip. I mean you.'

*   *   *

Watching the watcher was a perilous business, especially for a relative amateur, especially when the target knew his identity. It would have been easier to carry out the surveillance in the attic of a nearby house, but where the task was to follow a mobile client, different tactics were required.

Roberts made a mental list of all manner of people, activities and services that could give him justification to loiter – in the greatest possible variety of places and times. It would be a logistical nightmare, and he reluctantly accepted that he would have to carry props to support a range of disguises. His dislike of using such paraphernalia was tempered by the greater nightmare – Tavener detecting him. If Tavener used public transport, the risk was being spotted or failing to keep up. The same went for private transport. Cars quickly get noticed, no matter how plain or carefully driven. And the option of frequently changing vehicles or being supported by a second driver was off limits – nobody else could know about this game of cat and mouse – and nobody else was available anyway.

He decided to assess Jenny's schedule, considering the opportunities Tavener would have to sneak away and meet a contact, if that was to be the play. He would guard her where she was most vulnerable – away from home on quiet sections of the routes she took most often and which afforded ready escape routes for any potential assailant. He might assume that she would have means of detection and defence at home, so he would probably depart from his protection duties either after seeing her reach home or somewhere approaching it. He could be away all night if he wanted, but of course that could court the disaster that she was captured or eliminated while he was absent.

Roberts had taken a room in a cheap city centre hotel, masquerading as a specialist tradesman working away from home. His task of troubleshooting the heating control systems on an overdue office build would cover for his coming and going at all hours. He rented a second-hand car from a backstreet motor trader and parked a couple of streets from Jenny's home in Stoke Bishop on a likely entry and exit route. The pattern would be to watch and wait. If he was to tail Tavener he knew he could do it only once.

Jenny Noble-Franks had settled into her new routine working three days a week at Gray and Hartens' Bristol offices in Queen Square. From Monday through Wednesday she would depart home around six thirty to reach the office with time to read the early papers and financials and be prepared for the UK market's opening at 8 a.m. She would lunch at her desk from the fresh sandwiches and salads bought in for the team and head home around six, usually via the Clifton co-op to pick up groceries. But over the final couple of miles she varied her route.

So it was that on Tuesday, 17 November 1987, during his first day of observation, Roberts watched Jenny leave for work but not return – and not a sign of Tavener. All he could do was be patient and let the pattern unfold. The next morning she drove by in her dark blue VW Passat, followed half a minute later by Tavener rumbling past in his own mustard-coloured Rover 3500 V8. Subtle. Was he even taking this seriously?

That evening Tavener returned first, disappearing into the final turning towards Jenny's address, then after a couple of minutes reappearing to head back towards town. Ten minutes later, Jenny passed Roberts. After an even briefer delay, she raced back past him. Something was up. He started his car and spun round to trail her along Whiteladies Road. The priority was no longer to hold back to discover Tavener's possible other connections, his instinct was that what mattered now was Jenny's protection.

Tavener was out of sight but Jenny pressed on as fast as the early evening traffic would allow until she finally turned down Park Row and into a multi-storey car park. Roberts pulled up short, squealing a tyre as he wrenched the car into a side road just yards away. If Tavener was there and parked he could easily observe anybody entering below.

With Jenny heading up the levels, Roberts tugged the hood of his jacket over his head and chanced it by foot on the opposite side of the road, peeking across at the car park to try and get an idea of what might be happening. He figured Tavener's attention would now be turning inwards, to Jenny's approach. He headed past the multi-storey and out of view but saw nothing significant, then doubled back and slipped down a side alley to a basement door. Inside he paused and listened. Traffic was rolling past on both sides – Park Row behind and College Green Road in front. A couple of women burst through an upper door and started clattering their way down in heels amid end-of-work gossip. Roberts ascended the steps briskly, his head down. They passed each other without so much as a glance. He pushed on, stopping at the doors on each level, listening and peering round to find Jenny – and presumably Tavener.

On the fifth floor Jenny had pulled up alongside Tavener. He was standing motionless at the front of his car, hands thrust into his black mac, taking in the view across the city. She turned off the engine and sat in the car for a minute but he didn't look round. She stepped out and started to approach him.

'Strange way to get a girl's attention, wouldn't you say? All very cloak and dagger.'

No response. No turn to acknowledge her presence.

Jenny knew what games could be played, but not why he had chosen this one. She said nothing more.

Eventually, he turned.

'I wanted to see if you could shut up. Maybe you can, after all, Jenny.'

She was taken aback but remained silent.

Tavener resumed, 'So you think you're being stalked? A mutual friend says you could be under threat because you manage a substantial investment fund over which you have full authority. So here I am, sent to look out for you, to see whether you really are in danger.' He fixed her with a stare from his hollow eyes.

'Very well – and for that I am thankful to you and her. So why this meeting? Surely this is a significant gamble you're taking – for both of us.'

'To protect you, I need your assistance. We do not have the luxury of time for you to take a passive role in this, I'm sorry to say.'

'What do you mean?'

Tavener scanned around them, briefly looking over to nearby buildings which might have a view of the scene.

'Come with me,' he ordered, taking her by the elbow and marching her away from the edge towards a recess beside the stairwell.

Jenny's whole body tensed, caught in confusion as instinct and logic conflicted within her. She pulled her shoulder bag in front of her, clutching the leather seam, preparing to open it, but as they reached the recess Tavener pinned her into a corner, squeezing her arm and forcing it across her body.

'Is Lady Margaret the head of the organisation?' he demanded.

'Get off me!'

He twisted his grip, the pressure swelling into searing pain in her arm and shoulder. She couldn't move her right arm to get to the gun in her bag.

'I need to know you are who she says you are. What's the organisation called?' he spat. 'What's her cover name? Tell me, or you'll lose that arm.'

Jenny tried to wrestle herself from his hold which was thrusting her against the wall. As her face scraped the smooth concrete, Tavener's purchase weakened. She dropped the bag to distract him. Momentarily he let his attention follow it as it fell to earth. She spun round, flicked the hidden blade out and slashed his hand clear. Blood spurted from the gash across the fingers of his left hand. He applied pressure with the other hand to try and stem it, simultaneously landing a kick to her gut which sent her reeling into the wall. She collapsed, winded.

He reached inside his coat and withdrew his Beretta. The door to the stairs boomed open and Roberts entered, firing two quick shots at him. Tavener set his position and returned fire as Roberts rolled towards the cover of Jenny's car.

Roberts was hit. Tavener was not.

Disoriented and with thick red blood seeping from inside his thigh, Roberts scrabbled to locate his weapon. Jenny had frozen, engulfed by shock, trying to recover her breath. She watched as Tavener stepped over Roberts. Crack! A single shot to the forehead.

Tavener turned back to Jenny, who was shaking too wildly to undo her bag. Her eyes widened in terror as he stood over her.

'Last chance. Tell me what I want to know and you live. Are you even thinking of your family?'

She lowered her head and nodded. Tears started down her face. 'I am thinking of them.'

With every sinew in her being she thrust the blade through his ankle, splitting muscle from bone before he could evade her.

Crack!

24

Having enjoyed a *gelato napoletano* followed by an espresso, James Tavener sat and waited. The Caffè Antico in Cagliari, Sardinia, was so pristinely presented – its staff in formal *camerieri* attire, its fittings and décor in classical style with hints of art deco – that he could have been in any of Italy's finest establishments, in Rome or Milan.

At five minutes after four o'clock, two men entered and scanned the room for the individual they had never met. When Tavener identified himself with a sustained look in their direction, the nearest man gestured towards the door inviting him outside, onto Via Vincenzo and into a black Mercedes.

As the car eased away, Tavener sat distracted by pain, the streets passing by the darkened windows. It was only a couple of days since the shootings in the multi-storey car park and his bandaged ankle was still agony, even with double doses of painkillers. A hand reached over, offering the hood. He took it and slipped it over his head without discussion. Next he handed them his watch. It took a mere few turns through the maze of streets before he abandoned trying to place himself. Even the rises and falls up and

downhill were no help. He guessed he was heading north –
only the sea lay to the south.

It must have been two hours later, after prolonged twists
and climbs into the hills, that the car left the metalled
roadway and swept onto a gravel track. After several more
minutes of being rocked between the two heavies in the
back, they stopped. The guard on Tavener's right got out
and gabbled something in Italian at him before grasping his
arm and guiding him out of the car and into the building,
where the hood was removed. He gestured a respectful nod
in gratitude for Tavener's compliance and departed, leaving
him to take in the scene.

 Distant sounds of life echoed back through the
voluminous entrance hall – chatter and crockery being
handled in a kitchen, the clack of shoes on a hard floor. The
walls were clad in great panels of white marble, reaching
up to accommodate the marble staircases which swept
down on each side. A few modern ornaments, including a
wall adorned only with a line of eight brightly coloured
cooking pans, broke up the otherwise overpowering
minimalism of the place.

The doors at the far end opened.

'Mr James . . . Mr James . . . it's so good to see you.
Welcome! Please, this way.'

Despite the loose covering of a designer cream cardigan,
the man was noticeably lean. And tall, like Tavener. He cut
a manicured, immaculate image – not a hair out of place
nor hands that had ever seen a day's labour.

'You're limping. My boys treated you well, I hope.'

'Your men were most professional and courteous, thank you.'

They threaded through the mansion to a grand terrace at the rear, illuminated by soft electric and candle light. In the distance, only darkness. The sun had long set and there was not a single light beyond to offer a clue to their whereabouts.

The host signalled towards the firepit, which was promptly stirred back to life by a servant and logs added.

'A drink? You must be tired after the journey.'

'Please.'

'I thought you might. I gambled on opening a 1975 Romanee-Conti Grand Cru. I trust you like a good claret, Mr James?'

Tavener met his stare coolly, his eyes narrowing as he put his nose to the glass.

'I prefer a burgundy over a bordeaux actually, especially when it's served in a burgundy glass . . .'

They gave way to laughter.

'Salute!'

'Bottoms up!'

A stillness fell as the breeze settled and the house staff withdrew. The two were left alone.

'We will eat in a little while, but for now, some business. I know why you had to come here, of course. My associates admired your methods in Bristol.'

'You take great precautions, signore.' Tavener paused and looked across at his companion. 'Is that the correct form of address? I am afraid I don't know your name.'

'Yes, James, it is a little formal, but things are better without names sometimes. It's the way it has to be. I hope you understand. One cannot be too careful in establishing new relationships – finding new resources, I like to say. I think, in your profession, is it not "assets"?'

'An American influence perhaps, but yes. In my former profession.'

'So you eliminated two people. In a public place.'

'I had reconnoitred. Public, but not observed. And as a relatively new building, the top floors of the car park were seldom used and were empty at that time of day. The patterns were predictable enough.'

'And the woman?'

'She provided both very little and yet quite a lot.' His host leaned in to focus on Tavener's words. 'It's how she did it. I gave her a way out. She knew I meant business, having seen the fate of her would-be rescuer. Yet even with the most precious things in her world called to mind, she pressed the destruct button. From a professional angle, she was circumventing any option to properly interrogate her by precipitating the execution.'

'So you shot her and then left the scene. How were you planning to clear things up?'

'I wasn't – not once I knew I had support on hand.'

'You detected my men?'

'Who else would have found the only possible vantage point to keep eyes on me? I wanted to confirm both who they were and to know the scene was cleared, so I gave them no choice but to move in, for which I thank you.'

The man studied Tavener with a mixture of irritation and intrigue.

'What are we to learn from this?'

'That whatever organisation I am getting close to has a distinct thread of professionalism and commitment running through it.'

'How do you assess this organisation? Could it be the legendary "club" that our Russian associates have been whispering about? What is it they call it?'

He searched the floor for the words.

'The Architects' Club,' suggested Tavener.

'That's it. The Architects' Club. A mythical global network of sages and warriors, here to save the world from itself, and most of all, from people like us. It's ridiculous. Most governments are corrupt. People think we live in a civilised world. Pah! It's still survival of the fittest. With communism failing in the USSR, Gorbachev's perestroika will lead only to domination by the most powerful among the KGB and ruling machinery, not to democracy. You can sit back and do nothing, or you can gain from such chaos and opportunity. Too many people think they've hit the big time with a few million stashed away, a villa here, a yacht there, but I say if you're going to do something, do it well. Create a state, or control one. When a man controls

SAM EARNER

resources, infrastructure, financial institutions, then he can make his mark on the world.'

He sat back and took a long slow mouthful of wine, dabbing traces of red from his lips onto a crisp white napkin before continuing. 'With such opportunities at hand, the last thing we need is a bunch of heroes trying to get in the way. And it's my job – my intent, I should say – to see to it that they are destroyed, in whatever form they exist.'

Tavener looked ahead for a moment, reflecting on his host's words. 'Let me tell you what I have found and what I plan to do, signore. The focus of interest is information, not any treasure trove of priceless antiques or collections of silver, although they exist too. No, it's information, I'm sure of it. You see, the other person eliminated in Bristol was her ladyship's personal aide. He must have been scurrying about behind the scenes some months ago when she showed me an underground vault – it was empty, and I suspected it had been emptied just for me.'

'Emptied ... why? How do you know it contained information? Where did it all go?'

'It was an act of reconciliation between the two of us. The fact is, she needed to hire professional help in the light of an increasingly transparent world, especially if Mr Berners-Lee manages to progress his vision of global computer communications. Her secrets and treasures were bound to become known to the world sooner or later, but she is at odds with herself and can't let go. She can't bear to share these things with anyone else. I see now she was

330

trying to play a clever game, which could never have worked.'

'Oh, James, you have me. Please . . . what game?'

'She employed me as a security expert for her real concern, her "information repository" let's call it, but without me realising it. She tried to use her treasures as a pretext.'

'But why did she show you an empty space?'

'My lever for infiltration was always that I needed to know more. She took me to the vault and gave me a bunkum story about it being an old silver store, in the hope that I would shut up and ignore it thereafter. Regrettably for her, however, I then placed a number of, admittedly crude, but reliable surveillance measures around the place. When I was out of the way, they replaced the boxes of papers and files in the vault.'

'Do you have a next move?'

'I do, but only one. My cover is that I was snatched along with Jenny and Philip. Since nobody will be making contact by way of ransom, we three can only be assumed to be dead, and so I cannot return to her service.'

'You intend to return covertly and crack this vault once and for all then? But why now, if you couldn't do so before?'

'The vault has the only proper technical defences in the whole place. It is heavily fortified and entry is by keypad, with dated but functioning fail-safes, as far as I could tell.'

'So you put a gun to her head. Simple.'

'I put a gun to Jenny's head, remember? I wouldn't even get her ladyship to the door, not without a team, and I presume discretion is the byword here, if you are to succeed in your intent.'

'What then?' The two stopped as a servant appeared behind them. The host smiled at Tavener. 'Dinner?'

Once alone again, and eating their first course of *lorighittas* with a tomato and wild boar sauce, the conversation resumed.

'What then?' he continued impatiently.

'It occurred to me, why put a vault so far underground?' said Tavener.

'Because it's hard to reach, of course.'

'True, but it's not just that it's hard to reach. There are two gigantic floodgates at either end of this deep section of tunnel under the lake. You put the vault there so if all goes wrong you can flood the tunnel to deny access without destroying its contents. That's what I think.'

'But that means nobody gets to it.'

'Correct . . . unless you remove the water.'

His puzzled expression had been replaced by one of total bafflement. 'But how? *Dio mio!* James, I must admit, for a man who must have spent most of his life in a grey suit, you are anything but dull. Impress me!'

'Through the vault, of course.'

'*Mamma!*' He shook his head at Tavener and slid away another measure of red. 'Please, I can't take any more, my friend. No . . . wait . . . would this not destroy the material in the vault?'

'Not if you remove it first. Rothwell has a curious geography. The lake is man-made. There is an area of ground between the main house and a small village called Knaith to the south, where the land is lower than the lake – lower, in fact, than the tunnel floor. So the method of recovery from hitting the panic button might be to extract the material via another tunnel running away from behind the vault, then open the vault door to drain the tunnel into the low-lying land. That means that the main house's basement is never threatened by floodwater getting past the retaining doors.'

'But what's the point of all this if there's another way in? Surely it weakens the whole thing?'

'The point is – partly – deception. If an adversary sees thousands of tons of water flooding the tunnel and they haven't worked out the rest of the story, then they could conclude it's game over, wisest to simply abandon and move on. And, of course, every great scheme will have its flaws. You cannot have greatness without risk.'

'Have you searched for this other entrance?'

'I have, but to no avail. The terrain allows for the placement of another tunnel that could be very long. That means searching hundreds of acres of land, much of which is densely wooded and thickly overgrown.'

'So what are we to do, James?'

'There are two options. First – my recommended option but the slower of the two – we send in an assault team, which will cause Lady Margaret to panic, thinking the information in the vault is at risk. She'll press the button and flood the tunnel as a precaution. The rest of the world will be left to think it's all about silver and treasures.'

'The rest of the world means who exactly?'

'The authorities, police, MI5, and our enemies too – others from the organised crime community, or indeed anyone who might believe that someone holds information on them. The only people who could know differently would be other members of the so-called Architects' Club – and us.'

'Okay, okay . . .' The host mulled over the developing puzzle. 'So you think you know what sort of information exists?'

'No, not with any certainty. It's an educated guess based on experience – based on what I would consider worth protecting in the way that she is protecting it. It would be either information about others or information about themselves. Probably some of each. That's not saying much, I know. The clue to its value is in the efforts being expended to protect it, rather than just destroying it.'

'And what about discretion, something you have rightly identified as important, James?'

'That aspect relates to the prize. That's why we make it look like an attempted heist. It's still a big deal on one level, but commonplace on another. Just a gang trying to go big time. Hence the team would be briefed to go for the silver room or some other plausible high-value target. It would need to centre on the main house but not the vault. The team must not stop Lady M getting to the vault.'

'But wouldn't the rest of the world wonder why she flooded the tunnel?'

'My theory is they would conclude that the most precious treasures are in the vault, of course.'

'Hmm, okay. And may I ask where is this button exactly – to flood the tunnel?'

'It's at the vault door, in the middle of the tunnel.'

'So in operating the defence system, what? she drowns? isn't that a bit crazy?'

'As I say, a thread of professionalism exists, and a deception is much more convincing if there are no weak points. Fortuitously, the craziness resonates with the reason the tunnel system was originally built. One of the dukes didn't like to be observed so he conceived of the tunnels to allow him to move around undetected – a bit eccentric but it conveniently aligns with current circumstances. Call it heritage, call it genetics, call it what you like, her behaviour will look a lot more plausible when folk check the history of the place. Like great-great-great uncle, like niece,' said Tavener. 'Anyway, then we watch and wait.'

'For whom? She will be dead. Are there any others to take over?'

'That's the point. If any other members of the organisation exist and learn of the attack, and if the material is essential for them to operate, someone will return to get it.'

'If, if, if! That could take forever. Nobody might ever come. I don't like it. Too long. What else?' the host snapped. He stood up, threw his napkin onto the table and paced around, waiting for a response.

Tavener sensed the blood rising in his neck. He took a breath.

'Option two then. Quicker but dirtier. We send in a team to locate the alternative entrance. They report back with details of its construction, protection and so forth, and I infiltrate – exploit the weak part of the scheme.'

'Better. But why would this be dirtier?'

'There is the risk of the team being detected.'

'By whom? She is alone now, no?'

'True, up to a point. Her aide is gone. Her suspected main contact to the outside, Jenny Noble-Franks, is gone too. She has few visitors – the current one knew her late husband through fencing. She purports to do a bit herself. Whether that's true or a pretext for, let's say, finding some personal comfort, I don't know. But the more tricky issue is the college. Previous fuck-ups by those amateurs from Albania have got the principal thinking the IRA are snooping. With nobody taking him seriously he's gone as far as training a core of students to conduct armed standing patrols.'

'Boys with live weapons?'

'And nightscopes, radios, tripwires and flares. The latest was that they had reduced the cover to observation only. No rifles. But there is potential for complications.'

The host was silent for a moment, processing the complexities of Tavener's words. He rubbed his eyes and stretched back in his chair.

'Come, James. Let us go and sit somewhere more comfortable.'

James followed him to a sitting room on the other side of the house. It looked down onto a sizeable pool lit by myriad underwater lights that sparkled like tiny diamonds in the midnight blue water. The esoteric minimalism continued in this room too. There was a pair of soft leather sofas sporting modern lines in red tan facing each other in the centre. A smoked glass side table stood beyond them and contained crystal decanters and whisky and brandy glasses. A huge original painting hung on the wall facing out to the pool. Tavener couldn't believe his eyes. It was square with sides of over two metres, in either oil or acrylic, he guessed. The scene was of a swimming pool under a perfect blue sky, devoid of any signs of life except for the splash after someone had dived in.

'Brandy? Cigars?' the host offered.

As the drinks were poured, Tavener continued, 'You should know that her ladyship held a high-powered social event in the summer, mainly to keep people around the capital in favour. That is when I learned that the CIA and MI5 were involved.'

'Wow! You mean they're actually awake? Perhaps this club is real, after all.'

'There was a guy representing the governor of one of the British overseas territories. He seemed familiar, maybe an old CIA contact, but I don't think he recognised me.'

'Let's hope not. Right or wrong, the Virginia farm boys can be a real nuisance.'

'It doesn't matter. He's dead. He slipped away from the banquet and conveniently passed a device which I'd concealed near one of the staterooms in the Oxford wing. Lady Margaret had led a guided tour that day and he must have figured out the irregular geometry in that part of the house. It turned out that he uncovered a concealed staircase, went in and never came out. A few days later I got a visit from an old MI5 associate, and then a CIA team went in to follow his route and retrieve their man. They didn't find him and came out minus a team member.'

The host looked about him and tapped his cigar absentmindedly into an ashtray. It was out. He started the process of re-lighting it, quizzing Tavener in between short puffs and turning it to check for a glow. 'You're talking a proper black-ops team?' Tavener nodded. 'Armed . . . NVGs?' Another nod. 'So who or what in hell is down there?'

Tavener smiled. 'The one thing that has kept me alive this long is good instincts.'

'You haven't gone in?'

Tavener shook his head. 'Would you?'

The host stared across the room for a moment, then let out a long, slow billow of smoke.

'You'll find your first payment upstairs, James. Used dollar bills. Quarter of a million. The remainder when the job is complete. We'll continue this in the morning. Sleep well.'

'Buona notte, signore.'

25

The principal's kindness in coming to the class in person to get Bruce served only to highlight the severity of the situation. When tenderness is offered first, a heavy blow is sure to follow. They walked awkwardly along Class Corridor and up the broad wooden stairs to the library, the sound of floorboards creaking underfoot a welcome distraction from Hunter's attempts at informality. Yes, Bruce was enjoying lessons just fine that morning.

On arrival at his study, the sight of Miss Hamble holding the door open and a tray of tea and biscuits on the sideboard completed the onset of turmoil which was already eating like acid into Bruce's stomach. What had he done this time?

'Take a seat, Bruce. No here,' Hunter began, ushering Bruce over to the sticks of furniture which passed as "chairs: occasional" on an army married-quarter's inventory. He handed him a cup of tea. 'Sugar?'

'No thank you, sir.'

'Firstly, there's nothing to worry about.'

Naturally, thought Bruce.

'Your father has taken the precaution of reporting to the authorities that your mother did not return home last night.'

Bruce looked up anxiously. Hunter paused. 'All I know is –
and at this stage your father has to be circumspect in what
he divulges ... police procedure – your mother returned
briefly from work yesterday evening before heading back
out on an errand of some sort.'

Bruce nodded slowly in acknowledgement.

'Well, that's about all I can tell you right now. But I
wanted you to know straightaway and to hear it from me
directly. Do you have any questions, Bruce?'

Bruce pondered for a moment then shook his head. 'I
don't know what to ask, sir. What should I ask?'

'Would you like to call your father? I believe he is
required – and doubtless would want to be – at home. In
case of contact.' Bruce's eyes switched to meet Colonel
Hunter's again. 'In case your mother returns,' he rushed.

Bruce felt numb. What would it achieve? he thought.
Then he considered his father. 'Yes sir, I would like to call
Dad, if I may?'

'Remember that he has to be guarded about what he
says, Bruce. Just in case.' Hunter gestured Bruce to use his
desk telephone.

Bruce's attention spiralled down the telephone line,
entranced by the novelty of a ringtone normally heard only
on the weekly call home.

'Eight-three-o-two-one-six.'

'Dad? It's me. I'm calling from the principal's office.
Can you speak?'

Hunter slipped away, allowing Bruce to talk freely.

'So, he's explained what this is all about, and that we can't speculate – openly I mean – at least for now, son?' responded Charles Noble-Franks.

'Don't people need to be absent for twenty-four hours before calling the police, Dad?'

'Oh, I'm not sure. They never said so, and to be fair it never entered my head. It's just so unlike her. My main worry was that she'd run off the road or been mugged – that she'd be lying somewhere in trouble, injured. We wouldn't wait a day to start looking for her, would we now?'

Bruce and his father chatted as best they could. Charles' occasional vague or circumspect responses confirmed the principal's caution. It sounded like they had to protect against possible phone taps and the risk of information getting out through family members which could complicate any ransom demands, in case that possibility materialised. The demons of confusion and curiosity sprang to life in Bruce's mind. A ransom would mean a kidnap, but why?

They finished the call and Bruce hung up. His hand remained on the phone like a magnet stuck to iron, unable to let go. His thoughts centred on his lingering suspicions of his mother's dark side.

Colonel Hunter peered around the door. 'All finished, Noble?'

'Yes, sir. Thank you.'

'Well done. I can tell you're taking things a step at a time – which is as it should be, young man. I'll send for you the moment I have something more to report.'

*   *   *

Bruce's gloomy introspection was interrupted by the shrill ringing of the bell sounding for mid-morning break. Justin Hepburn grabbed his arm.

'Follow me. RSM's office. He's called a few of our entry together – I think it's about corps hierarchy.'

As they entered Kitchen Block more of their number joined them, pounding the polished lino to the CCF staff office door. Hepburn didn't hesitate but immediately rapped on the white gloss paint.

'Come!'

Inside, the others were already seated in a semicircle around Pitcaithly's desk. It appeared to be a quorum: six students for six platoons, plus a CSM. But what about a CQMS? Or was there going to be a reorganisation into only five platoons?

'Chaps, excuse the snap meeting. What with Remembrance last week and a few other things it's been hectic in here. Anyway, the end of term is fast approaching, senior entry has exams to focus on, and I have a CCF to run. So, apologies for not standing on ceremony but you lot will be the corps hierarchy in the new year. Rose will be CSM.'

Bruce took in the faces, and the reactions. Some grinned gleefully at the notion they had made it. Others wore the faces of men who knew they had an underlying task at hand, a serious task quite beyond the challenges presented by any normal year in the college's history. Beside him sat Justin Hepburn. Next was Arthur Rose, who clearly knew the score and was one of the straight-faced gang. Then Mike Heskell, who also looked quite sober. On the other side sat a smug Carl Loevenger. He hadn't changed his arrogant personality since first passing through Rothwell's hallowed oak doors and Bruce was as unsurprised as he was unimpressed that the next parasite was worming its way through the system. Smirking Carl Loevenger. A guaranteed liability to any covert plan. Finally, Jim Willmott. For all the allegations of being another grey man, Jim's shocked expression could be forgiven. Where the British army too often defaulted to promotion of the loudest, at least Jim was someone who sought information before opening his mouth.

Pitcaithly quickly came to the point. The group would loosely follow a standard training syllabus, but it would be used as a basis for focusing on more specific skills for the general defence of the college. Secrecy was paramount. Each student was to engage with his senior entry counterpart and arrange for a detailed handover.

'Any questions?' he asked as the bell signalled the return to classes. 'Noble?'

'Who will be CQMS, sir?'

'I haven't decided yet. Not a priority anyway.'

'With respect sir, the CQMS is a key part of the plan – to enable the swift distribution of arms and equipment. Nothing will happen without his team,' Bruce said.

Pitcaithly paused and looked over to Captain Pearce, a twitch of tension in his jaw muscle. He sighed.

'May I offer a name, sir?' Bruce continued to volunteer his ideas, as his colleagues squirmed in fear of the RSM's reaction. They could all be on defaulters before wearing the rank at this rate. 'Shaun Dodd.'

Loevenger piled in. 'Don't be a twat, Brucie. Dodd's a nerd. He couldn't command the respect of the clothes in the store.'

'Dodd's smart and reliable. And he's original in his thinking. His input – indeed critique – of any plans we cook up could be a useful reality check, sir.'

'Christ, do I honestly have to listen to this crap? You want your buddy to get a top rank in the corps, plain as, Brucie. Just because you think you can see in the bloody dark. What are you anyhow, a bat or something? Batman?'

'I think the expression is "blind as a bat", Carl,' snapped Heskell. 'So speak for yourself, old boy.'

While the exchange ran its last moments before Pitcaithly seized control again, Bruce let his gaze shift imperceptibly to Art Rose. He recalled the basic NLP skills that Shaun had set as holiday reading, and he casually took in Art's demeanour to check his reaction to Loevenger's blunder. Only Art could have let slip about Bruce's odd

345

talent. His face gave nothing away, but as Bruce's vision zoomed in on his skin tone he noticed the dilation of the artery in his neck and reddening around his ears. He was not his usual collected self.

'I will consider your suggestion, Mr Noble. Back to classes, gentlemen.'

That evening the group met secretly in the college chapel to achieve the real outcomes that the more conventional process would likely fail to do. All were present, except Carl Loevenger, who was collectively acknowledged as a risk to the whole project. They fell silent, letting Art speak first in deference to the regime which bound them.

'Guys, thanks for coming. Two issues to crack, as I see it. One: are we satisfied with current plans for our defence? Two: how to achieve our goals without Loevenger blowing it?'

Sensing that no secret undertaking is ever safe they hastened the discussion before anyone disturbed them, even though the chapel was hardly a popular venue with anybody who didn't need to be there.

'Tackle the Loevenger issue first, I say. Then we have a way clear to do what we need to do,' said Mike Heskell.

'Are we expecting a problem that might not exist?' Bruce asked. 'If he shouts his mouth off, he will incur the wrath of the entire CCF staff and the principal too . . . It might usefully guide his career elsewhere, if you get my drift,' he added, cognisant of the parallel with Jez Picher.

'My sentiments exactly,' Jim Wilmott agreed. 'However, if Loevenger does gob off about covert plans, it is also conceivable that rather than bringing about his own demise, he could get the hierarchy in the shit with the MOD. The college leadership will always be accountable for what the students do. He could even win plaudits for blowing the whistle, worst case.'

'What can we actually do, though?' asked Art. 'Do we just take the risk? After all, that's exactly what Willis is doing in giving him a senior NCO position. My concern is less about careers and reputations than whether he exposes his guys to dangers of his own making – in other words, if we ever have to deploy with arms, if we have to fight. He's a hair-trigger . . . excuse the pun.'

'All logical enough, but it still leaves us with the same problem: what can we actually do about him?' said Justin Hepburn.

Art stared through them. A grin crept across his face.

'What, Art?'

He whispered, 'Let's just say, as CSM I would be within my rights to relieve him of his command if I thought he was a risk to our troops in combat.'

'Sounds ominous,' said Bruce, frowning.

'What do you mean, Bruce?'

'He means a bullet in the back, if I'm not mistaken,' said Mike Heskell.

'Calm down, guys. Allow me a moment's indulgence. I mean I would just pull him out and put him at the back – running the comms cell or something,' said Art.

'He'd never settle for that.'

'He'll settle for what he's ordered, or he'll settle for my fist.'

Bruce trudged up to the dorms, his attention bent in upon himself like two steel barbs – distraught about his mother's disappearance but also preoccupied by his task at the college. The persistence of any thoughts other than for his mother at such a time filled him with a guilt he could almost taste. What was wrong with him to be so absorbed with the mysteries and demands of the college's other life when his own mother could be anywhere, suffering anything?

He had spent periods in a daze with the twin menaces circling around inside. Worst of all, while he labelled them as menaces for conscience' sake, part of him welcomed some verve in his life again, black though it was. The reality of such tangled plots was becoming a drug to him, standing in stark contrast to the humdrum routine of the academic – and even military – curriculum.

'Bruce . . . Bruce!' came Shaun's words through the fog.

He lifted his head from the wash basin to see the staring faces, to hear the hush where there should have been a hubbub.

'You with us this evening?' smiled Shaun. The din resumed.

'I'm nowhere, mate. Lost would be an understatement.'

They got back to their dorm before the other two occupants. In the precious few minutes available Bruce explained his turmoil.

'Welcome to the enigmas and contradictions of Tier Two, my friend,' Shaun said, but as ever he was just out of Bruce's intellectual reach. 'And I know that's not helpful at all, not until you've read your Wilber anyhow, so try this. Maybe both subjects stick in your mind because they are connected. It's called intuition – psychic intuition – to give it its proper scientific title.' Bruce's expression became fixed, his eyes so intense he could have melted a hole in the carpet. Shaun stopped speaking and looked at his friend enquiringly. 'What?'

'Well Shaun, as you would put it, you've unlocked something that was bubbling just under the surface. I must go to Bristol. Home. I must go home and stand in the street and look east. Then I will find my mother.'

26

Colonel Hunter caved in to Bruce's request to return home. What else could he have done? The surprise was getting permission for Shaun Dodd to accompany him, which Bruce engineered more by riding the wave of the first agreement than through any degree of subtlety or persuasive argument. Emotion and acting, not clever words, won the moment.

So it was that by Friday evening the pair were being driven back to Bruce's home by Charles Noble-Franks. The journey was difficult, tense. It was two days since Jenny's disappearance and every expectation of a plausible reason for her absence had long since evaporated. Charles was distracted and visibly disturbed. Bruce and Shaun exchanged concerned looks as he muttered to himself and stared through the traffic ahead, sometimes hardly noticing what was going on in the road around him. Twice he had to brake or swerve violently to avoid catastrophe.

The dual burden of his father's stress and his own anxiety was beginning to take its toll on Bruce. The drug of adventure had worn off and reality gnawed at an open wound. Trusting his intuition was fast becoming ridiculous and emotionally draining. But Shaun's temperament remained steady. Was he just not getting it? Or did he have some blind faith, the rationale for which eluded Bruce?

They pulled onto the drive. Now full of doubt, Bruce trudged into the house in pursuit of food, a hot shower and sleep. Shaun followed suit, taking in his new surroundings as he went.

Next morning Bruce ate a perfunctory breakfast of toast and tea while striding around the kitchen and driveway, inside and out, not quite knowing where to put himself.

'Did you sleep?' asked Shaun.

'B-i-t-s,' came the yawned reply. 'I dreamed of a fucking house of cards,' Bruce continued after the yawn snapped shut. 'I woke up from it, so I remembered it. It took ages to drop off again.'

'Archetypal maybe. It certainly fits the circumstances.'

'I must admit, Shaun, that I feel a bit stupid bringing you all this way. I only hope that the bizarre compulsion to follow my instincts leads to something other than total embarrassment.'

Shaun nodded supportively. 'We won't know unless we try.'

'Very well,' said Bruce, before turning to face the hallway. 'Dad, we're heading out for a while. Not sure how long for.'

Traffic on quiet suburban streets like Rylestone Grove could never be described as heavy, especially at half past eight on a Saturday morning. Standing there in the quiet, Bruce looked quizzically at his friend. 'Go on then, Shaun. Do your thing. I'm truly stuck. I haven't a clue what I'm meant to be doing.' Shaun's face broke into a knowing grin. It whispered, 'All will be well.'

'You were in the zone with this yesterday,' he said. 'You told me you just had to come out into the street and look east, Bruce. So look east.'

A watery winter sun hung low in the sky. Its distant embers threw a soft golden hue upon the empty tarmac and pavements. Bruce took in the scene. He looked to the ground and let out a heavy sigh, then looked up again, along the road and beyond, opening himself to whatever direction arose from within.

'I think we could be on for a bit of a walk, Shaun.'

'Lead the way, my friend.'

The section of street, which in fact faced southeast, soon curved to the right, up to a T-junction with Parry's Lane. Bruce stopped and looked left, towards the southeast again, straight towards the city centre.

'Christ.'

'What?' asked Shaun.

'I'm getting this by instalments. We need to cross the Downs. Next stop – Whiteladies Road. Apologies. This is extremely weird. I can't even begin to describe what I am experiencing. It's detectable, but so subtle, so fragile.'

'Stay with it.'

The pace quickened. It had to. As Bruce's hazy but powerful vision became stronger, it pointed to ever greater departures. Having covered the first mile to Whiteladies, now they had to get to its far end, through Clifton and past the university buildings another one to two miles hence. After the Wills Building, the mystical journey led them down Park Row, where it all but vanished.

Bruce halted, bemused. He turned about, peering up and down the street.

'Once more I am at a dead end, my friend. We've come this far and for what? Where now?'

'What does your gut tell you?'

'That's what I mean. Nothing.'

'If it was to guide you again where would you go? I mean, go on, walk somewhere, anywhere.'

Bruce eyed Shaun from within the bubble of his dilemma. There's no trying, he thought, only doing. He struck out, absolutely clueless this time, continuing along Park Row. And then, as the road opened to their right, they saw the police vehicles and security cordon at the entrance to the multi-storey car park. Passers-by stayed on the opposite side to avoid the scene, consumed as it was by a solemnity under the slow turning blue lights and murmur of detectives' voices high above.

Shaun craned to view the top. 'A house of cards, you say? Now, if that isn't one massive concrete house of cards … So there's the physical connection to the metaphor. There's also the allusion to the playing of card games –

poker perhaps – but either way there is risk, high stakes, danger—'

He suddenly stopped talking, realising the insensitivity of his words. But Bruce was dumbstruck. He knew what this meant.

'I can't believe what's just happened. Explain it, Shaun. How does a wild goose chase end like this? What are the chances?'

'So firstly, Bruce, you're saying that this police activity relates to your mother, and you feel certain of that?'

'Yes, this definitely relates to her. I could try to blag it with the PC over there to find out what's going on, but I don't need to do that. It would be an error – it would complicate matters when the "Who are you, sonny?" conversation started.'

'Are you sure? This is important. For you as well as your mum.'

'I'll be gobsmacked if we get home and I'm wrong.'

'What is it you expect to hear when you get home, Bruce?'

'Mum's missing, her car's missing. They've found the car, right? But that might be an inevitable outcome, so here's more: the car is locked and undisturbed. There's no sign of her.' Bruce stayed his trembling voice. 'How can I even conceive of this? How have I done this?' He winced, feeling himself being torn apart by the discovery of his powers of insight and what those powers had brought.

Shaun allowed Bruce a moment.

'Like I said, Tier Two. Psychic intuition. It's real. Doesn't make it nice, though. I'm sorry, Bruce.'

This time there was no blank look from Bruce. He was on to the next part of the mission. Across the street, at the entrance to a Victorian town house set high atop rising ground, was another constable. Like his counterpart at the car park, he stood solemnly in front of a quiet scene, in all respects unremarkable apart from the garland of police tape strewn across the doorway.

Bruce eyed the officer for a moment and examined the building behind him.

'We need to get back.'

Tired and hungry, the pair's attention had shifted from the wonders of the psychic level of consciousness to more fundamental matters, like food. They clattered through the back door and Bruce headed into the kitchen then towards the hall in search of his father.

Charles was slumped at the foot of the stairs, still as a statue, his hand resting on the black telephone receiver. Bruce thought he was staring into a mirror of time from his own experience in the principal's study.

'Dad?'

Bruce was met neither with words nor eye contact at first. Just a sigh long enough to end the world.

'Let's go into the living room. I have … I have news,' said Charles.

Shaun held back, mouth open, looking for guidance.

'Shaun, of course you may join us, but you don't have to. Up to you.'

Shaun responded with a tentative nod and followed father and son into the room. They sank into the nearest chairs. Where they sat wasn't important to them. Paying attention to Charles was.

'That was Detective Inspector Coombes on the line. They have found your mother's – Jenny's ...' His hands swept upwards to cover the streams of tears starting from his eyes, now screwed shut in agony. There was a silence that seemed to last forever, like an injured child whose first wails are yet to arrive after its lungs have filled with air.

Shaun looked at Bruce. His face was pale with grief over the horror that must be coming. Charles' anguish continued, his hand becoming a gnawed fist with saliva trailing over blood-drained fingers.

Bruce could bear it no longer. 'They've found her car, haven't they? They've found her car but no sign of her . . . of Mum.'

The words wrenched Charles from his turmoil. He stared in amazement, wiping the fluids from his face and clearing his eyes. 'How do you know?' He sniffed back more tears.

'I don't, but you started so I guessed. I'm sorry, Dad. I just wanted to help you get the words out.'

'Well, that's about the sum of it,' he sighed, 'and the fact that the police obviously think there would have been a ransom contact by now – hence the call rather than a visit, I suppose.'

They stayed there for hours, turning it all over, talking it all through, back and again, until finally exhaustion overtook them and a grim reality established itself.

Shaun returned to college while Bruce hung on for another week to help his father begin life without Jenny. Charles' notions of searching for her himself came to nothing. Each time he prepared to depart, calls or drop-ins from the CID brought home the fact that they had already checked all the places that he had thought of. By mutual consent, and under the imagined gaze of an absent matriarch, both had agreed that Bruce should return to his studies, that no more harm or disruption should befall this family.

Only three weeks later, term drew to a close. There was another parade, this time to send 66 Entry on their way. Once more Chapel Court was turned into a transport depot as parents' cars cut across it like mice chasing cheese, taking their precious sons home. Out of sight behind the frenzy was the next group of winter expeditionaries readying their kit, this year for Glencoe. Bruce saw what others were too hasty to notice. His stomach lurched for a moment at the memories it stirred of his departed friend. Only his father's soft tones inviting him home saved Bruce from reliving it all again.

A glum Christmas passed slowly, despite the best efforts of visiting brothers and sisters to bring cheer over dried-out turkey, bullet sprouts, black-edged roasters and forgotten gravy. Pete's wife, Denise, stood ready, of course, but held back as Charles forced himself to function in the name of the family and of his wife, missing and now presumed dead.

Bruce's return to the new year's snow was a reluctant relief from the growing suffocation of home. It ushered in a heady final six months at Rothwell. Two terms with 67 Entry as the seniors meant both his command of a platoon and a prefectship.

Each house had ten prefects. The cream were the four college prefects, the leader of which was either the head boy or deputy, with the two roles being split between the houses of Wessex and Lancaster. Each house also had six house prefects, of which Bruce was one. He had to assist with rotas for mundane domestic tasks given out to defaulters among the junior students. That aside, the task was to be a role model: to demonstrate and enforce the standards of attitude, dress, performance and behaviour befitting future army officers.

Although the main focus of their final six months was to nail three A levels, exams suddenly seemed less important when Pitcaithly gave word that over a pre-Christmas dinner with the college hierarchy (the first such event ever) Lady Margaret had urged Colonel Hunter to take full freedom to train across the estate. The intention was to encourage mutual recognition and benefit between the college and the estate. As the wine had gone down that evening, the options had gone up, with much merriment on all sides.

Pitcaithly was like a dog with two tails. Following a long lull in security incidents, the previous months had declined into ambivalence and passivity. He had contested in vain that observation-only measures meant skill fade at individual and team level, that nobody would shoot straight or apply tactics effectively if the need arose. Now fate had come to the rescue. Hunter would not dare risk ignoring the gracious invitation of the glamorous, internationally connected multi-millionairess across the lake.

A long-planned visit by the Chief of the General Staff in the second week of January 1988 brought further opportunities. Lieutenant General Sir Martin Brock was the former commanding officer of 22 Special Air Service regiment. Pitcaithly was always mindful that to have an edge unconventional techniques would be required for a truly effective defence of the college, and so he decided that rather than the predictable parade where the general would inspect ranks of boys turning white with hypothermia despite thermals squeezed under their uniforms, the college would perform tactical and physical demonstrations. These would be carefully choreographed to highlight capability and potential which was ripe for new tactical knowledge and innovations, if only they knew where to look. The subtext of this would be how the military staff at Rothwell hoped the borderless college grounds would remain unnoticed as a soft target for an IRA who were stepping up their campaign on mainland Britain. Perhaps a visit from the SAS would inspire the young men to hold the regiment as their greatest career aspiration, as well as serving a practical purpose. Pitcaithly knew the general would see right through his ploy, but hoped he would appreciate the sentiment behind it. While the RSM schemed and connived, college life pressed on as if there was nothing out of the ordinary.

*   *   *

'Guys, you'll need to set up for this one yourselves,' began Mr Campbell, the physics teacher. 'The oscilloscopes are stacked under the cupboards along the far wall. One between three should do it.'

'Standards are slipping, sir,' joked Dom Hughes. 'Mr Tavener stuck in the snow, is he?'

'Mr Tavener is no longer with us. Left a few weeks before Christmas. You mean you didn't even notice?'

No, we didn't notice, thought Bruce. How did we miss that?

'I believe his mother became ill. Maybe things have got worse than he expected. Anyway, it's self-help until we get a replacement.'

Shaun looked across the room at Bruce, now alert to the coincidence. But Bruce was fast becoming a newborn sceptic of coincidence. He felt adrenalin pulse as fantasy ran away with him, contemplating all sorts of random connections and unfathomable possibilities. Relief stayed the madness, however, when he realised that he was being squeezed within the coils of his own imagination. He jolted awake, darting his attention to Shaun who met him with a reassuring slow nod of acknowledgement.

Tavener. What were the odds that he should have featured alongside two ugly events in Bruce's life – by however tenuous an association? Present at Rory's death; absent after his mother's absence. It was an itch that could not be scratched, refusing to go away just as it would not reveal itself to him.

Bruce's thoughts were pushed into the background when General Brock finally arrived, breaking all the rules by using a Scout helicopter from the SAS's dedicated Army Air Corps flight, rather than a standard Gazelle from a regular AAC regiment. And the order included a white-out landing in the snow with an aircraft devoid of engine snow-guards. After all, why should a former SAS officer be concerned about whether a flying Meccano set loses its only engine and turns over during landing? He had experienced much worse than the inconvenience of a helicopter crash.

The general was curious and clearly impressed when he received an answer to his question about how they would proceed with a snow-covered parade square.

'No parade, sir. Demonstrations!' announced Pitcaithly proudly.

The sequence unfolded and the general got to speak with the students, which Bruce guessed he valued more than the bullshit of inspecting boys marching around having wasted hours polishing brass and leather.

For Pitcaithly the hard part was to employ his heavy Glaswegian accent, devoid of conversational niceties, to surreptitiously lead the witness. Indeed, after the third attempt to spark discussion on pulling old regimental strings in the college's favour, he was met with a grimace that made it clear that he should stop insulting his guest's intelligence. Deeply disappointed by his failure, the RSM conceded to following the visit plan without further petitions.

*   *   *

As the weeks slipped by and January bled into February, fresh overnight snow hardened life around the college. Even negotiating the few yards to the science block was a treacherous undertaking. Black leather shoes offered little grip over icy paths and visits to Nurse Eunice climbed as students crashed to the ground with comedic regularity, their books flying skywards. But while bringing perverse amusement by day, the conditions were a distinct liability by night.

Under Pitcaithly's reinvigorated college defence regime, Bruce found himself leading a night clearance patrol exercise. He was to navigate a large anticlockwise route, exiting the college purlieus via the cricket pitch to the south and returning after four hours by the north edge of Winter

Lake. Yet only a few hundred yards outside the estate gates snow began to fall again, and the team of eight slid about clumsily on the slightest uneven ground in their army issue DMS boots.

Bruce had selected a typically clandestine route, seeking cover from view and opportunities to execute snap ambushes amid wooded terrain and natural dead ground – ground hidden from obvious vantage points. They soon reached a large copse in an area favoured by Rothwell's white deer population. A drawback of using woodland, however, was that it increased the potential to make noise as they trod on fallen twigs and branches. It also impeded silent communication between patrol members who could not see each other so easily, even after their eyes had adjusted to the dark. With the aim being to locate, flush out and engage any enemy, walking through woodland also meant that slow, thorough progress was required.

Within the copse the team encountered sections of dense, impenetrable vegetation that forced them to split up. This would afford any enemy in lying-up positions ideal cover from detection. For Bruce this presented a moral as well as a tactical dilemma. He could bypass the tough parts to maintain group cohesion and progress, or he could have them hack their way through to determine that nobody was hiding there. He decided upon the latter, but he knew his strategy would be risky.

Gathering the team into a huddle – a tactical no-no, but now a necessary evil – he speedily issued his orders. 'We advance, W-formation at five-metre spacings. If you encounter a thicket, attempt to pair with the nearest person and clear it. Then continue. Acknowledged that formation will break. Stay on a bearing of three-thousand mils until clear of this wooded feature. Limit of exploitation is edge of open ground to south. Rendezvous southeast corner at 00:45. We wait until 01:00 for stragglers. Thereafter we retrace steps and priority is safety. Main party returns – white light – to locate stragglers in case of injury. It's a training exercise, after all. Clear? Questions?'

A murmur of assent sounded around the group. They spread out and began the task.

After five minutes the first clump of bushes, brambles and gnarled trees presented itself. Bruce scanned right and left to link up, but his team members on either side had already done so with others, leaving him on his own. He spotted Tim Jenkins' hunched figure vanishing into the gloom as he pressed his way into the undergrowth. He had no choice but continue into his own patch alone.

The going was near impossible. He stamped repeatedly just to advance a single foothold, then used his rifle butt and barrel to push into the tangled mass. Eventually the worst of it yielded and he found easier passage through a small space in the middle of the undergrowth. The dense branches all around and fresh snow made for a deathly silence inside. He took a breath. Despite the biting cold, perspiration was running down his back and his scrim net was chafing at his sweaty neck. As he strode out to get through the remaining vegetation, anxious to reconnect with his team, the floor of brambles gave way, his boots slid from under him, and he disappeared into the darkness below.

The blood was warm as it trickled down Bruce's forehead, following the line of his jaw into his parched mouth. His head spun with the cocktail of its metallic taste, the ringing in his ears and searing pain in his left arm. How far he had fallen he could not gauge. The pitch blackness and suffocating silence coincided with a familiar instinct not to act as the situation would suggest. Bruce did not call for help; he stayed still and quiet.

As he calmed, the ringing subsided and the pain softened to a blunt ache and rampant tingling in left shoulder and upper arm. It had to be *that* side, he thought. He shuffled his webbing back into place, bringing his ammunition pouches and knife scabbard into line from their contortions around his back. His rifle was lost. He removed his helmet, extracted his water bottle, took a swig then soaked his hanky and dabbed the blood from his face. Considering what to do next he ran his hand over the uneven rock around him. He resisted the urge to shine his torch. Slowly a heat picture began to emerge. The temperature difference between rock and air was so slight that he could see only the faintest of images, yet he could detect that he was in a narrow, roughly hewn section of tunnel, only wide enough for a single person to pass.

The luminous dial on his military watch read 01:15. He must have lost consciousness for a while. Above him he heard nothing from the others. He put a hand on his radio but chose not to try it. He switched it off. With the cold beginning to slow his mind and seize his body, he decided to seek a way out through the tunnel. He reached for his compass – still attached to its lanyard, thank God – held it clear of any metal about him, and watched the tiny luminous arrow point north. North towards the college. That would be the way out.

Steadily he moved ahead, cautiously trusting his thermal picture but remaining alert lest there be more holes waiting to swallow him up. He kept a close eye on watch and compass – disorientation of distance and direction were all but guaranteed underground. After ten minutes the tunnel widened to the size of a small room, the ceiling appearing to reach higher and away beyond his senses.

Bruce had paused and was taking another drink and sucking on a dextrose tablet, when the distant crunch of grit underfoot reached his ears. The lightest movement of air whispered upon his face, carrying with it an unmistakable and growing stench. It was the stench of decay and death. He edged to one side of the space, not daring to put a foot wrong. He got himself out of the direct line ahead so whoever might be approaching would not see him until they were in touching distance. His heart started like a hammer. Maybe this would be a source of help for him to find a way out, but who on God's earth could it be?

The footsteps grew closer. They were cautious, considered. They made no errors, disturbed nothing bar the ground that must be walked upon. And no light whatsoever. Bruce slid his right hand down to his bowie knife which was resting in its scabbard. He froze, finger poised upon the popper which he now could not release, for it would have clicked loud amid the hush. The footsteps entered the space, walked a few paces past his crouching figure, and halted. The grinding underfoot signalled a slow turning towards him, while the sound of sniffing filled the electric hiss of otherwise total silence. His pulse raced, his mouth and throat dry as paper, sweat beading behind his neck and upon his forehead. Yet despite the crushing fear and slide into his survival instincts, his perception of the thermal picture intensified. The surreal depiction of a humanoid creature emerged as etched lines upon an orange glow. The figure shuffled fully round, leaned in and peered straight into Bruce's face. Bruce stared back, aghast, right into its eyes. It came even closer, its warm breath reeking of decayed flesh clinging to stumps of teeth.

Bruce froze, his finger still hooked around the catch of his knife. The usual compulsion to act, to take the initiative, had abandoned him. He had no control whatsoever, no play to make on whether to treat this being as enemy or friend. Fear had overwhelmed him, making him incapable of movement.

'How do you see me?' the voice shrilled. Bruce recoiled, pressing his back into the wall. 'Nobody ever sees me. How do you?'

'Who are you?' Bruce trembled, finally remembering to breathe again.

A luminous flurry unravelled before him and only at the last instant did Bruce make out the blade coming for him. But too late. The ghoul speared him through an already weakened shoulder, pinning him against the jagged rock.

'Who are you?' roared the voice.

Spittle and fragments of matter spattered Bruce's face, occluding his eyes and mind in the same moment. But the assault had upset the stalemate. He popped the catch, unsheathed the carbon steel Buck and pressed home its long, precise point under his enemy's raised arms and into its torso. The roar turned to an unearthly howl of anguish as Bruce freed himself and barged his enemy to the floor. As never before his life rested on his next moves.

He got to his feet and paced into the tunnel – too dark to sprint – continuing towards the college, whence his attacker came. His sight was weakening but behind him the snarling and scraping of gravel told him what was coming. He scrabbled inside his pouch for his torch, but it was missing. Raising his arms to guide him, he bounced along the tunnel walls.

The steps behind were closing in on him. He kicked something on the floor, something metallic and tubular. Then another. When the magazine broke free and skidded along over the grit he knew it to be a rifle of some sort, but there was no time to fish around and pick it up.

The tunnel remained straight. Ahead was a faint light. As Bruce got closer it began to trace out a much larger space. With his assailant nearly upon him the light suddenly intensified to reveal a huge hall. Bruce broke into a sprint which kept him just out of reach. He entered the hall and headed towards the shaft of light emanating from the open door at the top of steps on the far side. He glanced back as the creature entered behind him; he rushed past a long table, and only then did he connect with the figure of Lady Margaret standing in the doorway, shotgun in hand.

'Move aside, boy!'

The chasing footsteps halted. Bruce darted aside as she raised the weapon to her shoulder, barrels up to her target.

'Get behind me. Quickly!'

Bruce squeezed past her, then turned, trying to see back to what had been pursuing him. Lady Margaret shuffled back into the cover of the door frame.

Then came the voice again. But it sounded like another voice entirely. This being could make all the timbres, tones and pitches of the devil's own orchestra.

'Amulet, what pleasure you afford of me – after all this time.'

Now the intonation was composed, with warm, rounded notes. Seductive.

'Stay back. That's all you have to do.'

'What? No name for me? Don't you remember the name of me?'

'You've been down here too long. Losing the power of speech. Why don't you just free yourself and be gone?'

He started towards her at funereal pace. Her eyes widened in fear. She knew how quick he could be, and how long it took to secure the bolts on the doors.

'Back!'

But he continued. 'And still no name. So sad.'

She brought the gun full into the aim and laid her view along its satin black barrels. He opened his arms and closed his eyes, then strode full at her.

She fired the first shot, then the second.

'Door!' she screamed. 'Bolt it!'

Bruce rushed to secure the door. Through the clearing smoke he looked, dumbstruck, back down the stairs at the smiling wretch, still standing, arms and hands open like Jesus, with hardly a mark upon him.

Lady Margaret dropped the shotgun in a panic, slammed shut the right-hand door, thrust home the bolts and dragged Bruce up the steps and back into the house.

27

'One rescue I call good fortune. Two is suspicious. How do you manage to appear every time I'm in trouble?'

'You're bleeding. Let me see.'

'I need to know. My mother is missing.'

Lady Margaret stopped her attempt to inspect Bruce's shoulder and met his stare. 'What do you mean? I cannot help with your mother. I am sorry about it, of course. But I don't see how it has anything to do with tonight. We haven't time to discuss all this anyway. Won't you be missed by the college? Shouldn't you be somewhere?'

'I need answers. And we need to talk. There are too many things that don't add up, or rather they do – in all the wrong ways, as I see it. What was that thing in there, anyway?'

She paused, holding a handkerchief to his wound. 'When you're fit – next weekend – come to the Woodhouse. But you must not be observed. Take the long way round. Approach through the woods.' Bruce nodded his agreement. 'You must not speak a word of what you have witnessed. That thing is no threat to the college.'

'Apart from stabbing anyone who enters its realm, that is.'

'We need to get you back into the house.'

'I'm starting to feel lightheaded.'

'Then we must hurry. I can't show up at the hospital with you in the back of my car again, as you rightly point out. When you're inside, call for help. They will have to get an ambulance for you.'

'But how do I explain my injuries?'

'Simple. You fell into a hole and were pierced by a splintered branch. Thankfully you found your way back. Your memory is hazy. After all, you're feeling quite lightheaded, are you not?'

'I'm going down this time. I'm destined to be the unluckiest officer in history is what they will think.'

*   *   *

After what he considered to be a sufficient period of time since the disappearance of Jenny Noble-Franks and Jim Tavener, Roger Gleeson made his way light-footed through the estate outbuilding which housed Tavener's ground-floor flat. As he stood outside the door, he scrutinised his collection of key templates, guessed a likely winner, checked around again, and let himself in.

As he had expected, clever Jim had bought time by giving the impression that he would return – he would probably have paid the rent in advance, too. It seemed that the place had not been touched since he had left and the dust had settled thick in the two months after the events in

Bristol. Gleeson knew his search was likely to be in vain, but he hoped that Tavener might have been forced to rush and make a mistake. Either way, he had to check. Otherwise he had no chance of getting back on the man's trail.

It would have been standard practice for Tavener to keep important items and documents packed ready for a rapid exit, so what remained were the remarkably few home comforts that any normal person would view as necessities. Keeping a careful eye on the windows and possible observation from outside, Gleeson started to examine the flat, room by room.

On a drab coffee table lay an open copy of the *Financial Times*. Gleeson peered down at it, spotting where Jim had held the pages, and here and there where a thumbnail imprint might have marked something for later attention. He looked up and around again. Through the crack in the kitchen door he spotted a mug beside the sink. Caught by impulse, he went straight for it. Perhaps Tavener had been in a rush after all. He had ditched the mug's contents but not rinsed them from the stainless steel basin. Residue clung around the plughole. Down the side of the mug ran a gluey streak of black coffee. Gleeson grasped the mug with a gloved hand and it resisted before unsticking from the Formica surface with a soft pop.

Rejuvenated in his purpose, Gleeson set about the place with more thoroughness and determination than he had intended. His thoughts ran hot with the emerging picture as he picked his first target – the internal stud walls. He headed for the bedroom and the built-in wardrobe. Flinging the doors back, he parted the bland jackets used as the deliberate character cover of a lab technician, and started tapping a knuckle down the back wall.

A mixture of frustration and excitement was welling within him. Tavener sat in the middle of a web of connivance and suspicion. He had departed the scene when Jenny Noble-Franks was reported missing – doubtless she was dead, her body never to be found. He was on the ill-fated Snowdon expedition. And after that expedition, on the night that the initial police interviews were held, Jenny would have returned to Bristol along a route placing her close to where two armed men were found assassinated behind a filling station. What was Jim Tavener seeking or protecting that was worth all the killing? The place reeked of conspiracy, yet signs of the source eluded him.

He withdrew from the bedroom and collected his thoughts. Tavener was among the best in the field and nothing important would be hidden in a way that meant it could not be quickly accessed. The only hope lay in the margin of pressured decision-making – that Jim had left something which he considered to be of low value or would soon become outdated and irrelevant. Closing his eyes, Gleeson took a moment to try and think like Tavener, a career spy turned fixer for hire. The man would have built a portfolio of information to allow him to form critical insights and thus penetrate the monolith that Lady Margaret had built to hide a suspected underworld of financial, business and political influence.

Tavener had always advocated modernity. He loved gadgets and working at the cutting edge of technology. Gleeson knew that the only significant development in recent times was a form of microdot which dissolved in water. Any agent in possession of microdots and about to be compromised could easily dispose of them without trace. The word was they could even ingest them to destroy the evidence.

Driven by this hunch, Gleeson checked all the areas in the vicinity of sinks, bath and shower. He figured that all would be in regular use, except perhaps the bath. Tavener would never waste time taking a bath. The build-up of limescale under a slowly leaking cold tap intrigued him. Although the only thing one could hope to find from Jim Tavener would be disinformation – false lines marked out in a newspaper, fake documents hidden behind walls that would lead a merry dance for months of investigators' time – here he could be on to something.

He removed the glove from his right hand and with his little finger gently felt his way up and into the spout of the bath's hot tap. There, hiding in the rough interior of the slightly furred pipe, were the telltale braille lumps fixed upon a square of acetate film. He teased the film free using his nail edge, then bagged it for examination.

He stood up, stared at the tap and shook his head. No time to run the tap, Jim? I doubt that. But we'll play the game all the same and take a look, old friend.

*   *   *

The unexpected blessing that befell Pitcaithly also served to distract Colonel Hunter and Captain Pearce from the latest calamity in young Noble's career. Bruce had resigned himself to a fraught interrogation by the pair, akin to the aftermath of his previous encounter with Jez Picher, but the unannounced arrival in Willis' office of an ex-SAS instructor, courtesy of General Brock, was clearly their priority. Bruce's explanation of events was plausible and his wounds were treatable without recourse to Sheffield General Hospital. Hunter could therefore rest easy and was free to deal with the general's gift in the shape of Barry Wilkes.

The visitor had barely finished introducing himself when Pitcaithly pushed the door open with his shoulder, trying desperately to juggle the stickies piled onto kitchen paper and spirited away from afternoon tea in the dining hall.

'Come on. Somebody grab some of these before the floor has them,' he laughed. Spotting Wilkes, he added: 'Looks like I'm a bun short!'

'Better than being a sandwich short, though. You must be Mr Pitcaithly, the RSM? I'm Barry Wilkes – call me Barry. I have been sent by a mutual friend and recent visitor to Rothwell. The general tells me you folks could use some training support?'

Pitcaithly nearly dropped the lot. He couldn't believe that General Brock had played his hand so well.

'Aye, great that you can join us! Aye, indeed! And it's Gordon, by the way.'

Willis and Pearce resigned themselves yet again to their familiar roles as the sideshow, while Pitcaithly basked in his PR success.

'Is there somewhere I can stow my gear?' asked Wilkes, huge camouflage Bergen rucksack over one shoulder and kit bags in hand.

'Of course, Barry. Please, follow me. Have you accommodation sorted?'

The voices trailed off as they headed out into the corridor.

Wilkes was classically SAS, as far as any stereotype could go that is. What most caught the eyes of folk lucky enough to glimpse into that community was the staggering range of their physical characteristics. Some were mountains of men, enormously broad-chested powerhouses that could haul huge weights and yet move like sprinters. But there were also implausibly small, wiry men, capable of carrying rucksacks full of ammunition weighing hundreds of pounds and who had the sheer aggression and determination to overcome any adversary.

In the middle were the less noticeable ones, like Barry Wilkes. Around five feet nine inches tall and twelve stone in weight, his was a honed muscular build that could bench press twice his weight and carry him through hundred-mile mountain marathons. His sandy hair and boyish but weathered looks suggested a youth, health and strength which belied his fifty years. But the clearest indication of his background was in his eyes. A look into the eyes, even in passing conversation, confirmed a deep inner toughness, aggression and self-belief. It said: *'I shall meet any challenge or die trying.'*

Wilkes was pleased with his accommodation, a spacious self-contained studio unit in the attic of Kitchen Block which allowed in the daylight from dormer windows at front and rear. He made himself comfortable, ready for the next four weeks that had been agreed as the timeframe for him to train the students to defend the college.

'When should we make a start, Gordon? Discuss your situation, requirements and so on?' he began. 'What's best? Do we need a formal session with your military staff?'

Pitcaithly felt a twinge of guilt in indulging his preferred agenda and not including the other military staff.

'May I suggest we discuss matters over a pint and get to the nub of it? That's probably simplest. Then we can decide how to involve others. Sound okay?'

'It's a deal. Pubs any good round here?'

*   *   *

A fixed but scarred Bruce stared back at himself in the mirror on his locker door. A shoulder broken then pierced, an eye cut across. What a mess. He tugged on his tee shirt and prepared for an excursion to the Woodhouse. It was Sunday afternoon.

'What are you up to today, Brucie?' enquired a prying 68 Entry loafer.

'Cleaning out the sports store, if you must know.'

'Ah, right. Good luck with that.'

Yeah, precisely. You don't want to invite yourself to that then? thought Bruce.

After a roundabout wander through the woods, he arrived at the glossy black front door of her ladyship's alternative residence. There they were alone and there was nothing to interfere with the discussion, bar enjoying Earl Grey, dainty sandwiches and Battenberg cake.

Lady Margaret had the challenge of gauging how much to tell Bruce, to satisfy his curiosity and keep him both loyal and silent. For Bruce, the priority was solving the riddle surrounding his absent mother.

'So, Bruce …'

'So …'

She would have to lead.

'How can I be of service?'

'By offering answers to some questions, my lady. For example, do you have any idea what has happened to my mother, who in a strange coincidence went missing about the same time as our shadowy Mr Tavener departed

Rothwell – the same Mr Tavener who was nearest to Rory McIntyre the day Rory died on Snowdon.'

'I am curious about how you mean to connect these events.'

'It was Tavener who nearly caught Rory and me in the tunnels.' Her face darkened. 'Yes, so there it is. Soon after, he ordered a check of boots for everyone going on the exped. I avoided it. Rory didn't. He wore the same boots in the tunnels. If Tavener wanted matching prints he'd have got them. Then Rory had an accident which nobody witnessed.' Bruce paused to force a response.

'The part I am missing is how I am supposed to know about Mr Tavener.'

'I don't know exactly. It's a hunch. But there seems to be a triangle: you, my mother and Tavener. Last year, after the incident with Jez Picher and our exploits in Colonel Hunter's office, I tested the water at home by mentioning your name. Dad didn't bat an eyelid, but my mother . . . she was too cool to be innocent, if that makes sense.'

Lady Margaret didn't reply. Bruce judged she'd got the message and was taking him seriously. She realised he wouldn't be fobbed off. However, the ensuing silence as she slowly circled the living room made him consider for the first time that perhaps there were things she couldn't tell him.

'Let me understand then, Bruce. You have been impacted by very tragic events—'

'Tragic events, plural? We only know that Rory's death could be described as tragic. I still hope that my mother will return, that there will be some explanation for her disappearance. So why do you refer to her situation as tragic, too? Is there something you know?'

Lady Margaret paused again, trying to control him, to rein in his understandable insistence.

'We will have to be mutually respectful, patient and unemotional, Bruce, if you are to get whatever answers I can give. I meant that your mother not being at home – her whereabouts and situation not being known – is tragic.' She waited a few seconds before continuing. 'You have been impacted by events that are most irregular and very disturbing. It would be natural to seek resolution, to make sense of things and even find a value in them – to believe that lives were not lost in vain.'

Bruce eyed her suspiciously but said nothing.

'That might explain how what we perceive as intuition is actually our minds retaining only the information that fits what we want to believe and filtering out the rest.'

'That is an interesting theory, my lady, but I have had some impressive results of late, thanks to my intuition.'

Now it was her turn to scrutinise him. Unlike his hostess, Bruce held nothing back. He described the means by which he discovered the crime scene in Bristol. And going back in time, he told her of his mother's almost unnatural calm when Jez's assault led to his hospitalisation, the curious detour on the way home at Christmas, and the sudden decision to sell their car. It all combined to make recent events harder to pass off as coincidence.

'We have all suffered loss at some time, Bruce. For you this has happened much earlier than we would like. I can only say two things. Firstly, it is my opinion that the longer your mother is missing, the less likely she is to return. You should be open and mindful of the fact. It could hold you up forever if you try to deny it. I'm truly sorry and feel horrid to say such a thing, but if you accept it you won't live your life looking backwards when it's time to look ahead. Secondly, it is also my opinion that time will eventually provide you with all the answers you seek, but you cannot circumvent the process.'

Bruce stared ahead and absorbed the message. It was a cruel irony that his intuition told him just what her cryptic words meant. His emotions collided as so many times before, his heart breaking because she was implying that his mother was probably dead. But – wrapped in disgust and guilt – his heart leaped too. In time, the mystery of his mother and Lady Margaret might come to light, maybe even Tavener's part too. He might even become part of whatever it was himself. Meanwhile, he would have to be patient and get on with his life.

Bruce looked up at her.

'May I have another cup of tea please, my lady? I think I need it.'

'Of course. Allow me.'

'Shouldn't you have assistance for things like this, my lady? Where's your aide. Isn't this the sort of thing he would do for you?'

'It was, Bruce. It was indeed.'

28

Rumours had spread fast about Barry Wilkes. The new boys of 70 Entry were awestruck as they sat on either side of him one lunchtime. It was March 1988.

Their task was, of course, to learn about whatever exploits he would share and what plans he had for the college. Every bit of information would be a form of currency, to be traded with a value bestowed upon the teller as if he were the owner of a copy of *Men Only* in a playground huddle.

Wilkes clearly had little experience in the role of master at a boys' boarding college and the table looked on as Jonathan Price and Steve Higgs, almost too young to shave, fixed him to the spot with their irrepressible grins. Wilkes smiled uneasily in return, eventually realising that it was he who must speak first.

'How are you liking life here then, boys?'

'Did you serve with the SAS, sir?' started young Higgs.

Heads shook around the table as his blundering registered. He flushed.

'Oh, okay . . . well, I'll answer your question first then. It seems to be the issue, after all.'

Wilkes knew well enough that the best way to keep things discreet meant quashing rumour. He advocated openness with responsibility. The boys could know why he had joined Rothwell but as part of the deal they had to respect operational security. Indeed, he himself, steely-eyed Barry, would be the single greatest guarantor of progress. If it was his will then it must be the SAS way, and nobody wanted to fail within the inspiring new regimen that was Barry Wilkes' elite training. His word was pixie dust. All would obey his every utterance absolutely.

'Will we be coached in non-conventional techniques, Mr Wilkes?' asked Price, as the conversation continued over jam roly-poly and custard.

'Perhaps, but first I need to see what you're like with the basics. It's essential to make sure those are solid, otherwise we can't build. There's plenty to go wrong, even in simple tasks. The complicated stuff can come later.'

'Does that mean you're training everyone, sir? I thought the focus was only on a core of older students who were over eighteen and could bear arms in an active rather than a training role,' came another, more senior voice.

'We have yet to make detailed plans, but you're half right. The primary focus is on the seniors, but I intend that everyone else can support that. Everyone needs to be competent. Make sense?' Acknowledgement rippled around as boys on nearby tables strained to listen in.

Lunch ended and the principal led the masters away as students stood in deference to the hierarchy. Wilkes was the last member of staff to exit through the double doors, a throng of boys eager to get ready for the afternoon's CCF activities bursting around and past him like the start of the Grand National. Bruce Noble was not much fussed about CCF these days and when he was jostled in the rush things grew ugly.

'Watch it, you fuckwits!' he yelled, as he lashed out but missed thumping a passing body.

Wilkes turned in surprise to see who was shouting. Bruce avoided his gaze, but that was not Wilkes' way.

'Problem?' he asked.

Bruce let out a heavy sigh. 'No sir.' He continued past Wilkes to the outside, head down.

Wilkes looked to others around him for a response, which came when Bruce was out of earshot.

'A few issues there at the moment, sir,' came the first cautious reply. Wilkes maintained eye contact with the student, continuing to seek information.

A second boy offered, 'His mother went missing. Just before Christmas. Not domestic, I mean. Suspected abduction, word has it.'

'Got it. Thanks. Maybe we cut him some slack then. Not normally like this, is he?'

'No, sir. And you should also know that he lost his closest friend at the college the winter before last. Fell from Snowdon.'

Quiet had descended on this remaining group of five or six students now surrounding Wilkes.

'Right. Well, not so lucky is he, poor kid.'

'And then there was the fight with Picher,' joined the next boy.

'Fights,' corrected another.

'Shut it, you idiots. What do you think Mr Wilkes will make of him if that's all you can say?' said a senior.

Wilkes examined each of their faces, moving swiftly from one to the next, before he turned and strode away.

*   *   *

Over the following weeks military training roared ahead. The guys were eager to prove that they had mastered the basics so they could taste the exotic, and as March passed to April their efforts were rewarded. Having coached, guided and scrutinised a concept of defence developed jointly between the CCF student commanders and the regular army staff, Barry Wilkes invited Arthur Rose, as cadet company sergeant major, to brief the ranks on the plan which would drive the next phases of training. With the entire college CCF mustered in the Great Hall, Art got onto the dais normally reserved for visiting senior officers to take the salute at the passing-out parades.

'You will each be given multiple roles, the tasks fitting your seniority. This is so we can step in for another team member if the need arises, and to keep juniors further from potential harm than more experienced folk. The tip of the spear, if you will, shall comprise students over eighteen who may carry arms combatively.'

From an overhead projector whose images covered the vast end wall, Art outlined the geography and defensive concepts. Detection measures set at a distance on likely access routes were intended to pick up vehicles coming into the estate at such a range that their occupants wouldn't expect to be observed. This early warning system would allow a small core of troops located around the main house – the inner cordon – to be bolstered by a first wave quick reaction force who needed to be at their posts in three minutes flat. The QRF would move into pre-reconnoitred ambush positions and set killing areas on likely infiltration routes beyond the inner cordon. A second wave – the general defence force – would bolster the inner cordon and defend remaining students from attackers attempting to enter buildings.

Art's briefing returned to the training plan.

'For the general defence guys, some will be outwards facing, at extra positions on the roof,' his pointer ran over the image on the wall, 'with your trusty SLRs. The component covering internal access routes and arcs will use SMGs.'

A muted groan echoed among a few who thought the sub-machine gun useless.

Wilkes stepped in. 'What was that? You mean you'd rather have a three-foot long weapon for fighting round corridors? This is close-quarter combat, gentlemen.'

Faces stiffened in the crowd. Art continued to speak. 'Phase One is complete when the QRF is deployed and the general defence force is stood to. What happens next is up to the enemy. The range of possible responses includes aborting their mission on being engaged by a QRF team. However, if all QRF teams miss them or fail to stop their progress we move to Phase Two.'

In its unconventional nature, Phase Two brought the first signs of SAS style. A small, fast-moving enemy with a proper plan could easily outmanoeuvre the QRF teams. It was Wilkes' assumption that they would reach the main house. Rather than chasing around in the wilderness, once out-flanked, the QRF teams would simply fall back to pre-determined positions near the main building. Five such positions were identified, from where the QRF members could fire back towards the college. Combined with sniper pairs on the roof and general defence shooters located in specified windows, all areas at ground level could be covered by observation and fire. Nobody inside would be on the ground floor, and all personnel not tasked to fight would take up safe positions away from windows on the upper levels. That would leave the way clear to fire upon the enemy near the house without undue risk to their own troops.

Art closed the formal part of his briefing. 'Questions?'

A few moments passed without a word from the floor as the information sunk in. Pitcaithly paced slowly along one side of the audience, scanning faces for signs of doubt. Then Wilkes looked up.

'Okay, let me ask this then. What's the hardest, riskiest thing that we haven't covered properly yet?'

A couple of hands went up. He pointed at one of the seniors but Pitcaithly intervened. 'Let's hear from the juniors first. Go ahead, young Prior.'

Charles Prior of 70 Entry was liked by his peers, even if he was unremarkable in stature or charisma.

'Identifying the enemy, sir.'

Wilkes peered back at him. 'Well done, you. Spot on. Identifying the enemy, indeed.' The soft hush of air circulating from the heating grates around the sides of the wooden floor was the only discernible sound in a space containing over a hundred and fifty people. 'Our sensors will only tell us that someone is approaching, someone we should know about but don't. That could be for a host of innocent reasons. So we're going to deploy and fire 7.62 millimetre full metal jacket into them, are we? And inside the building, there you are, a member of general defence, ready with your SMG covering that stairwell. The firing starts outside, then stops. Footsteps approach. The door flies open and … what? After all, it's kill or be killed. So you fire? Are you sure you know who it is?'

Colonel Hunter was watching from the back. His passive expression turned to dark concern as the images came alive.

*　　　*　　　*

It was not until the next Saturday evening began with the arrival of girls from St Imelda's that the college remembered there was more to life than military training. And while the cycle repeated itself, with juniors spying and seniors relishing the occasion, somehow this time it was different. Not least, such events were preferred after exams, not before. But Colonel Hunter sensed the mood. A weariness had befallen his kirk and something was needed to break the pattern, something to provide a contrast to the spartan regime into which every student had thrown themselves under Barry Wilkes' spell. So the decision was taken to hold the dinner dance before the exams, long enough before to allow minds to refocus in plenty of time.

Despite a dark period of introspection harbouring an ever ready anger, Bruce accepted Shaun Dodd's insistence that the evening would do him good. So at last he signed up to attend a social function, which meant that every member of 67 Entry would be there. 68 Entry would lead the defence of the college that night, and thanks to the sway that Barry Wilkes now held at all levels of the college, Colonel Hunter agreed to take the calculated risk of arming the juniors on duty. After all, the plan hung on real deterrence and Barry argued that would be more likely to work with real munitions sending warning shots rather than hapless posturing with empty magazines.

As he stood at his locker, Bruce made a few final checks that he was looking the part, dressed in smart casual attire of open-necked shirt, sports jacket, chinos and desert boots. A last yell from Simon Webb echoed down the corridor telling him that he was both last man out and late.

By the time he reached the crossroads at the end of Chapel Court all he saw was the tail end of revellers winding their way into the dining hall. The Rothwellians had randomly engaged with their guests to escort them into dinner, well, as randomly as natural selection gets, that is. Bruce sauntered up with a creeping sense of detachment, recalling that the guys were out for results. He simply could not be fussed with the inevitable peacocking that would follow.

He stepped into the entrance hall – everyone had gone through to the dining hall and they were now swarming around the temporary bar set up to one side. To Bruce's right the rarely frequented ladies' loo door swung open.

'Oh, bugger it, these things! Probably tucked my dress into my knickers too. Oh—' The tall, elegant and athletic figure could have been a statue of a Greek goddess brought to life in colour and motion, with dulcet tones and a softly perfumed aroma. She wore a fitted above-knee champagne silk dress with graceful folds and twists which coiled to her bust, revealing the perfect lines of bare shoulders and neck. Falling around those shoulders and that neck were long shining waves of auburn hair curving gently round her contours.

Bruce stopped in his tracks, turned to meet the deep brown eyes now fixed upon him, and gave an audible gasp.

'Yes?' she said.

'Er … is anyone escorting you into dinner?'

'Yes.'

'Oh.'

'You are, Bruce.'

'What? I mean, I'd be delighted . . . it'd be an honour, in fact.'

They walked slowly, reluctantly, towards the hall, as if from that very instant preferring each other to the formalities to come. The noise swelled when they finally crossed the threshold, heads turning to check the outcome of the final pairing. Bruce had to raise his voice to be heard.

'How do you know my name? Did someone mention me?'

'No, but I never forget a voice. Camelia Gordon, remember me? From last term. You were outside, hiding in a bush with a view of nothing and a very big rifle, as I recall.'

'That's impressive. Yes, how could I forget? You're the only girl I've ever spoken to at this place. Drink?'

Bruce slipped into the evening, forgetting his woes and intoxicating himself with her wonder. The natural mechanisms that must be at work, he thought, were fascinating. It was as if people could detect their compatibility in moments. She could have walked away the instant she discovered him. But no. First there was inquisitiveness – she started a conversation with him; next there was the development of the dialogue, and finally the commencement of a relationship, if only by way of exchanging names. Tonight they were engrossed, after an entirely chance meeting, which signalled a compatibility after very few words were spoken.

'Nice scar, by the way,' said Camelia, peering at the scored flesh around Bruce's left eye. 'How did you get that?'

'Ah, courtesy of a friend. And not much helped by a later accident.'

'Dear me, some friend. But it does give you a certain …'

'Ugliness?'

'Aura.'

Bruce avoided talking about deceased friends and abducted mothers. Instead he delighted in hearing all about Camelia, beautiful, understated, enigmatic Camelia. The evening slipped by apace and in no time it was the end of the dessert course. The moment the lemon cheesecake and cream had been consumed, the pattern of bodies disappearing through all available exits began. It was almost comical, like a playground game. As the numbers remaining in the hall reduced, the risk of detection by the supervising masters rose. When a critical mass had vanished the staff got to their feet and moved to guard the doorways, linebacker style. Bruce and Camelia were, once again, late.

As the final few pairs bungled their attempts to outmanoeuvre the hall police – there was Carl Loevenger having his attempt at 'She doesn't feel well and needs air, sir' being scuppered by the offer of a visit to nurse – Bruce noticed again how the flow of events could work both for and against you. When they should have had no hope of escape, the final panicked rush by others meant Bruce and Camelia realised they could walk straight out through the kitchens. Both stopped talking. They glanced around, mainly as a momentary distraction to buy thinking time. She turned and faced him.

'Shall we?' said Bruce.

They rose and swept across the empty dance floor and out of sight, like ghosts.

The idea of attempting intimacy among the mud and leaves of the nearby undergrowth left them mutually under-whelmed, so they picked their way past the tipsy whispers and hushed chatter of tentative new lovers to reach the perimeter road. From there Bruce knew of the perfect place to be alone.

He was mindful that venturing too far away from the house could cause real problems. Entering any ambush site or identified killing zones might start a panic among the stand-in defence team and make it impossible for the masters to sustain their good humour. Instead he led

Camelia through the darkness of the assault course, past the rear of Kitchen Block and up to the squash court. Not only did he know the code to the door's Simplex lock, but he also knew how to reset it so nobody could follow. In any case, darkness and drunkenness would deter any sustained attempts by others to gain entry. Once inside Bruce kept the lights off and guided Camelia upstairs to the viewing gallery.

'Our eyes will adjust soon. Sorry, but otherwise we will have no peace,' he whispered.

'That's fine. In fact, it's quite romantic, don't you think?'

'I guess, but thinking that you will be gone so soon is already making me sad. And in our few moments alone together I don't get to see you clearly. You are beautiful, Camelia. What else is there to say?'

'I'm not really,' she sighed.

For a few moments they said nothing. As their eyes adjusted to the dark the outline of the corrugated plastic skylights became faintly visible, creaking when the outside breeze moved across them. Suddenly the sense of emptiness in the room had gone. Bruce felt the warmth of her breath closing upon him as she sealed her lips to his. They slid to the carpeted floor in an embrace and their intimacy deepened.

'Do you have …?'

'Yes,' replied Bruce. 'Presumptuous, I know.'

'Prepared is another word. And why shouldn't you be?'

He fumbled around with it, with her – his first time. She continued to kiss him tenderly but Bruce felt the events of the day, the week, his whole run of tragedy at this place, all conspire to overtake him.

'Damn it!' he exclaimed.

She said nothing but stayed engaged with him, patiently.

'I'm sorry, sorry, Camelia. I don't know why … it's just no good.'

'Shush,' started her soft words of empathy. 'It doesn't matter, it just doesn't matter. I have lost myself in you tonight, Bruce. It has been very special. Let's just lie together while we still have time.'

He put his head back to the floor and slid his arms closer around her. With one hand he smoothed his open fingers through her hair.

'You're amazing, you know that? Most boys would probably act like idiots if they knew about my, well lack of performance tonight, like it's a failure and stuff. But . . . is it you or all girls? You are so far ahead of us boys. So mature about it. We have so much to learn from you. Thank you, Camelia.'

They basked in the moment.

For Camelia, his self-awareness and touch shared equal potential. It was rare to have somebody so focused on her, so sensitive and open.

'My middle name is Jane, by the way. My friends call me CJ.'

'CJ . . . that's nice. Camelia Jane. Sweet name.'

Below, the inevitable stabbing at the keypad and twisting of the door handle began. Muffled voices, occasionally punctuated by the odd expletive, signalled someone failing to input Bruce's new door code.

'Ignore it. We'll just have to wait here until they go away,' he said. 'Hopefully they'll give up soon,' he continued, exasperated as the door came under growing assault.

'My, my . . . someone is very needy,' she giggled, as the struggle with the lock went on.

'Christ, we'll be here all night at this rate!'

29

'Dragon Two: standby; Dragon One: go!'

Tavener released the Pressel switch on the secure radio and rubbed his eyes. *Let's light this place up and see what's what!* he thought. He reached for the binos to watch from the vantage point selected to observe his operation – the college cricket pavilion.

The pair in the Range Rover swung into the eastern estate access road which led to Obelisk Drive. The passenger jumped out, cropped the chain and opened the gate. They sped on towards their target. After Dragon One had covered the first of the two miles to the college, Tavener sent Dragon Two into action. This pair ploughed their way in from the west, along the main entrance route past the garden centre. The *No Entry* signs would be ignored by these visitors.

At an observation point near the Cadogan Obelisk two boys were watching the road.

'Hello Zero. This is Recce Three. Vehicle approaching at speed along Route Meridian. Dark all-wheel drive. Range Rover, I think. Over.'

'Zero. Received. Stand by.'

In the command cell set up in Willis' office in Kitchen Block, call sign Zero, the mood turned electric. In charge was Tom Warren, a 68 Entry student and son of a senior infantry officer.

'Jenks, get on the net and do a radio check with Recce One and Two.'

'On it.'

'Gen Three, illuminate the barrier lights. QRF Three, eyes on Objective Stone.'

On the far side of the bridge dividing Winter Lake and Serpentine Lake stood a small checkpoint – a single-bar barrier with signs instructing drivers to stop and dim headlights; ten metres away was a low-level sandbagged defensive position occupied by two sentries. This was Objective Stone. The pair inside followed procedure and cocked their SLRs.

'Hello Zero. This is Recce One. Unrecognised vehicle heading along Route Triad. It's shifting! Gone straight past the cottages. Heading your location. Black four-wheel drive. Over.'

'Zero. Roger. Out.'

The radio net crackled and fell silent. The faces of the radio operators turned to Tom.

'George, deploy QRF One to cover Chapel Court and the Mall. Jonesie, I want Gen Two over to the dining hall. Make sure everyone's inside, lock it down. Hard target.'

'Yes, Tom!' came the eager replies.

'And someone get upstairs and grab Wilkes.'

The net reignited. 'Zero, Gen Three on Objective Stone. Vehicle closing . . . slowing ... our location now . . . he's put his lights down.'

Against protocol, the radio operator held his transmit switch down so that the command cell could hear everything. Next to him, his buddy called out: 'Turn your engine off and step out of the vehicle!' He listened for a response, as the engine idled.

Inside the Range Rover the two men had to make a rapid decision.

'They have weapons.'

'It's just for show. They're only boys – second team tonight, he said. Not old enough to carry live ammo, remember. Anyway, this is what we're here for, you idiot. So drive!'

The engine erupted, powering the vehicle towards the barrier.

'Down!'

The boys took cover as the car smashed the wooden pole aside and careered towards the bridge.

'Zero, you get that? Over.'

'QRF Three. Target on Stone. Destroy.'

Gasps circled around the command cell.

'Repeat. Destroy.'

'Three. Roger. Out.'

Inside the dining hall the noise from the party was drowned by attack alarms – hand-held air horns sounding around the college. Outside, frantic footsteps were hurrying en masse through the undergrowth towards the hall.

On the opposite side of the main house, QRF Three was ready in its firing position in the rose garden. Its commander, Geoff Kirkman, followed the sequence for what was one of the more familiar rehearsed scenarios.

'Gun Group, lone vehicle approaching Killing Area Bravo. *Rapid* …'

He waited for the vehicle to appear on the bridge. First came the climaxing roar of the V8, then headlights breaking the crest burst into view. It had such momentum that it couldn't turn onto the perimeter road but slewed onto the grass bordering the cricket outfield.

'… *fire!*'

Two general purpose machine guns opened up with one-in-two tracer rounds. The red fluorescence caused by the ignition of every second bullet's tip as they flew allowed the firers to observe their fall of shot in the dark.

The rounds shredded the vehicle, setting it alight and stopping it near dead. Glass shattered, metal splintered and tore like tinfoil, bullets ricocheted into the distance like lasers in a video game. The engine cut out, leaving only the lame sound of flat tyres squelching their final few yards on mud punctuated by deafening cracks of gunfire. Underneath the Range Rover a blinding white light erupted as the magnesium in the chassis started to incinerate.

Geoff let the guns continue to fire. He wanted to be sure that the bodies convulsing in their seats would die quickly and not in the flaming carcass that was engulfing them.

Twenty seconds later the thunder of gunfire ceased and its last echoes faded into silence.

'Zero, QRF Three. Target destroyed. Over.'

'Roger. Secure and observe for further hostiles. Out.'

Barry Wilkes burst through the door of the command cell.

'Situation?'

'Unidentified vehicle broke through the bridge checkpoint at speed. It rammed the barrier, sir. It has been destroyed in Killing Area Bravo,' replied Tom.

Wilkes gave him an anxious look. 'Destroyed?'

'Sir.'

'Who was inside?'

'Two hostiles. Not identified, sir.'

'Hostiles? How did—'

Wilkes checked himself as the radio speaker spat out the next transmission.

'Zero, Gen One. Vehicle on Triad isn't going to stop. He's crashed the gate!' The sounds of bodywork shattering wood once again rang out in the background. 'Now heading along main drive to college.'

Tom looked to Wilkes, unsure of who would lead. Wilkes nodded, his face serious.

'Still yours, Tom. Doing fine.'

'QRF One, dark coloured four-wheel drive approaching your location at speed. Neutralise. Over.'

'QRF One. Roger. Out.'

Wilkes bolted out of Kitchen Block and into Chapel Court. As he ran, he drew his SIG P226, swiftly pulling and releasing the working parts to put a round in the chamber. The vehicle appeared on the final straight of the main drive, lights ablaze to dazzle anyone trying to take aim.

Fifty yards ahead he could just make out the concealed team members of QRF One on either side of the crossroads at the end of the drive. The four-by-four was closing fast, its engine screaming, spitting driveway stones from under its huge tyres. He sprinted towards the scene, passing the end wall of the courtyard and darting to one side for cover twenty yards behind the QRF.

QRF One commander Anthony Kemp gave his fire-control order: 'Numbers Three and Four: enemy vehicle to front. Two rounds, deliberate … *fire!*'

Four shots rang out in close succession. Two found the vehicle. One penetrated the windscreen, the other extinguished a headlight. Steam started from under the bonnet but the Range Rover continued at full speed.

'What's the boy doing?' Wilkes muttered. 'Give the bloody follow-up!'

Kemp was transfixed by the rush that was now upon them. No words came. Target fixation turned to paralysis. Barry recognised it. The car braked and slid past them, then made a right turn along the perimeter road towards the Mall. As it slowed to turn, Wilkes emptied his pistol into the side windows. Helmets of the QRF ducked in panic as the rounds punched into their target, but the intruders pressed on unscathed.

At last Kemp found his voice.

'QRF One. Vehicle has beaten us. Heading Mall. Over.'

Tom Warren's cool words continued, this time addressing the sniper team overlooking the Mall: *'Destroy!'*

Atop the parapet of the main house, Chris Brown shuffled to settle his stance. He took a deep breath and released it halfway out, switching his focus back and forth from the precise point of aim in the nightscope to the peripheral view of the whole scene. He decided where he would intercept the target if it approached the house.

It looked suicidal. Tyres squealed, announcing the wild swing onto the Mall. Before the vehicle could rebuild speed as it straightened up, Chris released his first shot. Developed from types used in winter Olympic biathlons, his long-barrelled rifle fired a high-charge 7.62mm round and was intended for single targets at very long range – six to nine hundred metres. Despite facing a moving target, the bullet hit the driver's centre of mass. The vehicle began to veer towards the corner of the Oxford wing which bordered the parade square. The rifle's weakness, however, was that it was bolt-operated. Chris had to reload as fast as his hand would allow. Trembling, he rushed.

'Fuck! Jammed the fucking case in the breech!'

'On it.'

Beside Chris was his back up, Alastair Lewin. He opened up with his SLR on the slowing Range Rover, a succession of rapid single shots puncturing the bodywork. From the passenger window a machine gun burst into life, spraying a score of bullets into the stonework in front of them and through the first floor windows below.

'Shitting Uzi!'

The boys dropped their rifles onto the broad parapet in a frantic dash for cover.

Below them the driver's door opened and a body was ejected. The vehicle's engine bellowed as it U-turned back up the Mall, steam billowing from the engine compartment.

'Report. Any contact call-signs. Report. Over,' Tom's voice hissed in their ear pieces.

Chris nodded to his backup. 'That's you, dummy.'

'Zero, Hawkeye. Target has gone. Via the Mall and towards the workshops. One times enemy lying on Mall. Over.'

*　　*　　*

'It's stopped. The firing's stopped. We'd better get back to the dining room. That's where they'll want us to gather,' Bruce whispered.

'Are you certain? What if it's still going on but nobody's firing?'

'We have to take a gamble, I guess. If we all congregate reasonably quickly then the masters won't take such a bad view of everyone's absence.'

'What? Are you mad? You mean take a gamble just so the teachers don't properly lock the place down and prevent future generations of Rothwellians from getting their leg over?'

'One has to think of his fellow man,' Bruce chuckled as he watched her reaction in the darkness. 'Shaking your head in disapproval is understandable, but I really do think it's over.'

They made their way down the narrow staircase towards the exit, Bruce leading.

'Hang on a moment, Bruce Noble. How did you know that I shook my head?'

But her challenge was deflected by the blast of an air horn and shouts summoning any absent seniors and their guests to the dining hall.

The scene inside was chaos. The soft disco lighting was obliterated by bright main lights under which there was nowhere to hide muddy knees, dishevelled hair and various states of undress. Red eyes screwed tight against the glare, and sweaty, flushed faces, swaying bodies, the occasional burp, the odd uncontrolled fart and a persistent odour of alcohol in the air confirmed that all hope of honour was lost.

'What a b-lood-y shower!' Pitcaithly strode in and took control before any of the masters could say a word. 'Roll call! Where's young Hepburn? Come on, Head Boy.'

'Sir, but surely 68 Entry should be handling this? I mean, we've all had a few to drink.'

'68 has handled the terrorists very well, thank you,' Pitcaithly snapped. 'Just because you're on a social doesn't mean you're off duty. The enemy will happily kill you under both circumstances. And anyway, between area defence and fire duties, 68 are fully tied up right now.'

Shocked looks were exchanged between Paul Kelly, Lancaster housemaster, and the history teacher Mark Fisher.

Pitcaithly sought to reassure them.

'Just a small fire and some burst pipes in the main house. The fire's out, but it's a bit of a mess in there.'

*   *   *

James Tavener put down the polystyrene cup of black tea he had made in the darkness of the cricket pavilion and sat, leg crossed ankle-upon-knee, looking over the scene through the broad windows of the upper level. He had tested and proved many assumptions. One: Hunter had indeed decided to go it alone. He had put live weapons in the hands of students – even a reserve team – and they were man enough to use them. Two: any doubt about how Lady Margaret would protect the vault had been further reduced, if not altogether eliminated. She had made no effort to reach the main house during the assault. Therefore the vault's main entrance must be secure – no one with sufficient explosives to blast their way in would have sufficient time to place and detonate them without challenge. Colonel Hunter would protect her estate as part and parcel of protecting his college. The flooding option must be a fallback plan – albeit crazy – should she be forced to open it at gunpoint. Perfect. And, finally, three: triggering the college's defence plan, including planned collateral damage, meant that both police and military authorities would be all over the place for months. Hunter would never again be able to instigate armed defence of his college – if indeed he even remained as principal – if indeed he was not court-martialled first.

A good night's work, Tavener thought, as he afforded himself a tot of '53 Hine cognac. The substitution of its native Baccarat crystal decanter with a silver hip flask was both a field operative's necessity and a privilege on such occasions. He slid the last drops down, savouring their Grand Champagne hot velvet edge before slipping out through the waiting window and away into the night.

30

Lady Margaret had never felt so alone. And so deeply sad. From the window of the master bedroom at the Woodhouse she lowered her binoculars from the desperate vision of men burning to death on her lawn, entombed in their metal coffin. Men sent to rob her? To kill her? No, worse. To rampage through the annals of an ancient society that had saved the world through the centuries. All courtesy of Mr James Tavener, no doubt.

Lucien Martell was now her only connection to the organisation, and he had departed months ago. Without Roberts she had no one to share her thoughts and fears with. The innumerable practical chores he had undertaken were another, but now very much secondary, burden. Human contact, trust and protection were what she craved.

The organisation had faced great peril many times before. Once found out, once access was gained and identities uncovered, its enemies would eliminate the membership in a clandestine global spree of throat slitting. Either entire families would be murdered, or husbands, wives, friends or lovers would wake to find terror and tragedy lying beside them in crimson sheets.

But to reach out now was to run the very risk that had brought her to this point. Globalisation, in its many forms, had stepped ahead of the ancient order. To act, to move, to communicate could today be a precipitous act. The organisation's enemies could now more easily detect the patterns and join the dots. And wealthy worldly-wise philanthropists who attempted to maintain low public profiles and did not play like mainstream plutocrats created most curiosity of all. The temptation to pick up the telephone, send the facsimile, the coded letter to call the cavalry via London, Paris, New York gnawed at her very soul.

Tavener was in the driving seat now. Any call to arms could just open the wound wider and give greater access to the soft belly of her community. For they were, by conviction, peace-seekers, who most often rescued mankind from the impending catastrophes of the day. No, she was alone. Only she could find a way to outlast the danger and conjure a next generation to take up the quest. Such thoughts churned through a sleepless night, made worse by the knowledge that others were fighting the battle for her. Yet she could only keep her distance as the college fought their common enemy to the death.

At mid-morning the next day she drove her tatty Volvo estate onto a Mall full of police vehicles and tradesmen's vans. College staff, including the usual cast of principal, housemasters, regular army staff and all manner of secretarial and maintenance support, flitted here and there, escorting investigators and ferrying files and pots of tea.

Amid the chaos she stood in the drizzle to contemplate the torn face of her ancestral home. Windows had been shattered in the dormitories above the banqueting hall. One bore the scorch marks of fire from curtains somehow ignited by bullets or bombs. To the right, further missing panes led the eye to trickles of water running down the pitted stonework.

She pressed ahead, through the college's side door and into the entrance hall. Colonel Hunter hurried out of his study, accompanied by a police chief inspector. The pair were deep in conversation and when he momentarily caught her eye she waved him on his way, signalling: Don't worry about me for now, Malcolm.

On the first floor she was relieved to see that only a few rooms were damaged. But what damage! It was hard to conceive how college students, having suffered an armed assault, could have taken control of the fire so quickly and with such rudimentary equipment. The fire piquet used a large cart with heavy spoked wooden wheels pulled by manpower alone. Upon it hung hoses, nozzles, ropes, axes, wrenches, sand buckets and ladders. Like its surroundings, it was antiquated in design and inadequate in an age of high technology. Yet somehow it did the job.

Dorm One with its wood-panelled walls was now a charred, blackened sarcophagus. Fragments of incinerated curtain material hung in shreds from the spindly remains of their supporting poles. Window panes had been affected by the heat in varying degrees: some had shattered, others cracked, a few were intact with frames showing signs of distortion. A pair of thick canvas hoses trailed from outside up the final steps and lay by the door, their nozzles in a pool of water like snakes drinking from a pond. A cluster of discharged fire extinguishers stood beside them.

Next door, in the first of the Lancaster House dormitories, the water to a pipe holed by a stray bullet had been turned off. Pale green fleur-de-lys wallpaper was peeling away and rolling to the floor in great sheets. The room was soaked; the sopping grey-blue carpet squelched underfoot and water seeped through the gaps in the floorboards to the rooms below. Lady Margaret prodded the floor with her walking cane, idly inspecting the sodden remains of a classic car magazine that had been cast aside in the furore before the gunfire started. The cane was a temporary and symbolic physical support, a substitute for absent moral support. Its polished ebony shaft was adorned with a silver spike at its end, while the handle bore a silver casting of a centurion's head.

Two juniors passed by, their arms loaded with clean laundry. It was ten thirty. In the upheaval wrought by the attack, the housemasters' wives, who managed the laundry service as well as acting as mothers to any boy down at heart, had decided to get the replenished stocks out a day early. The clear-up meant Sunday chapel was cancelled.

All efforts centred on the restoration of order and sufficiency.

'Excuse me, gentlemen. I was wondering whether anyone was hurt in last night's trouble?' Lady Margaret asked them.

The boys turned to each other, wondering who would reply. Eventually the smaller lad looked up: 'Whose mum are you, may I ask?' Aghast, the second quickly hissed 'No!' under his breath. The first started to blush.

'Ah, well, I am Lady Cadogan-Brandt. I am just visiting to find out what happened – that everyone is fit and well.'

The bigger lad jumped in: 'There's nobody injured that we know of, ma'am. Those not on duty retreated—'

'Withdrew,' the first boy corrected.

'Withdrew inside the building away from windows and stuff, so out of harm's way. But thank you for asking—'

'Checking.'

'Checking . . . eh? Oh, do shut up, Giles.'

Lady Margaret couldn't contain the grin that spread across her face at the comical pair of fresh-faced youths trying to say the right thing.

'Thank you, gentlemen. I am much relieved,' she said and continued on her way, deeper into the house.

It was undeniable that however great the military expertise responsible for the decisive results that night, they had all fallen foul of the timeless maxim that nobody considers the aftermath. The police response alone threated to derail the tightly packed college curriculum. It would soon be exam season and the Great Hall where examinations would be sat was the main police incident control centre. Other areas were also commandeered so that the whole machinery of gathering and documenting evidence – samples, exhibits and witness statements – could proceed swiftly. The situation was made worse by a media invasion that clogged roads with all manner of vehicles and reporters with camera crews seeking to access all areas and any potential witnesses.

After a few days the bow wave of criminal investigation ceded to repair and recovery work. The burnt shell of the four-wheel drive was removed from the cricket outfield and only singed grass, mud impregnated with melted and twisted fragments of metal, and sticky rubberised oily deposits bore testament to the lives that had ended there.

By Friday, six days after the attack, the police presence had dwindled to just two officers acting as liaison to the final few returning investigators eager to complete their business. They had been increasingly replaced by all types of tradesmen. The college staff sought to manage as much of the recovery effort as possible to minimise their embarrassment over the collateral damage to Lady Margaret's estate. At least that was how they saw things. But when it came to the more complex, sensitive or expensive surveys and repairs, there was no choice but to consult her. It was reported that water had penetrated the electrical supply to the silver room. When the fire service inspected the house and declared all fires extinguished, they had ordered that power be cut to that area to prevent the risk of electrical arcing and reignition. The silver room relied upon dehumidifiers to slow the onset of corrosion, oxidation and general deterioration. Now a proper inspection was required, and Lady Margaret was asked to attend.

Waiting in the hall were Colonel Hunter, stores manager Ted Grainger in his other role as head caretaker, and Mr Carmichael from Hoves and Brown electrical contractors. Hunter outlined the situation to Lady Margaret. She listened carefully and when he finished talking she looked at the others.

'Mr Carmichael, Mr Grainger, would you kindly excuse us? Just for a moment please?'

They slid away without a word.

'Malcolm, this is an unusual situation for me, to state the obvious. I am of course grateful for your sterling efforts, both in protecting the student body as I have said before, and now in the college's endeavours to make good the very unfortunate damage. Normally I would have my own support to confirm that plans were in order, people verified and so on.' He nodded sympathetically and continued to give his undivided attention. 'So please excuse what some might consider as leaning towards impertinence if I ask you about who you have hired for the various works.'

'Please, my lady. This is your estate. Ask anything.'

For an intense few minutes the questions and answers flowed back and forth. Some things needed to be checked – he would task Miss Hamble to confirm the outstanding details. All the while, Lady Margaret tried to suppress her deep longing for Roberts to be at her side, a longing made worse now it was clear just how difficult it would be to verify outsiders as trustworthy and not planted by potential enemies. Finally, she accepted the inevitable: trust would have to yield to risk. That this logic would apply to a situation likely created by Tavener sent a chill down her spine.

Past the entrance hall, outside the principal's office, was a sturdy and ornately carved pair of dark wooden doors. Always locked, they marked another internal house boundary between college and estate. Nobody ever went through them. She took two large iron keys from the pocket of her Barbour and unlocked the doors.

'Please wait here while I open the strongroom. I will return straightaway.'

The silver room had a small single door of thick steel secured by two key-operated locks and a hefty rotary combination device. It took a couple of minutes to successfully dial in the five digits, such was the accuracy required with the numbered dial that she never managed it first go. She returned to the three men waiting for her.

'This way, gentlemen,' she said, leaning for a second on her walking cane.

The trio shuffled along the dusty flagstones of the short dark corridor to the entrance near the end on the right. It was barely wide enough for a grown man to step through without having to turn sideways, and most would have to crouch slightly. Carmichael was invited to enter first: he had the lamp. He ducked, crept in and carefully swept the beam around inside.

'Oh my!' he exclaimed, unable to suppress his reaction.

'Didn't you say that the electrical lines ran through from the ceiling, Mr Carmichael?' Lady Margaret asked as his light wavered and flickered over the shining mass of candlesticks, salvers, goblets and jewellery boxes.

Like so much around the house and estate, first appearances could often be a veneer, a distraction from the true function beneath. So it was with the silver room. The modest door suggested a space the size of an average larder, but once inside the internal geometry defied expectation. The store extended for thirty yards ahead and ten yards across. Narrow walkways ran off a central aisle between sections of shelving filled with all kinds of silver ornaments and creations. The sight was a spectacle by itself. It took a while for the realisation to dawn, however, that what made it so striking was the absence of any other precious metals, certainly no gold.

Carmichael forced himself to focus on the task and cast his light to the ceiling in search of cabling. He spotted a pair of steel conduits routed along the top of a wall behind some high shelves and traced them along the room.

'There don't seem to be any problems so far,' he said.

The conduits turned at the end wall and descended into two dehumidifier units. Each had a fan a foot in diameter mounted in front of cooling vanes and a heat exchanger. Carmichael flashed the beam onto the right-hand unit.

'Ah, this could explain things.'

The actuator beside the fan had burnt out. On closer inspection he discovered the cause.

'There's something jammed behind the fan blades. Wait a moment ...'

He wrestled with the contraption, squeezing his right hand in to retrieve the item.

'Is that safe ... what you're doing?' Hunter asked, anxious to avoid any more injuries.

'It's fine, as long as nobody turns the power back on.' Carmichael winced as he pulled a small object out of the fan. 'There it is.' Turning to face them, he held up the broken shaft of a small screwdriver. 'What do we make of this then? There's no sign of water entering this room, you see. This is what caused the fuse to blow in the main board, which must be why the fire boys thought water had got in.'

'Well, it's irregular, and maybe that's a matter for her ladyship and the police, but at least you appear to have found the cause, Mr Carmichael. Good work,' said Hunter.

Lady Margaret felt her skin start with cold perspiration at the notion that the silver room had been infiltrated. Tavener knew the code and she was furious with herself for not changing it.

Carmichael continued, 'It will need a replacement electrical unit – and who knows how old this one is, begging your pardon, my lady.'

'No need for niceties, Mr Carmichael. Is there anything we can do while a replacement is sought?'

'I can disable this one so we can get the power back on and just run the other unit. Not ideal but better than nothing.' She nodded her agreement. 'Okay, I'll pop out to the van and fetch some tools then.'

The minutes ticked by. Hunter felt obliged to make polite conversation to pass the time, but Lady Margaret was of an entirely different mind and made little reply. The notion that Tavener was on the loose and had delivered his first treachery was haunting her. It was as if a phantom were watching her right there, from the gloomy recesses of the silver room itself. And now it taunted her: this place was known, its security broken. But why? Nothing quite fitted. The night attack had threatened lives, caused collateral damage, but had got nowhere near the silver room or the vault, and ultimately it had failed. Events didn't add up.

Carmichael's absence was becoming hard to ignore. Ted Grainger decided this was his matter to sort out and he set off to see what was keeping the man.

'Is there no one else who can keep watch while this room is open, my lady?' Hunter asked.

'There usually is, Malcolm, but today, alas, no.'

'I can nominate one of my staff, perhaps, if that would assist?'

'That is very considerate, but it would only take one item to go missing and that poor individual would be in a difficult position. I simply cannot ask that.'

At last footsteps were audible on the flagstones outside the room. Hunter gave in to his impatience and strode into the corridor to find out what the holdup was about. Lady Margaret looked on from inside, watching his profile framed in the small doorway. That was when the first pair of silenced pistol shots shattered Hunter's head into a mess of blood and bone. His corpse pitched forwards and thudded to earth as empty brass cases tinkled musically upon the cold stone floor.

She froze, breathless, her eyes struck with terror. Around the door appeared a hulking masked man, his head covered with a black balaclava, his gun trained at her chest. Behind him another figure passed by in the corridor, weapon pointed ahead.

The first man marched up to her, grabbed the hair at the back of her head and pressed the muzzle of the silencer to her mouth, splitting her lip.

'You're coming with us.'

His voice was calm, deliberate, and carried a rough-edged Italian accent.

'Move!'

He thrust her out through the door. She resisted his attempt to push her along the corridor, resting her weight upon the walking cane.

'What's this? What's wrong with you? Any fucking hold-ups and I'll end this job early.'

'I can't go quickly. It's an old riding injury,' she pleaded.

'That's not what I've been told.'

He looked to his accomplice. 'Now!'

The second man drew the pin from the grenade and rolled it along the corridor back towards the hallway. Taking an arm each, the pair dragged her away, round a corner to the old kitchen and the set of steps which ran down to the tunnels. As they started their descent the grenade exploded behind them, sending great shards of wood, sparks and thick smoke in all directions. Another fire to put out, she thought. But would she live to see it done?

*   *   *

As the deafening sound of air horns echoed through the corridors outside their study, Shaun spun round to look at Bruce.

'What? That's …'

'The attack alarm,' said Bruce. 'Again. And it was real enough last Saturday.'

Mr Cowley's voice carried down the corridor in between alarm blasts: 'Everyone, stay in your studies until we give the all-clear!'

Bruce peered round the door to see Cowley heading away to spread the word around Lancaster House. When the coast was clear he tiptoed out to his locker to retrieve the items he required. At first Shaun couldn't believe what Bruce was doing, but then he remembered: this was Bruce Noble. He stayed his compulsion to hiss words of incredulity and watched as Bruce thrust the katana in its scabbard through his trouser belt, stuffed throwing discs into jacket pockets, slung a bow across his back and chest and grabbed a handful of steel-tipped arrows. He couldn't resist what he saw as an essential piece of advice, however.

'In those shoes, Bruce?'

Bruce looked down at his tired black day shoes. 'Thanks.' He swapped them for his combat boots with their cheat's quick zipper fastenings. 'Tell Art I'm tunnel bound,' he proclaimed. Shaun gave him a quizzical look. Bruce provided the necessary clarification: 'Ah, yes, section under the lake.'

'With your non-bulletproof college uniform, combat boots and ninja gear?'

Shaun raised his eyebrows mockingly, but Bruce responded with a dismissive tilt of his head and pursed lips.

'Joking aside, Bruce, how does the sound of the attack alarm lead you to disobey a clear instruction risking, again, expulsion – but this time you are now only weeks away from exams – and conclude that medieval weaponry is required against an unknown foe, who is somehow supposed to be in the tunnels under the lake?'

Bruce grimaced, pausing to consider his words.

'You wouldn't believe me if I told you.'

'On the contrary, I'm probably the only person who would. Sweet dreams, were they, Bruce?'

'Dreams? Perhaps. And perhaps the consideration that last weekend's assault was obviously, deliberately misguided – men equipped and trained but sent to their slaughter. Why? Deception and complication: to get us thinking it's all over and to have this place swarming with cops so nobody will be bringing out the guns again. All of it was a cover for the real action, which I believe is happening now. The intention is not to kill us, nor to steal priceless artefacts. It's to get something else. And whatever it is, there's a specific location where it's kept.'

Shaun said nothing and regarded Bruce thoughtfully.

'Did you hear the word that went around earlier about her ladyship arriving on site?' Bruce continued. 'It's rather a coincidence that the only person with access to all areas should turn up just when she might be needed – by an enemy, that is.'

Bruce set off from his locker, carefully avoiding Cowley. The housemaster's voice could still be heard behind him barking orders at the boys to stay in their studies. He rounded the snooker table in the games room and crept outside. From there he would make his way across the gardens on the north side of the house and attempt to enter the tunnel system by the squash court behind Kitchen Block. Whether it was Shaun's words sinking in, or the cumulation of countless subliminal processes that had set him on this course, Bruce couldn't tell. Yet it was true enough: get caught like this and a promising career really would be over.

Two minutes later he arrived at the tunnel doors set in a high limestone wall that enclosed a courtyard containing the squash building, sailing store and a garage. At his back a wide, cobbled driveway curved down from the road to Chapel Court. Standing in front of the rickety wooden doors, he breathed a sigh of relief. The area was empty and everything was quiet, bar the last blasts of alarm horns within the college. Although he had never entered the tunnels this way, he guessed it must link to the one under the house and lake. So far so good.

He checked behind and around him constantly, as if old Cowley would at any moment magically float through a wall and catch him red-handed. He forced himself to slow his breathing, he had to calm down. It was clear he wasn't going to slip inside quickly and quietly.

The tumbledown entrance had been sealed with a bolt and padlock, a cheap affair, made of die-cast metal with a zinc coating to give some weather protection. As he contemplated his next move, he heard footsteps tip-tapping towards him over the cobbles of the long, curving slope. It was now or never. There was nowhere to hide. He remembered the pride Art took in the heritage of his Far Eastern weapons. He drew the katana and whispered, 'I hope this is as good as you say it is, Art. And sorry for the damage.' He slipped the blade in the gap between the doors and raised the sword as high above the bolt as he could manage, then rained his strongest blow down onto it. The blade cut through it like a butcher's cleaver through bone. A sharp *ting* rang out, echoing around the walls of the yard, followed by the sound of the severed metal clanging as it hit the cobbles.

'Who's there?' cried a voice. It was Mr Fisher. He must have been checking for any students still outside.

Bruce yanked the door open and darted inside, pulling it shut behind him. He sprinted into the darkness, only to realise he had forgotten to bring a torch. But as the shaft of light erupted at his back, he was curiously reassured by his oversight. Fisher could see nothing in the darkness that now engulfed him. He had omitted to bring a torch too. Bruce smirked to himself.

His plan, such as it was, started looking shaky after about fifty yards when the blackness was near complete. As the tunnel suddenly curved to the right, he crashed into the wall and decided to stop. His left hand had dug into the rough mortar as he swung his arms to run, and cold, wet grime from the wall mingled with warm blood oozing from his grazed knuckles.

Behind him there was no indication that Fisher was attempting to pursue him. Ahead was nothingness; he could barely see his hand at the end of his outstretched arm. Allowing his breathing to settle, he took a few moments to attune to the tunnel's haunting emptiness. He closed his eyes to encourage his mind to form a heat picture of his surroundings. As reliable as gravity, far more than his eyes simply adjusting to the darkness, his internal thermal vision came to life with its familiar faint orange hues. He lingered for a little longer than his gut wanted and noticed how the images shimmered when pockets of warmer air from the outside found their way in and drifted through the space.

Then, from deep inside, winding its way back along the arched brick walls, came the gentlest resonance of feet sounding upon the dirt floor.

31

Bruce's tiptoe advance slowed to a halt. Twenty yards ahead he could make out the tall, blonde-haired figure of Lady Margaret shuffling along the passage between two large men, under the intermittent glow of a single torch. He focused in to try and see exactly what was going on. One man had her arm pressed upwards into her back while the other was trying to light the way ahead and check the tunnel behind as they went. It made for slow progress and they hissed words back and forth in a foreign language while searching ahead.

Occasionally the beam flicked near Bruce, but the man holding the torch wasn't properly observing where the light fell. There was a sense of trepidation about him – he was going through the motions but not executing them properly. Surely he couldn't fear the dark, or being underground? Maybe both. When the light ran close, Bruce realised his heat vision diminished. A few moments of darkness allowed it to return, but it was fragile when interrupted and mixing it with looking at the torchlight was complicated. He was intrigued to find that instead of panicking when his key advantage was interrupted, he experienced a powerful sense of premonition.

Now and then the torch beam cast the outlines of Lady Margaret and her captors against the filthy red bricks, great black shadows, curved and misshapen, sliding like thieves along a wall in Victorian London. The image triggered something in Bruce. He had no idea what would happen next, yet he felt providence at work. Within this aura was an unmistakable connection to her ladyship, as if their minds had become joined. She was taking every opportunity the sporadic lighting and uneven surface afforded to wave her cane feebly around and prod for safe ground on which to walk, in this way continuing to slow their progress.

'Keep a-bloody moving, woman, or you're gonna pay.'

'I'm doing my utmost, you imbecile. Do you want me to fall? And where do you think you are taking me? There's nothing this way.'

She yelped as the first hood wrenched her arm further up her back.

They shuffled forward, their light cast here and there, Bruce keeping his distance. Soon the start of the descent under Serpentine Lake came into view. The trio headed down the gentle gradient and reached the flat section of tunnel beneath the lake. They passed the first huge flood retaining door, set back into the wall like a soulless sentinel ever ready for duty. It was an unnerving sight. Silent. Motionless. A colossus of iron and steel, eyeless and sleeping. Tread too closely, disturb it, and it would awaken, thunder into life and sweep you to oblivion in an eternal tomb.

Bruce descended the slope behind them and stopped short of the flood door. He peered ahead, slipping his katana into its wooden saya and bringing his bow to hand. Lady Margaret and her two companions were on the right-hand side of the tunnel nearing the iron door halfway along this deeper section. Bruce looked up and scanned the ceiling above them. He spotted the two circular constructions he had discovered during his trip down here with Rory. They were evenly spaced, one before and one after the iron door. He studied them for a second time, his heart leaping when he realised their likely purpose: to *allow* the tunnel to be flooded.

'This is it. Open it!' ordered the first man.

'I can tell you categorically that it's empty. Empty!'

The black eyes inside the balaclava stared back in hatred.

'You're wasting your time. Whatever you think is here, there's nothing,' Lady Margaret protested.

He took her hand from behind her back, squeezing it hard as he thrust it up to her face.

'You see this pretty little hand? If you don't get this door open now, I'm gonna start by putting a bullet in it. You understand me?'

Their raised voices resonated along the tunnel. The tension was rising.

'Fine, as you wish, but what you need to know before you start brandishing that thing at me, is that for this door to open, that one … and the other along there … must close. It's a security feature.' She pointed to each retaining door in turn.

The man's eyes narrowed. He allowed himself a glance at his accomplice, seeking reassurance, but he got nothing in return, except the focusing of the torch beam onto the pair of them.

'If this is a trick, you die . . . right here.'

Bruce defocused into the darkness of the floor at his feet as he nocked an arrow onto the bowstring. He observed his breathing, letting it become slow and rhythmical. Then he lifted his head once more to fix his gaze upon the target.

Lady Margaret began to punch numbers into the keypad. An unseen klaxon blasted into life. Above an electrical unit by the door an amber light struggled to revolve. As it turned, the rays revealed decades of dust and cobwebs covering its plastic prism. The retaining doors hummed then hissed and shuddered as hydraulic rams began steadily heaving them away from the wall. When they were half-closed, both ceiling ports screeched then slammed open, crashing into the sides of their frames like great cymbals as hundreds of gallons of lake water began gushing down.

'You crazy fucking bitch.'

The man raised the gun and pressed the muzzle hard to her forehead.

Bruce released the arrow.

The second attacker watched as his partner was struck deep in the neck. He turned to try and escape the torrent, giving Lady Margaret an opportunity to act. She ducked away from the wounded man in case he managed to fire his gun, but as the bright red blood erupted to cover his whitening face and dead, staring eyes, the gun fell away and he slumped into the deepening water.

Bruce dropped the bow and raced to get past the flood door but was too late, it had almost closed. He could only snatch a last look inside, watching as the second assailant who was running towards him failed to escape. The man stopped, wondering where else to go, then fumbled back round, torch in one hand, pistol in the other, to face his suicidal host. But Lady Margaret had unsheathed the sabre from inside the cane and in the blink of an eye all his terror of a watery grave was spared. She ran him through the heart.

*   *   *

After the flood retaining door slammed shut it took a few moments for Bruce to realise he had been encircled by black silence. It was the cold that did it, waking him from his trance. He presumed Lady Margaret had a plan. It didn't feel final. Surely she wasn't there to drown in her own tunnel? Having dealt with her enemies he hoped she would have headed through the centre door before the water engulfed her. But Bruce hadn't seen it open. A slow mechanical door could mean she perished before getting it closed behind her. His mind set like concrete upon the final images: the rate at which the water was rising, the centre door – her only hope of escape – still firmly closed.

The cold clawed at him now, but still he ignored it. He would not let go, could not let go, until he knew she was safe, that she had survived. Then behind him, footsteps. He turned to face the approaching sound and strained to conjure a heat image of who or what was coming towards him. The steps grew louder. They were quick, but there was no light. Who could move so briskly without illumination?

Bruce was caught between the impulse to help Lady Margaret and alarm over the approaching steps. With a growing sense of dread he remembered the one who could move in such a way. He prepared himself, once more reaching to find the hilt of a blade.

The steps pounded, like a giant pair of ghostly jackboots stomping unimpeded, relentless, towards a blind victim ripe for devouring. Bruce drew the katana and prepared to strike. He raised it up and behind his head. The boots marched straight up to where he stood. He flinched, unsure of the moment to strike.

'Stop!' The light erupted in his face. 'What are doing, Bruce?'

'Art?'

'Don't look so shocked. You wanted me to come. Wait, let me get these goggles off. They're bloody terrible around white light.' The green hue of backlight shone across Art's face as he yanked the night-vision goggles away and switched on the flashlight. 'Shaunie said I should get down here, that you asked for me. Except – small matter – down here is pretty big, and unlike some less judicious folk, I have never been here, so finding a way into the tunnels was a task in itself, never mind then going the right way.'

'Yes, of course. Sorry, Art . . . bit dumb of me,' said Bruce.

'So what's up? Why did you want me here? I mean, you're all tooled up. Shaun told me what you took.'

Bruce stared back to see the single weapon that Art was carrying, his prized Watan katana, still resting in its saya.

'I thought . . . mistakenly, it seems . . . that . . . well, it's rather ridiculous to say now I can hear the words coming . . .'

'What?' pressed Art.

'That the attack upstairs would shift down here.' Art looked at him, bemused. 'To blow the place up from below.'

'But we don't even know what the attacks are about.'

'As I said, it sounds ridiculous. Anyhow, it doesn't matter now. I was wrong. There is nothing here. Which is just as well, unless you can deflect bullets with that thing.'

'What's that?' Art asked, nodding towards the steel flood door.

'It's a door.'

Art's eyes narrowed and flicked back to Bruce.

'To keep the lake waters from flooding the college, I suppose,' Bruce continued.

Art stared at it quizzically. 'Usually closed, is it?'

'I guess so. But now you mention it, I'm not really sure. Perhaps it was automatically closed, triggered by what's happening upstairs.'

'Exactly. And whatever it is might still be happening, so we shouldn't stay here any longer.'

'Too right.'

They raced for the tunnel exit, aiming to make their way back unnoticed to their studies. Bruce attempted to play along convincingly while all the time being savaged by the notion that his unlikely soulmate and mentor was possibly breathing her last beneath the lake. All he could do was hope. Any idea about raising the alarm so she could be rescued was quashed by the impossibility of opening the door. But not only that, he was also constrained by her words at the Woodhouse and the connection that bound them. He was not to speak a word of this to anyone.

*   *   *

This time the turmoil was complete. Authorities, both from the civil and military sectors, swarmed to grasp control of a second major incident at Rothwell in a week. A circus had descended, comprising police, medics, officials from both the county and the parish councils, and even the local clergy (in addition to the college's own Anglican and

Catholic chaplains). Of course the local and national press added to the throng of people and vehicles cluttering the Mall and all adjoining roads. Then there were the various branches of the army: the Royal Military Police (Special Investigations Branch), the Intelligence Corps, the Royal Army Medical Corps, the Royal Army Ordnance Corps (to quarantine and remove the already impounded munitions), the Army Legal Corps and the Royal Engineers (to assist with the impenetrable tunnel doors, which would have to remain closed until extensive measures were taken to allow them to be opened for purposes of investigation).

Around the edges of various gatherings and impromptu huddles lurked men in dull but tidy suits. They would watch and listen over shoulders, hover in the shadows when statements were being taken, and wander wheresoever they pleased. MI5, probably. Special Branch, possibly.

The assassination of the principal was viewed as a likely terrorist act, but finding the door to the silver store open, its contents untouched, served as a source of confusion. Even poor Ted Grainger was unaccounted for. Two eyewitnesses from the student body had seen him enter, but not leave, the back of a tradesman's van, the last known sighting of him.

Through the disorder, the greater matter at hand soon emerged. The chief constable of Nottinghamshire had declared he would take a personal interest in the progress of the investigation for as long as Lady Margaret remained absent. And absent she very much remained. With Roberts gone and family links being both tenuous and distant, it was not until three weeks later that a chance social visit by Lucien Martell gave the police a solid lead for contacting blood relations rather than business associates and aristocratic acquaintances.

For Bruce, Shaun, Art and the rest of 67 Entry, those two weekends of April 1988 would never be forgotten. The events were the stuff of legend, but also deep sadness over the gruesome death of Colonel Hunter. For Bruce, the contrast with their academic obligations was almost unbearable. He had to empty his mind of vivid memories, memories cast with terror, excitement and paradox. Only he knew that deeper secrets existed, secrets which lay behind the multitude of strange events. And only for Bruce was the saga unresolved, infected by torment at the deaths, whether actual or presumed, of friends, loved ones and his mysterious protector.

The days passed into summer: the last exams, the last sporting fixtures, the President's Dinner, the passing-out parade, packing up and readying for the next phase, which meant university or Sandhurst. Bruce stayed the course, focused on his studies and did himself proud. Always preferring the path less trodden, he won an army cadetship to read Philosophy and Psychology at Imperial College, sponsored – very rarely indeed for a Rothwellian – by the Intelligence Corps. He would enjoy three years as a relatively rich student on Her Majesty's payroll, before heading to Sandhurst for the standard graduate course and then a career in military intelligence.

And so it was that on the penultimate day of term Bruce sat with his most trusted friend, Shaun Dodd, under the cedar tree above Winter Lake. The breeze was light, the sky clear and the sun warm. All around, crickets hid in the meadow grass and chirped a countryside chorus.

Bruce pulled the first can of cool cider from the bag.

'You know what, Shaun? I think we're going to be all right,' he said.

32

He had to wait longer this time, but the need to let the dust settle – whether dogs and their handlers in the woods, or forensic teams in the house, or the endless visits by investigators, counsellors, lawyers, and even the odd member of parliament, each knowing that *this* was the job they had to get right – only served as a silk lining to the patient execution of James Tavener's masterplan.

Finally the day arrived. It was late summer 1988. The college had fallen quiet and the resident staff had breathed a collective sigh of relief as they had a few weeks' respite before the arrival of 71 Entry. Although the nights were still short Tavener knew that the mood would be one of determination to put the past behind them, to forget what had gone before. He hoped this meant his next act would go unobserved.

Sunset was listed as 20:18 hours but Tavener would have to wait until nearer ten o'clock for the clear sky to deepen to midnight blue and yield the cover he needed. Having concealed his vehicle two miles away in woods to the south, he sweated as he hauled his gear to the entrance of the vault's secret tunnel. It was well concealed, sunk into a funnelled recess within a bank of dense woodland and surrounded by thick undergrowth. He clipped the brambles like a surgeon, cutting as little as possible to gain access to the heavy iron door. Then he sat and waited and listened for ten minutes, scanning the narrow scene all the time with his hand-held nightscope. Satisfied he was unobserved, he unpacked and assembled the equipment: a mini oxyacetylene cutting kit.

The door had no lock or handle; it was intended for exit only. In a testament to its dated design, the hinges were on the outside. They were shielded by sturdy iron covers to prevent access to the pins but Tavener figured ten minutes on each with a super-hot cutting flame might be enough to undo them before the acetylene mix expired. The flame cracked into life, throwing a blinding blue-white light over the scene. For an instant he recoiled, aware just how conspicuous he was, his hand moving towards his pistol for reassurance. He had to work with absolute focus. This place would not stand abandoned forever, and signs of attempted entry would invite a redoubling of effort by the organisation, despite its apparent weakness. He had everything to gain, but also to lose if he drew others to this spot before completing the job. Sweat ran afresh on his brow and down his neck as he set the cutting flame to work. One by one he overcame the three massive hinge assemblies. As the final, upper one separated, he squeezed to the side in anticipation of the door crashing down. But nothing moved. He took a crowbar, dug the toes of his boots into the sloping earth beside the entrance, climbed above it and used his body weight to prize the rusty top edge open. With just an inch gap the door yielded and parted from the frame. A shove with his boot sent it slowly past its balance point and into the brambles with a resounding thud.

Another pause and scan of the area showed only the faint outlines of willow branches drifting with the breeze, the scent of lily of the valley hanging in the air, the unbroken darkness of night painted all around. Satisfied he was still alone, he entered the narrow tunnel under torchlight and headed towards the vault.

He paced over the damp compacted earth through this smaller tunnel with walls of rough concrete sections assembled into the familiar semi-circular profile. After what must have been three or four hundred yards he reached another door, a stout steel frame into which was set a smooth rectangle of stone, identical to the inside walls of the vault. He had suspected this from the moment Lady Margaret invited him to see inside the empty room. The wisp of dust which rolled across the floor near the back wall had stuck in his mind. Now he was on the other side of the concealed door. It had no defences, no security measures. He ran the torch beam around its edges to find the mechanism that would release it. He slid the jemmy bar into place, slipped the catch, eased the door open and stepped inside.

Water lapped at his boots. Two inches of murky brown silt and lake water covered the stone floor. Whether the door had a slow leak or had been opened during the final showdown with Lady Margaret he couldn't tell. It occurred to him that if she had attempted to escape through the door while the tunnel was flooding it could have backfired. The pressure of rapidly rising water would likely force the door shut before the mechanism had opened it. Yes, it was a guess, but he felt a sense of satisfaction: the mechanism was slow and intended only to move the weight of the door, not overcome the force of thousands of tons of water. And how would anyone actually test the system to check that it all worked as intended? He peered at the back of the iron door opposite him and gazed through it, imagining the bloated, decaying body of her ladyship floating beneath the tunnel's brick ceiling.

No matter, he thought, as he returned his attention to the room. It was academic now. Shelves stacked with files, paper folders and documents were set along the walls. In the centre was a plain wooden table. Directly ahead was the iron vault door and the tunnel under the lake.

At first glance things appeared to be in a rudimentary order, with the oldest material running along the wall to his left to the corner diagonally opposite the iron door. The most recent entries were stored in box files ranged along the wall on the main tunnel side. He looked at the scene with relish. The prize all along was going to be information, specifically information about identities and roles. Maybe even plans. The right stuff would be priceless on the black market. Every organised-crime boss or state intelligence agency would pay handsomely to know who was trying to defeat, outwit or evade them; who had caused them so much trouble and pain, cost them so much money; who owed them and who should pay the price.

The clock ticked mercilessly in his mind. Logic directed him to the most recent information, but some instinct, an incurable curiosity, drove him to peek into the very oldest entries. These could point to when, where and how the Architects' Club was born. Indeed, he needed to see somewhere the name itself, 'The Architects' Club', actually written down.

He withdrew a likely-looking manuscript from the furthest corner and placed it on the table. The pages were some form of papyrus. His careful handling failed to avoid the first page snapping like a sheet of rice paper. *Idiot*, he scolded himself under his breath. The content appeared to be a form of hieroglyphics, or maybe ancient Hebrew. He couldn't tell. He moved along the shelf to something later, selecting a dusty scroll bound by a half-perished ribbon. The paper contained other forms of writing, perhaps ancient Greek, with symbols appearing to be versions of the modern Greek alphabet. An unsophisticated circle and cross could be theta; other letters, like psi and epsilon, were reminiscent of cuneiform. More recent exhibits contained pages from the eighteenth century. They yielded no names or lineages, but appeared to refer in older English to the decline of the Bavarian Illuminati following a Bavarian government edict issued in March 1785. He savoured the words, even though his purpose was to get tangible information rather than historical treasures.

It was the muted snap then quiet, rhythmical ticking emanating from the corner on the main tunnel wall side that stopped Tavener in his tracks. He abandoned the pages and strode round to find a jumble of cardboard boxes sandwiched between the ends of converging rows of shelves. He raised his torch and pointed it at the suspect items as if to interrogate them. He reached down and took hold of the box on top, which felt light, empty. He snatched it clear, then the next, and the next, fighting through the trash to the final piece. It was larger than the rest and made of thin chipboard, and when he lifted it from the water its lower edges fell apart.

Underneath, set upon a small metal stand and clear of the wet floor, was the source of the sounds. Although he was surprised, Tavener also acknowledged its inevitability. The faint red LCD numbers glowed back at him as they ticked away: 00:46, 00:45, 00:44 …

He felt the adrenalin rush within his veins, his mouth turn to sand, his hands stiffen in a dysfunctional clamminess. He trembled as he retrieved the miniature camera from his pocket and willed his legs to take him to the newest box files. His eyes scrambled in search of a clue, a date, anything to tell him which to reach for. He went for the top shelf, far right, ripping the file clear and slamming it onto the table. 00:36, 00:35, 00:34 …

He seized the first document, opened it, pressed it flat and snapped three or four shots. He turned the page. More frantic clicks from the tiny camera. Then the next page. He was peripherally aware of lists on the sheets. Names, codenames, organisations … 00:21, 00:20, 00:19 …

Just a few pictures from the leading pages of a document and random samples inside. Next document. Same drill. Turn, press flat, snap. Turn, press, snap. 00:11, 00:10, 00:09 …

He was right not to trust the accuracy of the timer. As the mechanism released and the hissing started, he leaped for the open door, his feet thrashing through the water as he sprinted back into the tunnel. The detonation sent searing white and blue flames after him. Air rushed in to fuel the fire and debris shook from the walls and ceiling, covering him in dust and mortar. The fireball flashed forth like dragon's breath and licked him white hot as he strained to get clear.

When he reached the night air, Tavener collapsed. His hair and camouflage clothing were singed and his lungs felt blistered. Lying back on the dewy brambles and scrub he drank in the cool, moist atmosphere. He fumbled the water bottle out of his pack, which he had left lying by the entrance. Lifting the bottle to his mouth, he took long desperate gulps to try and soothe his burning insides. He coughed and spat out stringy saliva as mild blistering took hold in his trachea.

After three or four minutes he recovered himself, sat up and peered back into the small tunnel. He suspected that the incendiary device had caused great damage but was it total? The characteristic white flash and sustained burning made him think of a phosphorous grenade. Perhaps that's exactly what it was. Another discreet favour courtesy of Colonel Hunter? Or payback from beyond the grave by Philip Roberts? And it would have worked, given a helping hand from a well-placed can or two of petrol to sustain the inferno.

He wondered about heading back inside to survey the damage, maybe to recover any unburnt material. The incursion would surely have set alarms off, but who would be around to hear them? He coughed again and laughed to himself in satisfaction. Even the few photos he had were likely to yield something very valuable; possibly a couple of hundred names or line items of various sorts, he reckoned. He stood up. The distant glow which had shone along the damp concrete walls had disappeared to be replaced by the first wisps of white smoke finally reaching the outside. That would need time to clear.

He decided to wait a little longer. He picked up the nightscope, climbed a few yards onto higher ground and scanned around him. Barring distant glinting from the eyes of white deer huddled in the corner of a field, there was no movement, no sign of life. He scrambled back down the slope and peered into the entrance. From deep within, something stirred. A faint clanging, then the slow build of a rumble. It sounded like a door swinging open. But the tunnel under the lake was underwater, so how would anyone have entered the vault from that side? As he tried to work out what was happening, the rumble accelerated to a crescendo and the torrent burst through the doorway, hitting him like a tidal wave and sweeping him away into the undergrowth.

Battered and cut from being dragged by the water through twists of brambles and tree roots, he finally got a handhold and wrestled himself clear of the swell. Like a beaten sewer rat, he crawled through the sludge, feeling the grainy mud prising its way beneath his fingernails and mixing into his cuts. He got onto his knees and fished out the small camera to check whether it had taken in water. Miraculously, it appeared to have survived intact. With this sole consolation giving him the strength to carry on, he limped away.

From his covert position on a nearby ridge in the woods, Lucien Martell had kept watch over the evening's events. He allowed himself a grin at the sight of Tavener skulking away with his prize. When he was confident that Tavener was clear of the area, he broke cover and stole into the night. He would be heading far from Rothwell. Treachery was at large. He had people to see and an organisation to rebuild.

About the author

Sam Earner is a former British Army officer, now providing consultancy services in the defence sector. He trained in Neuro-Linguistic Programming and has studied Ken Wilber's works on Integral Theory since 2002. He read Aeronautical Engineering at Bristol University and has a Master of Defence Administration degree from Cranfield University. Sam is married to Debbie and they live in Somerset as loyal subjects of a female ginger cat.